All Up In My Business

Also by Lutishia Lovely

Sex in the Sanctuary
Love Like Hallelujah
A Preacher's Passion
Heaven Right Here
Reverend Feelgood
Heaven Forbid

All Up In My Business

LUTISHIA LOVELY

KENSINGTON PUBLISHING CORP.

www.kensingtonbooks.com

DAFINA BOOKS are published by

Kensington Publishing Corp.
119 West 40th Street
New York, NY 10018

ISBN-13: 978-0-7582-3869-6
ISBN-10: 0-7582-3869-X

First Kensington Trade Paperback Printing: March 2011
10 9 8 7 6 5 4 3 2 1

Printed in the United States of America

*To the memory of my grandmother, Amanda Jane Harding,
whose country breakfast fare of fried eggs, salt pork bacon,
and fresh-baked homemade biscuits would assail my
senses before 6 a.m. and force me out of bed!*

ACKNOWLEDGMENTS

I appreciate you!!! Yes, you, holding this book, reading these words—you are the wind beneath my wings and the sun that warms my life. It is with a lot of excitement and even more gratitude that I present the first work in my brand-new series. Trust me, I can't wait until you get all up in my business and experience my new baby! And just as it takes a village to raise a child, I didn't birth this literary work alone. There were people helping me out and cheering me on every step of the way.

Like Selena James, for instance: editor, midwife, friend. Better than any Lamaze coach, she held my hand through labor pains, told me to breathe, and helped me push. Love you tons, sistah! Natasha Kern . . . you're a blessing. Not just my agent, but also a trusted navigator on my literary journey. A trifold cord is not easily broken, and I visualize this team together for a very long time and having lots and lots of young'uns! Kensington is a first-class publishing house, and the Dafina line lives up to its name: my unexpected gift. From the art department to sales, and from PR to management: a huge hug for helping keep me on the shelves and making sure I shine! My "baby" is cute because your hands have held her.

I independently published my first novel in 2004 and came out traditionally in 2007. The publishing industry can be daunting for a newbie and can be tricky to navigate. Those early years were tough, and lonely, which is why I love to life the circle of writers and supporters I now call friends. You all know who you are, but I'd like to holla at a few: Carl Weber, you are a creative mastermind who is gracious enough to share your expertise with those coming up behind you. You understand that there is room enough for all of us. Thank you for everything. Carol Mackey, you could have a big head (you know you've got it going on!), but instead you are one of the kindest, most humble, yet talented women in the game. You've supported writers for years . . . and now you're one of us! May all of your giving now come back as gifts. I'm talking sales, girl. Cha-ching! Pamela Samuels-Young . . . finally, an author to hang with on the West Coast! Authors Monda Webb, Tamika Newhouse, Teresa Gonzalves, Marcus Miller: thanks for your support at my *Heaven Forbid* release party! Page 59 Book Club, you know how to represent! Everyone who came helped make this night special. Najuma, thanks for the suggestion and all of the help. Debra Owsley, you too! Stuart McClean . . . your gallery is fabulous! Bruce Marigny, it's nice knowing a brothah with connections. Thanks for taking care of me. Curtis Bunn, the National Book Club Conference was as amazing as I'd heard. Ella Curry, see you at the next Chocolate Social. And yes, Trice Hickman, what happens in Atlanta . . . ☺

Loved catching up in LA with the "street lit clique": K'Wan, J. M. Benjamin, Nicola Mitchell, and newcomer Terry Wroten. Glad the New Yorkers survived the east vs. west contest! Pat "Cover Girl" Tucker, Cydney Rax, up-and-comings Michele Grant, Jessica A. Robinson, Jacqueline E. Luckett, and Kimberly Kaye at Foxy 105 FM . . . you ladies put the "s" in *sistahhood*. Much love . . .

Y'all know I love a book club and, as always, have to hug a few: Elite Mindseekers (next time, it's a bonfire on the beach!), Romance Slam Jam (hey, Miss Emma and Dee!), Seven Virtues, Natural Sistaz, Ladies of Legacy, Prominent Women of Color (big hug, Toni!), Royce and the Sweet Soul Sisters, Priscilla, Yasmin, and APOOO, Adrienne Dortsche and Black Women Who Read, Maria Akins and Urban Divas, Debbie Shaifire and Urban Fire, Charisse Cook and Women Enlightened by Books, Sharon E. Luckett and S.I.S.T.E.R.S., Toshika Jones and Babes on Books, and last but not least, LA's own . . . Janice Aaron and Odyssey's Book Club Network. You guys are some of the most loyal, voracious, and vivacious readers I know! Oh, and congratulations to LaShaunda Hoffman (SORMAG) and Tee C. Royal (Rawsistaz) for ten great years of author support. I'm sure I've missed somebody . . . that just means I have to write another book!

To *all* of the Lovely ladies and gent readers, friends, family, and especially Spirit . . . hugs and smooches.

Prologue

Oh my God! "Is that...No, it can't be!" Chardonnay Johnson slammed on the brakes, frantically looking up and down the street, and then over to the business complex that housed the Livingston Corporation. She cautiously rolled down her window, her breathing heavy as she continued to look around. Except for the faint noise that came from the boulevard she'd just exited, all was quiet. She didn't see any movement, no other cars except the few in the company parking lot of the headquarters for the restaurant where she worked—the parking lot where she had no business being this time of night.

"Zoe told me to mind my own business," Chardonnay whispered, her eyes once again fixed on the large something or other lying on the ground next to an open car door. "But, no, you just had to be nosy." Mere seconds had passed since Chardonnay turned toward the parking lot entrance and her headlights had picked up a massive lump on the ground. But these seconds felt like an eternity as she sat frozen, wondering what to do, while at the same time trying to convince herself that she wasn't seeing what she was looking at. The parking lot was large, and it was dark, so she almost convinced herself that she'd watched too many crime movies and was simply imagining things, that all she needed to do was turn around and go home. She'd go to bed, wake up, and arrive at her workplace, Taste of Soul, and find out she'd been tripping all along. "Girl, you need to get out of here." Chardonnay pulled to the side, preparing to make a U-turn in the street and get the hell out of Dodge. Her eyes darted between the road, the building, and the lump. *It's probably just some garbage bags,* she thought. She turned her car around but turned to take one last peek at the eerie-looking scene. In that moment, two things happened: It dawned on her who the car with its door open belonged to, and the "garbage bags" moved.

"Oh, no!" All thoughts for her safety aside, Chardonnay whipped back around and raced across the near-empty parking lot, pushing her fifteen-year-old Nissan Maxima to its limits. Her heart leaped to her throat as she drew closer, her headlights confirming suspicions that what had appeared as a massive lump of trash on the pavement was indeed a body. Her heart beat an erratic rhythm as shaky hands threw the car in park while simultaneously reaching for the cell phone. Chardonnay panicked. She locked her doors, then unlocked them. *Should I go to him? No, I should stay inside my car. Look at all that blood on the ground!* Chardonnay didn't think she knew Jesus but found herself calling his name as she dialed 911.

"Nine-one-one, what's your emergency?"

"Yes, Operator, somebody's been shot!"

"Someone has been shot?"

"Yes! I mean, I think so. He's on the ground. He isn't moving. He was, but he isn't now."

"Where has he been shot, ma'am?"

"I don't know!"

"Okay, calm down. Where are you?"

"The Livingston Corporation parking lot." Chardonnay gave the address. "You need to get here, quick!"

"An ambulance is on the way, ma'am. Did you see who shot the victim?"

"No, I just drove into the parking lot and saw him here on the ground. And there's a pool of blood underneath him." Chardonnay thought she saw a shadow run around the far side of the building. Seconds later, she heard screeching tires. Chardonnay's eyes went wide. All twenty-seven years of her life seemed to flash before her in an instant. She threw down the phone, put her car in drive, and raced away from the scene. She could still hear the operator coming through on speakerphone.

"Ma'am, what is your name? Ma'am, are you there? Please, calm down."

"Calm down, hell!" Chardonnay yelled. "I just heard squealing tires. It might be the killer! Look, I gotta go! I got kids."

1

Seven months earlier . . .

"Y ou've come up, my brothah! This place is off the charts!"
Toussaint Livingston moved around the new "man cave" in his
brother's house.

"I was hoping to have it done last weekend and invite y'all
over for Memorial Day."

"That's all right. The NBA championship game is coming
up. I know where I'll be watching."

What had formerly been a seldom-used, garden-level family room now resembled a gentlemanly sports club: Dark-
stained walls offset by white marble floors surrounded a pool
table, a poker table, oversized chairs, and well-placed ottomans,
and a wall-length, fully stocked bar anchored the room.
Framed, autographed photos of some of Malcolm Livingston's
favorite athletes lined the walls, along with a few famous jer-
seys, footballs, basketballs, and a Hank Aaron–autographed
baseball bat. Anyone seeing the man who now stood before a
signed Michael Jordan basketball, which was encased in Plexi-
glas and sitting on a pedestal, may have mistaken him for a professional athlete. A tautly muscled six foot two and two
hundred pounds, Toussaint looked ready to catch a pass and
then run for fifty yards, or hit a baseball out of the park. "Man,

he said, continuing to scope the room. "You make me want to fix up my place."

"What's stopping you?" Thirty-four-year-old Malcolm Livingston, Toussaint's older brother by eighteen months, proudly walked over to the bar that had been made to resemble the one in his favorite gentlemen's club. Aside from stocking almost every liquor known to man, the bar housed four beer taps and the necessities for serious drink-making: shakers, strainers, muddlers, slicing boards, and glasses of every shape and size. A full-sized refrigerator, with the front made out of the same wood as that on the walls, blended seamlessly into the well-appointed space. Malcolm couldn't wait until the next Super Bowl. "Huh? What's stopping you?" he asked again, pouring him and his brother mugs of ice-cold beer.

"You have a wife to handle the details. I don't have one of those or the time to do it myself." He accepted the beer from his brother and took a swig. "Ah. This is on point!"

"First of all," Malcolm said after he, too, had taken a long swallow, "you don't have a wife because you don't want one, and secondly, everything you're looking at was my idea— well, mine and the designer's. All Victoria did was let the woman in."

Toussaint's ears perked up. *Woman?*

"Yeah, I thought that would get your attention. Unlike the past two months when I've tried to tell you about the renovation and you were too busy to listen."

"I don't remember you mentioning a female."

"That's because I was trying to tell you about the design, not the designer, brother. Uh-huh, you wished you'd listened now, don't you? And she's fine too. . . ."

"What's her name?"

"Don't matter," Malcolm answered, purposely messing with his skirt-chasing sibling. "This one isn't your type, Toussaint. You like 'em tall and light, all polished and refined. Like Shyla. Alexis is a dark, bohemian-style chick."

"C'mon now, Malcolm. You know I like dark meat. Alexis? That's her name?"

Malcolm sighed and walked over to a rectangular coffee table. He reached down and pulled out a folder. "I know you won't stop until you've satisfied your curiosity, so here you go. This is her marketing material. And I'll tell you now—she's good, but she don't come cheap!"

"In designing or dating?"

"Ha! Definitely the designing but probably both."

Toussaint took the folder and sat on the dark leather love seat. DESIGNS BY ST. CLAIR was emblazoned across the front of the pocketed folder. He sipped his beer as he opened it and was immediately drawn to the photo of a woman on the folder's bottom left side. Toussaint's eyes widened as he hurriedly set down his beer. "I know her!" he exclaimed.

There she was, looking just the way Toussaint remembered—like a bar of dark chocolate. And, he imagined, probably tasting as sweet.

"What do you mean, you know her?" Malcolm asked.

Toussaint chuckled and sat back, his eyes still glued to her picture. "She got into a fight over me," he began. . . .

"Wait, wait!" Long locs flew behind the compact, curvy woman as she ran up to the parking meter attendant. "I've got a quarter." She hurriedly dug into her purse and pulled out a wallet.

The attendant, who'd just flipped open his pad, began punching in numbers.

"Don't tell me you're going to stand there and write up a ticket. I told you, I have the quarter."

"Look, when I got here, the meter was expired."

"We got here at the same time! Why are you going to charge a ridiculous fine when I'm standing here telling you that I've got it?"

"You should have thought about that before you came back late to your car."

"This isn't my car, but that's not the point!"

"What? This isn't your car? Then why are you yelling at me? You can't pay for someone else's meter time."

"Are you kidding me? How do you know who's paying for what?"

"I know that you aren't paying for this. This vehicle is being ticketed."

Alexis St. Clair knew she was being totally irrational, but she was livid. Recently, she'd received a citation for being parked in a nine-to-five no-parking zone. She'd been to a business meeting breakfast and had reached her car at 9:01. After finding out the amount of the fine—over one hundred dollars with court costs—Alexis had become incensed and decided to fight the charge. She showed up in court, but her very logical argument of why one minute should not equal one hundred dollars—with a timed and dated camera shot provided as evidence—was soundly shot down. She learned from a couple other citizens who were also fighting their tickets that a new company had taken over monitoring the streets of Atlanta. The number of tickets issued had gone through the roof. She'd been angry ever since, which is why when she saw yet another hapless Atlanta citizen about to get jacked (because in her mind it was straight-out robbery), she took matters into her own hands.

Hands on hips, the usually calm Alexis brushed aside the attendant and placed a quarter in the slot. "You cannot put a ticket on a car that is parked legally, and this car is now parked legally. So your ticket is null and void!" When she was really angry, a slight accent from summertimes spent with her St. Croix paternal grandparents surfaced. Now was one of those times. Her words were clipped and precise, her voice raised.

"Look, I've had just about enough of you," the short,

slightly overweight officer said with a huff. "If you don't leave now, I'll have you arrested!"

Toussaint, who'd been observing this exchange in rapt amusement, hurried to the scene. He'd enjoyed seeing a complete stranger come to his, or rather his Mercedes's, defense—had enjoyed watching her give attitude. Not to mention he'd appreciated watching her ample breasts heave with her movements, loved how her thick booty filled the back of her jeans. Yes, he'd enjoyed the show and the scenery but didn't want to see the sistah get arrested.

"Officer, there's no need for that. If you'll give me the ticket, I'll be on my way." Toussaint's comment was directed toward the officer, but his dazzling smile was on Alexis. "Thanks for defending me. That was impressive."

"Toussaint?" For the first time since the encounter began, the officer stopped punching his pad.

Toussaint turned to look at the officer. "Greg?"

"Man, how are you doing?"

The two men did a soul brother's handshake.

"I can't complain." Toussaint looked at the ticket machine. "At least not too much."

The parking meter officer looked embarrassed. "Aw, man, I wish I'd known. I've already processed it so, you know... maybe call the office."

"Oh, so if you'd known it was *him*"—Alexis whirled on Toussaint—"whoever you are"—and then back to the officer—"you wouldn't have written the ticket? Is that how things work? Not what you know but who you know? So Mr. Mercedes gets off scott-free if he *knows* somebody, but Ms. Infiniti here has to pay?" Alexis was now as angry that the officer might *not* give the ticket as she was when he was determined to give it.

"My goodness, we're feisty," Toussaint said, his flirty eyes scanning Alexis's body with admiration. "If it makes you feel better, baby, I'll pay the ticket. And I want to thank you for defending my honor by taking you to dinner." He reached out his hand. "I'm Toussaint Livingston. And you are?"

"Out of here," Alexis said as she turned to walk away. The man was obviously some muckety-muck who got life handed to him on a silver platter. People who got passes like that got on her nerves. His deep-set brown eyes, long curly eyelashes, wink of a dimple, and thick juicy lips had gotten on her nerves as well. She didn't have time for . . . none of that.

"But wait." Toussaint hurried after her. "What's your name?"

"I'm not interested."

"But it's just dinner!"

"I'm not hungry." With that, Alexis crossed the street and disappeared into downtown Atlanta's morning rush crowd.

Malcolm laughed as Toussaint finished his story. "She left you hanging, just like that? Alexis is a smart, talented designer, but that feisty filly you described doesn't sound like the woman I know."

"You haven't seen her fire, my married brother, but I have. And I want to fan that flame. This is the same woman. I'd know her anywhere."

"You mean you *want* to know her. But it doesn't sound like that feeling is mutual." Malcolm laughed again at the thought of his Don Juan brother being rejected. That didn't happen often. No wonder he was curious.

"Can I hang on to this?" Toussaint said, placing the folder under his arm as he stood and drained his glass. "I think it's about time for me to redo my house."

After Toussaint left, Malcolm poured himself another brewski and then settled himself into one of the room's oversized recliners. He opened up the arm, revealing an array of buttons that operated every electronic feature in the room. Smiling, he pushed the first button. A smooth pulley system began retracting a deep navy curtain along one wall, revealing a 125-inch screen. Malcolm popped the remote control out of its recessed cradle, also in the arm, and turned on the set. The television was set on ESPN2, and tennis was playing. It didn't matter to Malcolm. Aside from polo and maybe swimming, he'd never met a sport he didn't like.

Ah, yeah, that Nadal dude is bad. He watched the tall, muscled Spaniard race across the baseline and backhand a volley across the net. The crowd went wild, and the player clenched his fence. Malcolm noted Nadal's opponent was the equally talented Roger Federer. Malcolm reached for a bowl of salty pretzels, ready to enjoy a quiet Sunday afternoon watching the Wimbledon final. He turned up the volume, smiling. *This is going to be good.*

"Daddy! Daddy!" Brittany, Malcolm's rambunctious six-year-old, came bounding down the stairs. On her heels were his three-year-old twins. "We want to go shopping, get some ice cream. Can you take us? Please!"

"Where's your mama?" Malcolm asked, his eyes not leaving the screen. God knew that he loved his children, but he'd be lying if he said there weren't times when he didn't long for the good ole bachelor days. Like now, when he wanted to chill and watch TV—alone.

"She said she's tired. She told us to ask you!"

Malcolm fought to not show his irritation. Britt saw everything. One hint of a frown and she'd turn into the *Enquirer,* asking why he was mad at her or her mother. He swore the child was psychic, because as quiet as he and Victoria tried to keep their ever-increasing disagreements, Britt always seemed to sense their discontent.

"Look, Daddy's tired too. Let me rest awhile, finish watching this game, and then I'll take y'all out somewhere."

The twins begged to stay downstairs with him, but he bribed them into returning upstairs. Now he had to get ice cream *and* toys. Malcolm thought about his wife and this time didn't try to hide his frown. *What's really going on with you, Victoria? You've been acting strange for the past couple months. Ever since . . .* Malcolm abruptly turned off the set, poured the almost-full mug of draft beer down the bar sink's drain, and walked up the steps. Thinking about his marital situation had darkened his mood, especially as he thought of his footloose and fancy-free single brother. He imagined that even now Toussaint was making a date with the sexy interior designer at whom Malcolm could only look and not touch.

I love being married with children, Malcolm concluded as Brittany, the twins, and the oldest son, Justin, piled into his SUV and they headed to Lenox Square. *But I don't like it all of the time.*

2

Adam Livingston loved the taste of her thighs. Tender on the inside and crispy on the outside, nobody could fry chicken better than Candace, his wife. Even now—after living and working together for more than three decades—his mouth still watered at the thought of this juicy, dark meat. Whether the succulent morsels on his dinner plate or those he hovered over when between the sheets, Candace knew how to please him. Unfortunately, the way she sexed him and handled a bird aside, Adam knew that Candace in the kitchen wasn't necessarily a good thing. His wife rarely cooked these days, preferring instead to either eat at one of their restaurants or have their on-call personal chef whip up an intimate lunch or dinner with guests. Now, when Candace graced the kitchen with her presence, it usually meant a conversation was coming regarding something he'd rather not discuss with her—namely her extravagant spending sprees, plastic surgery, or the ongoing competition between their sons.

Technically, money wasn't a problem. The restaurant his parents had opened in Atlanta fifty years ago had grown into a soul food empire, with ten highly successful restaurants in seven Southern states. Additionally, the barbeque sauce his grandfather had created—which was slathered on their most popular menu item, baby back ribs—had been sold in grocery stores nationwide for the past five years. Still, Candace could spend money faster than Usain Bolt could run the hundred-yard dash. Just last year she'd renovated their kitchen to the tune of fifty thousand dollars, had their backyard relandscaped to resemble the scenic islands they'd visited on their thirtieth wedding anniversary, and had one of the guest bedrooms converted to a closet to handle her almost daily jaunts to Nordstrom, Bloomingdale's, and Saks. These renovations had increased the value of their mansion and had made Candace happy. So Adam hadn't complained . . . too much.

And when it came to plastic surgery, Adam thought his wife had had enough. She'd always been beautiful in his eyes, ever since he saw her walking across the Clark Atlanta campus back in the seventies. She'd looked like a Fashion Fair model to him that day, her dark caramel skin enhanced by the beige mini she wore along with similarly colored thigh-high boots. Her long, thick hair had matched the sway of her hips as she'd casually chatted with a friend. A couple days later, when he saw her in the cafeteria, he'd immediately gone over and introduced himself. She was even finer up close than she'd been from a distance, and after taking one look into the almond-shaped brown eyes that sat above a wide yet nicely shaped nose and luscious lips, Adam had gotten the distinct impression that he was looking at the mother of his children. This feeling proved prophetic—Candace became pregnant during her junior year, when Adam was a senior. They'd married that summer and welcomed their oldest, Malcolm LeMarcus, the following December.

Even after having their second son, Toussaint Lamont, Candace stayed slim. When she hit her forties and finally gained thirty pounds that didn't shed easily, Adam still thought she was fine. She was five foot seven, and to him, the extra weight hardly showed. Candace hadn't seemed that bothered by it, either, until her sister-in-law, his twin brother's wife, Diane, had commented on Candace being "fat" during a family get-together and had suggested liposuction as a quick way to take the weight off in time for their cruise to the Fiji Islands. Candace had been so pleased with the results that a tummy tuck soon followed, and breast implants followed that.

Any brothah would be pleased to squeeze a set of firm titties, even if he'd had to pay for them, and Adam was no exception. But a couple weeks ago, when Candace started complaining about her wide nose, Adam had shut her down immediately. "You're becoming addicted to this shit," he'd warned. "If you don't stop cutting on the body God gave you, you're going to become as obsessed as Michael Jackson was, may he rest in peace. You look fine, Can. Give it a rest." So he hoped she'd gotten the message, because he didn't intend to pay the highly skilled and equally expensive cut-and-paste doctor another dime.

That left the topic of his and Candace's sons. The midyear company meeting was in two weeks, right after Juneteenth, so Candace probably wanted to butter him up regarding some plan in the works—probably another of Toussaint's outlandish ideas. Adam loved his youngest son, but he swore that boy didn't have a fear bone in his body. Where Malcolm was more like Adam, in looks and demeanor, Toussaint was definitely his mother's child. Like her, he was brilliant, but he'd also inherited her impulsiveness and flamboyance. Toussaint had run an idea by him some months ago, an idea that Adam had nipped in the bud as quickly as he had Candace's nose-job suggestion. "We're trying not to have to sell the company, son," he'd patiently explained. "And to not take on more debt." Adam wasn't sure how the other players would feel about constructing more Taste of Soul locations across the country, but he hoped that his and Candace's vote would be the same—no f'ing way. The more Adam thought about it, however, the more he thought this might be exactly why he smelled chicken frying.

Damn, I have too much on my mind to argue with Candace about this right now.

One thing on his mind was the e-mail he'd just received on his smartphone from the woman who'd been trying to seduce him for the past two years. He'd met Joyce Witherspoon in the clubhouse after a golf outing. They had exchanged business cards, because she'd told Adam of her plans to start an event-planning business, and she wanted to contract with Taste of Soul as one of the catering partners. Her e-mails had slowly gone from strictly business to potential pleasure, even as she launched the successful, high-profile business that kept the Taste of Soul catering arm busy. Adam was flattered, and Joyce was attractive, but he had told her that he was happily married. Joyce's response had been quick and witty. "You're married, but are you flexible?" He assured her that there was no room in his bed for a third party, but she continued her erotic banter in various phone calls and e-mails. Adam reread Joyce's detailed description of what she wanted to do to him with her mouth and then pushed DELETE. He had always been faithful but could no longer ignore the fact that Joyce's constant flirtations and adoration was wearing him down.

I've got to do something about this . . . and soon. Adam picked up the *Atlanta Journal-Constitution* and pulled out the sports section, determined to take his mind off of Joyce's blatant suggestion. The only woman who'd be putting her mouth anywhere on him was cooking dinner in his kitchen.

Candace Livingston poured melted butter into the baking pan and then sparsely coated each buttermilk biscuit with the warm liquid before spacing the dough out evenly in the bottom of the pan. She loved cooking, especially now that she didn't do it often. It was a love she'd inherited from the grandmother who'd helped support a family of four by cooking for an affluent family in their hometown of Birmingham, Alabama. "The way to a man's heart is through his stomach,"

Amanda Long would tell Candace as she whipped up a slap-your-mama pound cake or an oh-no-you-didn't peach cobbler.

Candace smiled at the memory of those kitchen counseling sessions. Adam may think it was her small waist and big booty that had captured his heart, but Candace knew it was those candied yams and collard greens she'd fixed while they were dating. But somewhere between the birth of their first son and the opening of their second restaurant, the thrill had gone. She'd worked long, arduous hours at the Buckhead location, in the same tony suburb where they lived, and while it had been a labor of love, her joy for fixing food had been replaced with repulsion. There'd been days when she'd thought that if she fried, smothered, or baked another thing, she'd lose her mind.

Tonight she cooked with love, purpose . . . and just a little guilt. *Love* because when it came to cooking, she knew she could throw down. Adam loved food, and her fried chicken was his favorite. *Purpose* because she thought Toussaint's latest idea was a stroke of genius, that the timing for said idea was perfect, that Adam would surely be against it, and that if anybody could change his mind she could, by using various types of thighs. And *guilt* because a married woman of respectable society, with grown sons and grandchildren, had no business thinking about the things she'd been thinking about the past two weeks. *You have a good life,* she chided herself while turning over a perfectly seasoned, perfectly crisp piece of chicken. *Women would kill to be in your shoes.* Then she thought of her options, the special project that had been placed before her, and couldn't deny the excitement that thinking about it caused. As she set the table, lit the candles, and called her husband to a meal fit for a king, Candace knew she had some decisions to make. And she also knew that one wrong move, at any given moment, could turn her life upside down.

3

"Hey, Ace, how you livin'?" Malcolm poured himself a glass of cold lemon water as he sat next to his uncle. Adam's twin brother was named Abram, but everybody called him Ace, including his nephews and his children.

"Can't complain," Ace answered, looking around the room. There was a steady hum of voices as the players in the Taste of Soul restaurant empire conversed among themselves and waited for the midyear company planning meeting to begin. The bright and cheerful conference room décor, consisting of leather, mahogany, silk-covered walls, and freshly cut flowers, contrasted with the quiet atmosphere.

Zoe Williams, Ace's executive assistant and the taker of meeting minutes, entered the room and sat next to Ace's daughter. "I love that suit," she said, managing to set down a purse, folders, and an iPad without spilling the cup of coffee also in her hand. "I don't think I've seen it before." Zoe had commented on the suit just to make small talk and to keep from staring at the person who seemed to take all of the air whenever they were in the same room—Toussaint Livingston. While working to breathe normally, she tried to look sufficiently interested as her boss's daughter, who was home on break from studying abroad, went on and on about clothes Zoe couldn't afford. All Zoe wanted to do was stare at her boss's nephew and figure out how to go from Ace's assistant to Toussaint's wifey. Among the other non-Livingstons present, however, was the marketing manager, the woman Zoe would have to crawl over to climb into Toussaint's bed.

"Sorry for the delay," Adam said as he walked through the double doors of the large conference room. "That was an emergency call from our Dallas location. On top of the major challenges we're already facing, one of the cooks suffered a severe burn and was transported to the hospital by ambulance."

A variety of responses were heard around the room.

"Why couldn't he have been driven to the hospital by one of the employees?" money-conscious Malcolm asked. "Did the brother burn his feet up?"

A couple at the table snickered but quickly stopped when Adam cut them a sobering look. "This is serious," he admonished Malcolm. "Somehow, one of the large pots of hot grease tipped over, and this young man suffered third-degree burns on more than thirty percent of his body. He's got a long and painful road ahead, filled with surgery, skin grafting, and rehabilitation. Zoe, get me his information as soon as this meeting is over and book me a flight to Dallas for tomorrow afternoon. Oh, and send flowers," Adam added. "As for the rest of you, please keep this young man in your prayers."

"Jesus is the healer, hallelujah," Malcolm's wife, Victoria, said fervently, as if she were in church instead of a conference room and proving why she only visited the company offices twice a year. "I think we should pray for the young man right now."

"We can pray later," Malcolm quickly countered, concern mixed with obvious irritation. Since his wife had renewed her commitment to the Lord, their sex life had hit the skids, and he was more than a little upset. *We haven't had sex in two months. Why don't you pray that the Lord will heal those headaches you keep having?* Later, Malcolm would commend himself on the fact that he didn't say this out loud.

"I don't have to tell you what's going to come out of this," Toussaint said to his father.

"I know," Adam replied, motioning for Zoe to hand out the meeting agenda. "I've already got a call in to our attorneys, to make sure our liability insurance can take care of...whatever comes up."

After everyone had received their copy of the order of business, Adam nodded at Ace.

"Y'all know the main reason we're here," Ace said, his posture relaxed, his tone casual. "Like many businesses, this one is in trouble, for the short-term. Let me emphasize that. This downturn is temporary. We've weathered financial storms before, and we'll weather this one as well. But it's serious, and we want everyone around this table to know that. If we don't generate a large cash infusion, we'll have to file for Chapter 11 bankruptcy within six months."

This time the room's reactions were more audible. Zoe gasped, the CFO groaned, and a third person hid their shock behind a cough. But the Livingstons were as cool as cucumbers. Even in their own boardroom, no one ever saw them sweat.

"What this means," Ace went on, "is that we'd have time to get our stuff together and hold off these creditors who are calling in huge loans because of their own financial struggles. Filing bankruptcy is serious business, no doubt. But know this: In the event that this does happen, business *will* go on. No one here will lose their jobs." He fixed Zoe with a reassuring grin. "Businesses do this all the time, to buy time. That's all we're doing."

"I think it's a good option, Ace," Malcolm said.

Others voiced their opinion, and then Toussaint stood. He handed out elegantly bound copies of a business proposal.

"What you're looking at, ladies and gentleman," he began, "is your future—the future of Taste of Soul." He waited, making sure he had everyone's attention. He did. Especially for the ladies in the room who were not his kin, six feet two inches of creamy, chiseled chocolate was hard to ignore. "This is the blueprint for taking our company to the next level, without filing for bankruptcy. We all know that the twenty-first-century game for corporate America is expansion through mergers. It's time to go big or go home."

"Oh, here we go . . . ," Malcolm grumbled. He met his father's eye and knew Adam's sentiments were the same. Taste would always belong to the Livingstons, period. But a subtle nod from Adam silenced further grumbling from Malcolm or anyone else.

"This is what I propose," Toussaint continued, "a chain of Taste locations across America and throughout the world, franchises, along with retail establishments that carry an array of complimentary products. The goal is lofty—fifty new establishments in five years—but is achievable through partnership with high-level investors who can infuse this company with up to half a billion dollars cash immediately upon closing the deal. We will still control the business. All decisions will still be made by a Livingston majority.

"I know this plan is aggressive," Toussaint concluded enthusiastically as he prowled the room like a caged panther. "But I've done the research, crunched the numbers. Now is the perfect time to strike—while the iron is hot." He paused, gauging the faces of those seated around the large, mahogany conference table, and then took his seat.

"Thank you for a well-delivered proposal, Toussaint," Adam said sincerely. He didn't agree with his son's assessments but couldn't deny that they'd been delivered flawlessly. "As always, you came well prepared." Instead of voicing his objections, Adam looked around the room. "Discussion?"

"I'd like to know which iron is hot," Malcolm taunted

without looking at his brother. "The economy is still in the tank, unemployment is high, and the real estate market has yet to rebound. While what you're proposing may look good on paper, I don't think your plan will succeed in real life."

"All of the points you mentioned are exactly why this is the perfect time," Toussaint calmly responded. "Right now, premium real estate is available at bargain prices. Aligning ourselves with federal funding opportunities will help put people back to work. As for the tanking economy, I think our last-quarter profits are proof enough that no matter how low one's bank account, folks still have to eat. That is why ours is an attractive company to potential investors and entrepreneurs."

"What are your thoughts, Ace?" Adam asked his twin brother. Although their similarities were unmistakable, few knew these two were actually twins. Where Adam seemed to wear every rib, slice of sweet potato pie, and shot of cognac around his stomach, constant workouts and a lifetime of jogging kept Ace's body fit and trim. Adam kept his salt-and-pepper hair in a close-cropped style, along with a tidy mustache and goatee. Ace had shaved his head the minute the gray had started coming in and was still clean-shaven. Their personalities were different as well. Ace was prone to take the chances his more conservative brother passed up. Which is why he thought Toussaint's plan had merit and warranted further review. This is what he thought and what he gave as his answer.

Malcolm looked from Ace to Toussaint. "If we decide to expand, keeping the business a hundred percent in the family, where would you propose our next location be? Other Southern states? The Midwest?"

"It's all outlined in the back of the proposal I gave you," Toussaint said, leaning back casually in the tan-colored leather chair. He knew he'd baited the hook well and was patient enough to wait until the right time to reel everyone in. "All of the details are included in the extra reading material at the back of the binder, to be perused at your leisure. However, to answer your question, I think the next gold mine for this company is out west—locations in Los Angeles, followed by one on the Vegas strip."

Zoe's mind whirled even as she typed the meeting minutes on her iPad. The meetings were also recorded so that the final report she prepared could be as detailed as possible, but often she was asked to repeat a fact or figure that had been shared earlier, so she took notes on the spot in addition to having everything on a recorder. But it wasn't the talk of menus and revenues that had her thoughts going a mile a minute. She was thinking how good Toussaint looked in his tailored black suit and wondering whether he planned to move out west during the proposed expansion and whether she'd be able to make her move and work her magic soon enough to go with him. Before long, Zoe would realize she wasn't the only female in the conference room making plans.

Toussaint had plans too. He'd hurriedly left the office after the meeting and now bobbed his head to Marvin Gaye as he cruised through the streets of Atlanta in his shiny black Mercedes sport coupe. Though late, he was determined to keep the appointment with the interior designer who would turn his downtown penthouse from a casual bachelor pad to a millionaire showcase. Her first assignment would be to transform his living and dining areas into a contemporary, elegant yet understated paradise. Her second assignment, if the meeting went as Toussaint planned, would take place in the bedroom, where Toussaint would initiate a different type of layout—one where no clothing was needed.

4

Malcolm twirled a glass paperweight as he sat behind his desk. Papers covered the rich cherrywood, and both his inbox and outbox were overflowing as well. A stack of manila folders rested on the desk's left side, the only nod to neatness. Toussaint's proposal lay open directly in front of him, with certain points highlighted and others underlined. There was no denying that his brother's proposal was excellent. The details he'd included at the back of the folder certainly added credence to what Toussaint had presented in the meeting. Toussaint had a keen eye when it came to seeing the big picture of the Livingston enterprise. *Yep, I think your plan could definitely happen, baby brother.* Smiling, Malcolm opened his desk drawer, unlocked a special compartment, and pulled out a plan of his own.

"Burning the midnight oil, big bro?" Toussaint asked as he strolled into Malcolm's office.

"I could ask you the same," Malcolm replied as he calmly closed the folder he'd been reviewing and placed it back in the drawer. "I thought I saw you leave earlier."

"Yeah, had an appointment." Toussaint frowned, remembering how the second part of his meeting hadn't gone as planned. "I just came back for a couple things. I'm going to work from home tomorrow." He noticed his open proposal on Malcolm's desktop. "Oh, taking notes, I see," he said, and sat down in one of the plush seats facing the desk.

"Just doing as you requested—taking a closer look at my leisure."

"Still convinced the plan will fail?"

"You did your homework. But I'm adamantly opposed to splitting up the business. Our restaurant empire is the Livingston legacy, for our children and theirs."

"Exactly. My plan simply ensures there will be something to leave them."

Malcolm shrugged. "I noticed a few eyes light up at your plans to expand west, one pair being those of our very capable marketing manager."

Toussaint smiled at the mention of their marketing manager, Shyla. "You're just mad you can't hit that fine ass like I do."

"You're not going to be satisfied until you've slept with every single woman in the company," Malcolm said with a frown. "What about Alexis? Did you call her?"

Toussaint's countenance remained neutral. "I called her. We met."

"And?"

"It's all good. She's playing hard to get, but that's just getting me hard."

"You're thirty-two years old, Toussaint. It's time to think about getting married and settling down. Do you think that might happen with Shyla?"

"Naw, man, it's not even like that. Me and baby girl like to hang out, that's all. But speaking of marriage, what's up with you and Vic? It felt kinda chilly between y'all in the boardroom earlier."

"Nothing's up," Malcolm honestly replied. "That's the problem."

"Care to talk about it?"

Malcolm stood and walked over to the large windows that looked out over downtown Atlanta. "Not much to talk about, especially where my wife is concerned. Her focus is taken up with the kids and that holy roller church she's been attending. At one time, she swore she'd never worship where her mother attended. Now she can't curse, drink, or screw because she's 'living for the Lord.'"

"Whoa, wait a minute. You aren't buttering the biscuit?"

Malcolm had said more than he intended. "We'll get through it," he replied, coming back to his desk and picking up Toussaint's proposal.

"I sure hope so. You're only thirty-four. Y'all have at least thirty, forty more years together. You need to keep the home fires burning before somebody else starts looking hot to you."

"Hey, Shyla," Malcolm said as someone "hot" stuck her head just inside his office door. "You're working late."

"I was headed out and heard your voices. I don't mean to interrupt."

Malcolm waved her in. "You're not interrupting."

Shyla knew the picture she painted as she strode confidently into the room and sat next to Toussaint. Aside from being naturally beautiful, her makeup was flawless, her tailored Chanel suit fit to perfection, her three-inch heels emphasized her long, lean legs, and the new weave she'd just gotten the past weekend was worth every bit of the twelve hundred dollars she'd paid for it. "Your presentation was excellent, Toussaint. I looked for you afterward because I have a couple marketing ideas regarding the new markets that you might find interesting. But your secretary told me you'd left for the day."

"Had a meeting," Toussaint countered easily. "But I have some time now. Why don't we go back to your office and talk about it."

The two left Malcolm's office shortly thereafter, and everyone knew that talking wouldn't be the only thing happening once Toussaint and Shyla were alone.

Malcolm placed his key in the lock and turned the doorknob to their six-bedroom, six-bath, colonial-style brick home. It was a little after 10:00 p.m., and considering the fact that four children lived there—between the ages of three and eight—things were surprisingly quiet. He loosened his tie as he headed to the stairs and his new favorite room, the man cave. Like his father, cognac was his drink of choice, and like Adam, Malcolm's waistline was beginning to show how many meals this favored drink had chased down.

Malcolm placed two cubes of ice in a tumbler and poured two fingers of the amber-colored liquid into the glass. He took a drink, grimaced, and poured a bit more. He took off his tie, followed by his jacket, and sat down in the dark room without turning on the lights. *Here I am only thirty-four years old and feeling like an old man. Few friends, even fewer interests outside work, and no sex life. Man, you're pitiful.*

"I thought I heard the garage door open." Victoria startled Malcolm, whose back had been to her when she came down the stairs. "What are you doing down here drinking in the dark? That's what drunks do."

Malcolm took a deep breath and another sip of his drink before standing and turning around. "Hello, Victoria."

"Hello." Victoria crossed her arms and leaned against the massive fireplace mantel. "What's wrong?"

"Nothing." Malcolm retrieved his jacket, tie, and briefcase from the couch and headed out of the room.

Victoria quickly followed. "What do you mean, nothing? You come home and head straight for the liquor cabinet, without checking on your wife or your kids, and expect me to believe that everything is okay?"

"Don't try starting an argument, Victoria. It's not unusual for me to have a drink when I come home in the evenings."

"Yes, but in the dark?"

"Where are the kids?" Malcolm was ready to change the subject.

"Where do you think they are on a school night? In bed." Victoria turned and marched back up the stairs.

Malcolm followed her to the master suite. Victoria walked to her side of the oak, four-poster, king-sized bed, grabbed her Bible off the nightstand, and once again headed toward the door.

"Are you going to be long?" Malcolm asked her. "I was hoping we could...spend some quality time together."

Victoria snorted. "Oh, you can't speak but you can screw? That liquor's got you riled up and now you want to have intercourse?"

"The liquor has nothing to do with it," Malcolm said, slowly walking toward her. "It's been months since we've been intimate, Victoria. I need to make love to my wife and don't feel I should have to beg her."

Victoria put up her hand. Malcolm stopped a few feet away from her. "The Lord has spoken to me about that boy who got burned," she said in a firm tone that brooked no argument. "He told me to fast and pray for three days, to help bring about that child's healing. No food, only water."

"Good. Maybe you'll lose one of those rolls around your neck or your stomach," Malcolm shot back, hurt and angry that he'd been rejected—again.

"Perhaps I will," Victoria replied calmly, masking the hurt his jab had caused. "At any rate, I'll be sleeping in the guest room while I do the Lord's work." She walked to the door and placed a hand on the doorknob. Before opening it, she turned and said, "I would love for you to join me and the kids at church this Sunday. That's something we could do together. Good night."

5

Toussaint and Shyla entered the upscale Buckhead Taste of Soul location. The rich vocals of Aretha Franklin assailed them immediately, oozing from the bar and waiting area located at the front of the restaurant. Toussaint bobbed his head to the beat as Aretha spelled out the respect she wanted. His uncle Ace's suggestion from ten years ago—placing jukeboxes in the restaurants so patrons could have soul music along with their soul food—had been excellent. The idea was further enhanced when Ace's wife, Diane, had suggested that the main platters be named after soul groups. Now, instead of ordering a meat dish with a salad and sides, customers ordered the Otis Redding Rib Eye Platter or the Wilson Pickett Pork Chop Plate. A highlight from those early days was when the Godfather of Soul, James Brown, personally came in and christened his namesake—the James Brown Baby Back Big Snack, a half slab of succulent baby back ribs, served with potato salad, coleslaw, and tangy baked beans.

"I can't believe how crowded it is," Shyla said as Toussaint led them to a corner booth.

"What do you mean you can't believe it? I thought you knew!"

"Of course, Mr. Livingston, I'm well aware of this location's success. But it's three o'clock in the afternoon. I thought these heavier flows occurred mainly during lunch and dinner."

"If you'd patronize this establishment more, you'd know that it's always busy," Toussaint admonished gently.

"My waistline can handle this place only once or twice a month. Do you think you'd like me with a pudgy stomach and flabby thighs?"

"You know I like you nice and tight, baby," Toussaint drawled softly. Further comment was interrupted as their waitress came up to the table.

"Hello, Toussaint," she said with a wide smile. "You're looking nice today. Is that a new suit?"

"Hello, Chardonnay," Toussaint responded. "This is not a new suit, and you look nice as well."

"Thank you." Chardonnay preened. Like most women who worked at Taste of Soul, she fantasized about being with Toussaint Livingston. "I like that chain too. It's platinum, huh?"

Shyla cleared her throat. "Excuse me, but is Toussaint the only customer you see at this table?"

Naw, bitch, he's just the only one I wanted to speak to! "Uh, hi, Shyla."

"I'd prefer that you call me Ms. Martin, and, Toussaint, shouldn't she address you as Mr. Livingston? You are a top executive, while she's . . . well . . . at the opposite end of the spectrum."

Chardonnay ignored Shyla and looked at Toussaint. *Zoe said she'd bet money this skank ho was fucking you. I bet she's right.*

"You know we're not that formal," Toussaint said, smiling at Chardonnay. "Besides, we value *every* employee in the corporation, no matter their position."

Shyla wasn't ready to leave Chardonnay alone. *This troll is almost drooling, for God's sake. Toussaint would never stoop to the level of your ghetto ass!* "At Taste of Soul, we pride ourselves on excellence in every area." Shyla scanned Chardonnay from head to toe. "Your blouse is wrinkled, your shoes are not shined, and that blob of barbeque sauce on your skirt is disgusting. Do you feel this is the best you can do in representing us?"

Chardonnay looked down at the splotch, more to mask the fire in her eyes than anything else. She needed this job, or she would have already mopped up half the floor with Shyla's weave. Plus, she figured if Shyla was sleeping with Toussaint, she might have enough clout to get her fired. *You've gone and crossed the wrong sistah,* Chardonnay thought, even as she fixed her face with a look of embarrassment. *Didn't your mama ever tell you not to fuck with the person who was fixing your food?* "I'm sorry," Chardonnay said in a kind, soft voice. "I didn't notice the stain. I just finished serving a family with children. Should I take your order and then go and remove it, or would you like me to remove it first, while you two decide what you want?"

"Where's Jermaine?" Shyla asked. "I'd rather he wait on us. I don't like your fake, syrupy attitude."

"Now, now, ladies," Toussaint said. "Let's not fight. We're on the same team, and I'm ready to eat. We would love for you to take our order, Chardonnay," he continued. "What are the specials today?"

Chardonnay rattled off five different specials from memory, with specific details about each one above and beyond what was required. Her special care with customers brought her big tips, and she wanted to take special care with the man currently at her table. After taking their orders, Chardonnay smiled at Toussaint and apologized again to Shyla. "I'll bring your drinks and then take care of this stain," she said. "Thanks for pointing it out to me. I know I'm representing the company and want to look my best." With that she turned and walked away, knowing how the navy skirt that was part of her uniform emphasized her bubble butt and knowing that Toussaint was watching.

She was right. Toussaint watched Chardonnay's swaying backside until she turned the corner. "A bit hard on the help, don't you think?" he asked once he refocused on Shyla.

"She was rude and blatantly disrespectful," Shyla answered. "I'm surprised you didn't check her before I did."

"How did she disrespect you?"

Shyla rolled her eyes. *Men! Put a pair of titties and a big ass in front of them and they go deaf!* "Never mind, it's over," she said finally, not wanting to give Chardonnay any more air time. Shyla had more important fish to fry than the ones being prepared for Toussaint's plate. Such as getting a little platinum of her own—namely an engagement ring. "Given any more thought to my suggestion?"

"What suggestion?" Toussaint asked.

"My moving to your department and us working together. And about taking me with you when you move to LA."

Toussaint laughed. "Girl, the plans aren't even off the paper yet and you've already got us living in Malibu."

"Oh, please. You know your plans, at least phase one, are going to happen. You always get what you want, Toussaint."

Not always, Toussaint thought, remembering his interior designer's polite but firm rebuff the week before. And then, as if he'd conjured her up, Alexis St. Clair came walking toward him, followed by a handsome, nicely dressed older man.

"Alexis!" Toussaint said, rising and extending his hand. "I see that designing isn't the only place you have good taste."

"Hello, Toussaint," Alexis replied as she shook his hand. "This is one of my favorite places to dine, and that was so even *before* I met you." Alexis felt eyes on her and looked beyond Toussaint. From the look that was returned, she assumed the woman to be Toussaint's love interest. "I'm Alexis, Toussaint's interior designer," she said, wanting to nip any misconceptions in the bud. Alexis prided herself on living a drama-free lifestyle and intended to keep it that way. That's one of the reasons why, as fine as Toussaint was, and as much as she'd wanted to do otherwise, she'd refused his advances. "I never mix business with pleasure," she'd told him.

After introductions were made, Toussaint spoke again. "Would you two care to join us?"

"We'd love to, but we have business to discuss," Alexis answered. "Shyla, it was a pleasure meeting you. Toussaint, I'll see you next week." The gentleman with Alexis shook Toussaint's hand and nodded at Shyla before following Alexis around the corner to the restaurant's second dining room.

"Wow, Toussaint, keeping secrets from me. You didn't tell me you were redesigning your penthouse. And you've found quite the attractive designer to assist you."

"I don't tell you everything, woman." *For instance, I won't tell you that there's something about that sistah that turns me all the way on!*

While Chardonnay returned, sans barbeque stain, with their salads and placed them on the table, Toussaint pondered his latest prey. Alexis was a short, dark brickhouse who reminded him of Lauryn Hill. Her features were exotic, which in the conversation the week before, Alexis had attributed to her Caribbean grandparents. She wore her hair dreadlocked, the thick, long dreads falling almost to her waist. But it wasn't just her looks that drew Toussaint to her. Alexis was a study in contradictions: at once bold and shy, confrontational yet compassionate. She'd nailed Toussaint's personality and taste with one walk-through of his condo. And she had a subtle sense of humor that she unleashed at the most unexpected times. And there was something else, an alluring, mystical quality that he couldn't define. She was a puzzle, one that Toussaint planned on solving. *You always get what you want, Toussaint.* Toussaint planned on putting Shyla's words to the test. In the meantime, he steered their conversation back to a safe topic—business. "What are your thoughts for our holiday campaign?"

★   ★   ★

Back in the kitchen, Chardonnay waited impatiently for her order. "This is for Toussaint," she told the head chef, yet again. The two worked well together and were always teasing around. "Act like you know."

"Look, I put quality on the plate no matter who it is. Everything I do is quality, believe that." The chef's eyes roamed Chardonnay's body before he gave her a wink.

"Yeah, whatever, man. Just try not to burn the catfish."

A minute later, the chef put a perfectly prepared plate on the pickup counter. "Order up!"

Chardonnay immediately walked over and reached for Shyla's order. "Move!" she said to Jermaine, who was also waiting for a customer's plate.

"Aren't you going to wait and take these both out together?" Jermaine asked.

"Yeah," Chardonnay said over her shoulder. The head chef frowned slightly as he watched Chardonnay walk around the corner to the pantry.

As soon as Chardonnay turned the corner, she did what she'd planned—gave Shyla Martin a little something extra to eat. She returned quickly, just in time to see the chef set down Toussaint's order. She balanced the two plates expertly as she walked out of the kitchen.

Chardonnay hummed the Supremes track that had been playing in the bar when she'd walked past it on the way to the restroom. She laughed out loud as she imagined Shyla enjoying her extra creamy mashed potatoes. *Now, you haughty-ass heifah, that's just what you get!* She danced up to the counter to key in her next table's order.

"I saw you."

Chardonnay huffed as Bobby "Butt Stank" Wilson came up behind her. The man had been trying to get in her pants ever since being hired as a line cook two months ago. "Boy, quit jaw jacking and get outta my face."

"Baby, I'm getting ready to get all into yo fine ass. Unless you want me to just go ahead and tell management what I saw."

"Okay, nucka," Chardonnay said, putting a hand on her hip as she turned around. "Just what in the hell do you think you saw?"

"Not what I think, what I know. I saw you spit in that plate of food. And that was *after* you'd stuck your finger in your panties and then swirled it in the cabbage."

6

Zoe's phone rang. She crawled across the floor to answer it, trying to catch her breath along the way. She'd been laughing for a full two minutes, ever since Chardonnay had told her what happened at the restaurant earlier. She'd laughed so hard and so long that Chardonnay had finally hung up on her. At least that's what Zoe assumed. As she looked at the caller ID, she realized she was right. It was Chardonnay calling back.

"It ain't that damn funny," Chardonnay said as soon as Zoe picked up. "Zoe! I know your ass can hear me."

"Ooh, girl, wait a minute." Zoe took another calming breath. "I'm trying to catch my breath...wait." She took a couple more deep gulps and squeezed her eyes tightly together to shut out the picture that Chardonnay's story had created, the one that had her rolling on the floor laughing. "Did you really do that?" she asked once she could speak. "Did you really season a sistah's cabbage with some pussy juice?" The question sent her howling again.

"You ain't got no damn sense," Chardonnay chided. But Zoe's laugh was infectious, and pretty soon, Chardonnay found herself laughing again as well.

"Girl," Zoe said, wiping her eyes. "When you texted me

that you needed to talk, I was expecting anything but this. Whew! That's some hot ghetto mess action right there!"

"She asked for it," Chardonnay said as she fixed plates for her two young children. "Tangeray! Cognac! Come on in here and eat! Hold on a minute, girl. I'ma have to do a beat-down to pull these heathens away from the television. Tangeray!"

Zoe used the time it took Chardonnay to gather her kids around the dinner table to further compose herself. She went into the bedroom where she'd deposited her purse on the nightstand, pulled out a pack of Newport longs, and lit one up. Taking a deep drag, she slipped into a pair of bright yellow Pooh slippers and headed to the kitchen to pour herself a glass of her friend's namesake. Taking what was once a Peter Pan peanut butter jar, she filled it halfway and took a long swallow.

"Zoe, you there?"

"Uh-huh."

"Good, because I need your advice on part two of this shit."

"You mean there's more?" Zoe took her glass and headed back to the bedroom, wishing she'd copped some weed earlier, as she'd planned.

"Probably not, but a sistah can't be too careful."

"Chardonnay, I'm not following you. What's going on?"

"Bobby said he saw me."

"Saw you spit in sistah-girl's food?"

"*And* put my hand in my panties."

Zoe took another long drink of her chilled white wine as she pondered this tidbit. "Girl, young blood is probably just trying to get *in* your panties. He's been sniffing your behind from day one on the job."

"He's trying to apply pressure . . . says he captured what I did on his camera phone."

"And you believe him?"

"I don't want to."

"Did he show you?"

"Not yet. A large party came in and we got busy. I had to leave as soon as my shift was over to pick up the kids."

"So what's he want? Some money or something?"

"Hell no, girl. What do you think a jacked-up-looking fool like him wants?"

Zoe smoked her cigarette as she pondered this question. She'd brought a plate home from the restaurant but hadn't eaten, so the chardonnay had gone straight to her head. "Well, he's a stupid fool is all I can say. He knows you don't make much more than him. Don't know what else he could use the pics for unless he's trying to come up in the company. Or unless he's . . . Oh, damn."

"Exactly. He wants a little taste of that juice I stirred in Shyla's entrée."

"His ass is so hard up that he's got to blackmail somebody for sex?"

"Are you surprised? One look at his face and you can understand that shit. When God was handing out looks, he ran out of 'handsome' and just slapped a dose of 'butt ugly' up against Bobby's face."

Zoe laughed despite the relative seriousness of the situation. "Are you going to give him some?"

"Hell no! Have you walked close to Bobby lately? He smells like fifteen kinds of funk on a good day, and his breath is worse than a fart generated from refried beans. I'd rather kiss Uncle's pit bull in the mouth."

"Ooh, Chardonnay. Why you want to lie about a man like that? True, Bobby ain't much to look at, but he's a hard worker. He's always working double shifts. I even heard Mr. Livingston talking about how dedicated he is. You could do worse in a father for your kids."

"Oh, really? Then why don't you give him some? I'm trying to come up with somebody like Toussaint."

"Toussaint? Please, you're never going to get a man like him."

"Humph. You're just saying that because you want his ass. Girl, let me get off this phone. Yak is trying to beat his sister in the head with a rib bone. Don't tell nobody what I told you."

"Who am I going to tell? Bougie Shyla Martin? I might have to ask her how she liked the cabbage, though." Zoe started laughing again.

"Heifah, you'd better keep your mouth shut. I ain't playing."

"Girl, your secret's safe with me. I'll holla later."

The conversation she'd had with Zoe stayed with Chardonnay for the rest of the evening, even while she bathed her kids and got herself ready for bed, and even as she rolled up a blunt and settled on the couch to watch another crazy episode of *Bad Girls Club*. She thought about what it would be like to sleep with Bobby. And then she thought what it would be like to ride a fine brothah like Toussaint all night long. It was a no-brainer. If she was going to delve into the company dick pool, Chardonnay decided she'd aim straight for the top.

7

Toussaint smiled as he snuck up on his mother. He tiptoed up to the island in the center of the designer kitchen and placed a light kiss on her neck.

Candace screamed as the Caesar salad dressing she'd been making flew off the whisk and landed everywhere. "Boy! What is wrong with you?" She took the whisk and popped Toussaint in the middle of the forehead. "Trying to give your mama a heart attack?"

"Dang, Mama!" Toussaint said, still laughing as he walked over, calmly reached for a paper towel, and wiped the dab of salad dressing off his face. "You're about to turn that whisk into a deadly weapon." He reached for a few more paper towels and began looking on the floor for liquid spots to clean up.

"Oh, don't worry about it. Beverly can clean it up later." Candace was referring to the Haitian housekeeper she'd hired the year she turned fifty and decided she'd washed enough dishes and swept enough floors for her lifetime. She'd further justified the decision with the knowledge that the salary she paid Beverly fed her six family members who were cramped into a two-bedroom apartment on Atlanta's west side.

"I'm still adjusting to the fact that you have hired help," Toussaint said. He'd ignored his mother's suggestion and was now wiping a bit of dressing off the stainless-steel refrigerator door. "If you don't watch out, people are going to think you're bougie . . . trying to keep up with the Joneses."

"Please, son, you know better than that. We're Livingstons. The Joneses are trying to keep up with us."

Toussaint stuck his finger into the bowl of salad dressing. "This is good, Mama."

"Boy, get your finger out my food. You haven't changed a bit—still that rambunctious child who shot your cousin in the back of the head with a BB gun."

"Ha! That's why you love me, Mama."

"That I do, son. That I do. That's probably your brother," Candace said when the doorbell rang. "Unlike you, who walked into our home as if you still lived here and scared me half to death, your brother has manners and is ringing the bell."

A half hour later, Adam, Candace, and their two sons were seated around the massive mahogany and cherrywood table that anchored the Livingston's dining room. They'd just finished the Caesar salad and were digging into Candace's seafood lasagna with gusto.

"Victoria is going to be sorry she missed this, Malcolm," Toussaint said around a mouthful of food. "I bet y'all's cook can't compete with this dish . . . no way."

Malcolm shrugged. "Chef does all right. Of course, nobody can compete with Mom's cooking."

"I'm sorry she and the kids couldn't join us," Candace said, repeating what she'd said earlier when learning that only Malcolm would be joining them. "That new church she joined sure keeps her busy. But then again, it's been a long time since there's been a Sunday dinner with just the four of us."

"I can't believe July is around the corner and the year is halfway over," Adam said.

Toussaint nodded his agreement. "Fourth of July next week. Time flies when you're having fun."

Speak for yourself, Romeo. Malcolm reached for another slice of the bread Candace had made from scratch. He took a bite and groaned his pleasure. "Remember Malcolm Mondays and Toussaint Tuesdays? When y'all would have to eat what we cooked?"

"How could we forget?" Adam asked. "Some of the stuff y'all made could have killed me! Like that almost-raw pork you served covered in barbeque sauce? I think some of those worms are still crawling around inside me."

"Naw, Dad," Malcolm countered. "I think you've drunk enough cognac to kill anything living down there. Besides, I was, what, seven or eight years old when I baked that first slab of ribs?"

"And you were so determined," Candace added, smiling. "You looked so proud as you brought in that platter and set it on the table. Your father and I didn't have the heart to tell you that we couldn't eat that meat."

"You didn't have to. Toussaint spitting his bite back onto the plate was hint enough."

Everyone at the table cracked up at that memory and at the fact that Candace had diverted the boy's attention long enough to secretly microwave the ribs to a level of doneness. The conversation continued, largely revolving around cooking and food.

"Yeah, if your last name is Livingston, you've got to be able to burn," Adam concluded. "And thank God that now I'll gladly park my feet under Malcolm's table and eat anything he fixes."

"Well, you better make sure it's Malcolm and not Victoria cooking," Toussaint joked. "That girl's been in the family for over ten years and still can't boil an egg!"

Malcolm joined in the laughter, but the smile on his face didn't match how he felt inside. The family had often joked about Victoria's lack of cooking skills, but her stellar pedigree, good looks, and large bank account had overruled what would have been a deal breaker with a more common woman. Malcolm was embarrassed by the fact that hiring a chef had been a move of necessity as much as convenience—and not because Victoria was busy being a mother to four children. She was also a spoiled only child who had been the apple of her late father's eye, and she had always lived the life of a prima donna. From the second year of their marriage, Malcolm and Victoria's home had never been without a cook, housekeeper, or chauffeur, and after the first childbirth, they added a nanny. Malcolm's grandfather had put the situation into succinct order after tasting the omelet his granddaughter-in-law attempted during his first visit to their home after the wedding. The eggs were almost burned on the outside, runny on the inside, and she'd failed to wash the vegetables that were mixed in.

"Well, it must be what she does in the bedroom," his grandfather had said somberly after forcing himself to eat a few bites.

"Excuse me?" Malcolm had asked, confused.

"You obviously didn't marry her for her skills in the kitchen, son. If you didn't know how to cook, your family would starve to death."

"I'm looking forward to the Fourth and heading to Hilton Head," Malcolm said, changing the subject. The Livingstons owned a rambling, eight-bedroom, ten-bath home on this tony island, on land that had been in the family since purchased from the master who freed Malcolm's great-great-grandfather. "Even Justin is excited," he continued, speaking of his oldest son. "He's asked to bring a couple playmates along."

"Well, everybody's welcome," Candace said. "We've already reserved an additional villa to handle any last-minute additions to the guest list. It has four bedrooms, with two beds in each, so that should accommodate everyone. Toussaint, will you be inviting a guest? Shyla, maybe?"

"Shyla? Why would you think I'd invite her?"

Candace fixed her youngest son with a knowing look. "Not much gets past your mother. I noticed the way Shyla looked at you during the planning meeting. She handled herself quite professionally, mind you, but while you were presenting the expansion plans, love was written all over her face. And hers wasn't the only one," she finished, mumbling under her breath.

Toussaint chose to ignore the last sentence. He knew that Zoe also had a thing for him. And while he preferred dark chocolate, he rarely turned down a tasty sweet treat, no matter the flavor. Toussaint had wondered more than once how Zoe's administrative efficiency would translate in the bedroom, and he hadn't totally dismissed the idea of finding out. But she wasn't coming to Hilton Head, and neither was Shyla. "I might bring someone," he finally answered.

"Who?" Malcolm asked.

"You'll just have to wait and see, big brother," Toussaint answered, already envisioning Alexis in a skimpy yellow bikini. She'd turned down his first date request, but Toussaint was persistent and determined. When it came to challenges, he didn't back down, especially when the object of said challenge looked so delicious.

8

It was a rare day off, and Alexis St. Clair was bored to tears. She sipped coffee that had been liberally doused with hazelnut cream and wondered for the umpteenth time why she'd turned down Toussaint's offer to spend the Fourth of July with his family. It definitely wasn't because of the excuse she'd given him, that she never dated clients, even though it was true. No, the reason she'd turned down the oh-so-charming Toussaint Livingston was because she saw him for what he was—trouble with a capital *T.* She'd been caught off guard at their initial meeting, having forgotten the name of the man whose car she'd tried to protect months before. But she hadn't forgotten one detail about *him*—that tall, lean body, killer smile, and gorgeous eyes that had made her mouth water and her kitty cat wet. She'd never reacted to a man the way she had to Toussaint and knew she was treading dangerous waters by taking him on as a client. At the end of the day, it was an astute business decision. But personally . . .

As if it would help her erase these thoughts, Alexis shook her head and stepped away from the large bay window in her two-bedroom condo. She continued to sip coffee as she surveyed her kingdom—a cunning combination of Spanish modern and American contemporary, comfortably formal with hints of eclectic whimsy that showcased Alexis's style. The condo was small, less than a thousand square feet, but everything in it was quality and classy, much like its owner.

Alexis eyed her cell phone sitting on one of the ebony blocks. She thought about calling her best friend, Kim, but knew she'd be with her in-laws. Another best friend had joined the peace corps. Alexis had to wait until that friend called her. "Maybe I should call Mama," she mused out loud, picking up her cell. She held the phone in her hand and contemplated the possible outcome of the call. Would Mrs. Barnes be in a rare good mood, or would she be talking about Alexis's brothers and the latest trouble surrounding them? And how much money would she ask for? That was how the calls usually ended, with Mrs. Barnes asking for some money "to hold until the first." Of course, Alexis always sent the money, knowing she'd never see it again. It wasn't that Alexis minded helping her mother. She didn't. It was that much of the money went to support her unemployed brothers and alcoholic stepfather that Alexis couldn't stand. No, she concluded, calling Missouri was not a good idea.

"That's it, Alexis. Go ... anywhere!" She finished her coffee as she strode to her room, thinking of what she could wear that didn't need ironing. When she turned the corner and entered the hallway to her bedroom, her eyes went to where they often did—to the grouping of photos that artfully lined the wall on both sides. She stopped, focusing on one picture in particular. It was of a handsome, dark-skinned man looking proud and distinguished in a double-breasted navy suit. He wasn't smiling, but a devil-may-care twinkle in his eye belied the picture's serious tone. His evenly shaped lips were framed by a tidy mustache, and his hair, which was liberally streaked with gray, was combed away from his face. Thomas Alexander St. Clair was the first man to tell Alexis she was beautiful, the first to take her on a date, and the first man she'd loved. Her father was also the reason she was afraid to love again. But Alexis didn't want to think about that now.

Thirty minutes later, a casually dressed Alexis walked into Taste of Soul. The sounds of Archie Bell & the Drells immediately welcomed her. This quartet thumped out a mean beat, using drums, bass, guitar, and organ, and encouraged everyone to "tighten up" and "make it mellow." She reached for a take-out menu and began to scan her choices.

"You gotta do the ribs, pretty girl." A skinny, plain-looking man wearing a stark white apron spoke to her from behind the counter. "I cooked them myself, just for you."

"Then I guess I should try them," Alexis politely countered.

"Yeah, and you should try going out on a date with me too!"

"Stop harassing our customers, Bobby!" Chardonnay said, playfully smacking him upside the head as she walked up to the register. "Don't pay any attention to him, ma'am. He's *special*." Chardonnay and Alexis shared a laugh. "But he's not lying about the ribs. I just had them for lunch and they are bangin'!"

"Then ribs it is!"

"The James Brown Baby Back Big Snack or a whole slab?"

"Um, I think I'll take a whole one."

"And your sides? You get three."

Alexis reopened the menu. "Let's see . . . I'll have the barbequed beans, the collard greens, and the mac and cheese."

"You chose exactly right, sistah. Anything to drink?"

"No, I'm fine."

"For here or to go?"

"To go."

Bobby, who'd been standing by Chardonnay this entire time, took the printout from her hand. "Just sit and relax, pretty lady. I'm going to handle this order personally."

"Thank you, Bobby." Alexis couldn't help but smile as he spun on his heels and marched into the kitchen. She knew he was teasing, but the attention felt good, as did the camaraderie. Good food wasn't the only thing behind Taste's success. It was the people too.

Alexis took a seat and looked around the dining room. It was less crowded than usual, but several tables were occupied. Alexis's eye fell on the last booth on the far wall. Instantly, she remembered her encounter with Shyla, the person she'd thought was Toussaint's woman before he informed her that she was "merely a colleague." *Maybe he asked her to join him today, since I turned him down.* A sudden wave of loneliness washed over her, and Alexis sprang from the chair and walked to the jukebox, just for something to do. *Who Toussaint Livingston dates is none of my business,* she firmly told herself. Just then the songs changed. The Whispers crooned about saying yes, and Alexis wished she'd given Toussaint a different answer. *"Have you ever been kissed from head to toe?"* Alexis listened as Walter and Scotty sang a question straight through her heart and imagined that if she'd said yes, her evening would have entailed a very different type of fireworks than the ones she'd later watch from a promenade near her home. *He's trouble, Alexis, and you won't go out with him!* But her heart wasn't listening. Her heart was beating to a totally different drum. Her heart was saying yes.

9

All hail the power of Jesus' name, let angels prostrate fall
 Bring forth the royal diadem and crown him Lord of all . . .
   Victoria sat in the sanctity of her quiet master suite. Malcolm was at work, Justin and Brittany were at school, and the twins were at preschool. Their cook wasn't coming until later in the afternoon, and she'd given the chauffeur the morning off. She was blessedly alone in the house.
   Victoria leaned her head back against the velvety fabric that covered the chaise. Tears ran down her face as she raised her hands in supplication, proclaiming Jesus as the Lord of her life. As the last note of the classically arranged piece played, Victoria bowed her head, tears running down her cheeks. *Yes, you are Lord of all. You are all that matters.* She squeezed her eyes tight to stop the flow of tears and waited for the next song on the CD to begin, the next praise to the Most High that would block out her thoughts.
   "Holy, holy, holy," Victoria whispered, drying her cheeks with the lacy handkerchief that had rested atop her Bible. "Lord God Almighty. Early in the morning our songs shall rise to thee."
   Victoria stayed seated for the next fifteen minutes, bathing herself in the worship CD that her spiritual mentor had given

her. Her mentor was an older woman at the church she'd joined less than three months ago, shortly after visiting the doctor and hearing the news. The beep of her cell phone jarred her out of her devotion. She looked at the ID and frowned.

"What's wrong, Malcolm?" Victoria's carefully crafted peace was immediately shattered. "Why are you calling in the middle of the day?"

Malcolm's thought to remain calm throughout this phone call flew out the window. He'd received great news, which is why he'd called his wife. It was time to share what he'd been working on with her, something he hadn't wanted to do until he was sure of its success. He'd hoped the joy he felt at being one step closer to his goal could extend into the evening. Maybe not.

"Does there have to be a problem for me to call my wife?" he retorted. He stopped, took a deep breath, and continued in a softer tone. He and Victoria had been operating in a disconnected mode ever since she'd joined that church. Actually, they'd been disconnected for years, but this church thing took their dysfunction to new heights. Every conversation was a potential argument. Whenever he'd tried to broach the subject of what was going on, Victoria would claim she was too busy to talk and would either focus on one of the children, retreat to another wing of the house, or leave the house altogether. He hadn't noticed this behavior the first couple months, because his mind had been elsewhere. But ever since the Fourth of July celebration two weeks ago, when Victoria had spent most of her time lounging on a hammock and reading the Bible instead of engaging with their family, Malcolm had deduced that something was deeply wrong in their marriage. And he planned to find out what it was.

"I know I've been busy lately," he said, deciding to begin by placing the focus on himself. "I thought that I'd get out of here a little early, and we could drive up to Stone Mountain, have dinner at that restaurant we discovered last year, with the desserts you loved so much."

"It's Wednesday, Malcolm," Victoria said with restrained patience. "I have Bible study tonight."

"I was hoping that you'd consider skipping it for one night. I have some news to share with you."

I have some news too. News that I'm not ready to share. "God is to come first in one's life, Malcolm. Even before one's spouse."

"Is that what they're teaching you in that place?"

"Why don't you join me tonight?" Victoria said, her voice pleasant for the first time in their conversation. "Then we can learn together."

"So is that the only way I can get my wife back? To come to church with you? Is that the exchange? You'll give me some pussy if I spend time with Jesus?"

Victoria's hang-up was his answer.

Malcolm slowly placed the phone on the receiver. He rose from his desk and looked out of the company's tenth-story window. The Atlanta skyline beckoned him into the city, a place he rarely ventured unless for business. But looking out toward the Bank of America Plaza, Atlanta's tallest landmark, Malcolm realized how long it had been since he'd socialized outside his role as a Taste of Soul VP. He thought about his good friend Jon, a popular and prominent city councilman, and wondered if he still hung out at FGO, an upscale private club that catered to the city's elite. *It's time I get back into the swing of things, start living like the young man that I am,* Malcolm thought as he sat down at his desk, retrieved his key chain, and unlocked the drawer that contained his future treasure. Malcolm's pet project would benefit from him reconnecting with old acquaintances. He pulled out the top-secret folder and smiled, his good mood returning. *Yep, I'll stop by and see my baby and then it's on to FGO. . . .*

★   ★   ★

The CD had stopped playing, but Victoria remained where she was, seated on the chaise. Dozens of thoughts clamored for attention in her mind, but one was definitely front and center. Soon, she knew, she'd run out of excuses for why she'd been distant from both Malcolm and his family, why she didn't want to have sex and had begun sleeping in the guest room more frequently. *But how can I tell him, Lord? How do I explain a problem that only you can solve?* These were the questions that consumed Victoria's thoughts until she heard the sound of the nanny bringing the twins home from preschool and the cook arriving shortly afterward. How did she tell her husband— who hadn't wanted a third child when they had twins—that baby number five was on the way?

10

Malcolm straightened his suit coat and adjusted his tie as he rode the elevator to the top floor of the tall building, where FGO was located. Founded by a senator's son a half century ago, FGO—For Gentlemen Only—had been, until ten years ago, a male-only club. Now, women were allowed to frequent the establishment, under what was defined as a guest membership, but they could not formally join the club as a voting or chartered member. And the only way men could become members was to have another member in good standing refer them. Ironically, Adam and Ace had been referred by Victoria's uncle and had been members for over twenty years. Both Malcolm and Toussaint had been invited once they graduated Morehouse. Toussaint was a regular visitor, going there at least once a week. Malcolm, on the other hand, hadn't been to FGO in months.

"Mr. Livingston!" the host exclaimed, shaking Malcolm's hand enthusiastically. This elderly gentleman, with a dark, well-worn face and stark-white hair, had known Malcolm since he was a boy. "It's a pleasure to see you, sir."

"The pleasure's mine, Harold," Malcolm said, giving the host's shoulder an affectionate squeeze. They chatted briefly, inquiring about each other's families, Harold's beloved Atlanta Braves, and his second love after baseball—barbeque.

"Tell your daddy he still owes me from our last bet," Harold said, his eyes twinkling.

"Ha! Will do, sir. Will do."

"Malcolm! My man!" Jon Abernathy walked briskly toward his former college roommate and dear friend. "Who let the dogs out?"

"That should be my question," Malcolm answered as the two men exchanged a soul brother's handshake and quick embrace. "I thought I might find you here."

"What, did Victoria make you delete all of your single friends' phone numbers? I haven't heard from you in ages! Just last week I thought about driving over to Taste for a rib dinner, see if you were hiding out in the kitchen."

Malcolm laughed at Jon's statement. The Auburn Taste location, specifically the kitchen, had been where Malcolm could be found on most nights he wasn't on campus, especially during his undergrad years.

Jon led Malcolm over to the table where he'd been sitting. "Well, at least she loosened the leash and let you out tonight," Jon continued. "Good to see you, man."

"It's good to see you too." Malcolm signaled the waiter, who brought him a cognac, neat. He raised the glass in silent salute and took a sip. "So what's up, man? What's the latest around the way?"

"Oh, same old, same old," Jon answered. "Still fighting off the sistahs, running from wedding rings."

Jon had been a ladies' man for as long as Malcolm had known him. At five foot nine and around one hundred sixty-five pounds, he wasn't a big guy. But what he lacked in height he more than made up for with swagger and style. Jon was always impeccably dressed and expertly groomed. His weekly manicure and pedicure was routine, as were his trips to the barber. The spa in which he was part owner kept his dark skin smooth and soft, and the gym kept his muscles firm and abs tight. A marriage shortly after college, just before Malcolm and Victoria wed, had ended in divorce five years ago. Jon doubted he could ever stay faithful, and had vowed to be a bachelor for the rest of his life.

"How's your son?" Malcolm asked.

"Looking more like me every day," Jon proudly answered.

The two men continued talking casually, enjoying each other's company. Malcolm ordered another cognac and Jon had his Seven and Seven refreshed. They'd just finished lamenting the loss of a mutual friend, who'd died in a car accident several months earlier, when Jon stopped midsentence. "Damn," he said, under his breath. "Who is that?"

Malcolm followed Jon's gaze and saw a beautiful, dark-skinned woman with a bodacious body and long, thick locs, accompanied by a distinguished-looking older man. He recognized her instantly. "That's Alexis St. Clair. She's an interior decorator, and in case you're thinking of using a remodel as your line, save it. Toussaint already tried it and it didn't work."

"Maybe Toussaint's getting rusty."

"Hardly. She doesn't date clients, and right now she's redoing his house."

Jon watched the older man walk away from the table, leaving Alexis alone. "I'll keep that in mind," he murmured as he stood, straightened his tie, and walked to his target.

Malcolm shook his head, smiling at memories of him and Jon in grad school. They'd gotten in more trouble than the law allowed, with many of their young-adult antics known to them alone. It was only now that Malcolm realized how much he'd missed his friend. But they'd grown distant when Jon left Atlanta for Yale Law School and Malcolm became immersed in the family business. *I wonder if he still plays golf. Maybe we can hit the holes once a week and stay connected.*

"Malcolm, I thought that was you." Joyce Witherspoon had noticed Malcolm when she entered the establishment but hadn't wanted to interrupt the conversation. Now she sidled up to his table with her hand outstretched.

"Hello," Malcolm said while rising, his expression revealing his puzzlement. And then, recognition dawned. "Joyce! I almost didn't recognize you!"

"May I join you?"

"Please." Malcolm moved so that Joyce could sit on his side of the booth. "You look nice. Not that you don't when you come to the office, or I see you in the catering kitchen but... well..."

Joyce laughed. "I've been told I clean up well. And after wearing conservative suits all day while interacting with my clientele, I like to get girlie after hours." She especially took care with her appearance when she came to the club, and tonight was no exception. The Christian Dior silk, form-fitting dress that stopped a couple inches above the knee, not to mention her four-inch heels, made Joyce feel feminine and fabulous. The thick, permed hair that was almost always in a conservative bun swung loose and carefree around her shoulders, and the subtle fragrance that brought to mind flower gardens and springtime tickled the noses of those around her. She'd stopped by here on her way home, hoping she'd run into Adam. Even though he'd called her the month before and clarified—yet again—that there was no way he'd have an affair with her, that he very much loved his wife, Joyce was determined and patient. She'd always been attracted to older, successful men, and had carried a torch for Adam Livingston for years. She would most likely never stop hoping they'd get together. But now, here sat Adam's son, bearing a striking resemblance to his father. She'd always thought Malcolm handsome but had never considered how much he favored his dad. *Hmmm, I wonder if he's faithful to Victoria?* While Atlanta had come to be known as the "black gay capital," there was still a plethora of single, heterosexual men who would love to spend time with Joyce. She was attractive, smart, and her event-planning business already boasted an upscale clientele. But for some reason, the men Joyce found herself attracted to, the ones she felt most successful, most attractive, and most desirable, were also, usually, most married. "I don't think I've ever seen you here," she said once the waiter had taken her drink order.

"It's been a while."

"I'm sure a wife, four children, and the business keep you pretty busy."

Malcolm nodded. Suddenly, he didn't want to talk about Victoria, the kids, or Taste of Soul. He wanted to talk about a topic he hadn't paid much attention to lately—himself.

As if she'd read his mind, Joyce's next question provided the opportunity to do just that. "How do you know our esteemed councilman?"

"Jon and I went to school together."

"Morehouse, correct?"

"Yes." Malcolm shared a little of the good old days, when he was the big man on campus—large and in charge.

"I have a hard time envisioning you as a happy-go-lucky collegiate. You're always so serious when I see you, so grounded. You seem to lead the life of someone well established, but you can't be more than, what, thirty-five, six?"

"Thirty-four." Malcolm took a sip of the drink that had remained untouched since the waiter had brought it over. "I guess I did settle down rather quickly. I married young. Victoria and I had our first child two years later and our daughter two years after that."

"And you have twins, correct?"

"Three years old."

"Plans for more? You know, you can have eight and get your own reality TV show."

"Oh, no," Malcolm said, holding up his hands in mock surrender. "Four is more than enough." *And two more than I wanted,* he thought. "My baby-making days are over, at least the human kind. I have another baby I'm working on, though."

"Oh, really?" Joyce leaned forward and placed her chin in her palm, giving Malcolm her undivided attention. She'd never talked with him about anything but food and event business, and found him fascinating. "Tell me more."

Malcolm was just about to share his secret endeavor with Joyce when Jon came back to the table.

"Jon Abernathy," he said, sitting down and extending his hand to Joyce.

"A pleasure to formally meet you, Councilman. Joyce Witherspoon."

"Your face looks familiar. Where have I seen you before?"

"Any number of places. I'm an event planner and have organized several affairs for the city, including some campaign fund-raising events."

"Yes, of course. I knew I'd seen you before."

Joyce reached into her purse and pulled out a card. She'd hoped to learn more about Malcolm but felt that rather than wear out her welcome, now was a good time to take her leave. "Malcolm, I so enjoyed visiting with you. Jon, it was a pleasure to see you again. Please keep me in mind for any social event you need planned, large or small."

Malcolm rose and helped Joyce out of the booth. "Take care," he said, giving her a light kiss on the temple. Her fresh, floral scent was intoxicating, a turn-on, especially for a man who'd gone months without intimacy. Yet, he forced himself not to watch her as she walked away. Rather he turned his attention to his friend.

"So . . . how was your fact-finding mission?"

"Successful, Malcolm. You know how I roll."

"Oh, really, a date just like that?"

Jon had the decency to look sheepish. "Okay, more like an appointment. She just joined the Black Chamber of Commerce. I'm good friends with the president, and can, you know, help her out."

"Uh-huh. Who's that guy she's with?"

Jon shrugged as he repeated the name. "She introduced him as a friend. But since I didn't see a wedding ring, I'd say she's fair game." Jon looked over at her again. "*Very* fair game. She's even more beautiful up close."

Malcolm looked up and met Alexis's eye. She smiled and waved, and he waved back. "Guess I should go say hello," he said, easing up from the table. "She turned our family room into my personal paradise and did a bang-up job."

Is that so? Jon pondered as he watched her and Malcolm's easygoing interaction. *Well, when I get with you, baby girl, I'll be banging too.*

11

Zoe pulled into the fairly crowded Taste of Soul parking lot. It had been a long Monday, and the last thing she felt like doing was cooking dinner. It had been a while since she'd eaten at the restaurant of her employ. She walked into the bar area, which was also where takeout orders were placed. All of the bar seats were taken, as were most of the two-seater tables. Zoe waved at the hostess and spoke to the woman behind the takeout counter, who handed her a menu. Zoe swayed from side to side as the Commodores serenaded her with sweet love, followed by a love ballad from L.T.D. She'd narrowed her choices down to two when someone came up behind her and whispered in her ear.

"The greens are good, but be careful of the cabbage.... I'm just sayin'."

Zoe smiled. "You know you better keep your *sauce* out my shit," she whispered in an equally conspiratorial tone. "What you still doing here, girl?"

Chardonnay waved at one of her regular customers. "Workin' a double for someone who called in sick."

"I'm trying to decide between Marvin's Mellow Meat Loaf and the Tempting Temptations T-Bone."

"The meat loaf, hands down. Chef put his foot in it today, real talk. Plus, that special comes with three sides."

"Dang, my mouth is already watering."

"I'm getting ready to take my break. So I'll go ahead and put in the order with Chef, tell him to hold it for ten, and then you can join me in the parking lot for a cigarette."

"Bet. Hook me up with the greens, fried potato salad, and, of course, the mac and cheese. Oh, and add a slice of that sweet potato pie."

A couple minutes later, Zoe and Chardonnay sat in Zoe's Toyota Camry, puffing on Newports. "It's hot as Hades out here!"

"Yeah, they say this is going to be the hottest August Atlanta has seen in a long time."

"Sure feels like it." Zoe took a drag from her borrowed cigarette. Her New Year's resolution had been to quit smoking, but so far she'd only managed to quit buying her own. "Shyla been back?"

"Naw, that skank ain't been back in here. But this fine brother walked up in here today. His name's Q. He's a personal trainer and also owns a gym."

"What, you're getting ready to start exercising?"

"Yes, but probably not in the way you mean."

"Ha! You're a mess, girl."

"Uh-huh. Toussaint's been back, too, with another heifah on his arm."

"That boy has a woman for every day of the week."

"Shit, I wouldn't mind a day of the week with his fine ass." Chardonnay took a long pull off her Newport, followed by a swig of cola. "But you were probably right with what you said. Brothah like him would never look twice at a chick like me."

"C'mon now, I didn't mean that in a bad way. I was just saying—"

"You don't have to explain that shit," Chardonnay interrupted. "I know I'm not high black society, model material, rich or whatever. I know I'm a single mother with two bad-ass kids by two different fathers. But my pussy is still tight, and I can rival a video vixen when it comes to giving head. So don't count me out. 'Cause no matter what circle you travel in, an expert blow job is clout all day long."

"You're good peeps, Chardonnay. And one of these days a brothah's gonna see that."

At that precise moment, the back door to the restaurant opened and Bobby strolled out. He looked rugged and work-ready in a cool white top and loose jeans.

"Aw, hell," Chardonnay said. "Here comes trouble."

Zoe watched as Bobby approached. She took in his plain facial features while noting his tight, albeit thin, body and the muscles evident through his sleeveless white tee. *There's something about him* . . .

"What's up, ladies?" Bobby said once he'd reached the car and Zoe had rolled down the window on Chardonnay's side. "Tobacco all y'all smokin'?"

"What else would I be smoking with three more hours on my shift?" Chardonnay shot back. "You one ignorant-ass mutha—"

"What's that tattoo on your arm?" Zoe interrupted, overriding Chardonnay's insult.

"Aw, that's in memory of my moms. She loved flowers, roses especially. When she died a few years ago, I got this rose," he said, turning to show off the tattoo more effectively, "with the sun in the background on account of how she was the sunshine of my life. And then the cross running through it is because she was a religious woman. I ain't followed in her footsteps on that right there, but I think her prayers are still keeping a brothah protected, you know?"

"That's beautiful, Bobby," Zoe said sincerely.

Chardonnay stared straight ahead as Bobby walked over to her side of the car. She finished her cigarette and squashed it in the ashtray. "Your order's probably up," she said to Zoe. "And so is my break. Move, Bobby!"

"Damn, baby girl, you're so hot! I like that shit right there—bodacious!" Bobby's smile was lopsided as he opened Chardonnay's door and stepped aside.

"Bye, Zoe," Chardonnay said as she stepped out of the car. She brushed past Bobby and hurried into the restaurant.

Zoe waved to Bobby before going around to the front of the restaurant and picking up her special—Marvin's Mellow Meat Loaf with sides. She smiled when she checked her order and noted that Chardonnay had exchanged her collard greens for smothered cabbage. "Whatever, wench," she said, laughing out loud. She loved each green equally and was confident that the only seasonings in this serving were from the chef's pantry, not Chardonnay's panties.

It wasn't until she was almost home, with visions of meat loaf dancing in her head, that she remembered what she'd forgotten to ask her friend. What she meant to find out from Chardonnay the next time she saw her. What was up with her and Bobby? Had he told the truth? Had Chardonnay really been on Bobby's Candid Cell Camera, thus enabling him to blackmail her for a "taste" of her goodies? Or had she just been punked?

12

The house was quiet. Candace browsed through the materials for the upcoming Jack and Jill conference while Adam flipped through a *Forbes* magazine. The chef had cleaned the kitchen and gone home for the night, his dinner of filet of sole with braised vegetables and saffron rice a pleasant memory. A bowl of fresh, cut fruit chilled in the refrigerator, along with a bottle of sparkling white wine. Candace had turned down Adam's initial offer for a glass of bubbly but now thought it might be just what she needed. She had a lot on her mind.

"I think I'll have that glass of wine now," she said, rising. "And some fruit. You want some?"

Adam eyed her suggestively. "I sure do."

Candace laughed, even as thoughts of greed and indulgence interfered with her husband's flirtations. She'd been with the same man for three decades, enjoying two wonderful boys and a fairly stable family life. Adam had given her the world, without her even asking. "You're too good to me, you know that?" she whispered, walking toward him.

"Is that so? You're too good to me, too—looking good, that is. Those workouts are agreeing with you."

Candace twirled around, her soft cotton housecoat flowing around her. "Ooh, can you tell?"

"I'd better be able to tell something. You're working out now, what, three days a week?"

"Yes, if you don't include my Pilates class."

"Just remember, I like a woman with some meat on her bones and some junk in the trunk."

"I'll remember."

Just then a memory flashed in Adam's mind—the naked picture Joyce had sent him months ago, before the conversation in which he warned her to not call him again. He deleted the mental image quickly, just as he'd done from his computer. He was glad to be rid of her; he had all he needed right here.

Candace leaned down, placing a tender kiss on Adam's lips. "Wine or cognac?"

"I'll lay off the heavy stuff tonight and share the wine with you."

Moments later, Candace joined Adam on the couch. He put down the magazine and, once Candace had reclined beside him, reached over and began to massage her feet.

Candace closed her eyes, focused on her husband's ministrations. *It's these little things* . . .

"Can."

"Hum?"

"What's on your mind, baby?"

Candace's eyes opened slowly. "Nothing, Adam. Why do you ask?"

"Girl, don't even try it. I've loved you over half my life and know you probably better than I know myself. Now, talk to me, baby. What's wrong?"

Candace sighed. *Everything and nothing.* Crazy mood swings that she blamed on the change. But she didn't have the energy to verbalize all of what she was feeling. So she shared what she could. "Victoria stopped by today."

"Oh, really? She finally decided to rejoin the Livingston clan? What did she have to say for herself?"

"More than either you, me, or definitely Malcolm would

ever want to hear." Candace waited a beat and then continued.
"She's pregnant."

Adam calmly absorbed this news. He placed Candace's
right foot down and reached for her left one. "Again?" he finally asked. "I thought they were done having babies."

"Yeah, so did Malcolm."

"What is he saying?"

"That's just it. He doesn't know yet."

Adam's hand stopped in midstroke. "What in the hell is she
waiting on to tell him?"

"Courage. She's afraid of how he'll react, since he was so
adamant that they stop having kids two kids ago. Now, here
comes another one . . . and more weight gain."

"Why does she keep doing this, letting herself get pregnant? The girl's got a head on her shoulders. She knows how
babies are made. So what exactly is going on here, Candace?
Did she tell you that?"

"I think she's still trying to figure that out." Candace
shifted her body until she lay in Adam's arms. During their
conversation, Victoria had opened up more than she had in
the ten-plus years she'd been a Livingston. And now Candace
was called on to break the news that Victoria could not.

"I remember when those two got married," Adam said.

"Who could forget? Valarie Saunders just about drove us
all crazy . . . ."

"Wasn't that her prerogative as the mother of the bride?"

"If you say so."

"What was it, five hundred guests?"

"Fifteen bridesmaids and groomsmen on top of the best
man and maid of honor—and don't get me started with that
seven-course sit-down dinner and the orchestra flown in from
Japan."

"Ha! But the doves that flew away at the end, that was a
nice touch."

"It all was beautiful, really. Victoria was a stunning bride. And she and Malcolm were so happy. They could have floated to Barbados."

"It used to be you couldn't separate those lovebirds. I wonder what happened?"

"You mean besides four kids and another one on the way?"

"We had two, and it didn't change us."

Candace looked at Adam sideways. "We had our dry spells."

"Yeah, but we've always been happy."

"Umm. Speaking of happy," Candace whispered, reaching into her husband's boxers and massaging the treasure inside. "Let's go to bed. I want some of this . . . long and strong."

"I'll give it to you strong, but I don't know for how long." Adam laughed. "Am I going to have to start taking Viagra to keep up with you?"

"You just might," Candace answered. She rose from the couch and reached for her husband. "But now, for tonight, I'll take what I can get."

"And I'll give it to you, baby."

"Mmm, that's what I'm talking about."

13

Toussaint tried to focus on the expansion plans he'd worked on all morning, details he hoped would eventually materialize into the first Taste location on the West Coast. That he'd been staring at the same page for the past ten minutes without really reading it proved he was failing miserably at this attempt. No matter where he rested his eye, all he could see was what had made his heart almost stop the past Saturday night—Alexis walking into the dinner party he'd attended, on the arm of Councilman Jon Abernathy.

Toussaint had almost passed on the invitation. Ongoing developments at Taste had his schedule crammed full. On top of that, being temporarily housed at a one-bedroom condo in Buckhead while Alexis tore apart his living and dining room to create the masterpiece she'd shown him on paper was interrupting his groove. *No, brothah, Alexis is interrupting your groove.* Toussaint swiveled around to face the window and leaned back against his chair. It was true. While *her* plans to transform his home were proceeding nicely, *his* plan to tap her fabuluscious badonkadonk was way behind schedule.

To take his mind off his misery, Toussaint had finally accepted the Saturday night NAACP fund-raiser invitation from a longtime family friend. He'd called Shyla and invited her along. She'd suggested they get together that night, Friday, and they did—had dinner, took in the latest Tyler Perry, and finished the evening with a night of great sex.

They'd arrived at the soiree fashionably late. Toussaint had been his usual suave self, and Shyla had looked radiant beside him. Then, while standing in the local NAACP president's living room, he'd watched a stunning couple enter the room and cross over to speak to the host. Toussaint had immediately copped an attitude while an uncharacteristic and equally unjustified possessiveness of Alexis ran down his spine. Begrudgingly, he'd admitted that they looked good together. Jon wore a chocolate-brown tailored suit, a shade darker than his skin. Alexis's cocktail dress was a perfect tan complement, with bulky wooden accessories that added to her exotic allure. When Toussaint's and Alexis's eyes met, she'd stabbed him in the heart with her dazzling smile and friendly wave. Jon had looked in his direction then and placed a protective arm around Alexis's waist. Toussaint would have ignored them (as silly as that would have looked considering Alexis now spent more time in his home than he did and Jon was one of Malcolm's best friends), but Mr. Gray, the host, had chosen that moment to wave them over. The conversation had been forced and stilted, and shortly after that, he and Shyla had left the party. He'd called Alexis the next day and gotten her voice mail.

Toussaint sighed, turned, and reached for a folder. He consciously focused on the page full of numbers, determined to put his mind back on work, where it belonged. He'd rather think about malls and menus than the uncomfortable truth overriding all other thought—that for the first time in Toussaint's life, his cock was being blocked.

"Hey, brother, you got a minute?" Malcolm had opened

the door and stuck his head inside Toussaint's office without Toussaint noticing it.

"Sure, uh, come on in," Toussaint said, glad for the interruption. "I was just going over the numbers for the Los Angeles location." He offered the folder to Malcolm. "They're still pretty rough but you can get an idea—"

"This visit isn't about business," Malcolm said wearily, waving away the folder that Toussaint offered and sitting down heavily. "Have you talked to Mama today?"

"This morning. Why?"

"Did she mention anything to you?"

Toussaint's brow furrowed. "About what?"

"Something serious, by the way she sounded. I just got off the phone with her. She wants me to stop by after work."

"Why?"

Malcolm shrugged. "I don't know. She said she'd explain everything when I came over."

"Maybe I should call and ask if I need to come as well."

"She didn't mention you or Dad, which has me puzzled. It's been a long time since I've been summoned. And that's how it felt."

Toussaint leaned forward, putting his elbows on the desk and resting his chin on his hands. "You don't think this could be about their marriage, do you?"

Malcolm's head shot up, his face a question mark. "Mama and Daddy are cool as always. At least, that's how it looks to me."

"Looks can be deceiving."

Both men were silent a moment, remembering the shock waves that had reverberated through their social circle last year when a friend's marriage of thirty-five years disintegrated after a love-child revelation.

"Well . . . no use speculating until we know for sure what's up." Toussaint looked into the distance. That's what he'd been

doing since Saturday—speculating on Jon and Alexis and wondering if the player had already played *his* woman's instrument.
He frowned at the thought.

"Don't let it worry you, man," Malcolm said, misreading
the reason for Toussaint's serious expression. "I probably shouldn't
have said anything until I knew what she wanted."

"What's up with your boy Jon?"

The abrupt change of subject caught Malcolm off guard.
"Jon Abernathy?"

"Who else?"

Malcolm casually reached for the folder Toussaint had earlier offered. "Still doing his thing, far as I know. I saw him the
other night at the club."

"The FGO? You went there?"

"I know it's been a while. But, yes, I stopped by the other
night on my way home. Surprised I didn't see you. Jon was
there. And so was your girl, Alexis." Malcolm smiled, remembering how much he'd enjoyed hanging out with his friend.
"Soon as her date went to the bathroom, Jon was on it."

*So they just met? At FGO, when Alexis was with yet another
man?* Toussaint was totally baffled. How was it that she could
go out with other brothahs and not him? "Well, knowing
Jon—and Alexis—they're probably already working on a design for his house." Toussaint leaned back in his chair and tried
to sound casual. "By the time he finds out she doesn't date her
clients, it will be too late."

"Naw, I already told him you'd tried that route. He's trying
another one—the 'let's network' tactic. The good old bait and
switch."

"Damn, man!" So much for being casual. "Why'd you tell
him that?"

"Why wouldn't I? You aren't tasting the cocoa puff. Besides, everybody knows that Shyla is keeping you satisfied,
along with who knows how many others."

Toussaint snorted. "Shyla."

"Oh, so that's not the case?"

"I told you about me and Shyla—that's a casual thing."

"I don't know why. Shyla seems like a good woman, and our families know each other. We don't know anything about Ms. St. Clair, and believe me, Candace Livingston would make it her mission to find out!"

"Mama doesn't need to do a background check yet. I saw Alexis this past weekend. She was with Jon at the Grays' party Saturday night. He mention anything to you about that?"

"Oh, so that's what's up." Malcolm eyed his brother a moment. "Jon and I haven't talked since last week when he invited Victoria and me to that same affair. I wanted to go, but once again *Miss Holy* had plans, something to do with that datgum church where she practically lives."

"Victoria was always religious, but I've never known her to be a staunch churchaholic the way she seems now."

"You don't know the half."

"Do I want to?"

"Naw, man. Sounds like your life is way more interesting than mine. Especially since it seems Alexis has your attention but for whatever reason you haven't been able to get hers."

"Please..."

"Naw, c'mon now. It's not like you to beat around the bush when it comes to...well...the bush. You haven't asked about Jon in a long time, and now I find out you saw the two of them together this past weekend. Hmmm." Malcolm rubbed his chin. "Have we finally met our match?"

Toussaint's office phone rang, and even though the caller ID told him it was Shyla, he was glad for the interruption. It wasn't like a female to ever keep Toussaint out of the panties. He didn't want Malcolm to know he was slipping. "One moment," he said to Shyla when he picked up the receiver. And then to Malcolm, "Give me some feedback on those numbers.

We'll have more concrete information in two weeks, but those are enough to get the conversation started."

"Just don't think I'm going to forget the other conversation we were having. The one about—"

"Yeah, later, Malcolm," Toussaint quickly interrupted.

Malcolm smiled as he softly closed the door, then frowned when he remembered his next destination—his mama's house.

14

"Hey, Mama." Malcolm walked into what he knew was his mother's favorite room in the house besides the kitchen—the sunroom. It was a tropical paradise, filled with exotic plants, flowing fountains, a koi pond, and statutes bearing the same Eastern flavor as their landscaped backyard. Candace looked liked a queen, draped as she was across a gold velvet chaise. She wore a casual striped pantsuit made of soft, flowing fabric. She stood at Malcolm's greeting and floated across the room, her arms outstretched.

"Hello, son," she said, enveloping him in a big hug. "How was your day, baby? You look tired. Can I get you something to drink?"

"I don't know, Mama. Am I going to need it?"

Instead of answering, Candace called for the housekeeper, who returned in minutes with a spritzer for Candace, a spot of cognac for Malcolm, and a tray of veggies, crackers, and dip.

Malcolm watched the housekeeper leave the room and then took a sip of his cognac. "Okay, Mama, what is this all about?"

Candace took a deep breath. "I don't know how to say this except straight out. Victoria is pregnant."

Malcolm didn't move, barely breathed. Surely he'd heard

incorrectly. His brow furrowed slightly as he took another of his signature drink—Rémy Martin XO. *Mama didn't say what I think she said. There is no way in hell I heard Mama say—*

"Your wife is going to have another baby, son."

"What the f—" Malcolm began, standing abruptly. "Sorry, Mama."

"It's all right, son. I know you're upset—"

"Upset? You think this kind of news would simply *upset* me?" Malcolm threw back the rest of the cognac and slammed the tumbler down on the table. He began to pace. "That's why she's been tripping these last months, why she hasn't wanted me anywhere near her in the bedroom. That... She's gone and done it again, Mama. When she knows I don't want any more kids!"

"She says it was an accident."

"Well, maybe we can have another accident where she gets pushed down a flight of stairs."

"Malcolm, don't even joke like that."

"Who says I'm joking? We had this conversation before the twins were born and then again afterward. No. More. Kids! Damn!"

"Listen to me, darling." Candace walked over and stood before him. "Your wife knew you'd be angry, and you have every right to be. That's why she wanted me to tell you. She honestly didn't know what you'd do." Candace shivered, remembering Malcolm's comment. "I think you should stay here and speak with your father."

"How far along is she?"

Candace hesitated. "Too far along to do what you're thinking. It would be dangerous to have an abortion now, Malcolm. She's almost four months."

Almost four months. "So now she can tell me, since it's too late to do anything about it." It all made sense now—why she'd stopped dressing around him a couple months ago, refused his advances, spent so much time in the guest room. "I was a fool not to realize it," Malcolm concluded. "I should have figured it out."

"Baby, don't beat yourself up. Victoria's been big for a while now, never lost her stomach after the twins. Didn't look like she was showing at the Fourth of July picnic, and I was around her quite a bit that day. Even Mama didn't pick up on it, and you know that Marietta Livingston don't miss much." Candace had turned to gaze out the window as she talked. When Malcolm didn't respond, she looked around, just in time to see him leaving the room. "Malcolm, wait, where are you going?" She hurried after him. *Oh, Lord, where is Adam?* "Malcolm!"

Malcolm heard his mother calling him as he headed for the front door, and any other time in his life he would have stopped to answer. But tonight, Candace had told him more than enough. She'd given him a reason to divorce his wife.

15

Victoria rose from the side of the bed where she'd been praying. She looked at her watch as she wiped her eyes. *Candace has probably told him by now.* She got ready to go check on the kids and then remembered she'd had the nanny take the twins to the movies and had let the two older children stay with friends. She was alone. The house was too quiet, no sounds to drown out her thoughts. Victoria sat on the bed and wrapped her arms around herself, feeling a sudden chill that had nothing to do with the home's central air. With four children and an equal amount of housing staff, moments of solitude were rare. Now she realized that was a good thing. Silence amplified her thoughts, and memories . . .

Looking around the room, Victoria smiled. The place was immaculate, flowers abounded, and a bottle of Malcolm's favorite bubbly chilled on the buffet. She'd just finished lighting the last candle when the door opened.

"Wow," Malcolm said as he entered. "What's the occasion?"

"Hey, baby." Victoria's walk was seductive as she slinked toward her husband. She reached him and seared him with a kiss.

"Mmm, that is some greeting." He kissed her again. "What happened? Did you win the lottery?"

"Ha! Something like that."

"Seriously, baby, what did I miss? An anniversary, birthday . . . wait, where are the kids?"

"They're with your parents." Victoria reached up, loosened Malcolm's tie, and undid his first two buttons. "Come sit down, relax. Let me pour you some bubbly."

Malcolm walked to the couch. "So . . . we're celebrating."

"Uh-huh." After filling their glasses, Victoria joined Malcolm on the couch. She sat close, the silk wrap she wore teasing his body. He loved silk. That's why she'd worn it. "Remember what you said about the lottery?"

"We won?"

"No, but we are getting richer."

Malcolm barely heard her. He'd turned his body toward her, fingering the silky fabric as he eased it off her shoulder. The material, her scent, the setting, the bubbly had quickly put him in the mood. Since having children, alone time was sacred. He reached for her breast, ready to make the most of it.

"Malcolm, did you hear me?"

"Huh?" He exposed her breast and licked her nipple.

"We're getting richer."

"How?" He moved to the other side.

"We're pregnant."

Screech. Malcolm stood and walked over to the light-dimmer switch. Bright light flooded the room, killing the mood as much as had Victoria's announcement. He glared at her for a long moment. "I thought we'd decided to have no more children? I distinctly remember telling you I didn't want to have any more. We hardly have time for ourselves as it is!"

"I know, Malcolm. But I never agreed—"

"Oh, so your body, your babies? Is that how it goes? I'm just a sperm donor with no say at all?"

"No, Malcolm, not at all. I didn't set out to get pregnant...."

"I'm supposed to believe it just happened?"

"Yes."

"Well, guess what? I don't believe it."

The evening ended with their not speaking to each other and Malcolm sleeping on the couch. Eventually he came around, and even after discovering they were having twins, he resigned himself to another round of raising babies. He talked to her about him having a vasectomy—she had talked him out of it.

In the blink of an eye, Victoria was balancing newborns and toddlers. The children became her world, and her focus. She paid no attention to herself, or the fifty pounds she'd gained. In her children she found fulfillment; she felt wanted, needed. She hardly noticed when Malcolm began spending more and more time at the office, the club, the golf course, anywhere but home. By the time she realized anything was happening, their rift had become a chasm, with Victoria becoming more and more unhappy. Three months ago, she poured her heart out to her mother, who mentioned church....

A movement, soft but definitive, brought Victoria out of her revelry. She looked down at her stomach before placing a hand on the bulge. As she felt the movement again, Victoria smiled broadly, tears welling up instantly. It was the first time she'd felt this baby move. "Hello, pumpkin," she whispered, wiggling her stomach in hopes of getting the baby to move again. "I love you!"

When the phone rang minutes later, Victoria was still rocking the baby within herself. "Hello?" she said dreamily, her hand resting on the place where she'd felt its movement.

"Victoria?" Candace thought she recognized her daughter-in-law's voice, but whoever it was sounded much too happy, considering the soberness of the situation. "I told Malcolm about the baby, and he is not pleased."

Victoria's happy mood quickly dissipated, replaced by fear, which was quickly masked by the snobby, confident attitude she'd honed for decades. "What did he say?"

"What do you expect a man to say who has told his wife in no uncertain terms that he didn't want any more kids and finds out another one is on the way? He's furious, Victoria. And as I told you earlier, he has every right to be."

"Let's not do this tonight, Candace. I'm not in the mood."

"Neither am I. And neither is Malcolm."

Victoria changed tactics, along with her position on the bed. "Some husbands would be happy to learn that their wife is with child."

"Your husband is not one of them. But you got pregnant anyway. Children get older, Victoria. They grow up. They leave home. So even with your explanation, I can't condone what you did. You can't keep having babies to fill the hole in your marriage."

"Don't condone it—just accept it. You're getting ready to be a grandma again."

Is this woman crazy? Most of the time, Candace ignored Victoria's haughty attitude because anyone who met Valarie Saunders would see that the apple hadn't fallen far from the tree. And she knew another Victoria, the sweet, bubbly one her son fell in love with, whose house was immaculate and whose children were well bred. She hadn't seen this version of Vickie in quite a while. Candace took a deep breath and tried to tamp down an escalating temper. "Victoria, we need to talk, really talk. Technically speaking, your marriage is none of my business."

"Technically?"

"But you've got another baby on the way. Your kids need their father around."

"I would never push Malcolm out of our home, Candace. I love your son and can't see life without him."

"But he may be able to peep one without you. Has that thought crossed your mind, Victoria? A dissolution of marriage? Divorce papers?" After a moment of silence, Candace continued. "Uh-huh, I didn't think so. Now, when do you want to meet?"

16

"Mr. Livingston! Gracing us with your presence two times in as many weeks. Is it getting ready to snow in Atlanta?"

"I think we've already seen that," Malcolm replied, finding a soft smile for Harold, FGO's kind host.

"Yessiree, we have! But the first week in August?"

Malcolm gave Harold a pat on the back and walked into the club. For someone who'd been absent from the scene before last week, Malcolm felt a strange comfort in the surroundings—the dark oak booths and tables with stately gray fabric cushioning the chairs. There weren't many people in the club this rainy Monday night, Malcolm noted as he walked to a far booth and sat down. He looked dispassionately at the muted candle-style chandeliers, taking in the framed black-and-white pictures of Atlanta's finest that adorned the walls and finally resting his eyes on the large U-shaped ornate bar that anchored the room. There was one person sitting on a barstool, texting on her BlackBerry and sipping wine. She looked up at the same time he realized who it was. *Joyce.* She waved but didn't come over. *Good,* he thought. The only company Malcolm wanted right now was a Rémy Martin XO. Straight, no chaser. He placed his head in his hands and ran weary fingers over his face. When he opened his eyes, Joyce was standing beside him.

"Hello, Malcolm. Fancy meeting you here again."

"This is obviously your hangout spot," Malcolm responded without looking up.

"It would appear that way. I am here quite often. But I just received my guest membership a few months ago. Guess the excitement of being allowed inside these hallowed walls hasn't worn off."

Silence.

"I was going to ask if you were in the mood for company, but I think I have my answer. Hard day?"

"I've had better," Malcolm replied.

"It's been a rough one for me too. May I?" Joyce motioned to the seat on the other side of the booth and sat down after Malcolm nodded his agreement. "Lost a major client today," she went on. "One that would have given me an in to the 2012 presidential election arena—fund-raisers and what have you. I'd worked on that account for almost six months."

This information piqued Malcolm's interest. First and foremost, he was a businessman, and losses for Joyce's company, Silver Spoon Events, was potentially a loss for the Livingston Corporation's catering arm. "What happened?"

"Got undercut, big-time. Big event planners out of Los Angeles came in with figures I couldn't match. They're basically eating the cost to get their foot in the door. I'd have done the same thing if I could have afforded it."

"Doesn't look like you're doing too bad."

Joyce smiled. "I do okay, but not good enough to wave away six figures . . . yet." Joyce watched Malcolm sip the cognac the waiter had brought while she nursed her Pinot Noir. "Something happen at one of the restaurants today or . . . at corporate?"

"Naw," Malcolm said, leaning back and kneading his forehead. "Business is booming. Everything at Taste is just great." His comment dripped with sarcasm.

"Do you want to talk about it?" Joyce's voice was soft, caring. "Sometimes it helps to air it out."

Malcolm remained silent for so long that Joyce didn't think he'd answer her. She toyed with the idea of getting up and leaving, but something about Malcolm's demeanor kept her glued to her seat. He looked as if he could use a friend, and since Adam had rejected her blatant advances yet again, so could she.

"Victoria's pregnant." Malcolm surprised himself by sharing this news, then realized how much he wanted to talk about it with someone neutral, someone who wasn't a grandmother, grandfather, or uncle to the unborn. "Baby number five."

Joyce remained quiet, absorbing the impact of this news as much as Malcolm's obvious displeasure. *Goodness, they just had twins. And now another one?* "You don't sound too happy," she finally said.

Malcolm's laugh was sinister, hollow. Instead of answering, he downed the liquor in his glass and motioned to the waiter. He held up two fingers to indicate a double shot.

"Have you eaten?" Joyce asked. She was concerned at how much Malcolm was drinking in a short time period, especially considering that he had to drive home. Fortunately, FGO had an arrangement with the four-star restaurant located on the first floor. Orders could be placed by phone and delivered to the club.

When the waiter came over, Joyce asked about the day's special and then placed two orders. When asked, she declined another glass of wine, opting for lemon water instead. If necessary, she would be Malcolm's designated driver. Once she knew Malcolm would soon add food to the liquor in his stomach, she continued. "This isn't any of my business, Malcolm but both you and Victoria know how babies are made."

"I almost got a vasectomy last year," Malcolm said after a

long pause. "The wife talked me out of it, convinced me that since she was on the pill, there was no need to worry."

"No pill is foolproof. Most manufacturers leave room for error, claiming their products to be around ninety-eight-percent effective."

Malcolm snorted. "And here I sit, part of the unlucky two percent."

"Well, there's another way to look at this. Babies are blessings. I've always wanted a child."

"Why don't you have one? Come to think of it, why aren't you married?"

"Good questions."

"Seriously, Joyce. You're a smart, attractive woman. You obviously have a lot going for you. I can think of any number of eligible men here in Atlanta who would be lucky to have you."

"And they're not gay?"

"Well, there's that. ATL has become the black gay capital. But trust me, there are plenty of bona fide heterosexuals hanging in here, and then there's the rest of the country. You travel quite a bit, correct? Which means you're not limited to just looking in this area."

"Maybe I'm just picky. I had my sights on a certain gentlemen the past couple of years, but that didn't work out."

"Oh? What happened?"

"It's a long story, but the short version is that he wasn't available."

"Married?"

To your mother. "At the time we met, he hinted at some dissatisfaction with his marriage. I thought a separation was imminent. He's a wonderful man, worth waiting for. So I did."

"And now..."

"He's not going to leave her. So I've moved on."

"Good for you. You deserve someone who can give you as much as I'm sure you'll give him."

Joyce cocked her head and studied Malcolm. *You really are a younger version of your father. I wonder if you're as committed to Victoria as he is to Candace.* "You're a good man, Malcolm. I hope Victoria appreciates you."

Malcolm took a long sip of cognac. "Victoria appreciates the lifestyle and the children. She doesn't even—"

Malcolm became silent as the waiter appeared with rolls, two side salads, and piping-hot plates containing medium-well sirloin steaks; buttery baked potatoes, and carrot, corn, and green bean vegetable medleys. "I didn't realize how hungry I was," he said after a few bites. "Thanks for reminding me to eat. And thanks for listening. It's been a while since I felt I've been heard."

"That's what friends are for."

Joyce waited for the conversation to change from good food and big business back to babies and the state of Malcolm's marriage. When it didn't, Joyce decided it was time to go home. She'd had a busy day and another awaited her tomorrow. Still, she'd enjoyed spending the evening in the company of a handsome, intelligent man.

"Thanks for dinner," Joyce said after Malcolm insisted on paying the bill. "I've enjoyed the company but have probably kept you away from your family long enough. Are you okay to drive?"

"Yes, but I'm not ready to go home. Let's go back to my office and have coffee. There's something there that I want to show you."

17

September came in bright and balmy. Candace and Diane sat in Diane's airy dining room, sipping cappuccinos and poring over the program samples for the upcoming annual black-tie social.

"I like that one," Diane said, pointing to a design made from cream-colored linen paper that featured a scalloped border.

"Yes, that's nice."

"But this gold and purple design looks more regal and would complement the overall color scheme. This," she said, picking up the cream-colored paper, "might be too bland."

"Uh-huh."

"Candace Renee Livingston, where is your mind, darlin'? Because it certainly isn't on Jack or Jill. Never mind, I know what it's on, or more specifically, who it's on. I made some sweet potato ice cream earlier, with a pecan crunch topping to go with it. You want some?"

"Sweet potato?"

Diane walked the few feet from the dining room to the kitchen and kept talking. "Yes, from the Neelys cooking show. Girl, you know I love me some Pat and Gina. I think I've TiVo'd every show they've done and am trying to get in touch with them regarding our bid for a spot on the Food Network. Anyway, I was watching their show one day, and when I saw them whip up this dessert, I couldn't get into the kitchen fast enough. It took me a few tries to put a Livingston spin on it."

"Ha, you know how we do!"

"You know I had to add my creative flair."

"What did you do different?"

"The pecan crunch topping. They topped theirs with caramel syrup." Diane returned to the table with two bowls of ice cream topped with a generous helping of the pecan crunch.

"Oh my goodness!" Candace exclaimed after her first spoonful. "Girl"—she took another bite, and closed her eyes as she savored the flavors—"this needs to be on the menu, ASAP!"

"You think? Can we do that? Since I got the recipe from watching *Down Home with the Neelys*?"

"Unh-unh-unh." Candace didn't say anything further until she'd finished the last bite in her bowl. She wiped her mouth with a napkin and sat back in the chair. "I don't know what we have to do, but, baby? That situation right there"—she pointed to her empty bowl—"needs to go on the menu! Girl, that ice cream was so good it almost made me forget about Victoria."

"Is she coming to the gala?"

"Nobody knows what Victoria is doing these days. On any given day she's a piece of work and now with pregnancy hormones kicking in? Lord have mercy."

"Has she called you lately?"

"That child don't want to talk to me—hasn't called since we met almost two weeks ago. I know she don't like what I told her, but the truth is the light. The way this whole pregnancy situation went down was wrong on so many levels that when I got ready to talk to her, I barely knew where to start. Lying about being on the pill."

"You mean she wasn't?"

"Not regularly, if at all. Then, on top of that, to lie about it, get pregnant, and hide the fact—behind a church and a Bible,

I might add—until it was too late to have an abortion. That's some kind of nerve. Not that I would have wanted that, don't get me wrong, but she knows it's what Malcolm would have demanded, which is why she didn't tell anybody until she was sixteen weeks."

"How is Malcolm?"

"Still seething. He was thinking about moving out of the house, but thank God Adam talked him out of it. You know how our clique gossips, and that story would be front-page news before the sun went down. Be thankful for what you and Ace have, Diane," Candace said as she fiddled with the spoon in the empty bowl. "Y'all's marriage looks like the Neelys— happy and secure."

"Honey, you and Adam have been married longer than we have. We could probably take a page out of y'all's marriage manual. You want some more?" When Candace shook her head, Diane reached for the bowls. "I'll fix you a bowl to go."

We could probably take a page out of y'all's marriage manual. Diane's words repeated in Candace's head. She and Adam could probably write a book on staying together and raising kids. There was no doubt that their love was still there: strong, steady. It was this love that she banked on, hoped would remain, beyond her recent decisions. In a way, what she was doing was for her family, so that they could continue to see the vibrant, satisfied woman they'd always known. So far, her choice had proved everything she'd hoped and more. And for that, she was vibrantly satisfied.

18

Alexis was nervous, which was unlike her. She'd revealed her finished work to clients much bigger than Toussaint Livingston. Her talents had been requested and then applauded by people from the sports world to the hip-hop community. She'd designed rooms for political aficionados and some of the elitist members of black society—in Atlanta and elsewhere. *So why am I trippin'? You weren't even this nervous around Tyler Perry.* "What is wrong with you?" Alexis whispered to the empty room. She was acting as if she didn't know why she was edgy. But she knew.

Toussaint checked his look in the rearview mirror before getting out of the car. He didn't know which had him more excited—seeing his new living / dining showcase or seeing Alexis. As he turned his elevator key and pressed the penthouse button, he decided it was the latter. The elevator reached his floor, and he strode purposefully to the new, cherry-red door Alexis had had installed. Something about feng shui, Toussaint remembered. He opened the door, and his heart stopped. Before him was one of the most beautiful sights he'd ever seen. And the remodel he'd spent ninety thousand dollars on looked good too.

"Hello, Toussaint."

Toussaint stared at Alexis another moment before stepping farther into the room and looking around. The living / dining masterpiece he'd requested had been delivered, and then some. His home now looked like a spread right out of *Architectural Digest*. "Alexis, this is fabulous."

Alexis smiled and walked to where he was standing in front of the living room's best feature—the fireplace. "I just love how this turned out and am glad you trusted my judgment on the color of the mosaic inlay." The traditional red brick had been replaced by a sleek wall of marble in warm earth tones. The raised fireplace was now surrounded by a water feature that cascaded from the ceiling and disappeared into grooves on the floor base. Colorful mosaic tiles were inlaid just above this base and matched the floor-to-ceiling, large glass blocks that now served to separate the living and dining areas. Their vibrant shades, which included burgundy, gold, and turquoise, provided a punch of color to the subdued gray / navy blue / black color scheme and brought Alexis's whimsical signature style to the room.

"The controls have all been stored here," Alexis said, pushing a panel hidden in the heavy black steel mantel. She turned to the wall opposite the fireplace and pushed a button, and an Afrocentric picture, designed by local Atlanta artist Stuart McClean, receded into the wall to reveal a sixty-inch flat-screen television. She continued to point various details out to Toussaint as they walked around the room. Recessed lighting abounded and emphasized Alexis's smart use of wood, stainless steel, leather, and textured fabrics to design a look that was at once sophisticated and inviting. The dining room, with its expandable table that could seat up to ten people, reflected the living room's colors and textures, and the modern, square chandelier, gleaming with Swarovski crystals, rivaled the living room fireplace for wow and pizzazz. The curtains and floor-to-ceiling glass doors that shielded the patio now opened electronically, and the patio, filled with hearty plants and seasonal flowers, was now a true outdoor living space. "These vines will fill in and eventually give you complete privacy." Alexis motioned to the English ivy growing at the base of the four-foot trellis. Her tour of the new living and dining areas was complete. "However, if you want to take in the view, this entire fence is on a pulley and can be pulled to each side of the balcony."

"Beautiful," Toussaint whispered again. But he wasn't looking at the furnishings or the beautiful downtown skyline clearly visible from his balcony. He wasn't even commenting on the deep blue September sky or the leaves tinged with yellow, hinting at autumn's imminent arrival. He was looking at Alexis.

"I'm glad you like it," Alexis said. She turned, and her heart jumped. Toussaint's eyes were boring into hers, and when he unconsciously licked his lips, her eyes were drawn to them like moths to a flame. *Was he always this handsome? Did he have that slight mustache the last time I saw him, and were his lips this full and succulent-looking? Of course he was!* Suddenly she was all too aware of how well his tailored suit fit his broad shoulders, how nicely the light wool fabric flowed over his lean hips and long legs. Alexis performed this once-over in seconds, although the image would stay branded in her mind for days. She tried to look at him with a casual, yet businesslike stare. What she didn't know was that the obvious desire she saw when she looked into Toussaint's eyes was exactly what he saw as he looked into hers.

Toussaint took a step toward Alexis. She took a step back. "I want you to see my bedroom," he whispered.

"Toussaint, I—"

"For ideas on how you'd redecorate it... that's what I meant. And my guest bedroom too."

Alexis let out a long, silent breath. She was hot all over, and while she'd so far resisted Jon Abernathy's advances, she wanted nothing more at the moment than to be in Toussaint's arms, *and* in his bed. "I already have my next client lined up," she said, a bit too breathy for someone trying to sound businesslike.

"I'll wait." Toussaint allowed his eyes to travel and take in Alexis's long, disheveled locs, the perfectly fitting pantsuit that hugged her breasts and her booty, and the manicured toes visible in jeweled sandals. He imagined sucking those toes, one by one. His manhood leaped to attention. Toussaint quickly turned and walked from the outdoor space back into the penthouse. He didn't stop until he was behind the small and classy bar area located between the living and dining areas. "Would you like something to drink?" he asked, just to calm himself before his burgeoning erection embarrassed them both.

"I really should go."

"A glass of champagne to celebrate what a fabulous job you've done. And then I'm taking you to dinner."

"Oh, no, Toussaint, I couldn't . . ."

"Did that sound like a question, woman?"

"No, but . . ."

"But what? Do you have an appointment or a meeting?" Toussaint continued before Alexis could respond. "Cancel it. For the moment, I am not your client. So I am taking you out for an evening of dining and dancing. And you might as well take the pout off that beautiful face of yours, Alexis St. Clair. You're mine tonight. And I'm not taking no for an answer."

19

Toussaint wasn't the only one not taking no for an answer. Neither was Quintin Bright, owner of Q's Bodybuilding & Workout Center and Candace's personal trainer. "Push, Candace," he barked authoritatively. "Two more minutes." He stood in front of the stair climber, urging her on.

"My legs are burning," Candace panted, willing her legs to press down on the pedals. "I. Can't."

Q stepped closer and placed his mouth right next to Candace's ear. "You can and you will, do you hear me?" he growled. "I don't train quitters. Now, come on. Let's go!"

"Argh!" New beads of sweat popped out on Candace's forehead as she gritted her teeth and bore down. Q had continually increased the tension on the device, making her work harder and harder to push down. Right now it felt like hell. But there was no doubt her thighs were toned.

"Thirty more seconds. Don't stop now. I'll do these last few with you."

Q hopped up on the stepper next to her, with resistance twice that of hers, and pushed down with no problem. His thigh muscles bulged, and pecs rippled as he executed the moves. He'd toned his body to perfection, and it showed. He looked over at Candace, whose eyes were squeezed shut with the effort of finishing her task. "Keep your arms tight. Two more."

Candace finished and wobbled off the machine. Quintin reached out and caught her. "Good job, Candy. Abs next."

Candace bent over, panting heavily. "I can't, Q. Not right now. Just give me a minute."

"I'll give you the time it takes to walk over to the ab board. Drink some water. You're all right."

Candace rolled her eyes. "You're a slave driver," she hissed, taking a long drink from her water bottle.

"Wait, not too much. Short sips, woman. You know better than that."

The two walked over to the ab bench where he changed the incline to once again push Candace further into perfect fitness. She knew it would be pointless to argue, so instead of doing so, she simply lay on the bench and waited for his count to begin.

Q lightly spotted her as they began. He placed two fingers on her abdomen so that he could feel the muscles tighten. "Good, Candy, keep using your abs. Relax your shoulders. Lift from the core only. That's right...nineteen, twenty."

After two more repetitions on the ab board, Candace's workout was over. She lay on the mat where Q stretched her muscles, ensuring that they'd remain lean and not cramp. He raised her leg up and over her head, something that Candace couldn't even imagine three months ago. He sat in front of her, legs spread; he placed his feet on her ankles and pushed gently, and when she moaned, "Q, that hurts," he pushed a little more. Finally, Q mouthed the words she longed to hear, the music to her ears at the end of each workout.

"We're done, Candy. Get ready for next time."

Forty-five minutes later, Candace walked into the master suite she shared with Adam. He came out of the master bathroom at the same time. "There you are."

"Yes, baby." Candace walked over and kissed Adam on the cheek. "Were you looking for me?"

"As a matter of fact, I was."

"You know I work out every Tuesday, Thursday, and Saturday."

"I know. I had an appointment over by that gym, so when it was finished, I stopped to see if you were there."

Candace's heart stopped. "Oh?"

"Yeah. I saw your car but couldn't find you."

There was a reason Adam saw Candace's car at the gym. She kept it there as part of the cover-up.

"Hmmm, that's strange. Did you ask the person at the desk to look for me? I was probably in the shower. Or I might have gone to the juice bar a couple doors down from the gym. Did you look there?"

"No."

Candace breathed a sigh of relief.

"Called your cell phone, though," Adam said as he walked into their oversized closet. "Got voice mail."

"I don't have my phone on me while I'm working out, Adam," Candace replied. "Plus, I'd turned the ringer off earlier when I met with the Jack and Jill committee and forgot to turn it back on." She took a deep breath and walked over to the closet. "I'm here now. What do you need?"

Adam, who'd replaced his slacks, shirt, and tie with a sweat suit, turned and faced his wife. "You," he said, pulling her into his arms. "I was going to take you out to lunch, but now I guess it will have to be dinner instead. And then," he continued, kissing her temple, "when we get back home, I want dessert." He kissed her then, conservatively yet caringly.

Candace kissed him back. She immediately deepened the exchange, her tongue swirling, probing, even as her hands reached for his buttocks and pressed him to her.

"Whoa, Can, slow down, baby. I said I wanted you for dessert, not an appetizer!"

"Why can't I be both?" Candace countered, nibbling his ear. Even though she'd just endured an arduous workout, she was ready for more pumping.

"Later...after dinner. I'm headed back to the office but will pick you up—say, six-thirty? Our reservations are for seven."

"Sure, Adam. That sounds fine."

Later that evening, Adam treated Candace to a fabulous dinner. The Thai food was excellent, and from the kanom jeeb chau moung dumplings, to the tom kha kung soup, to their main courses of duck breast and braised lamb tenderloin, the couple enjoyed the food and each other. And, as promised, Candace was Adam's dessert, and he was hers. Both went to sleep fully satiated, especially Candace, who later that night enjoyed a second helping....

20

Zoe sat behind her desk, which was situated just outside Ace's office. She tried to look professional, consumed with Taste business, while she typed instant messages to Chardonnay, who had the day off.

What do you mean you saw it?

Zoe placed papers in her inbox while she waited for Chardonnay's response.

That nasty dog pulled it out while we were both in the pantry.

LMAO! ::silently:: Girl, shut UP!

If I'm lying, I'm dying.

Well...?

Well, what?

Well, what's he working with?"

Damn, girl, I gotta admit it. His face is a problem but his dick look good.

He's not that bad, Char, probably cleans up nicely. Just needs a woman's touch.

Yeah, he needs a touch all right...from a plastic surgeon.

LOL! Ooh, got

Zoe quickly closed the IM window as Ace approached her

desk. "These letters are signed and ready to go. Do you have the report that I asked for earlier?"

"Yes, Mr. Livingston. I just need to print it out."

Ace nodded. "Put it on my desk. I want to look at it before the meeting."

"Yes, sir."

Ace started for his office, then turned around. "Oh, and, Zoe..."

"Yes?"

"I appreciated the information you gathered online, regarding America's changing eating habits and focus on health. These are topics we in management are already discussing, but I appreciate your proactive contribution to this ongoing dialogue."

"Thanks, Ace. I just love being a part of what's going on here."

Ace nodded. "We see you."

Once Ace returned to his office, and Zoe had given Ace the printout, she hurriedly reopened the IM screen. She knew that Chardonnay would wonder what happened and then eventually figure out she'd been interrupted. As Zoe scanned the screen, she realized it had taken her friend a minute to realize they'd been interrupted.

Got what?
Hello?
You mad because I'm talking 'bout your man, Zoe?
You might as well go on after him 'cause you ain't never gonna be Mrs. Toussaint. :)
Okay, Mr. Boss Man must have walked out and put you on lock. Hollah later...

Zoe closed the IM screen and went back to work. She tweaked a PowerPoint presentation, separated the day's mail, and filed the stack of papers that had piled up on her desk. She then went to the restroom where she freshened up her makeup and spritzed on perfume. She popped a mint in her mouth, took another look at herself in the mirror, pulled in her stomach, and proceeded to the conference room and to her fantasy man.

Zoe was the person who prepared the room for meetings and as such was the first to arrive. Shortly after she'd filled the pitchers with lemon water and placed them on the table along with napkins and glasses, Adam, Malcolm, Ace, Toussaint, Shyla, and a couple others joined her. She was hoping to sit next to Toussaint and share some small talk, but Shyla quickly claimed that spot. It didn't matter. As soon as everyone was seated around the table, Adam began the meeting.

"I have some good news," he said, sitting up in his chair. "Torrance Edwards, the young man who was burned back in June, is doing much better. He had his last skin graft last week, and his family seems pleased with how he's progressed thus far. Additionally, all of the lawyers have finally agreed on a settlement amount. Our insurance covers it, so we should be able to close the books on this ordeal in the next few weeks."

Shyla was itching to ask what he'd received but knew that was not her business. She made a mental note to ask Toussaint later.

Zoe wondered about the settlement amount as well. *That could be one way for Char to quit her job,* she thought in jest. Zoe loved her job and respected the Livingstons too much to ever suggest doing something so underhanded as getting hurt on purpose to collect insurance money. But goodness knew that Chardonnay's other option—meeting a man with pockets deep enough to take care of her and her kids and who didn't sling crack—looked less likely with each passing day. Cognac was seven and Tangeray was five. Pretty soon there would be no more babies needing a daddy. But Chardonnay would still need a man.

"Regarding the company's financial picture," Adam continued, "we've had a bit of a setback. The bank has decided not to grant an extension on our loan payment. We've put in an application for an additional line of credit. It's imperative that it go through."

"Or what?" Malcolm asked.

No one answered. Everyone knew that bankruptcy loomed ever closer on the horizon.

Adam cleared his throat and looked at his twin brother. "Give us some good news regarding operations, Ace."

Although by most corporate ladder structures, Ace, as COO, was beneath Adam, who was CEO, these two brothers shared equal power at the Livingston Group. Adam valued Ace's opinion almost as much as he did their dad's, and he never made a decision without consulting him—and vice versa. As for Ace, he'd always preferred operating behind the scenes and possessed a calm confidence that allowed him to not be affected by Adam's more vocal role in the company. It was an interesting switch, because outside the office, Adam was the more conservative one while Ace livened up the party. As Ace succinctly shared his information and answered questions, his proficiency and expertise was evident, as was his subdued swagger. "Even though we've had to overhaul both the Dallas and Houston kitchens as a precaution against further accidents," Ace concluded, "operations are running smoothly."

Adam nodded at Ace and poured himself another glass of water. "Toussaint has submitted a second, more extensive plan regarding the expansion he introduced at our biannual meeting. We've tabled the franchise idea—"

Toussaint shifted, causing Adam to look at him.

"For now," Adam continued, nonplussed. "However, after carefully reviewing the other parts of his proposal, I've concluded that further discussion is warranted, especially the idea of branching out into other markets. Toussaint?"

"In Los Angeles, there are two major soul food restaurants, M&M Restaurant, which has two locations, and a place called Aunt Kizzy's Back Porch."

"What about that chicken and waffle place?" Ace asked.

He and Diane had vacationed in Los Angeles the previous year and had dined at Roscoe's House of Chicken 'n Waffles.

"Researched them too," Toussaint replied. "Roscoe's has definitely made a name in LA, with five locations that stretch from Pasadena to Long Beach. But they don't qualify as a bona fide soul food restaurant. Nobody out there has what we're bringing. I'll be flying out there the first week in October to visit these establishments and continue my development research."

Two pairs of ears perked up at this news. Shyla's mind went into overdrive for a way she could accompany him. Something had changed between them, and Shyla was almost certain it involved another woman. Toussaint had been distant for the past two weeks, and they'd been intimate only once. His excuse that he'd been too swamped sounded legit, but Shyla knew different. Toussaint was too virile, too sexual, too potent to be celibate for long.

Zoe also fantasized about rendezvousing with Toussaint on the West Coast. But she knew that's all it was, a pipe dream. She remembered Ace's earlier comments and decided she'd do better to focus on climbing up the corporate ladder instead of into Toussaint's bed. After all, she reasoned, Shyla had done that, and where had it gotten her? Zoe looked at Toussaint laughing at something his uncle had said and noticed the dimple she wanted to touch with her tongue, the sparkling white teeth against smooth coffee skin, the long tapered fingers that casually straightened a pin-striped tie, and imagined laying her head against the chest upon which that tie rested. She groaned inwardly, even as she began gathering her things to go back to her desk. *I'll focus on the promotion. That's my best shot to get ahead. But damn, like Chardonnay said two weeks ago, a woman can dream.*

21

Chardonnay took one last drag from her Newport 100, flicked it out the window, and rolled her eyes. *Damn. I would have to roll up the same time as Bobby.* She took out her compact, powdered her face, and then used gloss to freshen her lips. Her delay tactic proved unsuccessful. Bobby had time to wait. He always arrived to work at least thirty minutes early and often stayed to finish his work even if he was off the clock. But Chardonnay was too outdone to be impressed. After two months, he was still begging to taste her juice and threatening to expose her with what he swore he'd photographed. Chardonnay sat for a couple minutes while the latest cut from her favorite artist, Fantasia, finished playing on the radio. Then she huffed, puffed, grabbed her purse, and reluctantly exited her car.

"Thought you were never gonna get out," Bobby yelled from across the parking lot. He posed against his Hyundai as if it were a Bentley.

Chardonnay decided to ignore him.

"You might want to stop swinging that onion long enough to come check out what I've got for you."

"Whatever it is, I don't want it," Chardonnay said over her shoulder. Since seeing Bobby's appendage three days ago, she'd visited Q's gym and had seen something even bigger. She'd gone in and inquired about membership. Q recognized her from the restaurant and gave her the tour. When he asked if she had any other questions about the equipment, she mentioned the one that interested her the most, the one he'd forgotten to show her. He took her to his apartment and "showed" her for the next three hours.

"Chardonnay, where you going?"

"Didn't you hear me? Whatever you've got, I don't want to see it."

"Even if it's the phone with your pics on it?"

This comment stopped Chardonnay in her tracks. Bobby had told her that he'd left his phone on an overnight trip to Louisiana, that this was why he hadn't shown her the pictures. She'd thought he was lying, and that they didn't exist. *Is this fool telling me the truth? Only one way to find out.*

Chardonnay turned around and marched over to the car. She wanted to slap the smug look off of Bobby's face, but in light of what he might be holding in his hand, she thought better of it. "Let me see," she said from about two feet away.

"C'mon over here, baby girl. I won't bite."

"Coulda fooled me with those fangs in your mouth."

"Damn, why you want to hurt a brother?"

"I ain't got all day, Bobby. And I don't have time for games. If you have something, show me. If not, leave me the fuck alone."

"A'ight 'den." Bobby punched a couple buttons and then, holding the phone firmly in his hand, turned it around for Chardonnay to see.

Chardonnay's heart had sped up as she waited, but now she let out a loud guffaw. "What? Is that all you got?" The picture was from behind and showed someone holding something in their hand, with their head bowed. Chardonnay confidently put her hand on her hip. "That picture don't tell shit."

"That's just the first one. It's like a movie right here." He punched up the next picture.

Chardonnay squinted as she viewed this one. It was taken from behind as well but showed someone with a plate in their left hand, while their right hand was clearly between their legs. "That's just someone with a plate of food," Chardonnay said, her voice missing some of its previous bravado. "It ain't me." Still, she moved closer, waiting for the next piece of evidence.

Bobby clicked the next picture. "This ain't you either?"

Chardonnay closed her eyes. Her heart sped up at the same time. Bobby had switched from the camera function to video. As the camera rolled, Chardonnay watched as she turned to the side, where she clearly could be seen stirring her finger in the plate. She then picked her nose (*damn, I forgot I did that!*) and swirled it in the plate again. The camera captured the broad smile she had on as she left the pantry. Her hand had been caught in her coochie, instead of the cookie jar, and it had all been caught on tape.

Chardonnay fell back against the Hyundai. "Damn, Bobby, this is some messed-up shit."

Bobby laughed. "Ain't it? Who in their right mind would do some shit like that, contaminate a customer's food? Lawsuits have been won on less evidence, and if the FDA found out, they could shut the restaurant down!"

"I'm not talking about what I did," Chardonnay hissed. "I'm talking about your lowdown ass. How you gonna dis a sistah, who's trying to make it just like you?"

"Oh, I'm the muthafucka? Just because I caught you being a very bad girl? Ha! I'm not gonna try and blackmail you, Chardonnay. I could, but I'm not. Now here's what you can do for me. Lighten up, and give me a chance."

Chardonnay let out a string of expletives while digging for her cigarettes. "Bobby, you need to delete that shit, for real."

"And you need to stop tripping and go out with me."

"Fine, okay? Fine! I'll go out with you. One time. Then...
will you leave me alone?"

"If you want me to."

"And delete the pictures?"

"Absolutely."

"Then come over this Friday. I'll give you my address
when we close up."

Bobby watched Chardonnay as she walked away. He began
to get hard just watching, thinking that in a couple days that
ass would be his. *It wasn't pretty getting here, but we're here now.
And once I get you, I don't intend to let you go.*

22

"Baby, really, I'm fine." Toussaint reached for his glass of wine on the bar and walked toward his open patio doors. He'd worked almost nonstop the past three weeks and had taken the afternoon off, partly to rest and partly to enjoy the luxurious surroundings to which he was still becoming accustomed. The redesigned environment made him feel so good that for the first time in his life, he'd rather stay home than go out. The only thing missing was someone with whom to share his castle. Someone like Alexis. Everywhere his eye landed, he saw her touch. "Yeah, sorry, Shyla, I'm still here...just distracted."

Shyla paced in her office. *By whom?* It took every fiber of her being for Shyla not to ask this question out loud. But if one thing the corporate world had taught her, it was to be patient. Shyla knew that a trip with Toussaint to LA would make all the difference, would put the magic back into their currently stale relationship. Shyla knew she could hang with the women in LA. While not conceited, she knew she was beautiful. It didn't matter that the hair and breasts had been purchased; they were still hers. The perfect bone structure, long, lanky build, and intelligence had come courtesy of good genes and a stellar education. Shyla knew she was the right woman for Toussaint. Taking this trip together would prove it to him.

"Have you given any more thought to my accompanying you to Los Angeles? I want to talk with you about the proposal I submitted to the Food Network. I really think we have a shot, but time is of the essence. We could talk out there, away from the office distractions. This is a huge opportunity, Toussaint. I wouldn't take it lightly." Shyla hoped she sounded professional, instead of desperate.

"I checked out your proposal," Toussaint replied. "It's tight, no doubt. As for LA, we're still working out the personnel for that trip. Ace mentioned coming, and Aunt Diane may join us. I wouldn't pack any bags yet, Shyla, but like I said before, I'll let you know."

"That sounds fabulous. In the meantime, I'm also expanding my marketing ideas for the West Coast expansion. Nothing too detailed, just some ideas I've been kicking around since you announced the concept."

"That sounds good, Shyla. Copy Daddy and Ace on it."

"Absolutely." Shyla smiled, her confidence growing. *If he wants me to copy Adam and Ace, then he's going to give whatever I send him serious consideration. And after that, I'm as good as shopping on Rodeo Drive!* Shyla made a quick mental note to put her hairstylist on standby. LA weaves were some of the best in the world. Shyla wanted to make sure hers was fresh for the trip. "Oh, Toussaint, one more thing—"

"Shyla," Toussaint interrupted. "Ace is calling."

"Call me back. Maybe we can get together tonight. I miss you."

Toussaint switched calls without responding to Shyla's invite. *It's time to end things with her.* Later, he decided, after returning from Los Angeles. "Hey, Uncle."

"Hey, Toussaint. I know you're busy, so I'll be quick."

"Are you kidding? I always have time for my favorite uncle."

"I'm your only uncle, fool," Ace said, smiling. He'd been Toussaint's "favorite" uncle for decades. "Listen, me and your aunt Diane were talking about the LA trip. We're definitely coming."

"That's great!" Toussaint suddenly thought about Alexis, and how much he'd love for her to accompany him on this trip. He knew that his aunt and uncle would love her. His mother, he was not so sure. When it came to Candace and her sons, nobody seemed good enough. "Maybe we can squeeze in a Lakers game."

"Sounds like a plan. Oh, and there's one more thing. There's someone else I'd like to accompany us on this trip. I've been thinking about promoting her, and how she handles this trip would help me decide."

"Um, well, Uncle, I'm not sure how productive Shyla would be on this trip. She and I . . . Well, things might get complicated with her along."

"That's why you shouldn't shit where you eat, son, but that's a conversation for later. And it's a moot point where this is concerned, because I'm not talking about Shyla. I'm talking about Zoe Williams. You know that we like to promote from within, and I've had my eye on her for a while. She's an excellent worker: smart, dedicated, goes above and beyond the call of duty. With Shyla poised for a director position, it's time to consider the corporate ladder. Zoe has shown a real knack for marketing and PR and has expressed an interest in those areas. When we go to LA, I'd like to bring her with us."

23

Toussaint had barely begun to digest his uncle's suggestion to have Zoe join the team heading to LA when his phone rang. One look at the caller ID put a smile on his face.

"Hey, beautiful."

Pause. "Hi, Toussaint."

"You're a hard woman to reach. What's a brothah got to do to get a return phone call?"

A longer pause. "Be patient." Toussaint's throaty laugh produced a tingle between Alexis's legs. "I'm sorry it's taken me so long to call back. This latest project has me swamped."

"Is that project's name Jon Abernathy?" Toussaint was surprised this had come out of his mouth, but since it had, he eagerly awaited her answer.

"Jon? He's not a client."

"Neither am I, not anymore. So what is it, Alexis? Why will you go out with him and not me?"

Alexis paused, taken aback by the intensity in Toussaint's voice. "We did go out, Toussaint. And as I said when we had dinner—"

"*Appetizers*," Toussaint corrected. "You ran out before the entrée arrived."

"That was an emergency. My mom was stuck at a..."

Greyhound bus station. "She was in a bind." Alexis wasn't ashamed of her mother's choice of transportation, but rather why she'd been on the bus in the first place. Alexis's alcoholic stepfather had wrecked her mother's car during a road trip two states over, a trip he hadn't told Mrs. Barnes he was taking. He also hadn't told her he'd emptied the bank account. It hadn't been until she'd arrived at the bus station to purchase the ticket that she found out about this hitch in the giddyup. As usual when financial troubles came, she'd called Alexis, who had left the restaurant, and her date with Toussaint, and gone to the bank to deposit money into her mother's account.

"I understand. Things come up. But I'm ready to cash in that rain check you offered before running out on me. I want to see you, Alexis. You know I'm feeling you, girl, and I think you're feeling me too. What are you afraid of... falling in love?"

"I've heard that's not a good idea where you're concerned. Your reputation of playing the field precedes you."

Toussaint's response wasn't immediate. The conversation wasn't going as he'd planned. For once, Toussaint's whorish ways embarrassed him. But he'd never denied his lifestyle, and he wouldn't start now. "You've heard correctly. I've been around. But what does that have to do with us?"

"Everything."

"Why?"

Alexis closed her eyes and tried to still her erratic heartbeat. It had been years since she'd opened up to a man, since she'd taken a chance on love. And with this man, well, the potential pitfalls were enormous. But then again, she reasoned, nothing ventured, nothing gained. "You're right, Toussaint. I am feeling you. A lot. And quite honestly, that frightens me. I know I come off as strong and invincible, but... well... it's a long story."

"Why don't I pick you up at eight, and you can tell it to me. Over dinner."

Alexis's heart fluttered, even as a shiver of fear ran through her. Toussaint was one of Atlanta's most eligible bachelors—a woman's dream. The last man who was everything she'd ever hoped for had left her unexpectedly. Still, Alexis faced her fears, knowing that any given journey began with the first step. "Here's my address. Are you ready?"

Toussaint smiled as he typed her address into his phone. "I'm ready," he whispered, confident once again. "The question is . . . are you?"

24

The afternoon passed quickly, and a little past seven-thirty, Toussaint climbed into his Mercedes and headed to Atlantic Station and Alexis's loft. When he arrived, he wasn't disappointed. Alexis's home was a study in brilliant contradictions—just like her.

"Your home is perfectly put together, but I wouldn't have expected anything less," Toussaint said after they'd exchanged greetings and hugs. "I would have never considered purchasing a loft. But this . . . nice."

"Thank you. Lofts have come a long way from what one thought of in, say, the seventies or eighties."

"Do I get the grand tour?"

Alexis hesitated, but when she couldn't quickly think of a logical answer to the contrary, she nodded her consent. Her living and dining area was basically combined, much as she'd designed Toussaint's home. Floor-to-ceiling panels of shimmering beads, along with strategically placed floor rugs separated the spaces. Her kitchen was top-of-the-line, a fact that impressed Toussaint.

"I love your kitchen. Do you use it much?" he asked.

"Yes."

"What? Are you telling me you're beautiful and can cook too?"

Alexis warmed at the compliment. "I do all right."

"You know you're talking to a Livingston, right?"

"I kept that in mind as I gave you my answer."

This banter helped to ease the unspoken tension swirling between them. Alexis turned and led the way down the hall to the bathroom and bedroom suite.

"Wait, who're these people?" Toussaint had stopped to look at the black-and-white portraits lining Alexis's wall.

"Family, mostly."

Toussaint leaned closer to the portraits. The first one, of a handsome man dressed to kill, caught his eye. He looked at the portrait and then gazed at Alexis and back again. "This your father?"

"Yes," Alexis replied softly.

"You look like him."

Alexis didn't know why, but Toussaint's keen observation caused her to choke up. "We should probably get going," she said, returning to the living room without looking back to see if Toussaint followed. "Did wherever we're going require reservations?"

"Yeah, but we're good." Toussaint took another long look at the man on the wall. He hadn't missed how Alexis's demeanor had changed when Toussaint had mentioned him. He also noted that the tour was over.

"Where are we going?" Alexis asked once they'd settled into Toussaint's car.

"Someplace special." Toussaint's smile was boyish, charming.

"You're not going to tell me?"

"No."

Alexis crossed her arms in a huff. Toussaint laughed and turned on the satellite radio. The pulsating sounds of Latin jazz oozed out of the Bose speakers.

"Thanks for taking a chance and going out with me," Toussaint said sincerely.

Alexis glanced at him before answering. "You're welcome."

Conversation flowed fairly easily as Toussaint cruised down I-75. Not only was he a gentleman, Alexis decided, as he'd opened her car door and helped with her seat belt, he was knowledgeable too. During the short ride, they discussed food, travel, and Atlanta's social landscape. Alexis relaxed.

Toussaint noticed and smiled. The evening with Alexis was going exactly as he'd imagined. She was smart, edgy, yet down-to-earth in a way that reminded him of his mother. There was something about being around her that, quite simply, just made him feel good. He changed lanes and took the Peachtree exit.

"Ah, we're going to one of my favorite restaurants I see. I bet you guys eat at Taste all the time. I'm not complaining," she hurried on. "Who better to patronize the establishment than the owners?"

Toussaint smiled. "Couldn't have said it better myself."

Alexis's brow furrowed when Toussaint passed the block on which Taste was located and continued toward the business district. *What restaurant is out here?*

She didn't have to wait long for her answer. Within minutes, they were pulling into the Livingston Corporation parking lot. Alexis's confusion deepened. "Why are we going to your office?"

Instead of answering, Toussaint exited the car and then went around and opened her door.

"You ask a lot of questions, woman. Come."

Alexis sat back in the seat, playing the potential seduction in her head. He'd take her into the near-empty building, down a darkened corridor, and then show her his office, which she was sure had a nice comfy couch. It was naïve of her to think a tiger could change his stripes in one day. "That's okay, Toussaint. I'll wait out here."

"You'll be waiting a long time. The dinner is five courses."

"This is where we're having dinner?"

"Yes."

Skepticism showed on Alexis's face.

"Trust me," Toussaint whispered, reaching for Alexis's hand. "Satisfaction guaranteed, or your money back."

As soon as Toussaint opened the center doors at the end of the hall, a heavenly smell assaulted Alexis's nostrils. It was a symphony of odors, she decided—herbs and spices, something sweet made with cinnamon and nutmeg and one of her favorite smells in all the world...baking bread. "What is this place?" she asked with the wonder of a five-year-old.

Toussaint smiled appreciatively. She'd passed an important test—loving food and its preparation as much as he did. "This is the test kitchen. Everything on the Taste menu starts here, and we're constantly refining, making subtle changes. One of our primary goals is to make our Southern cuisine as healthy as possible, without compromising on taste."

"But you still season with pork, correct?"

"We do, but as you may have noted, we're constantly adding turkey and chicken alternatives."

"I have noticed, and those dishes I've ordered are delicious. Since they are so tasty, why don't you eliminate the pork seasoning altogether?"

"And have my great-grandparents rise from the dead?" Both Alexis and Toussaint laughed. "We have two powerful votes keeping pig in the pot—Marcus and Marietta Livingston."

"Your great-grandparents?"

"Their kids, my grandparents. They're retired but are still very active in the decisions affecting the company they founded. My grandfather often jokes that when he meets his maker, it's going to be with a rib in one hand and a pig foot in the other."

They continued talking casually as Toussaint showed Alexis around the kitchen.

"So where's the person fixing this food?" Alexis asked when the tour was over.

"You'll meet him soon."

When they reached the elevator, Toussaint punched the button for the tenth floor. Alexis was silent, a little intrigued and a lot impressed with the man beside her. He was sometimes perceived as arrogant or cocky, but the Toussaint she was witnessing tonight was funny, kind, and sexy as hell.

"Wow, this is impressive," Alexis said as they stepped off the elevator into the lobby of the Livingston Corporation. The lush, tan carpet anchored a room filled with mahogany furniture, striped cushions, lush plants, and silk-covered walls.

"I'll give you a tour later if you'd like," Toussaint said. "But now, my queen, dinner awaits."

Once again, Toussaint took Alexis's hand and led them down the hall. This time, Alexis was acutely aware of how smooth his skin was, and how large his hand. He held her hand gently yet firmly, like he could protect her, like she belonged to him. She refused to ponder the fact that she liked the feeling.

Toussaint opened the door to the company's private dining suite and stood back. "After you."

Alexis had one word for the room she entered—exquisite. When she turned to look at Toussaint, her eyes shined with unshed tears. She hadn't been treated this special since . . . *No, not now, Alexis. Stay in this moment, with this wonderful man.* "Flowers, champagne, a private dinner . . . all of this for me?"

Toussaint's laugh was deep and sultry. "This is just the beginning, love. It's all of this, and so much more."

He led her to the table and pulled out her chair. Once she was seated, he retrieved the bucket of champagne from the buffet and sat it on the table. He quickly poured two glasses. "To a dinner uninterrupted," he said with a smile.

"Cheers."

Immediately, the master chef for all Taste restaurants, Oliver Bouvier, came out of a side door. Oliver was a robust and kind soul, with tanned, weathered skin and kind eyes. He was born in Cuba, and even though he'd come to America when he was seven years old, his accent was still quite evident.

"Mr. Livingston," he said taking Toussaint's hand and bowing. "*Bonita*," he said as he kissed Alexis's hand.

"Oliver is our executive chef, overseeing the menus at all of the Taste of Soul locations. When he's not traveling to our different sites, or here, creating new, culinary masterpieces, he gives his capable sous-chef a break and heads to the Buckhead kitchen."

"Ah, my favorite restaurant," Alexis said. "Now I know why!"

"You honor me, señorita, with your beauty and your words." Oliver announced the first course, salmon mousse with capers, and left the room.

"Bet you were expecting soul food," Toussaint said, his eyes twinkling.

Alexis laughed. "I was, and I'm pleasantly surprised."

"Next to my mother and grandmother, Oliver creates the best soul food I've ever tasted. But he's classically trained and can master cuisine from any region of the world."

Over the next two hours and five courses, which included everything French and nothing Southern, Toussaint and Alexis got to know each other. Toussaint plied her with funny stories about growing up in the Livingston household while Alexis spoke of summers in the Caribbean.

"Tell me about your father," Toussaint suggested after a lull in the conversation.

Alexis's smile was bittersweet. "He was amazing," she began. "My hero. Tall, handsome, with big, strong arms and an even bigger heart. My parents divorced when I was little, but he'd visit me faithfully every week. We'd go on dates, just him and me, simple things: going for ice cream, to the park, or to the movies. During those times, he made me feel as if I were the only person who mattered in the world.

"We remained close through my high school years and college. Then I moved to New York, determined to break into the design world, and didn't see him as much. I should have tried to go home more, see him more often. I didn't know that..." A huge lump in Alexis's throat prevented her from speaker further.

Toussaint's heart clenched. In this moment, the strong, feisty woman he admired was replaced by a vulnerable, frightened child, still mourning the loss of her father. He didn't have to ask if that was what happened. Her loss was palpable. Wanting to take her in his arms but knowing now was not the time, he simply placed a gentle hand on her arm. "I'm sure he was a fine man, to raise a daughter like you."

Alexis nodded, using her napkin to wipe the tears that threatened at the corner of her eyes. "He died suddenly, a heart attack. I didn't get to say good-bye." This time she couldn't stop the tears as they poured down her cheeks.

Toussaint reacted before he could think. He stood, lifted Alexis from her chair, and walked them over to a love seat positioned in the corner of the room.

"I'm okay," Alexis said, trying to wiggle out of his arms.

"Shhh, no, you're not. And it's okay. It's okay to miss him. It's okay to cry."

He sat with her then, cuddled in his arms. And it was here that for the first time, Alexis truly let go, the first time she'd felt safe enough to mourn her father.

25

Malcolm's eyes sparkled as he and Joyce stood at the counter of his engineer's lab. The baby that Malcolm had worked on for almost two years, the one that he wanted, was finished. The excitement hummed like electricity throughout his body. He'd planned to have Victoria by his side during this moment—the unveiling. That Joyce was here instead of a room full of Livingstons felt different, but nice. This was Malcolm's moment. It was rare that he hadn't had to share the spotlight with his brother, father, uncle, or mother.

Since sharing dinner at FGO three weeks ago, Malcolm and Joyce had forged a fast and deep friendship. During that dinner, and later at the lab, where Malcolm swore Joyce to secrecy before revealing his project, they discovered common interests and shared goals. Joyce was attentive and supportive, a good listener. Malcolm didn't realize how much he missed what he used to have with Victoria—friendship—until he felt it again with Joyce. He knew that Joyce's attraction went beyond business, that the feeling was mutual. If not for the legacy begun by his great-grandfather, and Malcolm's determination not to be the one to break the tradition, he would have slept with Joyce that night. Malcolm was a Livingston, however, so he'd done what Livingston men did. Instead of bed partners, he and Joyce became business partners. Malcolm, under his newly formed limited-liability company, had agreed to be a sponsor for Loving Spoon Enterprises, as well as a business consultant.

The engineer-turned-cook who had brought Malcolm's idea to life now stood on the other side of the counter. Malcolm had met Luis three years ago at a food industry expo in Indianapolis. Now, here the three stood, at a nondescript warehouse near downtown Atlanta, where Malcolm had nursed his dream. "Malcolm, I present to you the Soul Smoker!"

Joyce clapped enthusiastically while Malcolm moved closer to his creation. The stainless-steel cylinder, measuring twenty-four inches long with a circumference of thirty inches, looked state-of-the-art, with various gauges and buttons at the bottom. Two bolted hinges secured the door, which ran the length of the cylinder. Inside were various skewers to hold the cooker's choice of meat—whether chicken, steak, chops, or a slab of ribs. Spritzers were strategically placed from top to bottom, with a holder at the top of the cylinder where the liquid and residual fat that would baste the meat was placed. Finally, there was another area where those who preferred wet ribs could place the sauce. An automatic timer distributed the sauce when the meat reached its appropriate tenderness based on how much the meat weighed; a number that was calculated by the machine, once the meat was placed on the skewers. With Malcolm's Soul Smoker, novice cooks, seasoned chefs, and everyone in between could skewer a piece of meat and then leave the kitchen. They could run errands, watch television, or clean the house and within an hour have fall-off-the-bone barbeque that was perfect every time.

"And now for the real test," Luis said, moving to another smoker with the red ON light gleaming. "I had my wife prepare this slab of ribs precisely according to the instructions that will accompany the device. I wanted to make sure the directions were easy to follow. I've also had a neighbor roast a

whole chicken, and my father marveled at the steaks he produced." The engineer opened the smoker door, unlatched the
skewer, and placed a slab of sizzling ribs on a platter.

Malcolm and Joyce looked at each other, their eyes dancing with anticipation. Malcolm reached for the knife and fork
set resting beside the platter. He didn't need either, really. The
sauce was creamy, the slabs fork tender. He pulled the end
bone away from the rest of the slab and took a bite. The meat
fell into his mouth, succulent and tasty. He pulled another rib
off the slab, closed his eyes, and tasted the meat critically, with
a palate honed from a lifetime of eating barbeque.

Malcolm cut yet another rib, placed it on a saucer, and offered it to Joyce. She pulled half the meat off the bone with
her teeth, closed her eyes, and chewed. "Yum." She finished off
the rib and licked her fingers. "That was amazing. May I have
another one?"

Malcolm's smile widened. He separated the remaining ribs
and gave Joyce one of the thicker ones from the middle of the
slab. "What about this one? Is it as tender as the smaller ribs on
the end?" Malcolm's face resembled that of a ten-year-old,
waiting to find out whether he got to keep the puppy.

Joyce couldn't answer because she was eating. "This is so
good," she finally eked out, still chewing. "Malcolm, you've
done it. Get ready, QVC viewers. The Soul Smoker is coming
to your kitchen!"

Malcolm, Joyce, and Luis high-fived; then Malcolm en-
veloped Joyce in a huge hug, lifting her off the ground.

"Malcolm, you're a genius. I'm so proud of you." Joyce
kissed Malcolm on the cheek.

He kissed her back, on the mouth. It started out innocently
enough, but as Malcolm's lips touched Joyce's, his body was reminded of how long it had been since such an intimacy had
occurred. Soon, tongue swirling replaced the chaste exchange.
Joyce deepened the kiss. Malcolm's lips felt better than she had
imagined, and she felt safe and protected in his arms.

Luis cleared his throat, which drove the haze of lust from Malcolm's brain. He ended the kiss abruptly and stepped back. "I'm sorry, Joyce. I got carried away."

"It's okay," Joyce replied breathily. She hid her disappointment at Malcolm's change of demeanor behind a bright smile. "This is an exciting moment." *One that will hopefully end up at my house.* Beyond that first night—when Joyce had let Malcolm know she was attracted to him, and he had let her know that he was faithful to his wife—Joyce had been platonic in her actions toward him. But she'd never stopped hoping. . . .

"How many slabs did you make?" Malcolm asked Luis.

Joyce hid her smile. *Yes! Wrap one up for us to eat later, baby!*

"I fired up three of the smokers to use different settings, play around with them a bit."

"Excellent! Wrap the tenderest slab up for me, and place a smoker in my car trunk. It's time to head over to my parents' and introduce them to the newest member of the Livingston barbeque family."

"Sure you don't want to stop by FGO for a celebratory drink?" Joyce asked as she and Malcolm walked to his office.

"No, I want to go see the folks."

After seeing Joyce safely to her car, Malcolm went to his and reached for his cell phone. He was surprised when his parents' home phone went to voice mail. It was after nine. He called his father's cell phone. "Hey, Dad. Where y'all at?"

"Hey, son," Adam answered. "I'm over at Toussaint's, marveling at his upscale bachelor pad. Your mother's at home, though."

"If she is, she isn't answering the phone. I got voice mail."

"Maybe she was out back. Try her cell."

"I did, same thing."

"Hmmm. Well, I don't know what to tell you, son. She didn't mention any plans to me. What's on your mind anyway? Everything all right with Victoria and the baby?"

Not by a long shot, was what Malcolm thought. "She's fine," was what he said. "I had something to share with you and Mama, but it can wait."

"Are you sure? I'll be leaving here in a few minutes."

"I'm positive. It's just a little something I've been working on, that's all. I'll run it by you later."

"Look forward to it."

"Bye, Daddy."

Malcolm looked at his phone and contemplated taking Joyce up on her offer to have a drink. But he didn't feel like a night at the club, and after the kiss that happened earlier, going to Joyce's house was out of the question. He knew what would happen behind her closed doors.

"I can't keep living this way," Malcolm said aloud. He turned the ignition and headed home, knowing that something had to change. And soon.

26

Candace hurried into the private shower at Q's Bodybuild-ing & Workout Center. Normally, she cleaned up at home, but her workout had run long, and Candace didn't have time to drive across town before meeting Adam at Ace and Diane's. Candace didn't feel above the other members, but after men-tioning her aversion to public bathrooms and showers awhile back, Q had offered her the use of his personal dressing room.

The water was hot and exactly what Candace needed. As usual, the workout had been grueling, and Candace was sore. After toweling off, she went to the bathroom. Again, she expe-rienced itching, and a yellowish discharge. *I thought I was over these yeast infections. I haven't had to deal with this in a long time.*

An hour later, Adam, Ace, Candace, and Diane sat around the dining room table.

"As usual, your food is delicious, Diane," Adam said, just before putting another heaping forkful in his mouth.

"It sure is," Candace agreed. "I haven't had meat loaf in a while. You put sausage in this, huh?"

"Uh-huh," Diane replied. "Just to shake it up a little bit."

"I taste a few more different ingredients too. I know how you do it, though, always trying to twist a dish."

"I'd get bored otherwise, fixing the same thing the same way," Diane responded. "This time, I added capers and black olives. Then I countered the tartness by adding a touch of molasses to the barbeque mixture I slathered on top."

The clink of forks on plates replaced conversation as the foursome enjoyed a meal that included rosemary roasted potatoes, fresh green beans, and homemade rolls. Small talk slowly resumed as the couples retired to the den for slices of lemon pound cake, before the men retired to Ace's study for brandy and cigars.

"I talked to Victoria today," Diane said once the men had left the room.

"I called earlier, got her voice mail," Candace replied.

"She got your message—told me she was praying with one of her church members when you called."

"How'd she sound?"

"Not too good, to be honest with you. She said she's experiencing severe back pain. The doctor has put her on part-time bed rest. But the sonogram was clear this time."

"What's she having?" Candace asked.

"A little girl. She's already picked out the name—Victory."

"Victory? What kind of name is that?"

"I kinda like it," Diane replied. "But it'll be interesting to see what Malcolm thinks."

After another pause, Diane changed the subject. "Those workouts are agreeing with you, Candace. You actually have a glow about you these days."

"Girl, any glow you see is from that pound cake you put your foot into." Candace tried to remain nonchalant, even as her heart quickened.

"I don't think so," Diane said, eyeing her sister-in-law closely. "I might want to check out your personal trainer myself, because whatever he's doing is sure working for you."

★   ★   ★

In the study, Ace looked up as his brother returned from the restroom. "Everything come out okay?" he jokingly asked. When Adam didn't respond, Ace looked up. "You all right, twin?"

"I don't know," Ace said with a frown. "I felt a bit of a burning sensation when I took a piss just now."

"You ain't been out creepin', have you?" Ace said this in jest. No Livingston man had stepped out on his wife in more than fifty years.

"No," Adam replied. He sat down in the leather recliner opposite his brother and carefully relit his cigar. "But that shit don't feel right."

"You might want to have old man Bronson check you out if it don't go away." James Bronson was not only the Livingston family physician, but also a trusted family friend. "Probably nothin', though."

"You damn right it's nothing," Adam replied, even as he adjusted himself in his pants. "Ain't been nobody for me but Baby Girl in over thirty years. So I know I don't have to worry about shit."

27

Malcolm bounded out of bed and was out of the house by seven o'clock. After pouring himself a cup of the ever-present coffee in the break room, he went back to his office and was immediately buried in work. There had been a sizable spike in expenses at several Taste locations, and Malcolm spent an hour in a conference call with the managers. The rest of the morning was spent approving expense reports, talking with human resources, and reading a myriad of reports. As the noon hour approached, Malcolm's stomach growled. *Perfect timing.* After giving his assistant instructions regarding a report he was drafting, he headed to the private dining room attached to the catering and taste kitchen.

The room was buzzing with conversation, but all talk ceased and all eyes turned as soon as Malcolm walked into the room.

"Smells good in here, son," Adam said. "But there's an unfamiliar chef in the kitchen with Oliver, and both of their mouths are closed tighter than the lid on the pickle drum. What's going on here?"

"Don't mind your father," Candace said, coming over to hug Malcolm. "He's so nosy. And I am too. Did you cook the barbeque I'm smelling?"

Malcolm greeted Diane, Ace, and Toussaint, who were seated at the table. Diane and Ace engaged him in small talk, while Toussaint texted on his phone. "We need to get this meeting started," he said without looking up. "I have a conference call with some LA Realtors at two o'clock."

"Slow your roll, little brother. Good things come to those who wait."

"That may be, son," Candace answered, "but I won't be waiting past one-thirty. You know I work out on Tuesdays."

"We're waiting for one more person, and then we can begin."

"Oh, is Victoria coming?" Diane asked. Candace had told her this was a Livingston meeting. "I thought the doctor advised her to stay in bed."

"No, Victoria won't be here."

"Then who could—" Diane paused as the door opened.

Four sets of eyes looked to see who was behind door number one.

"Hello, everyone!" Joyce enthusiastically greeted the room. She walked over and gave Malcolm a brief hug. "Sorry I'm late."

Candace and Diane exchanged looks, as did Adam and Ace. Toussaint's brows rose in question. "Joyce, this is a surprise," he said.

"Today's meeting will be full of surprises."

Before anyone could respond to Malcolm's cryptic answer, Oliver and the unfamiliar cook came out of the kitchen. Malcolm stood and introduced him to the table. "Everyone, I'd like you to meet a brilliant engineer-turned-closet-cook, Luis Sanchez. He's the mastermind behind the technical aspects of this device and is assisting Oliver in today's presentation."

Those around the room nodded or said hello, curiosity evident on their faces. Luis placed the large box he carried on the table, next to Malcolm, and then returned to the kitchen.

"Would you like me to bring out the salads now, Malcolm?" Oliver asked.

"Yes, please." Once Oliver returned to the kitchen, Malcolm stood. "As you all know, this has been a rather interesting time in my household. What you didn't know is that Victoria's unexpected—and untimely—pregnancy was not the only new project under way.

"Dad, about five years ago, I mentioned an idea to you—an invention, of sorts. The desire to see this idea come to fruition never left, and today it is my pleasure to tell you that not only has this idea been realized, but also soon it will be in millions of households." Malcolm smiled at the mixture of expressions around the table—a delicious blend of curiosity, expectation and, in Joyce's case, joy. He opened the top of the box, leaving the cooker exposed and sitting on the box's bottom. "Ladies and gentlemen, I present to you the Soul Smoker!"

Stunned silence filled the room for just a moment, and then everyone started talking at once.

"What is a soul smoker?"

"What in the world?"

"Where did you get this contraption?"

"Oh, my goodness, what have you gone and done?"

Malcolm smiled and held up his hands. "I'll answer all your questions, promise." He paused while Oliver brought out the salads. No one touched their plates but rather continued to look at Malcolm expectantly. "This device will allow the novice barbecuer to make slabs as good as the pro. It's a combination cooker and grill, where one can place their meat in the cooker, walk away, and return an hour or so later to perfectly done meat—every time." He continued the presentation, opening the smoker and walking them through the steps to prepare meat inside it. He passed around the detachable parts, including the skewers and sauce holder, and explained how the timer and other controls worked.

"You have been busy, big brother," Toussaint said, his expression unreadable. "Is it patented?"

"We're in the final stages. Unlike a copyright, a patent is a long, complicated process that's already taken us a year and a half, and that was without this final product fully completed. It will take another six months, we're guessing, to have the patent, but we can still implement part two of this national plan."

"National?" Toussaint asked. He dug into his salad.

"Yes, I am planning on marketing this product nationwide."

"How?" Ace asked, finally picking up a fork, spearing a broccoli floret, and dipping it into tahini dressing.

"That's where Joyce comes in," Malcolm said, smiling at Joyce. "She has a major contact that will ensure me high visibility in target markets."

"Are we talking newspapers, Internet, television, what?" Diane's interest was piqued, especially since she knew Shyla was working on an independent campaign for when Toussaint's cooking episode aired on the Food Network.

Candace put her fork down and wiped her mouth. "Joyce, how did you get involved?" For some reason, the secrecy surrounding the whole affair didn't sit well with her, and neither did this woman who seemed just a little too cozy at her son's side.

"It was a fluke, really. He mentioned needing national exposure for a project he was working on, and I mentioned my contact. That's pretty much it."

"Interesting." Candace didn't believe for a minute that was all there was to it, and she planned to have a talk with Malcolm later to find out how right she was. Immediately, a pang of guilt shot through her. *You've got your nerve questioning someone else's morality. Take a look in the mirror, sistah!*

Luis brought out another smoker. The strong smell of barbeque oozed out of its openings. He sat it on the table next to the clean smoker and plugged it in. Malcolm explained how the slab inside had been cooked and that a chicken had been prepared in yet another smoker. He wanted his family to experience the smoker's ability to grill the perfect meat no matter the type.

For the next thirty minutes, the family oohed and aahed over the barbeque made in Malcolm's smoker, which the chef served with fried potato salad. The meat was fall-off-the-bone tender, as it had been the night Malcolm and Joyce tried it, and had been moistened perfectly by the automatic sprayers inside the cylinder. Likewise, the sauce that had been brushed on internally was just enough to coat the meat. Extra sauce was provided, but no one used it. Everyone said the meat was perfect straight out of the smoker.

"I hate to eat and run, but you've given me a real reason to work out today," Candace said, rising from the table. She walked over and hugged Malcolm. "This invention is fantastic. I'm proud of you, son."

"I concur, big bro," Toussaint chimed in. He and Malcolm exchanged a soul brother's handshake. "We can put one of these in every Taste of Soul across the country, and around the world." Toussaint's comment made it clear that he fully intended to see his dreams realized, as had his brother.

"Brilliant ideas from brilliant sons," Candace cooed, smoothly diffusing the all-too-familiar competitive energy. "I want one of those in my house before midnight," she whispered to Malcolm.

Joyce glanced at her watch. She was hoping to spend a few moments alone with Malcolm, but the rest of the family seemed in no hurry to leave and she had an appointment. "You were great today, Malcolm. It felt special to be here. Thank you so much for including me in what I'm sure will be a rousing success and for allowing me to share this moment with you and your family."

"You're welcome," Malcolm said. He gave Joyce a brief hug. "Your encouragement these last couple months really helped me push on through to the project's completion. I appreciate you."

Joyce warmed all over. At first, she'd approached Malcolm with the sole purpose of getting Adam out of her head by getting Malcolm into her bed. But now, her feelings for him went beyond lust. In the short time Joyce had gotten to know Malcolm, she'd found him to be an intelligent, compassionate, focused, and faithful man, one whom any woman would be blessed to have. She didn't want to admit it, but Joyce was in love with him. "I know Victoria wishes she could have been here. She must be proud of you too."

Before Malcolm could respond, his father walked up. "Good job, son," Adam said, eyeing both Joyce and Candace as they hurried out the door. "Didn't know you and Joyce had gotten so friendly."

"We're helping each other out with some shared goals is all."

"You sure about that? Joyce is an attractive, unattached woman. She hasn't hit on you, flirted, or nothing?"

"Why do you ask?" Malcolm asked, his brow furrowed. His love life was a rare topic between father and son.

"I know things are strained between you and Victoria, but you know that when it comes to stepping out on your wife . . ."

"I know, Dad. We have a legacy of faithfulness to uphold."

"That's right."

"So that's what you stayed behind to find out? Whether my relationship with Joyce extends beyond business?"

"Just looking out for your best interests, son." Adam turned to leave. "Come by my office later. I want to run some things by you."

Adam left the conference room with an urge to use the restroom. Once again, it burned when he peed. *Damn, that felt even worse than last night.* As he washed his hands, he remembered what Ace had said. *You might want to have old man Bronson check you out if it don't go away.* Adam felt that Ace was right, and when Malcolm stopped by to see him later that day, Adam's office was unoccupied.

28

Candace turned off her phone as she walked up the steps to Q's gym. The door opened as she reached it.

"You're late," Q said as she passed him.

"I know, business luncheon, couldn't be helped."

Q gripped the towel that was around his neck and eyed his client slowly. "So, Candy, are you ready to work off that meal?"

Candace took off her jacket and smiled.

Adam paced Doctor Bronson's office, too keyed up to sit. It wasn't just the earlier experience in the office bathroom that had him on edge, but also the conversation he'd had with Candace last night.

"It burned when I took a piss just now," Adam said as he crawled into the bed. "Anything going on with you?"

"What do you mean?" Candace asked, not looking up from the *Ebony* magazine she flipped through.

"Everything all right when you use the bathroom?"

"Now that you mention it," Candace said after a long pause, "I have noticed a discharge. I think I might have a yeast infection."

"That shouldn't make my dick burn, should it?"

Candace shrugged.

"I think I'll go see Doctor Bronson."

"Are you sure, baby?" Candace quickly asked. "It's probably nothing."

"You're probably right."

Candace had not replied, and when Adam reached over to hug her, she'd stiffened. This unusual behavior had caused him to ponder other moments that at the time he'd ignored but now seemed strange. Especially since he was standing in Doctor Bronson's office because whatever was burning hadn't gone away.

Adam tried to distract himself by flipping through a medical magazine, but he tossed it aside as soon as Doctor Bronson entered the room and closed the door. "Well, James, what'd you find out?"

James Bronson walked over and sat in the chair next to Adam, the friend-turned-patient whom he'd known for over twenty years. Bronson looked older than his fifty-seven years, largely due to his near-white hair and premature wrinkles. His ruddy, freckled face, a nod to his half-Indian heritage, was a mask of calm as he turned and faced Adam. "Well, friend, there's no easy way to tell you this. You've got gonorrhea."

"I've got what? Man, you're bullshittin' me."

"No, ran the tests myself, keeping it confidential, like you asked."

"Well, you need to run them again, because there's no way I've got the clap!"

Doctor Bronson ignored Adam's outburst. "You need to speak with . . . whomever you're sleeping with," he continued calmly. "Have them get checked out as well so they can be treated. The sooner the better, Adam. This disease isn't anything to play around with."

"Are you listening to me, James? I've been faithful to Candace since the day we married, man. Now I'm telling you, there's no way in the world I've got that shit."

"And I'm telling you that these results don't lie. And gonorrhea doesn't just happen out of nowhere." Doctor Bronson said nothing further but stared at Adam with unblinking gray eyes.

Adam stared back. Realization dawned. "Wait. You don't mean to say..." Adam stood and began pacing again. He stopped at the window, looking without seeing the colorful oak leaves on the tree just beyond him, and then turned back around. "Are you trying to say what I think you're trying to say? That Candace is cheating on me?"

"Brother, as your doctor, I can only tell you the results of these tests. For any other information, you'll need to ask your wife."

"Q, please," Candace panted, ignoring the sweat that rolled off her naked body. "It feels so... it feels..." Her brain too discombobulated to put together a complete sentence, she gave up trying. "Mmm."

"Whose pussy is this, huh?" Q lifted his face from where it had been wedged between Candace's legs. Instead of waiting for an answer, he dipped down and used his tongue as a sword, spearing the flesh between her nether folds and swirling her nub with a fencer's precision. His head was buried so deep that anyone watching would have wondered how he breathed, since his nose seemed to be immersed as deep as his tongue. "Who does this belong to? Huh?" he asked again when he finally came up for air.

Candace whimpered, incapable of saying anything more.

Q spread her lips as wide as they could go and then dove into her paradise. He made deep, purring sounds, lapping, nibbling, sucking, and then lapping some more. Candace's legs began shaking violently as an intense orgasm seemed to erupt from her very core. She moaned against the sweatshirt she'd stuck in her mouth moments before, knowing if she didn't her screams would reverberate off of the gym's front door.

But Q wasn't finished. Before she could catch her breath, he flipped her legs to the side, moved behind her and plunged his nine-inch sword into her still-quivering heat. Candace didn't think it possible, didn't think she had any more energy, but within seconds she was writhing against him, encouraging him to go faster, deeper.

"Uh-huh, you love this big dick, don'tcha? Don'tcha?" Q placed his hand under Candace's knee and lifted her leg higher. They were positioned on a long, padded bench in Q's private office. Candace had one foot on the floor and one on the bench while Q, with one knee on the bench as well, effortlessly supported the rest of her weight. The office door was locked, and his phone had been forwarded to voice mail. As always, Candace had been booked for a ninety-minute session. The first sixty minutes had happened out on the gym floor. Now, Q was finishing her workout. "Ain't nobody ever gonna be able to push these buttons like I do, baby," he murmured as he spread her cheeks wide and continued his assault with one hand while cupping her breasts with the other. "That's why you're gonna keep coming back to me."

He motioned Candace to lie on the bench, positioned himself on top of her, and proceeded to pummel her with his juicy, thick dick. Candace moaned louder and louder until Q placed a hand over her mouth. "I know you wanna scream, Candy, but you gotta squash that shit."

"I'm trying to but..." Candace panted between thrusts.

"But it's good, right?"

"Uh-huh. Feels...so...good..."

"How about this?" Q's motion went from in and out to side to side.

"Ooh..."

Q grabbed her hips and pumped harder, faster.

"Yes, yes!" Again, Candace's orgasm was intense. She began to cry from the pleasure.

"Ooh, yeah, cry over this good dick, girl." Q slowed down, pulled out to the tip, plunged in, and repeated.

"Oh, baby, there are no words . . ."

"We ain't through. I'm just getting started."

"I can't, baby. I've got to go."

"I want some more of this." Q's stamina was legendary, his sexual prowess hard to refuse.

Candace complied when he lifted her to a kneeling position, straddled the bench, and plunged right in. Soon she was mewling once again, in the throes of ecstasy.

After another twenty minutes, Q neared his peak. "You want me to come for you, baby?"

"Yes, oh yes!" Candace didn't even want to think about what time it was.

"You want me to come inside you?"

Oh, hell no! Even though Q was wearing a condom and Candace felt she was practically through menopause, the thought of anyone but Adam releasing inside her almost made her go dry. "Pull out, baby," she said at last. "Come for me."

She took a hot shower. Candace's legs were still a bit wobbly as she walked to her car. Q was always good, but today he'd been exceptional. He'd sexed her hard and long, just the way she liked it. *If only Adam had his stamina and size.* Candace felt guilty for even thinking such a thing. Adam was a caring husband. He loved her the best way he could and didn't deserve her unfaithfulness. "I've got to end this," she muttered. *And I'll end it . . . just not today.*

Once buckled up inside the car, Candace fired up her phone. There were several missed calls, including one from Adam. *I'll see what he wants when I get home.* She put on her headset, tapped Diane's name on her cell phone, and pulled out of the parking lot as Diane answered.

"Where are you?" Diane said. "All of the women are here, and we're ready to begin."

"I'm on my way," Candace said, searching her mind for a lie that might work, hoping she wouldn't need it.

"What held you up?"

Q's nine-inch pole. "Traffic. There was an accident. I'm only about ten minutes away and—Ow!"

"What's wrong?

"Uh, it's nothing."

"Let me get off the phone so you can pay attention to the road. Hurry and get over here but drive safely."

Candace disconnected the call and gripped the wheel. She tried to dismiss what she felt, but, no, there it was again—an intense itchy feeling inside her vagina. Candace squirmed, adjusted her pants, and tried to quell the feeling. She'd meant to go to her doctor, get an antibiotic for the yeast infection but...

"Oh, shit!" Candace swerved, almost hitting the car in the next lane.

Last night, she'd thought nothing of it, but now it all made sense—Adam's burning, her itching, the discharge she'd assumed was from a yeast infection. *Maybe this isn't a yeast infection at all. Maybe it's . . .* "Calm down, Candace," she said aloud. "You always use condoms with Q." *Except for that one time, remember?* Candace's hand flew to her mouth. *Oh, no, could it be?* "No, it couldn't be that. Please don't let it be that."

Candace tried to calm her nerves as she turned onto her sister-in-law's street. She always praised Q on how he gave her good loving. Now she was praying that he hadn't given her something else.

29

Adam pulled into the circular drive of their Victorian mansion, noted the immaculately landscaped lawn around him and Candace's Mercedes parked directly ahead. He viewed these trappings of the good life dispassionately, as a myriad of thoughts whirled in his mind. He'd been conflicted since leaving the doctor's office: anger, hurt, puzzlement warring for dominance. As with every challenge in his life, Adam decided to face this one head-on. He reached for the car door handle with a sure hand, gathered his briefcase with the other, and walked resolutely to the front door.

Candace's heart began to pound rapidly when she heard the sounds of Adam's hard-soled shoes clicking against the foyer's marble floor. She'd rushed home after the meeting at Diane's house and had been both surprised and relieved that Adam wasn't there. She'd gone straight to the kitchen, relieved the cook, and started cooking. She'd chosen a sweet and spicy coating for the fried chicken this time, and along with navy beans, homemade coleslaw, and jalapeño corn bread, she had put together another Livingston favorite—a deep-dish apple cobbler.

She cocked her head to the side, listening for Adam's footsteps. Noting the silence, Candace reasoned that he'd either gone up the stairs or into the den, both carpeted areas of their home. *Should I call out to him? Maybe fix him a drink?* Candace didn't know what to do—whether to be proactive and go to him or feign ignorance of anything wrong and stay in the kitchen. She decided on the latter, opening the oven door and checking the food.

Her round ass bent over was the first thing Adam saw as he turned the corner. Unwanted thoughts flooded his mind as he noted its large plumpness, prominently displayed in a pair of fitted stretch pants.

"Is there something you want to tell me?" he asked calmly from just inside the room. Just like that. Straight, no chaser. No greeting or preamble needed, and none given.

Candace whirled around. "Oh, baby, I didn't hear you come in." She took a step toward Adam, noted the scowl on his face and the tightness around his lips, and knew right then and there that the dinner she'd meticulously prepared would go uneaten. "What's wrong?" It was not the question she'd planned to ask but one that came out of its own accord.

"That's what I'm here to ask you, Candace. What's wrong? Are you okay? Or is there something you want to tell me?" These last words were delivered even lower and more calmly than the first, as Adam walked into the room toward his wife.

Candace took a step back as her heart raced. She'd seen this demeanor from her husband before and knew what it meant—that he was highly upset and working with great effort to not go smooth off. It was a mood not often seen. The last time she had seen him like this was when a businessman had swindled Adam out of over a hundred thousand dollars.

Uh-oh. How do I handle this? What should I say? Think, Candace! She decided to play the ignorant card and not say more than she needed to, before she had to. "Adam, why are you upset? Did something happen at work?"

"No." Adam stopped about a foot from Candace and put his hands on his hips. "Something happened after I left the office. After I stopped by James's office and had him check out that little problem I mentioned last night." He stopped but continued when Candace said nothing. "Are you going to stand here and act like you don't know anything? Because as mad as I am right now, woman, you'd do well to not make me drag shit out of you." Adam clenched and unclenched his hands.

Candace's eyes widened as she noted the gesture. She swallowed hard but remained silent.

"Oh, cat's got your tongue now? Nothing to say for yourself?"

"Adam, I . . ." Candace reached out a hand toward him.

Adam flinched away. "Who have you been fucking?!" he bellowed.

Candace reared back as if struck. She may as well have been. In all the years they'd been married, Candace had never heard Adam yell the way he just did. Adam had never laid a hand on her in a violent way, but the thought that he could flitted across her mind. She took a step back, and then another. "Adam, I don't know—"

"Don't lie to me, Can. Don't fuck somebody behind my back and then stand here and lie to my face. If you're going to break our marriage vows after three muthafuckin' decades, the least you can do is be honest about it. Who. Are. You. Fucking?"

Candace stood staring at the man who'd won her heart over thirty years ago, the father of her children, the man with whom she wanted to grow old. Adam was right. He didn't deserve what she'd done, or her lies. Adam deserved the truth. Candace bowed her head and spoke barely above a whisper. "Q."

"Who?" Adam asked, taking another step toward her.

"M-my personal trainer," Candace stuttered as she took another step back and bumped up against the large island in the middle of the kitchen. "It was only one time," she continued in a rush. Technically, this was true. They'd only done it raw one time. "I didn't mean to, Adam. I . . ."

"You didn't mean to what, Candace? Cheat on me with some lowlife or give me the got-damn clap? Which one?"

Candace's head shot up. "No!"

"You heard me. That diseased muthafucka you're screwing is why my dick is itching and why it burns when I piss. You have *gonorrhea*, Can, and you passed it on to me!" Adam seared Candace with a scathing look, then whipped around and stormed out of the room.

"Adam, wait!" Candace began, hurrying behind him. "I can explain . . ."

"Don't try and explain shit to me right now," Adam said, quickly turning around to face her, his arm out to stop her progress. "And don't come any closer, Candace. I mean it. I've passed up a boatload of pussy to stay faithful to you, and this is how you thank me? No. Don't come to me and say another word. Matter of fact, you'd be wise to get your shit and get as far away from me as you can right now. Give me a chance to try and calm the fuck down. Because if I have to look at you a moment longer, I don't know what I'll do."

30

Malcolm's invention was still on Toussaint's mind as he rolled up his sleeves and washed his hands. *You pulled a fast one on us, brothah. Now I have to step up my game.* The Livingston family competitiveness was legendary, and Toussaint now felt even more pressure to succeed on the Food Network show. Which was one of the reasons he was in his kitchen on a Thursday night.

Like most Livingston men, Toussaint loved to cook and was as at home in the kitchen as he was in the bedroom. As he placed vegetables and herbs on the prep table and set out appropriate bowls, knives, and other cooking utensils, he was reminded of how little time he'd had to cook lately, and how much he missed it. Preparing for a potential show on the Food Network gave him the perfect excuse to stand behind a stove, as did his dinner guest.

It hadn't quite been a week since the dinner with Alexis, where she'd broken down about her father. They'd talked for two more hours—about fears, hopes, and dreams—and had had brief phone conversations during what had been a busy week for both of them. Tonight was the first chance they'd had to see each other since then, and Toussaint was preparing a small feast. He wanted everything to be perfect.

The smooth sounds of Kem blended seamlessly into those of Blu Cantrell, Corinne Bailey Rae, and other neosoul artists as Toussaint prepped his vegetables. He'd decided to try out some of the health-conscious, upscale soul food he planned to feature on the menu at the West Coast Taste location and on his network show: sautéed greens with tomato and fennel, black-eyed peas and arugula salad, wild rice, and baked mahi-mahi with a barbeque glaze. He planned to serve the entrée with spicy corn bread but would make sure that Alexis left room for dessert—maple-glazed yams in a puffed pastry.

He'd just removed the fish from the oven when the door-bell rang. He smiled, and there was a pep in his step as he walked through the dining room, quickly lit the candles in the living room, and continued to the front door.

The seductive greeting he'd planned died on his lips as he looked out the peephole. "Mama?" he asked after opening the door. "What are you doing here?" He then noted the carry-on next to her. *WTH?* "Mama, what's going on?"

"I've messed up, son." Candace stepped forward, and Toussaint quickly stepped aside for her to enter his home. "Your mother has screwed up royally, and I don't know if this problem can be fixed."

Toussaint watched, dumbfounded, as his mother passed him and walked into his living room. She plopped down on the couch and put her head in her hands. It was her first visit since he'd had the house decorated, yet she said nothing. It was as if she hadn't noticed. Toussaint's concern increased exponentially. Something was very, very wrong.

He walked over to the couch and sat beside her. "Mama, what is it? What's wrong?"

When Candace looked up, her eyes shined with tears. "It's me and your dad, son. We had a fight."

"Daddy hit you?" Toussaint asked incredulously.

"No, but I may have felt better if he had. I deserve it."

Toussaint's mind raced with the possibilities of what could

be wrong. He thought about Malcolm and the problems that Victoria's pregnancy had created in their marriage. That couldn't be the case with his mother, could it? *Do women get pregnant at fifty-three?* "Maybe a glass of wine will help," Toussaint said as he rose from the couch. "Is merlot okay?"

"Thanks, Toussaint."

Toussaint was almost to the bar area of his dining room when the doorbell rang again. *Alexis.* As Toussaint thought her name, he also remembered the food in the kitchen. He rushed to the kitchen and turned off the burners, and then hurried to the front door as sounds of light knocking pierced the stark quiet. Candace looked toward the door, and then around the room. Belatedly, she took in the lit candles, heard the light music playing, and noticed the huge transformation to her son's home. *Damn. I'm interrupting.* She stood as Toussaint brought his guest into the living room.

"Mama, this is Alexis." Toussaint's introduction was perfunctory at best. He'd barely spoken to Alexis before pulling her inside the room, still reeling from the comment his mother had made.

"Hi," Candace said dismissively. She reached for her luggage without waiting for Alexis to reply. "I shouldn't have barged in here like this, son. I'm leaving."

"Are you sure, Mama? You seem pretty upset."

"I'll be okay. Oh, and I like what you did to the house."

"Alexis is an interior designer. This is her work."

There was an awkward silence as Toussaint awaited his mother's response. Since she had been a subscriber to *Architectural Digest* for years, he felt that even in her disheveled state, she'd be impressed with Alexis's handiwork. If she was, she didn't say it. Candace simply reached for her purse and walked to the door.

Toussaint followed her out. "Mama, what is this about?" he asked again after he'd shut the door. "What happened between you and Daddy?"

"Never mind, son. Don't worry about it. I shouldn't have come here and involved you in our personal affairs. Everything's okay." Candace said this, but she didn't believe it.

"Is that why you're rolling up in here with luggage, your eyes full of tears? And ignoring my guest? Because things are okay?"

Candace ignored his questions. "I'll be staying at a hotel tonight. If you need me, call me on my cell."

Toussaint watched his mother get in the elevator before slowly turning around and going back inside the penthouse.

Alexis still stood where he'd left her. "I'm sorry to have interrupted."

"It's okay. I wasn't expecting her."

"Is everything all right?"

That's what Toussaint wanted to know. And after his mother had come to his home, ruined the seductive mood, and destroyed his appetite, he was determined to find out.

31

"That's fucked up," Ace said as he sat in his den, his expensive Cuban cigar burning unnoticed. He still couldn't believe what his brother had just told him. "I'm sorry, man."

Adam was in his library, nursing his third tumbler of cognac. He shifted the phone to his other ear. "I still can't believe she cheated on me. I mean, I had no idea!" While calmer than two hours ago when he'd confronted Candace, Adam was still quite upset. "And with a nasty clap-carrying dog at that. What in the hell was she thinking?"

"She wasn't thinking. That's clear." Ace paused. "Did she tell you who it was?"

"I could tell she didn't want to, but yeah, she told me the sorry muthafucka's name. It's that thug who owns the gym."

"Her personal trainer?"

"Can you believe that shit? Here I've been blocking Joyce twenty ways from Sunday while that bitch has been taking her workout to a whole other level."

Ace winced at the name Adam called his wife. He understood the anger but had never heard Adam call her that, not in over thirty years.

"I hope that muthafucka is worth what it's getting ready to cost her."

Ace sat up. "Now, man, I know you're angry. This shit is beyond fucked up. But don't do anything now that you'll regret later, nothing that will cast a shadow on the business."

"I don't give a damn about the business right now!"

"Well, think about the Livingston legacy, then, about Mama and Daddy. God only knows how they'd react if they found out."

"If? You mean when, don't you? Man, I'm divorcing Candace as soon as my attorney can draw up the papers."

Ace wisely held his tongue, knowing that his brother wasn't in a place to hear reason. Ace thought about Diane and their sex life. Then he tried to imagine finding out that she'd given his good loving to someone else. He couldn't even imagine it but felt that he'd probably feel the same way his brother did right now—ready to put her out of his house, and his life.

"Do me a favor, Adam," he finally said. "Hold off on calling the attorney. Just for now, until after the business trip with Toussaint to LA I'm helping him prepare—the schedule is jam-packed until then. But once I get back, we'll put our heads together and work this thing out." Ace did have a hectic schedule, but more importantly, he wanted Adam to have a chance to calm down and think more rationally. "Twin . . . will you do that for me?"

Adam's smile was bittersweet as he heard the endearment. It's what most family members had called them and what they still called each other. "I don't know about anything getting worked out, but yeah, I'll wait until you get back from LA."

32

Candace pulled up to the valet parking area of the Ellis Hotel. She'd read about the extensive renovation done on this historic landmark and had commented to Adam about spending a weekend there. The irony was that it was precisely because she'd spent time with someone else that she was now at the Ellis, alone.

Thankful for a relatively fast check-in and a near-empty lobby, Candace kept her head down as she took the elevator to her floor. She'd prayed that nobody she knew would be there attending a meeting or on a rendezvous, and it looked as if her prayers had been answered. *So far, so good.* She eyed the room numbers as she hurried down the hall. *Almost there.* Candace slipped her card in the slot and eased into the spacious, well-appointed room. Its modern, sleek décor made her think of Toussaint's new digs that she'd barely noticed, and the woman he introduced, whom she'd noticed even less. Thoughts of her son temporarily diverted her from the ache that throbbed in her heart and the tingling that she now clearly felt on her vagina's outer lips.

A free spirit during her early days, including the uneventful loss of her virginity at age sixteen, Candace had considered herself careful when it came to sex. With a steady stream of partners until Adam, and in almost thirty-five years of marriage, she'd never had a disease. *And the one time I decide to be unfaithful, the one and only time, this is how I get caught. Me. With gonorrhea.* It's a disease she would have thought beneath her, impossible for her to contract. But she had it. And all because of a man named Quintin Bright.

Candace's cell phone rang. She thought it might be Q returning her call but saw Ace and Diane's number instead. She hesitated in answering, not sure if she wanted to talk with either of them or hear what they had to say.

"Can't hide out forever," Candace told herself. She answered the phone.

"Candace, Ace just got off the phone with Adam. What is going on, girl?" Diane's voice was a mixture of shock and concern.

"What did Adam tell Ace?"

"That you've having an affair! Tell me that's not true, Can."

Candace sighed. "I could, Diane, but I'd be lying."

"Oh my God, Candace. I had no idea you and Adam were having problems."

"*We* weren't having problems. I was. Well, I wasn't either, exactly. It's just that . . . it just happened."

Diane, who was sitting in the dining room where she and Candace had discussed another troubled marriage earlier in the month, got up and paced the room. *Was she having this affair while talking about her son's marital woes?* "How does an affair just happen, Can? And why didn't you feel you could talk to me about it?"

"I don't know," Candace said softly. "I guess cheating on your husband isn't something you discuss over coffee."

Both ladies were silent as they pondered the gravity of Candace's actions. "Where are you?" Diane finally asked. "Ace said Adam put you out."

"Downtown. At a hotel."

"Candace! You know you can stay here."

"I know, but . . ."

"No buts. Where are you?"

"I'm at—" Candace's answer was interrupted by a beep in her ear. "Hold on, Dee. On second thought. Let me call you back." She clicked over to the new call without waiting for a response or saying good-bye.

" 'Bout time you called me back. How long have you been infected, Quintin?" It was the first time since meeting him six months ago that Candace had used his full first name.

"Infected? What the hell are you talking about?" Quintin knew exactly what she was talking about. It's why he'd called. But her accusatory tone had immediately put him on the defensive, and as he'd done since he was five years old and was threatened with a whooping for stealing, he resorted to what had become a natural defense mechanism—playing dumb.

"Oh, so you haven't had any symptoms, Q? No burning sensation when you use the bathroom, no swelling or discharge? And just how many women at the gym are you screwing besides me?" Candace realized that she could have casually chatted with any number of Q's women while jogging on the treadmill or using the unisex sauna.

When Q replied, his tone was soft. He was busted, knew it, and felt bad about it. "I just found out, baby. That's why I'm calling. So you can get treated before, you know, you're with your husband again."

Candace was close to tears. "It's too late for that," she choked. "He went to the doctor today and found out he has it."

"Aw, shit, baby." A lengthy pause. "You okay?"

"What kind of asinine question is that? Hell no, I'm not okay!"

"I mean, what went down when he confronted you?" When Candace didn't answer immediately, Q became angry. "He didn't hit you, did he?"

Candace knew it shouldn't happen, but her heart warmed

at the protective tone in Q's voice. His thugalicious swagger was part of what had drawn her to him in the first place and then kept her coming back. That and the big, thick dick that had poked her insides. Too bad there'd been a big bad disease on the end of his rod. "No, he didn't hit me," she finally said. "But I wouldn't have blamed him if he did. He put me out, though. I'm at a hotel downtown."

"Where?"

Candace told him.

"I'm coming down."

"No, you're not."

"Baby, I don't want you to be alone tonight. I'll be there in thirty."

"Wait, Q!" He'd hung up on her. *Dammit.* "You're the last person I need to see tonight," Candace mumbled as she dialed his number. The call went directly to voice mail. "Q, It's not a good idea for you to come here. Call me back." Her phone beeped. *Great, Diane.* Now that she was alone, Candace realized she wanted to be left alone. "Hey, Diane."

"Candace, where are you? Ace and I want you to come and stay with us."

"I'm at the Ellis Hotel, and actually, Diane, I'm okay. I'm going to stay here tonight."

Diane frowned as she pondered Candace's words. *Oh my God, she's with the other man.* Rather than ask about this out right, Diane chose a roundabout approach. "Fine, I'll come to you. Maybe it will help to talk."

Candace's phone beeped. *Why is he texting me? I said to call!* "Hold on, Diane." Candace punched her message box.

Uh-uh, Candy. Ima be witchu tonite.

"Candace, what is it?"

"Look, Diane. I have to go."

"Let me come down and hang out, Can. I'm worried about you . . . being by yourself."

"Don't be! Look, I just need to chill. I'll come by tomorrow, okay?"

When Candace called Q again, the call went to voice mail. *This shit is over, Q. You're going to be in for a surprise when your ass is left knocking on the other side of the door!* That decision made, Candace walked over to the minibar, opened a bottle of merlot, and, realizing she hadn't eaten since lunch, ordered a sandwich from room service. She slowly sipped the wine and pondered the events of the past few months and of the years before that. She remembered her wild teenage days, and her joy at discovering how good sex could be. She replayed her first dates with Adam and the first time they'd slept together, how she'd been a bit disappointed but not deterred. Adam was more conservative and not as endowed as some of her former lovers. But what he lacked in size he made up for in commitment.

With marriage, kids, and a business, the years had passed quickly. She'd been happy for the most part. It wasn't until she'd walked into the new, upscale gym and laid her eyes on the owner that she acknowledged just how unfilled a part of her life had been. Q must have noticed it, too, because he flirted immediately, made her feel sixteen again—the age she'd lost her virginity. She hadn't planned on having an affair with him. It just happened. One day, after an entire session of flirting, Q had offered to let her use his private area to take a shower. He walked in naked to dry her off, with his massive sword standing out to greet her. And that is when her first real workout in over thirty years had begun in earnest.

"Do you want it?" he asked softly, the tip of his huge weapon already poised for entry.

"Yes."

"Louder, baby, I didn't hear you."

"Yes!" came her fervently whispered reply.

He lifted her, held her against the tiled wall, and seared her with several inches of power, passion, youth, and will. She moaned and groaned in spite of herself, knowing that she should stop him while wanting him to go on forever. He pummeled her with his manhood, opening her up beyond her wildest thoughts, swiped her nipples with his hot tongue, and teased her rear with his middle finger. Finally she'd crumbled, unable to stand. And there, on the shower floor, beneath a flow of water, he'd taken her again, from behind, until they'd both convulsed with massive climaxes, soaked to the skin and to the soul.

He'd dried her off then, as promised. Before leaving, he simply said, "Good work, Candy. Get ready for next time."

He'd screwed her after every workout since, and she loved it. "But that's over, Candace," she said sternly, getting up to replenish her wine and stop her tingling nana. "Over!" *I'll make an appointment with Doctor Bronson tomorrow, go stay with Diane and Ace, and start the process of trying to get Adam to forgive me and get my marriage back on track.*

A soft knock at the door caused Candace's heartbeat to quicken. She breathed a sigh of relief when a quick peek revealed it was the bellhop with her meal. It wasn't until she opened the door that she found he wasn't alone.

"Q, I told you not to come." Even as she said this, she took in his tight black T-shirt, his baggy red shorts, and his long, strong legs.

"I know." His dark-eyed stare was piercing, and Candace's hands shook as she signed the bill.

The bellman left. The hotel door clicked. The lovers were alone. Candace frowned at Q. He took two steps and stood directly in front of her. "Do you really want me to leave?"

Candace looked up. She meant to look into his eyes, but her gaze came to rest on his bow-shaped lips, then dropped down to the hard chest lightly sprinkled with curly black hair, and down farther to what was surprisingly a burgeoning erection.

Q stepped even closer, so close that his shirt grazed Candace's breasts. He enfolded her in his arms. "Do you want me to leave?" he asked again, his breath hot against her ear.

Candace shook her head as her arms encircled his waist. Wordlessly, she took his hand and walked to the room's sitting area. *Just one more night,* she reasoned as she and Q shared the dinner she'd ordered and finished off the wine. They didn't make love right away, but rather talked, more conversation than they'd ever had—about Q's background, Candace's marriage, why she would cancel her gym membership, and why this would be their last night together. And this time when he fucked her, Candace decided to let him in raw. They were both already infected, he didn't have AIDS or HIV (the only paper she'd demanded he show her), and this was the last time. The last time in life that she'd have this man's gorgeous, skilled dick inside her. So she opened, Q entered, and, stroke after powerful stroke, he replaced the day's pain with the pleasure that had caused it all.

33

The next day, Malcolm entered Toussaint's office and closed the door. Toussaint stood and came from behind his desk, anger and concern evident in his hastily hissed words. "Man, what the hell is going on? I've been trying to reach you all morning!"

Malcolm slumped onto the dark brown leather love seat in the sitting area of Toussaint's large, corner office. "I've been over at the house. Talking to Dad."

"Mama showed up at my doorstep last night," Toussaint said, joining Malcolm on the couch. "She had a carry-on with her. What's going on with her and Daddy, man?"

Malcolm shook his head, wearily rubbing his forehead and then his eyes. "Mama cheated on Daddy," he said finally, a sigh accompanying these words of doom.

Silence filled the air. "You're bullshittin'," Toussaint said after he'd found the air to breathe again. "You're bullshittin'," he said again, louder this time.

"Keep your voice down," Malcolm whispered. "We have to keep a lid on this shit!"

Toussaint stood and paced his office. He stopped at the window and looked out, not seeing the beautifully colored leaves announcing October's arrival. "Who with?" he finally asked without turning around.

Malcolm joined Toussaint at the window. The conversation continued but instead of looking at each other, both men stared out into a world turned crazy with one simple line: *Mama cheated on Daddy.* "The owner of the gym where she works out—her *personal trainer,*" he finished sarcastically.

"That young, thug-looking muthafucka on the billboards around town?"

"Quintin Bright. He just turned thirty."

"Damn. I can't believe it."

"Me either. And neither can Daddy."

"Aw, man. I know he's upset."

"To put it mildly. I've never seen the old man tear up before . . . but he did this morning. Yesterday he was angry. Today he's just hurt."

"But how could it have happened, Malcolm? How could Mama do this? The last time we were all together, they seemed to be grooving like always."

Malcolm didn't have an answer.

"What's Daddy going to do?" Toussaint looked at Malcolm, his eyes, questioning as he awaited the answer.

Malcolm walked over to a table containing a water pitcher and four crystal goblets. "That's the million-dollar question, brother," he said as he slowly filled his glass.

"Do you think he'll divorce her?" Toussaint's question was more to himself than Malcolm. "No, that can't happen. Livingston men don't cheat or divorce."

"And Livingston women don't . . ." Neither son wanted to think about what their mother had done. "Is Mom still over at your house?"

"No, she didn't stay." When Malcolm shot Toussaint a questioning glance, he continued. "Alexis came over and Mom left."

"And she didn't say where was going? Because Daddy said he put her out."

"She's at the Ellis Motel." Toussaint walked to his desk and grabbed his cell phone. His office line beeped at the same time.

"Look, I've got to go talk to Ace. Daddy's not coming in today, so we need to rearrange some meetings. Then I'm going back over to the house. You're calling Mama, right?"

Toussaint nodded. "Need to find out how she is and hopefully . . ." Malcolm was out the door before he finished the sentence. "Man, this is messed up." Toussaint hit speed dial. "Mama, where are you?"

Candace cringed at the concern mixed with anger mixed with judgment she heard in her son's voice. "I'm all right, son. On my way over to Ace and Diane's."

"Damn, Mama. How could you? After thirty-something years! And with a young-ass thug?"

"I know I messed up, Toussaint. But this is still your mother you're talking to. This situation is between me and your father."

"Evidently not," Toussaint retorted. "If things had stayed just between you and him, we wouldn't be having this conversation."

"I don't expect you to understand," Candace said, sighing. "And I understand your anger. Things got out of hand. But don't worry, son. I'm going to do everything in my power to fix this and make things right with your dad."

"You know this doesn't just affect you, right?" Toussaint unexpectedly felt the urge to cry. "I love both of y'all, can't imagine y'all not together. And think of what will happen if the public finds out? It'll be a PR nightmare."

"Don't worry," Candace repeated. "That's part of what Diane and I will talk about. And hopefully I'll be back home tonight, with your dad, to work out the rest."

34

Ace was still reeling from last night's drama and was hurting for his brother. He'd not been surprised when Adam hadn't come to work, and he wondered if he'd be in the office on Monday. *Is a weekend enough time to recover from someone taking your heart and stomping on it?*

Shyla waited patiently for Ace to continue. It was obvious his mind was elsewhere. "Ace, you were saying?"

"Sorry, Shyla, a lot on my mind. I was saying that since you're meeting with the Food Network next week, I thought this would be a good opportunity for Zoe. She will basically be coming along in an assistant capacity. But as your star continues to rise to the level of director of marketing, as it is currently poised to do, I'd like to groom her for a junior management position in that department. This trip will show her another side of business operations. How does that sound to you?" Ace studied Shyla's calm expression as he awaited her answer. He knew she'd planned to rendezvous with Toussaint in LA, and that she'd be pissed to learn that Zoe was going instead. Yet this anger wasn't written all over her face. *Impressive.*

"I think that's a great idea!" Shyla replied, thankful she didn't actually choke on the lie. "The idea of me being promoted, that is." Shyla chuckled and tossed her hair, hoping her devil-may-care act was convincing. "Zoe seems to be a determined and capable worker. However, I didn't know she aspired for a marketing career."

"Her taking this trip was my idea, as are the thoughts of her moving to the marketing department. One of the secrets to our success in employee retention is that we promote from within. Zoe has been with us for three years and has done an excellent job. She's excited about her future here."

"And so am I," Shyla readily agreed. "I'll schedule a meeting right away and—"

"Ace, I need to—" Malcolm burst through the door to Ace's office. "Oh, sorry, Uncle. Didn't know you were in a meeting."

"It's okay, Malcolm. We were just finishing up," Ace answered from the sitting area on the far side of the room. "Come on in. Get back to me as soon as possible," he said to Shyla as she rose to leave. "And keep what I've shared with you regarding Zoe's future promotion confidential."

Shyla left Ace's office and couldn't reach the other side of the building fast enough. Her four-inch heels clicked a hasty rhythm on the hall's bamboo flooring before being silenced by the thick, plush carpeting of the common area between the business development and marketing wings.

Shyla felt she deserved an Academy Award for her performance in Ace's office. In truth, she was livid at the thought of Zoe going to LA instead of her. Not only was it a bad idea in terms of the business, but also it would totally ruin a perfect opportunity for her and Toussaint to have quality alone time. It had been a month since they'd been intimate, and Shyla was more than ready for some Livingston love. That's why she, and not Zoe, should be taking the trip to LA and exactly what she planned to tell Toussaint just as soon as she reached his office.

★   ★   ★

"I thought I asked not to be disturbed," Toussaint barked into the intercom.

"I'm sorry, Toussaint," his assistant replied. "But there's someone here to see you."

"Who?" The last thing Toussaint wanted to do right now was talk to anyone about business. He hadn't been able to focus on work since Malcolm left his office.

"Alexis St. Clair."

Toussaint started, then smiled. *I don't feel like seeing anybody, except her.* "Sorry for snapping at you, Monique. Please, send her in."

Toussaint stood and walked around his desk. When Alexis came in, he motioned for her to close the door and then opened his arms. She stepped into them, hugging him tightly, breathing in the woodsy scent she so adored.

"To what do I owe this unexpected visit?" he whispered.

"Would you believe I was in the area and decided to stop by?"

"Baby, I'd believe just about anything you told me."

"I was interviewed by a potential client just down the street. That gave me the perfect excuse to stop by, see how you're doing, and find out if everything is okay with your mom. I probably should have called. . . ."

"No, Alexis," Toussaint said, hugging her tighter and lazily running a hand down her back. "I'm glad to see you." Reluctantly, he released her but reached for her hand and led them over to the sitting area he and Malcolm had recently occupied. "Would you like something to drink?"

"No, I'm fine. Can't stay long." The ensuing silence was interrupted only by a soft gurgle from a fountain in the corner of the room. Alexis's eyes shone with something akin to love as she watched a myriad of emotions play across Toussaint's face. Her heart flipped. She ignored both that and the tingling feeling that began when her gaze went from his eyes to the full, lower lip that he nervously gnawed. "Want to talk about it?" she gently prodded.

"My parents . . ." Toussaint eyed Alexis intently, then turned and stared out the window.

"I'm a good listener, Toussaint. And a confidant who can be trusted. What you share will go no further, if that's your concern."

"They're having problems," he tentatively continued. "A major one, in fact. It seemed to come out of the blue. I can't tell you the last time I heard my parents disagree, much less argue or have to deal with . . . something like this."

Alexis didn't know what to say. She wouldn't dream of prying for details and couldn't quite relate to his parental angst. Her parents had separated when Alexis was a child. Except for a handful of occasions, she'd interacted with each of them one-on-one. As for her mother's current husband, whom Alexis refused to think of or address as stepfather, she was thankfully long gone from Missouri by the time he came on the scene. "I'm so sorry," she said at last. "I can't imagine the pain you must be feeling. But try and think positive. Your parents have been together for a long time. They've undoubtedly weathered other storms. Choose to believe that they'll weather this one as well."

Toussaint's eyes sparkled as he looked at Alexis. "Come here, baby girl," he whispered seductively.

Alexis scooted over and allowed herself to be wrapped in Toussaint's embrace. Her presence alone was his comfort; further words were unnecessary.

35

"He's with someone," Monique said as a fast-walking Shyla passed her desk.

"With who, Zoe? It's okay."

"I wouldn't," Monique hastily replied, nervously twisting her thick, blond hair, her deep blue eyes as wide as those of a deer caught in headlights.

The frantic tone of her voice caused Shyla to turn around. "Why? Who's in there?"

Toussaint's assistant hesitated. She'd been on the job less than six months and was still learning the ropes. Besides, this soft-spoken daughter of a single-mother librarian found Shyla's verbose personality frightening. "I, uh, think it's personal."

Shyla looked hard at Monique and then at Toussaint's closed office door. "Okay, then. Well, tell him I'd like to see him. On second thought, never mind. I'll send an e-mail." Shyla turned and walked back down the hallway. But instead of leaving the area, she ducked inside the small break room at the end of the hall. After pouring herself a cup of coffee that she had no intention of drinking this late in the day, she stood and pretended to look at the poster board on the wall near the door. Whoever was in Toussaint's office would have to walk by this door on the way out.

She didn't have to wait long. Just after reading an Avon party invite and rolling her eyes at what she considered a mother's lazy attempt at selling Girl Scout cookies by simply posting the order form, Shyla heard Toussaint's low yet unmistakable voice. She turned slightly, pretending to read the notice at the board's right edge. A low murmur, followed by the light, seductive laugh of a woman, told Shyla the couple was almost to the door. She looked up just in time to meet her adversary's eye as Alexis casually looked into the room. *The designer! He's still sniffing after that little twit?* Shyla had seen the woman only one time, when they'd met at Taste. Shortly afterward, the meeting had been forgotten, as had the woman. *But that's around the same time Toussaint went MIA.* Shyla's eyes narrowed as certain puzzle pieces began to fall into place, and she didn't like the picture coming together.

Shyla hadn't asked Toussaint about his interior designer or thought any more about her than she did the parade of other women she knew Toussaint occasionally screwed. She knew for a fact that for the past three years, she'd been the most constant woman in her lover's life and believed it was just a matter of time before he tired of the pussy parade and settled down— with her.

After waiting a beat, Shyla marched back down to the assistant's desk. "What's her name?" she asked, as if she had every right to know.

"Who?" Monique asked, not open to being interrogated or getting in the middle of office mess.

"You may look stupid, but don't act that way, okay? I know it was Toussaint's interior decorator. I just don't remember her name." Shyla tapped a finger against her arm as she impatiently awaited an answer, then tried a softer tactic. "I'm sorry, Monique, let me start over. I'm thinking about surprising my mom with a makeover to her dining room and want to talk with Toussaint's friend. But I don't want to ask him because he'll try and talk me out of it."

"Why would he do that?"

"Because he knows that I know that they slept together, him and the designer. He'll think I'm still jealous and want to cause trouble. But that couldn't be further from the truth. I just want to get the best person to do my mother's house, and from seeing her work up close and personal—when I spent the night at Toussaint's house—I know she's the best."

Shyla let these revealing words settle like a blanket around Monique and suppressed a smile as the assistant's eyes widened with understanding. "Oh, I'm sorry, Shyla. I didn't know…" Her face reddened with embarrassment as she fiddled with the charm bracelet on her left arm.

"Many here have speculated but few truly know for sure. So let's keep this just between us, okay?"

"Her name is Alexis St. Clair."

"Ah, right. Alexis. Now I remember. Thanks, Monique. When it's time for your raise, I'll put in a good word." Shyla winked, turned, and walked briskly away. *Ignorant female. But she might come in handy.* Plus, she was plump and plain, a departure from the last woman who'd worked for Toussaint. Shyla had breathed a sigh of relief when the former assistant got married and moved to D.C. It meant one less pretty woman to turn Toussaint's head. At least in the office. But that only left about a zillion outside the workplace. Including one certain interior designer who was about to learn that there was already a Mrs. Toussaint Livingston on the horizon. And her first name was Shyla.

36

Zoe watched, shocked, as Chardonnay laughed while her son rapped with the music. It wasn't the genre she had a problem with but the choice of song. Her good friend's seven-year-old was spewing expletive-filled lyrics about female body parts, Uzis, and crack, as if the song were a nursery rhyme. "Cognac, stop that!" she finally shouted, exasperated.

"What?" Cognac wore a pair of sunglasses and an over-sized, sideways baseball cap.

"Singing that disgusting song, that's what!"

"Why?" Cognac asked in an indignant voice that was underscored by scrawny arms crossed over a chest that had the nerve to be puffed out.

"Because you can't talk like that around your aunt Zoe, that's why!"

"I can too!" Cognac continued rapping as he mimicked the videos he'd seen, bobbing his head with his shoulders hunched over. The only thing missing was his blunt and a beer.

"Boy, shut the hell up. I'ma have Q beat that ass when he comes over, like he threatened the last time. Go on in there and clean your room. Go on!" Chardonnay lit a cigarette and then reached for the stereo remote and changed CDs. Soon the tamer sounds of Alicia Keyes drifted throughout the living room.

Zoe watched Cognac completely ignore his mother's directive, opting instead to retrieve a bag of chips and a box of juice from the kitchen and then walk back through the living room like he owned it. He eyed his mother defiantly as he walked past them and out the front door. "Oh, hell no!" she exclaimed, reaching for her own pack of cigarettes. "Are you going to let him get away with that?"

"Girl, I can't control his bad ass." Chardonnay reached into her cigarette pack, pulled out a half-smoked blunt, and lit it.

"That's why you need a man around, and that's why I think you should stick with Bobby. Q's fine and all, but he doesn't sound like the settling-down type. At least, not any time soon."

"Maybe not, but as long as he's laying the pipe like he's doing, I sure as hell ain't sending him nowhere. I thought Bobby was big, but unh-unh-unh . . ." Chardonnay made smacking sounds and licked her fingers.

"Is that all you think about, girl, getting some?"

"Just about."

"What about the pictures Bobby has on you? Have you thought about that? And what would happen if the Livingstons ever found out?"

"Girl, those pictures are long gone. He deleted them the first night he was over here."

"How do you know he doesn't have copies?"

"Baby, after what I put on him? Trust and believe, that evidence is history. His nose is wide open, sniffing behind me like a puppy dog."

"See, that's what I mean, Char. Bobby really likes you. He seems to be interested in you for more than what's between your legs."

"Girl, please. Nobody's marrying Bobby's tore-up ass."

Zoe looked at her friend a long moment. "Why do you talk about him like that, Char? I've seen the dogs you go out with, the dealers and players. Bobby might not be that much to look at, but he's got a steady job and seems to genuinely care about you. And didn't you say he fixed your car last week?"

"Yes, he did, and my screen door too. I'm gonna keep him around until he fixes all that's broken, and then lock him out of the very door he repaired!" Chardonnay laughed, took a long drag on the blunt, and started coughing. "Here, you want some?"

"No, I'm good."

"What, since you got offered that trip to LA you don't get high no more? Trying to go corporate, all Shyla Martin and shit?"

"Please, I'm hardly trying to be like her. But I am cleaning up my act. I had my annual review last week. Ace is very pleased with my work and says I have a bright future with the company. I don't want to mess this up."

"Aw, hell, girl. You gonna believe that? His old ass is just trying to get some."

"No, Char. Ace isn't like that. He really believes in my abilities—he even said that if I decided to go back to school, the company will pay for it."

"Yeah, whatever." Chardonnay got up from the couch. "You don't drink no more either?"

"Yes, but I don't want anything."

"I sure hope your ass don't turn into a fuddy-duddy."

"A who?"

"That's what my grandma used to call women who were stuck-up or plain or didn't know how to come correct with they shit."

"Oh, and you think that's me now?"

"Don't stop being fun—that's all I'm sayin'."

"So . . . is Bobby coming over tonight?"

"Why are you always so interested in Bobby? I think it's because you've got a closet crush on him."

"He just seems like a nice guy, that's all. I went to Taste for lunch the other day. He came up to the counter and asked if I'd seen you. Last week, I told you, remember?"

"Yeah, yeah, yeah, and so what?"

"He's not really ugly, Chardonnay. If he did something to his hair, got his teeth fixed, and maybe got a few facials for his bumpy complexion, he'd look all right."

˥ "Then why don't you go out with him, Zoe?" Chardonnay sat back on the couch, positioned a tray on her lap, and began rolling another blunt. "I tell you what. He'll probably be calling later, after he gets off work. Why don't I give him *your* number, and *your* address, and *you* can fuck him? How's that sound?"

Their conversation was interrupted by Cognac's loud wail as he came back into the living room.

"Boy, what the hell is wrong with you?"

"I hate Dontae!" he wailed. "He hit me!"

"Hit you? Did you hit him back?"

Cognac shook his head.

"Bring your ass on over here." When he came within reach, Chardonnay snatched him close to her. "Put your hands down away from your face." She grabbed his chin, turned his face this way and that, and seeing no blood, concluded he wouldn't die soon. "Shut up, boy. You're all right. Now take your ass back outside. And don't come back in here until you hit him back. Bust him right in his face, here me? If you don't go hit him, I'ma beat your ass. Understand?"

Cognac nodded and ran out the door. "Dontae! Where you at? I'ma beat your ass!"

Chardonnay took a puff of her newly rolled joint and howled. "Ha! That's what I'm talking about. That's my little man right there!"

Zoe sighed. Although the scene was a normal one for the Johnson household, today it made her sad. "I'm outtie, sistah," she said, reaching for her purse. "I think I'm going to go by the mall, see if I can find a cheap suit to take on my trip."

"Miss Fuddy-Duddy," Chardonnay sang as she rose from the couch and began picking up toys scattered across the living room floor. "Just make sure you get some of that Toussaint dick while you're Miss Biz-ness in LA. Otherwise, that trip won't have meant a damn thing."

Zoe's retort was interrupted by a knock on the door. When Chardonnay opened it, six feet of oh-my-goodness and Lord-have-mercy walked in, dressed in a black muscle shirt, jean shorts that rode lean, powerful-looking hips, and sandals. His presence seemed to fill the room. While she didn't agree with Chardonnay's choice, she had to admit that he beat Bobby out in looks, hands down.

"Hey, Q," Chardonnay said, pulling him farther into the room. "This is my friend Zoe."

Zoe stood. "Nice to meet you, Q. Chardonnay, I'll call you later."

"You don't have to leave," Chardonnay countered while almost pushing her best friend out the door. "I'll call you later, hear?"

Zoe waved without looking back. From the look of raw anticipation on Chardonnay's face, Zoe doubted she or anybody else would hear from her tonight.

37

Zoe pulled her shiny new Honda Accord into the mall parking lot. It was relatively empty for a Sunday night, which made her happy. She loved to shop but hated crowded clothing stores. But she needed something to rid her of a worsening mood. Between Cognac's cursing-filled rapping and Q's booty-call appearance—reminding Zoe of her empty apartment—she'd lost the high Ace's news had brought her. Zoe left the car and hurried toward the mall entrance, sure that nothing could cheer her up like a clearance rack.

Two hours, a couple hundred dollars, and a peanut butter smoothie later, Zoe slowly strolled through the near-empty mall. She felt good about her purchases, which included a light blue silk pantsuit she thought both professional and sexy, two slim-line skirts that deemphasized her hips while highlighting her assets, a pair of black pumps, and a small bottle of her favorite perfume.

Satisfied and a bit tired but still not ready to go home to an empty house, Zoe walked back to the music store she'd just passed. Her eyes lit up when she saw a bin full of CDs directly ahead with a sign announcing fifty percent off. She placed her bags beside her and dove into the R & B and hip-hop section as if she were digging for gold.

"Damn, baby, you out of music or what?" a teasing voice whispered close to her ear.

She frowned, pissed at the stranger who had the nerve to invade her personal space. "What's it to—Oh, hey, Bobby."

"Hey, Zoe. What up?"

"Nothing, just out spending the check that I just earned."

Bobby peeked around her and eyed the bags at her side. "Look like you're doing a pretty good job. And digging through those CDs like somebody's chasing you."

"I guess I did get a little excited. A sale sign will do that to me."

"Is that all it takes?" Bobby snorted. "Wish I could say the same for your girl. Looks like nothing I do can please Chardonnay. And I really like her too."

"Chardonnay's bark is worse than her bite."

"I know, but she's always dogging a brothah out. What's up with that?"

Zoe shrugged. "She tries to come off hard, but she's a good person when you get to know her."

"The 'get to know' is the problem. Don't want to let nobody behind that tall-ass wall she has around her heart. Look, do you think she'll like this?" Bobby reached inside a bag from a jewelry store, opened a small box, and showed Zoe a heart-shaped necklace set with tiny diamonds. Zoe thought it was a sweet gift but knew Chardonnay would complain that the stones weren't bigger. "That's nice, Bobby."

"Yeah, but do you think Chardonnay will feel that way?"

"What woman doesn't appreciate a man who buys her jewelry?"

"True dat. She'll like it," Bobby said, as if trying to convince himself. He offered Zoe a lopsided smile.

Zoe took in Bobby's slightly worried expression and smiled. *Maybe I can help this brother, and in the process help Chardonnay, Cognac, and Tangeray.* "Bobby, you have a nice smile, but can I ask you something? And please, don't get offended."

"Can't guarantee that, but go for it."

"Have you ever considered getting your teeth fixed? I mean, these days they have all kinds of—"

"Girl, my grill's been jacked up since I put the last baby tooth under the pillow at my grandma's house. I ain't sensitive about that."

Zoe visibly relaxed. "Good. Then why don't you think about having some cosmetic work done, getting caps. That would probably do wonders for your fa— That would probably change your whole look." Zoe continued to eye him critically. "And your hair has a nice, natural curl. Maybe a little texturizer—"

"I ain't got time for all that," Bobby interrupted. "Plus, I'm over a hot grill six days a week, ten, sometimes twelve hours a day. That shit wouldn't last in my head."

"Well, maybe get a nice cut, then. Or maybe even shave it off. Have you thought about that?"

"Look, Zoe, I know I'm not all that to look at and whatnot. But I'm a good man. I'm just a line cook right now, but this is just the beginning. I'm going places. That's what I told Chardonnay. But she don't believe me."

"Maybe that's because of how you got with her. Using those pictures you took to blackmail her, Bobby? Forcing her to have sex? Not cool."

Bobby showed the lopsided grin that Zoe decided was a cross between a smile and a smirk. "She ain't complaining."

"Not to you."

"She tell you she didn't like the dick?"

Zoe realized she was on a road that she didn't want to travel. "What about her kids?" she asked, changing the subject. "Do you get along with them?"

"The little girl's a sweetheart, little Ray-Ray. But me and Yak got some business to handle. Little man thinks he runs the house. Somebody needs to get in that ass; then we'd be all right."

Zoe nodded, further convinced that Bobby was just the man Chardonnay needed in her life. "Why don't you go to the toy store over there?" she said, pointing across the aisle. "Since you bought Char a present, you might want to bring her kids one too."

Bobby fixed Zoe with an appreciative gaze. "I like how you think, Zoe. You're pretty cool."

"I try."

"Hey, do you think . . . Naw, that's all right."

"What?"

"I'm not around kids and wouldn't have a clue about what to buy them."

"And you want my help."

"Do you mind?"

Zoe almost declined, but then thought again about the home where no one was waiting for her. "Not at all," she said, grabbing his arm. "Let's go."

38

"Dad?" In a rare move, Malcolm had used his key and let himself into his parents' home when both his phone calls and doorbell ringing yielded no response. It was Tuesday, and Adam was still not at work. Malcolm's concern had deepened to the point where he'd left the office to check on him. Stepping into the foyer, he noticed that copies of the *Atlanta Journal-Constitution* lay just inside the doorway and that the heavy, royal blue curtains that covered the living room windows were still drawn.

"Yo, Pops, you in here?" He kept walking, past the formal dining room, down the hall, and into the den. There, Adam sat in the dark, nursing a tumbler of cognac. It was nine a.m.

"Dad," Malcolm breathed, almost tearing up at seeing his father look so broken. A man who was usually dressed impeccably, even in casual wear, now wore a wrinkled T-shirt and baggy gym shorts. He didn't have to ask how he was doing. "Not too good" was written on his face. Malcolm sat down in the wingback chair facing the love seat where his father sat. "A little early for that, don't you think?"

"Yes," Adam said, slowly bringing the glass to his mouth and taking another sip.

"I'm worried about you, Dad."

Adam set the glass on the side table. "Don't be, Malcolm. I'll be okay."

"What about your marriage? Will that be okay too?" Malcolm hadn't meant to ask this, had thought to give his dad the opportunity to bring up the cause for his angst. The words seemed to flow of their own volition, and once out, Malcolm realized how badly he wanted to know the answer.

Adam leaned back against the love seat's soft, tan leather and rubbed dark-circled eyes that had seen little sleep. "For the past two days, I've been thinking about divorcing your mother, how it would be to live without her, and all of the ramifications." Adam shook his head slowly. "I can't imagine life without her, but I can't imagine sleeping in the same bed with her either, ever again."

Malcolm needed to digest those words. He rose, walked over to the bar, and poured himself a ginger ale. "We've got to do something, Dad. If Mama stays away too long, people are going to talk."

"Have you been talking to my brother?"

Malcolm shook his head.

"That's what Ace said when he called this morning."

"Oh, so you answered his calls but not mine."

"I was in the bathroom when you called earlier. Just hadn't gotten around to calling you back."

The sleek and modern Howard Miller grandfather clock ticked off the passing of time in an otherwise quiet room. Malcolm glanced at his watch, aware that he had a conference call with the restaurant managers in one hour.

Adam drained his glass and got up to pour himself another drink. "How's Victoria?"

"Victoria?" Malcolm asked, surprised by the abrupt subject change.

"Yes, Victoria, your wife. How is she doing? And speaking of marriages, how are y'all doing?"

Now it was Malcolm who felt that a shot of alcohol might not mix too badly with the coffee and Danish he'd consumed on the way to his parents' home. "All right, I guess."

"The baby or your marital state?"

"She looks healthy enough," Malcolm said, rising to open the curtains on the room's double windows just for something to do. "But our marriage . . . it is what it is."

"It was wrong of her to get pregnant and not tell you, son. But the baby is on the way now. Can't change that."

"Nope, sure can't."

"And I guess you could stay mad for the next eighteen years, but what good would that do?"

Malcolm didn't answer. How could his father, who even now was dealing with a wife who had stepped out on him, understand the dilemma involving a wife who wouldn't even make love to her own husband? The phone in Malcolm's pants pocket vibrated against his leg. "Hello?"

"Hey, handsome."

Joyce. "Hello."

Joyce noted Malcolm's serious tone. "I'm sorry, are you busy? Am I interrupting?"

"Yes, but that's okay. I have a minute."

"Okay, good. I just wanted to invite you to dinner tonight. I have some QVC information to share with you," Joyce hurriedly continued after feeling that the invite had sounded more like her real intentions instead of the strictly professional ones she wanted to convey.

Malcolm closed his eyes against the sexiness of Joyce's voice. So far, he'd done well to withstand her subtle advances, had ignored the allure of her sweet-smelling perfume and curvy body.

"I'm thinking McCormick and Schmick's, around seven?" Joyce prodded when Malcolm didn't answer.

"Uh, yes, seven is good. See you then." Malcolm walked

over to the bar, placed his empty glass into the sink, and turned to face his father. "Toussaint and I want to have a family meeting, here, with you and Mom."

"Just us, not your wife?" Adam knew his son and hadn't missed the subtle shift in his expression as he listened to the caller. He'd bet a thousand dollars that Joyce was the person on the phone and the one his son was meeting later tonight. It hadn't gone without notice that Joyce's e-mails to him had stopped shortly after the partnership with his son had started. He knew for a fact how dangerous someone like Joyce could be to a marriage, and soon he would have to have the conversation to make sure Malcolm understood this too.

"Let me know if you need me," Adam said as he walked Malcolm to the front door. "I'll take a shower in a minute and do some work from home."

"So you won't be in at all today?"

"No, son. I still need to sort this whole mess out between your mom and me."

The two men hugged as Malcolm prepared to walk out the door. "Oh, and, son." Malcolm stopped, turned around. "Make sure that there aren't two Livingston men who are thinking of breaking a fifty-year legacy and divorcing his wife."

39

While Malcolm enjoyed his time with Joyce, Victoria lay miserable in their master suite. "No, Mom, it's too late for you to come over." Victoria repositioned herself in the bed and winced as pain shot down her back. "I'll get the maid to bring me some tea, maybe sit in the tub for a bit."

"Good thing you have a maid to help you," Valarie said. "Because your husband surely isn't." Valarie hadn't approved of Victoria marrying Malcolm. She'd wanted her to marry a prominent doctor whose father had been a vital member of the Clinton administration. She was still smarting over the fact that he and his parents had dined with President Obama. If her daughter had listened, that could have been her! "I'm livid about the way Malcolm is treating you, darling," she continued. "It is neglect, plain and simple. You deserve better."

"Who? Someone like Charles?"

"Well, I wasn't going to mention him but..."

"Mom, not tonight."

"I'm worried about you, Victoria. And Malcolm, well, he ought to be ashamed..."

Victoria pulled the phone away from her ear as her mother continued to bash Malcolm. Valarie's attitude toward him was partly her fault. She probably shouldn't have shared so much of her marriage with her mother, especially the problems they'd had for the past five years. But she had. Every time Malcolm did something to upset her, Valarie's shoulder was the one Victoria cried on.

"Men like him have no control of their physical urges," her mother was saying when Victoria began to listen again. "Having that many children is shameful, even when you can afford it. It's people who live by their baser, lower natures who carry on in such a manner. I'm surprised you've put up with it this long, Victoria, and . . . Victoria? Are you listening to me? Victoria!"

"Mom, I have to use the restroom. I'll call you later." Victoria eased off the bed, waddled to the restroom, and then left the master suite for the guest room where Malcolm had slept for over a month. She opened the door slowly and breathed in his scent as she reached for the light switch. She swept her hand across the comforter and took in the messy desk, the only part of the room that the housekeeper was not allowed to straighten. *He left in a hurry. I wonder what's going on?*

Victoria walked over to the desk, realizing how little she'd thought about her husband since her last missed period. She looked down and spoke to her stomach. "Since your appearance, me and your daddy have rarely talked at all."

Victoria idly picked up a folder and began flipping through it. Her brows creased as she saw drawings of some type of grill. *Is this a product the restaurant plans to endorse?* She continued to flip through the pages and was just about to set the folder back down when a card fell out and landed on the swivel chair seat. She reached down and picked it up. " 'Joyce Witherspoon,' " she read aloud, " 'Owner. Silver Spoon Events.' " Victoria sat down and for the next half hour went through the folder and other papers on her husband's desk. She was shocked to learn that the grill she'd seen wasn't somebody else's product, but her husband's invention. *And he hasn't said a word, not one word!* She also saw several memos from J. W., with a variety of marketing plans for Malcolm's perusal. "Who are you, Joyce Witherspoon? And how involved are you with my husband?"

Tonight she missed him. For probably only the second or third time in the past five years, Victoria admitted that she missed Malcolm. That wasn't always the case, or at least it's not what she often allowed herself to think or believe. But for the past three weeks, since she'd been put on partial bed rest and hadn't been able to attend the near nightly church services that kept her mind off her marriage and on the Lord, Victoria had begun to long for what she'd never truly had—a healthy relationship with her husband . . . and herself.

Malcolm sat and sipped his cognac, feeling relaxed as he looked around the near-empty restaurant. He'd talked to Candace, and while his mother sounded slightly better than his father had, he could still hear the tears in her voice. To hear Candace Livingston in a weak moment was rare but was made somewhat better by talking to his aunt Diane, who said Ace had gotten Adam to agree to see Candace that weekend.

And then there was the state of his own marriage. After a week of trying to do the right thing and warm up to both his wife and her pregnancy, the situation had quickly fizzled back into a state where each spouse simply tolerated the other. For the past two weeks, only the Livingston men's track record of remaining married had kept Malcolm from filing divorce papers. Now, as he watched Joyce's sexy approach—tailored black suit, black pumps, and a bright smile—he wondered if even the legacy was enough.

40

Bobby rubbed his hands together nervously, looking in the mirror for the umpteenth time since he'd left the dentist's office two days ago. He still couldn't get used to the reflection in the mirror. What a difference a few facials, a haircut, and a set of even white teeth made. *Damn! Who knew?* It had been a week of transformations since his chance encounter with Zoe at the mall, and he'd taken his first vacation in eighteen months. After talking with Zoe, he'd gone home and spent the next two hours online, looking up dental offices specializing in cosmetic surgery and dermatologists who treated adult acne. During his family visit in New Orleans, he'd gone on a makeover journey and felt he'd been handled "from the rooter to the tooter." He'd been so excited about it that he'd called Zoe as soon as he got back; then they'd met so she could be one of the first to see the results of her pep talk.

As soon as he saw his girl's familiar red Maxima pull into the parking lot, Bobby reached for the bag on the seat next to him. In addition to the purchases he'd made at the mall the night he saw Zoe, he had several items from New Orleans, including an official Saints' Super Bowl T-shirt. *I can't wait to see her in this and nothing else,* he'd thought when purchasing one for himself, one for Chardonnay, and two more for the kids.

He hoped that she would see him tonight. Bobby wasn't one for tapping strange slits on short notice. He hadn't seen Chardonnay in a week, hadn't had sex in three. He missed her, but tonight he needed her too.

Chardonnay frowned when she noticed Bobby's car in the restaurant parking lot and saw a shadowed face inside the car; then she saw his car door open. *Damn! He's back.* Chardonnay wouldn't tell anyone, even Zoe, that for as much as she dogged Bobby, she'd kinda missed him while he was gone. She'd been disappointed when he'd canceled on her the previous Friday, and after finding out Q was also busy, she had gone out, bought a bottle of her daughter's namesake, brought home the T.I.-looking tenderoni who'd sold her a dime bag, and proceeded to screw the boy senseless her entire two days off.

"Hey, Char," Bobby said through her rolled-up window.

Chardonnay huffed before rolling down the window. "What the f—" she began as she turned her head. But what she saw left her momentarily speechless. *Whoa. He did clean up pretty good. Just like Zoe said.* For a moment, she entertained the thought that he was a good man and that he might make a good baby daddy, but the moment was short-lived. Char was known for dating pretty boys; it didn't matter if they were drug dealers, ex-gangbangers, jobless, or thugs—just as long as they could screw and were fine. Bobby could hit her spot, but at the end of the day, he was a cook. Gangsters got respect; diamond-sporting dealers received mad street love. And Q owned his own business. How could she hold her head up in the hood on the arm of a man who fried food for a living?

"It's about time you got that grill straight," she finally said. "And your skin looks better. But don't stand there grinning like the cat who stole the canary. You still ain't all that."

The comment wiped the smile off Bobby's face and caused the hand holding the bag to go limp. The bag plopped on the ground beside him. "Why you have to cut a brothah, Chardonnay? I walked over here to give you something. For you and the kids."

"Well, why are standing there flapping your yip-yap, then?" Chardonnay asked through a cloud of cigarette smoke. She took in Bobby's hurt expression. "Louisiana must agree with you, all right? You look...different." Bobby raised his eyebrows. "Okay, better. But check this out, I gotta be inside in ten minutes. It's not my birthday, so what's with the gifts?" Chardonnay kept up her tough-girl act, but inside she was moved that Bobby had thought of her while on vacation. *Maybe Zoe's right. Maybe this man does deserve a chance.*

Bobby's mood was subdued as he walked around to the passenger door and got in Chardonnay's car. He hadn't expected her to turn a flip, but he hadn't expected her to dis him either. A part of him thought about keeping the heart necklace, maybe even give it to Zoe, since her heartfelt suggestion had been the impetus for a transformation that made him feel good. *But I bought it for this girl, here. Maybe it will make a difference.* . . . He turned puppy-dog eyes at Chardonnay and handed over the smaller bag. "These are for Yak and Ray-Ray."

Chardonnay took the contents out of the bag and held up the first one.

"What the hell?"

Bobby's crooked smile returned as he reached into the larger bag he still held. "I got us one, too, baby. Figured we could all wear them to Stone Mountain."

"And get beat down? Yo ass ain't in N'awlins," she drawled. "You're in Atlanta, man. Cardinal country, ya heard?"

"Yeah, but y'all got love . . ."

"Humph, I don't know about that. But I like the idea of us going to Stone Mountain. You might have to buy us something else to wear there and save these tees for when you take us to New Orleans."

"Really? You'd come home with me? Meet my family?"

Bobby's mood lightened considerably at thoughts of he and Chardonnay making a real go of things.

"Don't get ahead of yourself," Chardonnay said, reaching for the other bag. She looked up in time to see Shyla's shiny Lexus pull into the employee lot. "Oh, hell no. Look who's decided to go slumming and park back here with the regular folk."

Bobby looked up and saw Shyla Martin pull her car into a parking space two cars down. He knew there was no love lost between her and Chardonnay, but he didn't have anything against her. "I like that ride."

"F that tramp and the horse she rode in on. Ooh, Bobby, these for my kids?" Chardonnay smiled at the remote-control car and Dora the Explorer doll, both of which she knew her children would love. "Oh shit," she exclaimed, looking at her watch. "I'm going to be late." Chardonnay hurriedly opened her door. "Get out!"

"But you haven't seen what else I got for you!" Bobby said, scurrying out the door so that Chardonnay could lock up her car.

"I'll see it later," Chardonnay said, taking her time crossing the parking lot so that she could finish her cigarette.

Bobby didn't miss the gist of Chardonnay's words—that she'd see him later that night. Knowing that, he felt okay to end the convo for now and get to work. He didn't even take it personally that, while she didn't have any more time to talk to him, she had a couple minutes to hang out with Newport before clocking in. As he reached the back entrance to the restaurant, Shyla and a man Bobby didn't recognize approached the door. "Ms. Martin," he said, stepping forward to open the door.

Shyla turned for a quick thank-you, but then took in his new and improved appearance and stopped in her tracks. "Bobby! What happened? You look great!"

Bobby's grin was immediate.

"Ah, just a little sumpin-sumpin. I guess this is what a vacation after eighteen months will do."

"Well, you look quite nice. Your clothing is impeccable." Shyla turned and noted Chardonnay approaching, taking a last drag off the cigarette before flicking it behind her. "Some employees could learn a lesson or two from you," she said, loud enough for Chardonnay to hear her. Then she turned and flounced inside.

Yeah, I got your lesson, wench, Chardonnay thought as she stepped inside and began her shift. She made a point to trade tables with Jermaine, just so she wouldn't have to breathe Shyla's air. But Chardonnay took note of Shyla's flirty demeanor and wondered just how things were between her and Toussaint. *I wonder how cute you'd think you were without Toussaint for a sex mate or without Taste for a job.* Chardonnay stopped, as this last thought that popped into her mind took her by surprise. What she wouldn't give to somehow make Shyla lose the job that gave her status and the right to look down her nose at everybody else. An image of Shyla, down-and-out, sans weave, designer clothes, or luxury vehicle danced in Chardonnay's head. *That sistah needs to be brought down a peg or two. And I might be just the sistah to do it.*

41

Adam tensed as the front door opened. He relaxed a bit when he heard Malcolm laugh at something Toussaint said. *Just my sons . . .* Then he heard her voice. *And my cheating wife.* It had been two weeks to the day since Adam had put Candace out of their home. He'd thought he was ready to see her, yet in this moment realized there was no getting prepared for this conversation. There had never been a family meeting like this.

Malcolm was the first person to enter the den. He noted that it looked much as it had when he'd visited earlier in the week: papers strewn around, a couple more tumblers added to those already sitting on various tabletops. *Where's the house-keeper? Did he make this room off-limits while he drowned his misery?* Malcolm thought these things in the seconds it took him to walk over to where Adam stood, looking out the window. "Hey, Dad."

"Malcolm." There were footsteps. Adam turned and stared at the den entrance.

Toussaint came around the corner, carrying a coffee tray. "In case someone wants coffee, or gets hungry," he said by way of greeting. He set down the tray that included mini-bagels, cream cheese, and thin slices of prosciutto, then walked over and hugged his father. "It's gonna be all right, Dad," he whispered.

One minute went by, and then another. Malcolm walked over to the bar and poured himself a drink. "You want one, Dad?"

Adam nodded. Malcolm looked at Toussaint, who declined. Instead, Toussaint poured himself a cup of coffee and began munching on a croissant.

"Where is she?" Adam asked when another minute had gone by. Now that his sons, brother, and sister-in-law had talked him into seeing his wife, Adam wanted to get started. *The sooner we talk about this mess, the sooner . . . the sooner what?* Adam didn't have an answer to that question, and suddenly wasn't in such a hurry to see his wife.

"Let me see where she is." Without waiting for an answer, Toussaint went in search of his mother. He didn't have to go far. She was in the kitchen, staring out the window. "Mama," Toussaint said, his voice soft, comforting. "Let's do this. The sooner you come in, the sooner we can put this family back together."

"But what if your father doesn't want that—can't accept that?" Candace asked, her wide eyes brimming with unshed tears. "I'm so ashamed. That he would only talk to me with y'all here is just . . . A mother shouldn't have to do this in front of her children."

"We're big boys," Toussaint said. "And we're here for both of you. We're not here to find out what happened. We don't need or want to know what went on. That's business that you and Daddy can discuss after we're gone. Malcolm and I just want to see y'all stay together. That's the only reason we're here." Toussaint walked over and hugged his mother. As she clung to him, he recalled an incident years ago, when the tables were turned. He'd been twelve at the time and had experienced his first heartbreak when Trina "Juicy" Willis dropped him for the neighbor with the high-top fade. "Hang in there, baby. You'll feel better," is what his mother had told him. And now this is what Toussaint told his mom as they walked back into the den.

"I'm sorry." These are the first words Candace uttered as she turned the corner and saw Adam and Malcolm, looking like the older and younger version of the same man, sitting on the couch. Even their posture was alike: both men with their right leg resting on their left knee, with a tumbler of cognac in their left hand. "Adam, there are no words to tell you how sorry I am that this happened," she said, walking farther into the room and perching herself on the wingback chair across from the love seat where Adam and Malcolm sat. "I know forgiving me won't be easy. . . ."

Adam stared hard at his wife. Through his anger, he noted the dark circles under her eyes, her skin's sallow appearance, and the tightness around her mouth. He hadn't been the only one suffering. "Are you sorry it happened, or sorry you got caught?"

"Both," Candace quickly replied. "But sorrier that it happened." She looked between Malcolm and Toussaint. "When I think of what I've done to this family, I'm just sick about it."

"What were you thinking?" Malcolm blurted out. "I know it's not my business, but . . ."

"It is your business, son," Adam interjected. "It's all of our business. Because what affects one Livingston affects us all, and it affects the business. That's why we can't be selfish, caught up in just thinking about ourselves and our own fleeting pleasures." These words were clearly meant for Candace even though he spoke to Malcolm. Only now did he turn to Candace. "And it's a good question too. And one I want to know. What in the hell were you thinking?"

"I want to share some things with you, Adam. I want to tell you everything. But I think this part of the conversation needs to happen just between us."

"Yeah, and if you'd been thinking about things that just

needed to happen between a man and his wife while 'working out,' " Adam said using air quotes, "we wouldn't be here, now, would we?

Silence filled the room, punctuated only by the ticking of the grandfather clock. Adam stared at Candace; she looked at the floor. The brothers looked at each other.

Toussaint spoke. "Dad, Mama's right. Malcolm and I don't need to be a part of this entire conversation. The only reason we're here is to speak our minds when it comes to this family, this marriage, remaining intact. Being the only single one here, I'm probably the last one to give advice on the matter. But when two people love each other, I don't think there's anything too hard to overcome, anything broken that can't be fixed. I love both of you, and more than anything else, want to see you happy. I just hope you continue finding that happiness together."

Adam looked at his son, his face a mask. He took a sip of his drink and remained silent.

"Marriage isn't easy," Malcolm said after a pause. "And unlike Toussaint, I am speaking from experience, present experience," he emphasized. "But we're Livingstons. We work things out." At this moment, an image of Joyce Witherspoon flashed through his mind. How sexy she'd looked the other night when they'd gone back to his office to work on the promotion outline and how the smokers would be incorporated into her catering events. How after unbuttoning her pink silk blouse, he'd buried his head in the valley of her breasts before nudging aside her lacy black bra and tonguing an already pert nipple. How she'd encouraged his actions by wrapping her arms around him and opening her mouth for a deep, wet kiss. Had it not been for a late-night cleaning person, Malcolm would have taken her right there, on his office floor. "We work things out," he finished softly, wondering if this could be true when you no longer loved your wife.

"Y'all can go," Adam said. He broke his gaze away from Candace long enough to look at his sons.

"Does that mean you and Mama will be all right, that she can come back here?" Malcolm asked.

Three sets of eyes stared at Adam and awaited his answer. He nodded.

"And everything will be fine? I mean, you were pretty angry, Daddy. You're cool and all?" Toussaint had never known his father to be a violent man, but anybody could strike if pushed far enough.

"I've never hit a woman," Adam said, draining his glass and resisting the urge to pour another drink. His stomach was telling him that he'd imbibed more than enough, and he decided to listen. "Your mother and I will be fine."

42

After hugging each of their parents, Malcolm and Toussaint left. The ensuing silence was deafening as Candace nervously twirled her wedding ring, searching her mind for the right words to say, the words that would allow her back into the master suite and into Adam's heart. "Thank you for letting me come back, baby," she began. "I've missed you..."

Adam snorted.

"Truly, baby, I've missed us. That other situation, it just happened. It never meant anything."

"Then why did you do it?"

"Stupid, and like you said, selfish." Candace stood and began pacing the room. "Adam, you know how wild I was when we met, how I was the life of the party, liked to smoke, drink. All of that changed when we got married, and I wanted it to change. I wanted to be upstanding and respected, like your mother, and to fit into the Livingston legacy. But even then that felt monumental to a woman like me. I gladly gave those things up, baby, and honestly, thought it was all in my past.

"Then I met... Then I started going to the gym and suddenly that part of me was reawakened, the part that lived life dangerously and only for the moment. I guess it was a midlife crisis of sorts, trying to recapture my youth.

"But it wasn't worth it," she continued, coming to Adam and kneeling in front of him. Her eyes again shone with unshed tears. "If I had it to do over again, I'd do things much differently. Is there any way you can forgive me, baby?" Candace's voice broke as she asked the question. "Is there any way we can put this marriage back together? I'll do anything."

"I had a woman chase me for two years," Adam said, looking down at Candace kneeling in front of him. "Well, I have had a lot of women give me rhythm, but this one was more aggressive than the rest."

Candace's eyes widened. "Who?" She got ready to sit next to Adam, but upon seeing him stiffen, returned to the wingback chair.

"Joyce Witherspoon."

Candace nodded. She didn't doubt that Joyce had gone after her husband, and thinking back to the meeting where Malcolm introduced his smoker, she wondered if Joyce was now pursuing her son. "But you didn't sleep with her, because of the legacy."

"I didn't sleep with her because of my marriage vows," Adam retorted. "Because of my love for you!" When Candace's head dropped in shame, Adam's voice softened. "And the legacy may have helped a little bit. I ain't gonna lie. When you've had something drummed in your head from the time you were ten, how decades of faithfulness are now resting on you, it's a pretty strong deterrent. Who wants to be the man to break a tradition borne by a slave? But it wasn't only that. It was you. You've always been the only woman for me, Can. Since the day I saw you walking across the campus, looking like Angela Davis's sister, or a seventies Erykah Badu.

"I'm going to forgive you, but I don't know how easily I'll forget. I can't tell you what it does to me, knowing you've been with another man. That another man has put his hands on what's mine." A surge of anger passed across Adam's face, and his hands clenched. "I guess we'll just take it one day at a time."

Adam and Candace talked for another hour. Then she made lunch, and they ate together, before Adam dressed to go to the office.

"Will you be home for dinner?" she asked as he prepared to leave.

"I've been out of the office for a couple days, so I imagine it will be ten or so when I get back. Oh, and, Candace?"

"Yes, Adam?"

"I've put your things in one of the guest bedrooms. See you in the morning."

Candace stared after her husband as he walked to the Mercedes in their circular drive and drove off. She was still standing there moments later, absorbing Adam's words and the reality that life was still not back to normal. *He's let me back into his heart, but not into his bed.* Turning away from the window, Candace climbed the steps to arrange her new sleeping quarters. *You gave him gonorrhea, Candace. What did you expect?* She was back in the house, and considering the circumstances, that was a big step. For now, Candace determined, it was enough.

43

"You did the right thing." Ace slapped his brother on the back before walking around to the swivel chair behind his desk and plopping into it. Not only was it TGIF, but it was also thank-God-that-last-night-Candace-had-gone-back-home. "I know it was hard, brother, but it was right."

"Yeah, I know." Adam loosened his tie and leaned back in the comfortable leather chair, one of two placed directly in front of Ace's massive cherry oak workplace. It was ten-thirty at night, and the Livingston Group executive offices were quiet—he and Ace the only employees still there. Adam had relished being back in the workplace, had found it therapeutic to focus his mind on something other than Candace's betrayal. He'd also enjoyed receiving the news that the Livingston Group had experienced a six percent increase in profit during the last quarter and that another large U.S. chain had agreed to carry all three flavors of Taste of Soul barbeque sauce—original, tangy, and extra spicy. He'd also enjoyed reading Malcolm's detailed report regarding operations and had agreed to accompany his son on his next site visits. The day had reminded him that the situation at home notwithstanding, Adam Samuel Livingston had a lot to be thankful for.

"Diane is sure happy to see y'all back together," Ace said.

"She loves her sister-in-law but was glad to get her house back. I don't know what it is with women, but they seem to like to be the only queen bee in the hive."

"Yeah, Candace was glad to be home."

"What about you? Glad to have her back?"

Adam shrugged. "I guess so." He became quiet then, his brow furrowing as he stared into the distance.

"Talk to me, twin. What's on your mind?"

Adam shook his head, remaining silent.

"Uh-huh. Well, then, let me tell you what's on your mind. The man who had your woman." Ace waited for Adam's response. "Am I right?" he prodded.

Adam nodded slowly, anger showing in the way he ground his teeth.

"Man, I can feel where you're coming from, but I hope you're not thinking of doing anything crazy. You know our circle is like a fishbowl. Anything happens and everybody will know about it."

"And then again, maybe nobody will." Adam finally looked up, fixing his brother with a determined stare. "Because I'm telling you right now, Ace. Quintin Bright is getting ready to learn a lesson. Nobody fucks with a Livingston and gets away with it. Nobody."

44

Zoe tried to contain her excitement, but the truth was she was beside herself. Her first time traveling on business and her first trip to LA. *Can life get any better?* It could, she decided, if somewhere between Georgia and California she ended up in Toussaint's bed. That she would get a chance to work with him more intimately was already a plus, she decided. And without Shyla sticking to him like white on rice. Yes, Zoe decided, life was looking pretty good indeed.

"Well, don't you look adorable," Shyla said in mock friend-liness as she stopped in front of Zoe's desk. She looked across the hall, into Ace's office, and saw that he'd heard her. That was her intent, for him to think she was fine with her new role of mentor. For what she had in mind to work, everyone had to think that. She turned back to Zoe and lowered her voice. "Is that a new pantsuit to celebrate your first plane ride, dear?"

Forget you, wench! Zoe smiled but remained silent. She knew Shyla was as fake as snow in Disneyland, but she also knew that now was not the time to start a fight. "This is my first trip to California," she replied cheerily. "I've been to Vegas, Denver, even the Grand Canyon, but never to LA. And to get the invaluable experience of working in the field with seasoned pros like Ace and Toussaint," Zoe continued, her voice now raised slightly so that Ace could hear her words. "I can't wait to contribute to this company's success!" She watched as Shyla rolled her eyes and knew she'd hit her mark.

"Well, don't worry that it has taken you longer than usual to understand the reports I gave you," Shyla continued, turning back to the side so her words would carry across the hall. "These charts and graphs will start to make more sense once you take a few classes, continue your education. As it is, you're doing amazing for someone who only finished high school." She again turned her back to Ace and lowered her voice to a whisper. "You did finish, correct?"

What I'm going to finish is putting a foot up your ass, Zoe thought. "You're so funny, Shyla," she said. "I'd love to chat, but we leave in two hours, and I want to make sure I have everything. Not that I can miss my flight, since we're taking a chartered plane. But you probably already know that. I'm sure you've done it *many* times."

Shyla shot daggers at Zoe with her eyes before spinning and flouncing off angrily, her strides brisk and purposeful. *I can't believe it! A chartered plane?* Shyly knew that the corporation had an arrangement with a charter company and traveled this way when necessary. Unfortunately for Shyla, her trips had never occurred during one of those times. Granted, the few times she'd traveled with Toussaint had been in first-class, but chartered? Shyla hadn't thought she could get any angrier about the fact that the would-be junior marketing manager, and not the soon-to-be marketing director, was making this trip to LA. But she'd thought wrong. Shyla was livid. *I've worked too hard for this company, and for you, Toussaint, and if Zoe thinks she's going to step over me to get to you, she's got another think coming!* As soon as Shyla reached her office, she told her secretary not to disturb her and then closed her door. Without breaking stride, she walked to her desk, pulled up her address book, and reached for the phone.

"Executive Travels, Linda speaking."

"Hey, Linda. Shyla Martin. I need to book a trip to LA. No, no, not on the company account." Shyla swiveled around and narrowed her eyes. "This is personal."

"Do you know how happy you've just made me?" Toussaint stood looking out the window of his corner office. He could have sworn that the sun just got brighter, and the leaves looked greener.

"I'm pretty excited too," Alexis answered. And she meant it. She'd been working tirelessly, almost nonstop, building up her business and her bank account. "I haven't taken a real vacation in almost three years." But time off from work wasn't the only reason she was excited. She was excited to spend time with Toussaint and was ready to tell him that she was in love.

"I've decided to take a few personal days myself. After business wraps, we're staying on the coast a few extra days— just the two of us."

"Sounds . . . romantic." Alexis's heart skipped a beat, remembering her and Toussaint's conversation the previous weekend when they'd met for dinner. First they'd talked about his parents and how relieved he was that they were working things out. Then the conversation turned more personal.

"Sounds like everything is looking good for them."

"Yes," Toussaint answered, his eyes turning sultry. "Almost as good as you're looking to me."

"Thanks," Alexis responded, suddenly shy.

"You look good enough to eat, baby, better than this steak."

"Toussaint, I don't know if I'm ready. . . ."

"Lexy . . ."

Alexis's eyes shot up to meet his. "Why'd you call me that?"

Toussaint shrugged. "That's what I call you late at night,

when I'm thinking of you and wishing you were with me. It just slipped out. Do you mind?"

"No, I like it, actually. My dad nicknamed me that."

"I wish I'd met your father so I could thank him for making you."

Alexis smiled.

"And so he'd know that I'd fallen in love with his baby girl."

Alexis swallowed, her heart so full that she could barely breathe. *He loves me?* "How can you say that? We haven't even been intimate."

"That's how I know. These feelings don't have anything to do with sex, Lexy, although I do want to sex you, real, *real* good."

"What about Shyla? And the other women? I don't do casual relationships, Toussaint, and I don't share. Have you ever been monogamous?"

"No, but I can be."

"If you've never been, how do you know?"

Toussaint reached out and took her hand. He raised it to his lips and kissed it. "I'm going to tell you something that I've never told another woman. If we make this official, this dating thing, you'll be the only woman. I won't be with anyone else. You have my word."

"Sorry, Toussaint, but I have to take this call. Talk later?"

"For sure." Toussaint smiled as he hung up the phone, giddy with the variety of surprises he had in store for Alexis St. Clair, including the five-carat bracelet of pink and yellow diamonds that he was picking up at Tiffany in Beverly Hills. Soon, however, Toussaint would discover that when it came to planning surprises, he wasn't the only one.

★　★　★

"Hey, pretty lady, I thought that was you." Coming back from the restroom, Bobby had spotted Shyla in the bar area of the restaurant.

Shyla barely looked up as she swirled the wine in her glass. She'd left the office shortly after Ace and Zoe, depressed that they were on their way to LA without her. "Bobby."

"Aw, baby, what's brought that ugly frown to such a beautiful face? Tell me who it is so I can kick his ass."

Shyla almost smiled and then realized Bobby's comment meant that she was wearing her feelings on her sleeve. That was something Shyla Martin couldn't afford to do, especially anywhere near her place of employment. True, she worked in this restaurant's executive offices, but this was close enough for jazz. "Aren't you still on the clock?" she asked, her voice harsher than intended.

"I'm on break, but you're right. I probably should get back in the kitchen. Where I belong." Bobby was all too aware of Shyla's position in the company and that she wasn't one to be messed with or taken lightly. "I hope I didn't offend you by calling you beautiful. Just a fact, you know, not meant to sound like I'm flirting or being disrespectful." When she didn't answer, Bobby turned to leave. "You take care, Shyla, all right?"

Shyla drained her wineglass. *What was I thinking, to come here of all places? As if doing so would take my mind off of the fact that Toussaint is probably screwing Zoe right now.* "That's all right," Shyla murmured, sliding off the barstool and heading out the door. Her travel agent hadn't been able to fly her out today without it costing an arm and a leg. *But tomorrow night, Toussaint, I will be back where I belong—in your bed.*

45

"Is this your first time on a private plane?" Alexis asked as she waited with Zoe in the private lounge. She'd been pleasantly surprised by the down-to-earth nature of the woman she'd just met, given that her only other encounter with a Livingston employee had been with Shyla, whom she'd met with Toussaint by chance at Taste of Soul.

"Yes," Zoe giggled, happy that she and Diane Livingston wouldn't be the only females on the trip. She got along with her boss's wife well enough, but then again, Diane was the boss's wife.

"Mine too." Alexis smiled as she swirled the straw in her banana smoothie. "What a way to start my vacation!"

Zoe stopped digging through her purse, the lipstick she looked for forgotten. "Vacation?" She'd assumed that Alexis was here on business, a consultant of some kind—public relations or research. "You're not here to work?"

Belatedly, Alexis realized she'd said too much. But it was too late to put the cat back in the bag. She was on a business trip with him for goodness' sake, with his uncle, aunt, and coworkers. Why was she trying to keep it a secret? Soon, everyone would know that she was Toussaint's woman. Alexis realized she liked the sound of that. "No," she said slowly after digesting the implications of that singular answer. "I'm here as Toussaint's guest."

"Oh." Zoe returned to digging in her bag, searching for the nonchalant attitude she needed to put on her face. With Shyla out of the picture, Zoe had assumed the coast was clear. Instead, she realized, she'd be dealing with yet another admirer.

Alexis watched as Zoe's energy shifted. It was subtle but definite. *Oh, no. Her too? Is there any woman under sixty not attracted to this man?*

"I'm sorry." Zoe pulled a tube of lipstick from her purse and opened it while smiling at Alexis. "It's none of my business. I'm just surprised. This being a business trip and all. I just assumed—"

"No worries," Alexis responded. "This is a new experience for me too."

The uncomfortable moment passed, and the two women chatted amicably. Zoe very much wanted to dislike Alexis but found herself warming to the woman who'd pulled herself up by her bootstraps and made a name for herself in the world of interior designing. Unlike Shyla, Alexis was successful, but relatable; she didn't put on airs. She had a quiet, unexpected sense of humor and a subtle accent that came through when she lowered her voice. By the time the Livingstons arrived, along with yet another surprise—business development manager Drake Benson—Alexis felt she may have found a confidant, and Zoe believed she'd met a friend.

Several hours later, the party of six—Ace, Diane, Toussaint, Alexis, Drake, and Zoe—sat around a large table at their first research spot: M&M Restaurant. They'd been seated by a cheery hostess and had placed their beverage orders. The air was casual, but Toussaint's business mind whirled as he took in the clean yet average surroundings. His body fairly hummed with excitement as he envisioned a hip Taste of Soul spot, the sounds of soul music pulsating through a dining room that sparkled with brass, crystal, and white linen. Finger-licking-good food would be served by waiters and waitresses with down-home charm.

"What are you having?" Diane asked Alexis.

"Hmmm, I think I'll start with the barbeque hot links. But the wings sound good too. I'm hungry, which is probably why everything on here is making my mouth water!"

\Diane laughed, intrigued at the woman Toussaint had dared bring along on a business trip. Not that such actions were unheard of—she knew that sometimes other managers brought along a spouse or significant other depending on the trip locale—but for the last year or so, Diane hadn't seen Toussaint publicly with anyone but Shyla. While staying at her home, Candace had mentioned both her concern and relief that Toussaint was still single—concern because she believed it was time for him to settle down, and relief because at least if he wasn't married, he didn't have to deal with the ramification of cheating on one's spouse. But Candace had mentioned how steady things were with Toussaint and Shyla. Diane doubted her sister-in-law knew about this gorgeous chocolate-drop, dreadlocked sistah now sitting beside her.

"What are you all having?" Alexis asked the table at large.

"I think I'll try their hot wings," Zoe responded.

"I'm curious about these oysters," Diane murmured, her mind focused on the menu.

"Why don't we order everything?" Toussaint suggested. "That way we can sample it all."

Soon, the table was laden with some of M&M's finest cuisine: chicken, both smothered and fried; beef short ribs; meat loaf; liver and onions; and oxtails, a menu item that Ace had to admit impressed him.

"They're falling off the bone, man. Gotta give it to 'em," Ace said as he wiped his fingers with a napkin. "Ribs can't touch ours, though. That special injection and marinating process we do? They don't know nothing about that there.

How's that succotash?" he asked Diane while reaching a fork into her food.

"I guess that's a moot question," she said with mock sarcasm as she waited for Ace to taste the forkful he'd taken from her plate. "Pretty good, huh?"

The conversation continued, centered mainly around the food that was being consumed. When Ace's and Toussaint's focus turned to business, Zoe, Diane, and Alexis discussed shopping and plans to visit the famed garment district before leaving LA. Having learned her lesson earlier, Alexis let Zoe and Diane take the lead in conversation. She didn't want to spill any more information, like the fact that she and Toussaint wouldn't be flying back with the others, but rather were taking a later, commercial flight instead. At the moment she thought this, she looked up and found Toussaint's eyes boring into her. He smiled and winked surreptitiously before swirling a piece of corn muffin into the gravy on his plate. He ate the bite and then licked his fingers while glancing at Alexis again.

Alexis fought against squirming, having become hot as she clearly got his message. Later on, he planned to sop her up, just like that.

46

"I'm stuffed," Alexis announced as she swept past the door that Toussaint had opened and entered their spacious hotel suite. "I can't believe we ate all that food!"

Toussaint walked over to Alexis, took her in his arms, and kissed her senseless. "Hmmm," he said once he'd come up for air. "I've wanted to do that all day." He turned Alexis around and began kneading her shoulders. "You know what else I want to do?"

"What?" Alexis giggled as Toussaint's finger hit a sensitive spot on her back.

"I want to get you out of these." Toussaint jiggled her pants. "And I want to see all of this." He sculpted her body with his hands while placing feathery kisses at the nape of her neck. "But you're not ready." He buried his nose in her vanilla-scented hair before stepping back and turning her around. "I've wanted you since the moment I laid eyes on you," he continued. "Please, Alexis, can I have you tonight?"

Alexis didn't reply. When she walked a few steps away from him, Toussaint's heart sank. He knew what she was afraid of—his past, all of the women—and couldn't blame her for how she felt. He understood that guarding her heart was as much about her father's sudden death as it was about hurt from past relationships. He knew this, but it didn't make him feel any better. No, he knew that the only thing that could help him now was burying his throbbing penis into Alexis's honeypot and loving her all night long. He was ready for commitment. Until he met her, he hadn't realized he'd tired of life in the fast lane. How could he make her understand?

Alexis's next actions showed him that he already had. She pulled the knit top he'd fingered earlier over her head. Toussaint's mouth watered as he beheld the chocolate globes bubbling over a beige lace bra. Her eyes locked with his as she reached for the zipper on the side of her slacks, unzipped it, and after maneuvering the fabric over her curvy hips, let the pants fall to a puddle at her feet. Toussaint's eyes darkened with desire. A smile flitted across her face. He thought that with her conservative nature, she'd wear bikini underwear, but the lacy thong matched her bra, and as much as Toussaint loved seeing her wearing them, he couldn't wait until she wasn't.

"Come here," he quietly commanded. She obeyed, stood in front of him, lips parted, eyes questioning. He grabbed her gently, reverently, and brushed her lips with his. She put her hands on his hips, and her touch sent an electric jolt up Toussaint's spine. He pressed his tongue into her mouth, hot and probing, slow and deliberate.

Alexis returned the kiss with equal fervor. She outlined his lips with her tongue and nipped the bottom one before wrapping her arms around his neck and swirling her tongue with his.

Toussaint raised his head and looked deep into Alexis's darkened eyes. *Yes, this is the fire I knew was burning inside you.* He took his thumbs and ran them over her lace-covered nipples. They hardened instantly. Alexis closed her eyes.

"No, open them. Look at me, Lexy. I want to see your desire." When she complied, he reached for the front clasp, unsnapping it. Her large, firm breasts caused his heart to stop, and he immediately placed one in his mouth. He sucked, then licked it while swirling his thumb over the other one. Alexis moaned, and he pulled her close, the evidence of his desire hard against her stomach. He'd dreamed of this moment for a long time and refused to rush it.

Alexis, however, had other plans. She was on fire and boldly reached for Toussaint's belt buckle. Toussaint laughed, delighted that she was as ready as he. He undid the buttons on his shirt and pulled it off, his undershirt and pants quickly following. Again, he took her in his arms, flesh against flesh, and plundered her mouth. His shaft hardened and lengthened even more as his hands palmed her round, ample ass. He squeezed it tenderly, parting her cheeks and running a firm, thick middle finger down her crease. He locked eyes with Alexis as he slid down his boxers. Her eyes widened as his massive weapon jumped out to greet her.

"I'll be gentle," he said, correctly guessing her fear at his size. "We'll take our time, baby. Because this," he said, gently grabbing his dick, "is for you, and only you. Are you sure you're ready for it?" Alexis nodded. "Good."

Toussaint gently took her hand and led her to the luxuriously appointed bathroom. He knelt in front of her, hooked his fingers on both sides of her thong, and pulled it down. He placed a tender kiss on Alexis's flat stomach and another one in the small V-shaped patch of hair at the top of her heat. Cupping her buttocks, he buried his face in her scent, wanting to devour her. Reluctantly, he stood. "Let me wash you."

They entered the oversized shower, and soon Toussaint and Alexis were covered in soap bubbles. Toussaint took the sponge and leisurely became acquainted with every inch of Alexis's body. When he handed her the sponge, Alexis became shy, keeping her eyes away from the big black dick that kept poking her thigh as she washed his chest. When she turned him around to wash his back, her eyes quickly traveled down to his sculptured buttocks, which had two deep dimples just above his cheeks. His back was taut and strong, his shoulders wide, his legs long. *All this is mine?* Alexis swallowed and felt herself grow even more wet. She fairly tingled with excitement.

"Touch me." Toussaint turned so that he and Alexis once again faced each other. Alexis looked into Toussaint's eyes as she tentatively reached for his erection. She looked down at the beauty of it, the tip shaped like a perfect portobello, a large vein running the length of its underside. His dick was rested above a sac that was perfectly symmetrical and soft as silk to the touch. She looked up as she stroked him lightly. Toussaint sighed and closed his eyes as she lightly ran a finger over his tip.

"Unh-unh, eyes open, remember?" Alexis became emboldened then and wrapped her hand as far as she could around his shaft. Her fingers barely touched. Still stroking, she leaned into him and began placing whispery kisses on the broad chest lightly covered with springy black hair. He quickly lifted her chin, lowered his head, and scalded her with a kiss that was hungry, urgent, as he buried his hands in her locs and ground himself against her. "Now...I want you now," he whispered. "I can't wait any more." He quickly turned off the water and carried her, wet and wanting, to the middle of the king-sized bed. Alexis closed her eyes as Toussaint immediately opened her legs and buried his head between them. She thought his assault would be ravenous, but he surprised her by licking her nub ever so lightly and then blowing air on the wetness.

"Ahhh..." Alexis hissed, grabbing the comforter with both hands, as if she needed to hold on for dear life. Toussaint kissed her thighs and then began licking her nub and inner folds as one would an ice-cream cone—slow, deliberate, rhythmic.

"You taste so good, baby," Toussaint whispered as he widened her even farther and continued his assault. He looked up and stared into her eyes as he placed one, and then two fingers inside her. "You're so wet...." He heightened her pleasure by tonguing her button while he probed for her sweet spot.

Alexis's deep moan and sustained shudder told him when he'd found it. "Yes, baby, let go. Hmmm." Toussaint lapped her nectar, kissed her swollen nub, and rolled over. He held her tightly in his arms until she'd caught her breath. When her breathing slowed, he spoke. "Do you want to taste me?"

Alexis rose on shaky knees, still throbbing from Toussaint's delicious lovemaking. She'd never been pleasured so thoroughly, and she wanted so much to give Toussaint the kind of delight she'd just experienced. She touched her tongue to his tip, then swirled it around the mushroom cap. Toussaint swiveled his hips and placed a light hand on the back of her head, encouraging her. Alexis opened her mouth wide and took in as much as she could, her saliva glistening on his shaft. With each moan, each thrust, she lavished more and more love on him, using both hands to rub and massage his massive member, from the base to the tip. In a totally intuitive move, she lowered her face to his balls and tickled them with the tip of her tongue. Later she would learn that this was one of Toussaint's most sensitive areas. His quick intake of breath suggested that she was on to something special.

It was enough. He had to have her now, had to make her his, and his alone. Toussaint rolled them over. He kissed Alexis slowly, deeply, once again placing a finger inside her. Using circular motions, he again brought her to the brink of climax, until he felt her love juices building, and she got wetter and wetter. He placed in another finger and gently widened her, preparing her for his girth, his length.

"Now," Alexis whispered, surprising herself. "I want you, Toussaint. Please..."

"Okay, baby," Toussaint replied as he reached for the colossal condom lying on the nightstand. He quickly rolled it on, and then, bracing himself on either side of her, sank down, slowly, beginning his dick's long, slow, tortuously tantalizing journey to her core. After several moments, when he was fully inside her, he kissed her long and deep, waiting until she'd fully adjusted. Now, he knew, it was her turn to take over the dance, to move at her leisure. It didn't take long. Slowly at first, and then more quickly, Alexis began moving her hips in a circular motion, mimicking the way Toussaint's tongue moved in her mouth. She placed her hands on his buttocks and pressed, hard, before once again mimicking Toussaint's earlier action and sliding a finger down the crevice of his ass.

This was almost his undoing. He rose up, slid out to the tip, and plunged back in, over and again. His eyes closed, and his mouth became slack in ecstasy. Alexis's moans became soft whimpers. *Mine.* He pulled out and thrust again. *This. Is. Mine.* Toussaint turned her on her side and raised her leg. He couldn't get deep enough, pound hard enough, squeeze her tight enough. But he tried. For the next two hours, and in more positions than even he knew existed, he tried to show Alexis St. Clair just what she meant to him. She tried to do the same. As the sky began to lighten, announcing the dawn of a new day, Toussaint and Alexis climaxed together, one final time, then fell asleep knowing one thing for sure: Their lives as they'd known them would never be the same.

47

"Are you Quintin Bright?"

"Who's asking?"

Adam stepped closer to the man who was three to four inches taller than him. He'd purposely waited until his brother went to LA to make this visit. Like many twins, he and Ace shared an uncanny intuition. Adam was sure Ace would have sensed what he was about to do and talked him out of it. "The husband of the married woman you fucked—and gave a disease to—that's who."

Quintin crossed his arms, suddenly understanding why his assistant manager had shown this stranger to his office. This was definitely a confrontation best handled behind closed doors. He cast Adam a lazy smile, then walked over to a bench and casually sat down. "I think it's more like she fucked me, man. That Candy..." He shook his head and let the sentence hang in the air. "Sorry about the clap, though, brothah. Did you get that taken care of, dog?"

"There's only one dog in this office," Adam snarled. "And if you ever come near my wife again, you'll find out that my bite will be worse than your bark."

"You don't scare me, muthafucka. If you'd been taking care

of business at home, we wouldn't be having this conversation. I can't say I won't miss Cotton Candy, with that soft, fat—"

Adam's arm pressed against Quinton's throat, cutting off the rest of his sentence. Adam had moved faster than he'd done in twenty years. He had thrown Q down on the bench, straddled him, and began to choke him before he'd realized it. Soon, two pairs of strong hands were lifting him off the man who was twenty years his junior. He jerked away from the assistant manager and personal trainer who'd heard the ruckus, and without another word, he turned and left.

Still breathing heavily, Adam settled into the driver's seat of his roomy Mercedes. He hadn't meant to lose his temper that way, had sworn he'd stay on the high road with that lowlife. But hearing him describe his wife's anatomy made him snap. A part of Adam wished he'd gone toe-to-toe with the youngblood and given him a good old-fashioned ass kicking, because then maybe his anger would be assuaged. As it was, he was still livid, Q's cocky grin as Adam turned and left was etched in his mind. He sped away, heading for the office.

As Adam pulled into his reserved parking space, he reached for his phone. He flipped his finger through the list of names until it landed on one he'd programmed in but felt would never use. Soon he heard ringing, announcing that he only had seconds to change his mind. After a few moments, there would be no going back. Not that Adam would want to. His mind was made up.

"Jon Abernathy."

"Jon. Adam Livingston."

"Mr. Livingston? Wow, sir, to what do I owe the honor of hearing from one of our more esteemed citizens?"

"Ha!" Adam relaxed as he heard the son of a dear old friend pontificate like a pro. "Boy, you talk more shit than a sewer line. You're an apple that didn't fall far from the tree, God rest the soul of your father."

"You know what they say about politicians. We call it like we see it and say it how it wants to be heard. But with you, my words are genuine. You're building an empire—no small feat."

"Trying to, but you're right. It's hard work trying to conquer the world."

"Is that why you called, Adam? Need a little help to win the battle? Not that you're not already well manned, with Malcolm at your right hand." Jon didn't care whether Adam noticed he hadn't mentioned Toussaint, who he believed was responsible for Alexis's short-term interest. Jon had felt she'd be the perfect woman at his side, another cover to keep tongues from wagging and his secret from getting out.

"No battles, per se, but I do want to run something by you, see if you can do me a favor. I'm coming to you in the strictest of confidences, you understand. Whatever is spoken during this conversation is between me and you. Do I have your word, on your father's honor?"

"You have my word, Adam. What can I do for you?"

Adam repositioned himself and watched as a couple employees came out of the Livingston Group headquarters. One of them waved at him. He waved back. "What kind of contacts do you have with the state's health department?"

"I can . . . take care of things when I need to. Is there a problem with one of your restaurants? Have you received a citation from the Board of Health?"

"No, my business is fine. It's another business I'm concerned about. See, my wife used to go to a gym, over in Atlanta Central. That new one that just opened up last year, Q something or other."

"Q's Bodybuilding & Workout Center?"

"Yes, that's it."

"I've been there a couple times. Popular place. Looks to be top-notch too."

"Well, looks can be deceiving. I have reason to believe

there are a number of serious code violations going on over there. The owner's carelessness...jeopardized my family. My wife used to go there, and, I don't want to go into detail, but let's just say I think the place should be shut down."

Jon, who'd been sitting behind his desk, now stood and paced his office. "Wow, I don't know, Adam. That's a tall order, to get the state officials to close a business. Of course, if the public's safety is an issue, I can understand your cause for concern...."

"Our families go back a long way, Jon," Adam said, his calm voice belying his rising anger. "That's why I called you, why I feel I can count on you. The gym might look professional and well kept on the outside, but the things happening on the inside are not cool—in fact, they're a detriment to society."

"What aren't you telling me, Adam? Is there some type of illicit activity happening over there?"

"There's no telling what all is going on in that establishment, behind the scenes. I would breathe a deep sigh of satisfaction, and be eternally grateful, if I saw that place put out of business or closed down for several months. That would undoubtedly cause a financial strain, of course, but where public safety is concerned, a man's gotta do what he's gotta do." Venom dripped, silent but deadly, from this last sentence.

Jon stopped midstride, aware of how Adam's voice had changed. Something deep had happened between Adam and the gym owner. Jon was sure of it. And the more he listened, the more he felt he had an idea of just what had happened. "And you say that Candace was somehow affected by this situation, these...violations you suspect are happening?"

"My wife, my entire family, was affected, Jon. I just want to make sure this doesn't happen to anybody else, at least not for a long time."

Jon's brow furrowed as he reached for his electronic Rolodex and began scrolling through names. He quickly came to the one he needed. "Let me see what I can do," he said to Adam. "I'll make a couple calls, pull in a favor or two. It might not happen immediately, and it might not be forever, but if you want things shaken up at Q's Bodybuilding & Workout Center then a rumble is about to begin."

48

Shyla settled into the backseat of the town car, her being in LA feeling somewhat unreal. Her smile was cunning as she remembered how easy it had been to get what she needed from Toussaint's unsuspecting assistant. "The Ritz-Carlton," she told the driver, scrolling through the notes feature on the iPhone for her reservation confirmation. She then reached for her briefcase and pulled out the copy of Toussaint's itinerary that Monique had given her. Glancing at her watch, she scanned the day's schedule. It included site visits to several shopping malls, lunch at Roscoe's House of Chicken 'n Waffles, afternoon meetings with commercial Realtors, and dinner at a restaurant near their hotel in Marina del Rey. Shyla thought about surprising Toussaint at the restaurant. After all, she and Diane worked closely together; Shyla knew for a fact that Diane valued her opinion. She'd even dropped a hint once that Shyla would get along well in the Livingston family. It was a comment that had been delivered in jest, when Diane had happened along a still-working Shyla well after nine p.m. Shyla had laughed along with Diane, as if taking her words lightly. But she'd viewed her words as prediction not pun, and she had never forgotten them.

No, Shyla, that wouldn't be wise. She hadn't been asked along on this business trip, and even though she'd used vacation days and her own money to fly here, her actions may be viewed as a usurping of authority instead of an ambitious climbing of the corporate ladder. Shyla decided it best to keep this visit a secret, between her and Toussaint alone. If he wanted to make her presence known—which he probably would after the night of love she had planned—then so be it. By then it would come off as his idea, her being there at his invitation. *Ah, yes. Me, Toussaint, Ace, and Diane.* "Sorry, Zoe, but your fantasy is over," Shyla whispered. *And my impromptu rendezvous is about to begin.*

They arrived at the Ritz-Carlton. The driver hurried out to open Shyla's door but was beaten to it by the doorman, who rushed to greet them. After paying the driver the fare and a generous tip, she walked confidently to the head concierge. Looking like money in a crisp, white Herve Leger dress and four-inch Burberrys, and carrying a matching bag, she reached the desk and flashed the boyishly handsome employee standing there a dazzling smile.

"Hello!" he gushed, his blue eyes sparkling. "Welcome to the Ritz-Carlton. How may I help you?"

"That's what I'm here to find out," Shyla seductively replied, leaning over to reveal creamy, tanned orbs highlighted by a push-up bra. "See, I'm here to surprise my husband. It's our one-year anniversary, but he was called away on this dastardly timed business trip." She fixed her mouth into a perfect pout, knowing the fiery-red Lady Danger MAC lipstick showed off her lips to perfection.

"That's too bad," the young man said to her lips before his eyes dropped to her breasts.

"That's how I feel," Shyla cooed. "Especially since I got all waxed and plucked, ready to give him his . . . anniversary present." Shyla reached into her bag and pulled out Toussaint's itinerary, while discreetly showing the concierge the stack of crisp, one-hundred-dollar bills folded inside. "According to the itinerary he gave me, he's at dinner right now. But if I can get a strapping young man such as yourself to help me, I can sneak into his room and . . . be his dessert later."

Laughter abounded as Toussaint, Ace, and Diane enjoyed the casual and comfortable ambiance of Aunt Kizzy's Back Porch. They had just ordered a variety of themed dishes, such as Cousin Willie Mae's Pork Chops and Miss Flossie's Chicken and Dumplings, with sides of okra, collards, and macaroni and cheese.

"Now, aren't you glad you came with us, baby?" Ace asked Diane as he leaned over to give her a kiss.

"Just don't forget you promised me a trip to Tiffany tomorrow. *That* was the trade-off for me not going shopping with the girls."

"I might join you on that trip to Tiffany," Toussaint said casually, taking a swig of his ice-cold Red Stripe.

Diane jumped on the comment like white on rice, the opening she hadn't even known she was looking for. "So tell us about this surprise guest, nephew, Miss Alexis St. Clair. Squiring you on a business trip? Sharing your suite? Now, I know it's none of my business—"

"So why are you asking?" Ace interrupted.

"But what happened to you and Shyla? I thought wedding bells were following you two around."

"You thought, or she led you to believe?" When Diane shrugged, Toussaint continued. "You don't even have to answer. I know you like Shyla. Mama does too. And don't get me wrong—she's a smart, beautiful woman who's good at her job. But there are no wedding bells in our future."

"And Alexis . . ."

Toussaint couldn't keep the smile off his face. "Alexis is . . . different."

"She redesigned your place, right?"

"Yes, Aunt Diane, the place you've yet to come see, though I've invited you numerous times."

"Well, I guess I'll get over there now. Seeing as how the living room isn't the only thing she...rearranged." Diane leaned back, not for a moment missing the light in Toussaint's eyes or the look on his face. She'd seen her husband wear that look, knew what she'd done to put it on his face. *His nose is so wide open, I could drive a truck through right now.* "She seems like a nice girl. But what do you know about her?"

"Enough to know that I want to know more."

"My feet hurt, and I'm wearing flats!" Zoe fell into the back of the cab, happy but exhausted. She'd fallen in love with the fashion district, an area near downtown LA that was roughly ninety blocks of wall-to-wall shops. Three hours had gone by like minutes. She was already planning a return trip to LA for shopping alone.

"Just remind me to never again invite myself shopping with two clothes fanatics," Drake said, piling into the cab beside Zoe while Alexis got in on the other side. "No wonder you see husbands in shopping malls with dazed looks on their faces!"

"Oh, quit your complaining. You know hanging out with us has been the height of your trip so far."

Drake snorted. "Hardly." But inside, he agreed. He'd had a secret crush on Zoe for months and had wanted to ask her out ever since his last relationship ended. But he'd been too afraid to ask, too hesitant to find out if this seemingly strong black woman liked any milk in her coffee. But now this business trip had given Drake Benson, the son of an English father and Irish mom, the chance to find out.

"I'll tell you what, all this shopping has worked up an appetite. Which one of you ladies is going to treat me to dinner?"

"I'm going straight to my room," Alexis said readily, planning to order room service, eat a good meal, and then invite her ravenous lover to join her in a long bubble bath followed by an even longer night of lovemaking. "But I did notice a restaurant by the pool. Looks nice."

"So, what do you say, Zoe?" Drake asked in a voice he hoped was casual. "Going to compensate me for carrying your bags across half of downtown?"

More than anything, Zoe wanted to trade places with Alexis. She knew exactly why Alexis was going straight to her room and knew which appetite she'd have satisfied. *Who did I think I was to even think I could come here and get with Toussaint? Fool! You're so stupid!*

Zoe stopped her thoughts, not wanting to ruin what had been a perfect day. "What the hell," she said, shrugging, with a glance in Drake's direction. "I guess your services are worth a salad or side dish."

"Who are you kidding? This is an expensed dinner. You'll probably order the most expensive thing on the menu. We're getting ready to dine like royalty."

"Au contraire, Mr. Business Development. I'm always mindful of the company's bottom line."

"She's bucking for a promotion," Drake whispered conspiratorially to Alexis. "Guess we need to drop her off at McDonald's."

"Humph. Only if you want a happy meal. I'm doing lobster tonight!"

The three laughed, then became quiet, content to gaze out the window and watch Los Angeles pass by. Zoe marveled at the palm trees and all the other vegetation, and Alexis had forgotten how crowded the city was. Drake's hand itched to reach over and clasp Zoe's, but he contented himself with the knowledge that he'd have her all to himself, at least for the time it took them to eat dinner.

They reached the hotel and walked directly to the elevators. One opened up right away. "I'm going to put down these bags and take a quick shower," Zoe said as they watched the numbers light up.

Drake nodded. "Do you want me to meet you in the lobby, or will you stop by my room?"

"I'll stop and knock. Be ready." The elevator reached Zoe and Drake's floor. They waved good-bye to Alexis and then went to their separate rooms.

Alexis sighed and leaned back on the elevator wall. She was deliciously exhausted, having gotten less than four hours of sleep. *But so did Toussaint, and he worked all day,* she reminded herself. A nice meal, a bubble bath, and she'd be good as new. Her va-jay-jay fairly tingled in anticipation at the thought of what was ahead.

Shyla looked at her watch. *He'll be here soon.* She giggled softly, her earlier trepidation having been replaced with excitement. For a moment, when she'd first entered the suite, she'd become frightened, taken aback with the obvious evidence of a woman's presence. She'd guessed that Toussaint would fuck Zoe but hadn't really wanted to believe it. But after calming down with a quick shower and a couple glasses of wine, she'd regained her confidence, remembering that she was Shyla Martin, soon-to-be director of marketing for the Livingston Group.

After rearranging the tray of hors d'oeuvres and making sure the champagne was properly chilled, Shyla walked to the floor-length mirror. She'd carefully chosen the dress she now wore, a satiny gold-print mini with nothing underneath. She'd gone back and forth on how to meet him. Naked in bed? Covered by bubbles in the Jacuzzi tub? By the door, with a bottle of wine and a glass? Finally, she'd decided on a sexy approach, which is why rose petals were strewn across the bed and candles lit the room. Her hair was down and around her shoulders, and her makeup was immaculate. She gave herself a final look in the mirror, satisfied that the nymph picture she'd paint from the middle of the king-sized bed was just the one

to harden Toussaint's shaft and bring him panting to her waiting wetness.

The sound of a card being pushed into the slot jolted Shyla
from her reverie. *Oh. He's here!* She looked around quickly and
then slid onto the bed, positioning herself in the middle. Grabbing a handful of petals, she sprinkled them on her exposed
thighs, even as she flipped back her hair to expose creamy
shoulders. She licked her lips, raised her chin, and felt like a
vixen. Finally, tonight, she'd have Toussaint all to herself.

Alexis dropped the bags just inside the door, kicking off
her shoes in one fluid motion. She walked directly to the table,
where earlier she'd seen the room service information. She'd
decided to place her order, schedule it for thirty minutes later,
and take a shower before Toussaint arrived. She wanted to be
ready in case he wanted her now, like she did him, and didn't
want to prolong the inevitable with a drawn-out bath.

She sat down and began looking at the menu. "Oh, for
heaven's sake," she murmured, realizing that nature's call prevented her from focusing. "I need to get out of these clothes
anyway." She hurried to the master bath, a frown beginning to
form as she smelled the scent of . . . *vanilla?* Alexis smiled. *That
rascal. He beat me here.* "Baby, are you filling the room with my
favorite—"Alexis turned the corner and stopped in her tracks.
"What the hell?"

Shyla hid her surprise at seeing Alexis instead of Zoe.
*Hmmm. The plot thickens. Obviously this surprise visit was timelier
than I realized.* "You don't look like room service," she said
calmly, leaning back deeper into the feather pillows."Were you
Toussaint's bed warmer last night while he awaited my arrival?" Shyla took delight in the look of horror on Alexis's face
and continued. "Oh, he must not have told you that you were
just one of several women he invited on this trip. The man's
insatiable, but, from the look on your face, I guess you know a
little bit about that by now. But don't worry, I learned a long

time ago that since I am going to be Mrs. Livingston, I'd better get used to sharing him with the rest of the world."

This last sentence jolted Alexis out of immobility. Without a word, she walked to the closet, pulled out her suitcase, and quickly threw clothes and shoes inside. She marched to the bathroom and retrieved her toiletries, not even looking at Shyla as she passed back by the bed. Alexis was numb with the myriad of emotions roiling within her; she could barely breathe. *Last night. Magical. Perfect. I've got to get out of here!*

"Wait. Are you leaving? I'm sorry, Alexis. I can't believe Toussaint didn't tell you I'd be here today." Shyla hurried off the bed.

"Don't!" Alexis growled as she turned and gave Shyla a look that stopped her dead in her tracks. "Come any closer, and I might not be responsible for my actions. I don't know who invited who, or what is going on. But I know that any man who will sleep with someone like you is no man of mine." With that, Alexis turned and walked out of the room, her head held high. She put on the shoes by the door, grabbed the bags containing her newly purchased items, and headed to the elevator. *Just let me get to a cab and get to the airport.* From there, with a ticket back to Atlanta in her hand, she could formulate her future, and breathe again.

The elevator dinged. Alexis's hurried entry into it was blocked by a solid, hard chest. "Baby!" Toussaint said, opening his arms and wrapping them around his honey.

"Get your hands off of me, Toussaint!" Alexis said, wriggling out of his grasp.

Toussaint stepped back and only then noticed the bags and Alexis's luggage. His brow creased with a deep frown. "Alexis. What is it, baby? What in the world has happened?"

Alexis maneuvered her things around him and into the elevator. "I don't know, Toussaint," she said softly as the doors were closing. "Ask your *wife*."

49

"My what? Alexis!" But it was too late, the elevator doors had closed. Toussaint frantically pushed the down button and jumped into the next elevator as soon as the doors opened. He reached the lobby and ran toward the entrance.

"Did you see a woman just now?" Toussaint asked the concierge. "Black, thick locs, carrying a suitcase and bags?"

The same man who had helped Shyla with this surprise nodded. "Just helped her get a cab, sir."

"Where was she going?"

"I'm afraid that's confidential information, sir. Would you be needing a cab as well?"

Toussaint's long strides were already eating up the space between the front door and the elevator. He ran a hand across his face, perplexed beyond belief at what could have happened to cause Alexis to leave. And then it hit him. *Shyla. Somehow, she got Alexis's number and called her.* It still didn't make sense. What could Shyla have said that would make Alexis pack her bags and leave? *Alexis is here, with me. Shyla is in Atlanta.* Or was she?

When the elevator doors opened, a fast-moving Toussaint almost collided with Zoe, who stepped out of the elevator at the same time.

Drake was directly behind her. "Hey, man, where's the fire?"

Toussaint grabbed Drake's arm. "Where is she?"

"Whoa, who?"

"Don't 'who' me. Your jogging partner, Shyla. Where is she?"

"In Atlanta? Heck, I don't know. Calm down, man. Let me go!"

Toussaint released Drake's arm. "Sorry, Drake. Didn't mean to grab you like that." He turned to a wide-eyed Zoe, who shrugged and shook her head before a question was asked. Toussaint pushed the button to his floor, a sinking feeling enveloping with each floor passed. "She wouldn't," he whispered. But he knew that she would. When it came to Shyla Martin, Toussaint wouldn't put a thing past her.

"Shyla!" Toussaint yelled as soon as he'd opened the door to his suite. "Shyla, I swear to God if you're here . . ." He walked into the master suite and stopped short. "You've got a lot of nerve."

Shyla cringed at his palpable anger. She'd thought Toussaint might sleep with Zoe, but never once had she considered that he'd bring an actual love interest on a business trip. And judging from his reaction, Alexis was much more than a passing fling. Thinking of the nasty encounter they'd just had made Shyla sit up straight. Had he run into Alexis? *Uh-oh.* With each passing moment, Shyla realized just how bad her idea was to surprise Toussaint. "Sorry, Toussaint," she said, easing off the bed and standing to face him. She knew it was time to do damage control. "I took some vacation days, wanted to surprise you. We've both been so busy back in Atlanta. I wasn't thinking—"

"Exactly! You weren't thinking!" Toussaint took a couple steps and stopped. "Shyla, I'm going downstairs to have a drink. When I come back, I don't want to see any evidence that you were here. And when I get back to Atlanta, I don't want to see any evidence that you're still with the company. Do you understand?"

"Toussaint, I said I was sorry. And I mean it. I never would have come here if I'd known you had company. But what does this personal mistake have to do with my job?"

"You're getting ready to have a lot of time on your hands to figure that out. I'll be gone no more than ten minutes. Don't let me return and find you here."

50

Alexis couldn't stop shaking. After crying almost all the way to the airport, she'd blown her nose, pushed back her shoulders, and dared another tear to drop from her eye. Still, she couldn't help but wonder, *How could things change so quickly?* One minute, she was living a dream, and now she was trying to claw her way out of a nightmare. Love, snatched away, just like that. Of its own volition, a scene began to play in her mind. Of another time, and another love suddenly gone.

Alexis hoisted the backpack onto her shoulder and then balanced Chinese takeout in one hand and her phone in the other, all while navigating the streets of midtown Manhattan. The week had been grueling, but finally she'd secured an internship at a design shop. But all that started next week. Right now, there was something else on her mind—home. She hadn't been back in a year, and even with all the drama that came with St. Louis, she was ready to see family, especially her dad. Checking her phone once she reached the bus stop, she wasn't surprised that she'd missed several calls. "Baby girl, it's your daddy. Been trying to reach you, but I guess it's hard to catch up with an up-and-coming design superstar. And, yes, you're right. Those hang-ups was me. You know I don't like to talk in this thing, like a recorder. Okay, that's it. Just call when you can. I love you, baby girl."

Alexis smiled as she listened to her father's message. She saved the message and continued to listen. There was a call-back from an earlier interview saying they'd hired someone else, her soon-to-be ex-roommate saying she'd sold the refrigerator (yay, more cash), and then a call from her mom.

"Lexy, it's me. Call right away. It's an emergency. Call me."

The way her mom sounded alarmed Alexis. Her heartbeat sped up, and her palms became clammy. She couldn't punch in her mother's number fast enough. "Mama, it's me. Call me back. I've been working all day, just now checking messages. Call me. I'm worried. Okay, bye."

Alexis continued listening to the messages, becoming more frightened with each passing moment. The second message: "Lexy, call me! Your daddy's been rushed to the hospital." Alexis had never heard her usually laid-back (translation, *inebriated*) mother so frantic.

The third message, an hour later, her mother's weary voice: "Alexis, you need to call me. It's your mom."

Alexis was standing in line to board the bus when her phone rang. "Hello? Mom, what is it?" Alexis yelled.

"It's your daddy, baby."

"I got your messages. What's wrong? Where's Daddy?"

"I'm sorry to have to tell you this, baby. Your daddy's dead."

Alexis stood stunned, watching without really seeing the bus take off. Then she crumpled to the sidewalk, convinced in that moment that one could indeed die of a broken heart.

Shyla's unexpected appearance had been like her father's sudden death. Alexis's father had been in great shape and only fifty-five years old. The drunk driver who'd hit his car head-on had been seventy-two—and lived. This is why she hadn't wanted to open her heart up to Toussaint, or anybody else. Because she'd never wanted to feel this kind of hurt again.

Digging her nails into her arm, Alexis leaned forward. "Excuse me, how far are we from the airport?"

"We'll be there in about ten minutes, ma'am."

Alexis pulled out her BlackBerry and looked up flights on Southwest Airlines. There was a flight to Atlanta that left in two hours. She started to make the reservation, then stopped. *Atlanta is the last place I want to be right now.* Without a second thought, she hit speed dial.

"Hey, Kim."

"Hey, Lexy! What's up, girl?"

"Ha! I don't have to ask what's up with you." Alexis decreased the volume on her phone as the wailing on the other end got louder. Then she realized how much she wanted to wail too.

"Yeah, little man here is pretty unhappy."

"I can relate," Alexis mumbled.

"Huh? I couldn't hear you. Wait a minute, Lexy. This boy is taking his nap." A pause, and then Kim returned. "Bruce would kill me if he knew I was still sneaking his son a bottle, but desperate times call for desperate measures. Now, what's going on?"

"Oh, girl, nothing really." It had seemed like a good idea at the time, but now Alexis didn't want to share her latest romantic woes. It seemed as if every time she talked to Kim about a man, it was about one she *used* to date.

"Something's wrong. I can hear it in your voice. Talk to me."

"Remember the man I told you about, the one for whom I broke the no-dating-clients rule?"

"Toussaint?"

"Oh, right, I told you his name."

"You told me more than that, Lexy. You're really feeling him. Oh, Lexy, don't tell me . . ."

"Okay, I won't."

"What happened?"

Alexis gave Kim the condensed version of what transpired in LA.

"What did Toussaint say when you confronted him?"

"I didn't."

"What? Uh, hello, am I talking to Alexis St. Clair? Because the Alexis I know would hardly let a brothah off without getting cussed out at least!"

"Honestly, Kim, I was so shocked, my emotions so scrambled, all I wanted to do was get out of there, away from them."

Kim was silent a moment, pondering what her dear friend had told her. "You need to at least find out for sure what happened," she finally said.

"Isn't it obvious? She was in our suite, Kim!"

"But who's to say how she got there. Women like her will do anything to get the man they want. Trust me, I know."

Alexis couldn't argue. Kim would know. Her husband used to be a professional baseball player. Kim had dealt with several zealous females in the years she'd been married who'd given the words *bold* and *determined* new meaning.

"I don't know your guy, and we haven't talked much, but from the little you have told me, Alexis, he at least deserves a chance to be heard."

Alexis sighed. "I guess you're right, but I'm not ready to face him. Wait, Kim, hold on." The unfamiliar number on call-waiting had an Atlanta area code. Alexis thought it could be a client. She clicked over. "Alexis St. Clair."

"Alexis, it's Zoe. Are you okay?"

Alexis's back stiffened. "Did Toussaint ask you to call me?"

"No! Alexis, please don't hang up. I'm in my room, alone. Toussaint has no idea I'm calling. But let me tell you, girl, he's worried sick! Almost choked Drake because he thought Drake knew about Shyla!"

"Did you know about her?" Alexis remembered Kim on the other line. "Zoe, hang on." She clicked over. "Kim, let me call you back."

"Are you sure you're okay? You know there's a guest room in Dallas with your name on it."

"Thanks for the invite, sistah. I'll keep it in mind." Alexis's friendly voice once again turned stern as she clicked back over. "Zoe, I need to ask you something. Just what do you know about Shyla and Toussaint?"

Zoe took a deep breath before answering. "Listen, Alexis. Toussaint's my boss, indirectly, so I don't want to get caught up in some mess. But I can tell you this: Shyla and Toussaint used to see each other, but I don't think that's still the case. I do know that she wanted to come on this trip and was furious when they brought me instead. I've never seen Toussaint as mad as he was earlier. And I'll tell you something else—Shyla ran out of this hotel as if the devil were chasing her. Bags and all, she's gone."

"You saw her?"

"Uh-huh. Me and Drake were sitting at the bar, waiting for a table. I saw girlfriend flying through the lobby. And she looked none too happy. In fact, she looked scared as hell."

They talked a few more minutes. Zoe assured Alexis that what happened at the Ritz would stay at the Ritz, and Alexis thanked Zoe for the call. Arriving at the airport, Alexis felt better getting out of the taxi than she had getting in. But she still wasn't ready to go home, alone.

Alexis approached the ticket counter with a new thought in mind. She knew what she needed and where she needed to be. Her brothers may have been deadbeats and her stepfather a drunk and her mother their enabler. But they were all the family she had. And right now, that's what she needed—family. Alexis made the reservation and headed toward her gate. She would be all right, as soon as she got to St. Louis.

51

Chardonnay turned her head from side to side, still adjusting to her freshly done weave. "Are you sure it don't look like too much hair?" She was sitting at Zoe's dining room table, watching her friend try and act like a chef. "Ooh, olives in meat loaf? That sounds nasty!"

"Unh-unh. Bobby told me this little trick."

"You seem to talk to him an awful lot. I think y'all screwing."

"Some women can have men friends and not screw them, Char."

"But what would be the point?"

"In-tee-ways . . . these," she continued, holding up a gooey red blob, "are sun-dried tomatoes, soaked in olive oil. Both of these add what Bobby and Oliver call texture, those layers that make our food taste so good."

"What, you're going to conquer the marketing department and then go for chef? You trying to put Taste of Soul on lock!"

"No, I'm just trying to learn how to cook. One of these days, I'll have a man up in here and don't want to have to order pizza every night."

"What's his name . . . Bobby?" Chardonnay's laugh was hollow and didn't reach her eyes.

Zoe took a deep breath and ignored Chardonnay. She knew what her friend's crass, hardened exterior was all about—trying to shield the hurt little girl who still lingered inside her. But Zoe was done preaching to someone who didn't want to listen. It was her life. If Chardonnay wanted to end up alone and bitter, that was on her. "Like I told you when I came back from LA, " she said, reaching for a pan from a bottom cabinet and dumping the meat loaf mixture into it. "It's all about me right now. I'm motivated to better myself, get my degree and make a career with the Livingston Corporation. You might think about the company's college program, Char. You can apply for one of their employee scholarships, where they help pay for any classes geared toward the food industry."

Chardonnay stood abruptly. "You got some wine? I need to get my buzz on, shit."

Zoe nodded toward the refrigerator. "You're in there."

Chardonnay smiled as she pulled out a bottle of chilled white wine. "Damn, I'm cool just like this too. And taste even better."

"Girl, please..."

The two friends enjoyed a companionable silence while Chardonnay opened the bottle, poured a large glass of wine, and leaned back on the counter. Zoe placed her hands on the meaty mixture and began sculpting it into a loaf. While she did so, she thought back to a week ago, when she was in LA and Shyla's unexpected appearance had caused the feces to hit the fan. She still couldn't believe how fast things changed: Shyla got fired, Drake was given the temporary title of marketing manager to go with that of business development, and Zoe was shifted into the marketing department as a junior manager, directly under Drake.

"I still can't believe Shyla's crazy ass," Chardonnay said, as if reading Zoe's mind. Zoe had kept her word to Alexis and not told anyone what happened. But as usual, Chardonnay had a way of finding out everything, and once prompted, Drake admitted that he'd been the one who'd spilled the beans. "Bogarding her way into Toussaint's room and ruining his new thing. But then again, that's what he gets for being so fine."

Instead of responding, Zoe placed the meat loaf in the oven, poured herself a glass of wine, and joined Chardonnay at the table. "What time is Ray-Ray's father bringing the kids back?"

"I didn't tell you? His new woman is trying to play wifey. They took the kids to Six Flags and are keeping them overnight. No rug rats for twenty-four hours!"

"And you're hanging with your BFF instead of a hardhead. I feel all warm and fuzzy."

"Don't get it twisted, sistah. I'm just stopping through. Company's coming over later."

"Q?"

"Hell no! I found out why his ass went MIA—nucka had gonorrhea. Can you believe that shit?"

"I can't believe he had it, and I can't believe he told you!"

"He knew about it the night you met him, said he didn't tell me because he was using protection. Then guilt started eating him up, and he told me to get checked. Luckily, I'm straight."

"This feels like a warning to me, girl. You'd better be careful."

"Girl, you don't have to tell me twice. As much as I hated to, I dropped his ass. Back with this little tenderoni I met a while back. Looks like a younger version of T.I."

"A younger version of the rapper? Who's all of what, twenty-five?"

"T.I. is at least thirty years old. Young blood is twenty."

"Damn! Kinda close to the cradle, don't you think?"

Chardonnay shrugged, lighting a cigarette. "He's five years older than I was when my stepfather took my cherry."

Zoe had been shocked to learn that Chardonnay's stepfather had raped her, and that Chardonnay's mother called her a liar when told what happened. This revelation helped Zoe understand some of her friend's behavior—her negative outlook, her rampant marijuana smoking and multiple sex partners. It was a classic example of looking for love in all the wrong places and yet not seeing love when it stared her in the face. "I think you should call Bobby, tell him you want to go to a movie."

"I'm done with him, Zoe. He's getting too serious. The minute he deleted those pics from his cell phone, his days were numbered. And now his number's up." Chardonnay reached for her purse and stood. "See you later, chickie. Time to test out my new man."

52

Adam and Candace sat in the quiet of their den. He reached for the cup of tea that Candace offered and took a tentative sip. "This is good."

"Thanks. You want a slice of pound cake? Diane made it."

Adam nodded, and she soon handed him a saucer. They ate silently. Candace was grateful beyond measure for something so simple as enjoying quiet time with her husband. Almost three weeks had passed since she'd come back home, and she was still in the guest room. Slowly but surely, however, familiar routines returned: evenings spent talking, catching up on the day, Adam reading the paper, Candace reading a book or working a Sudoku puzzle. They'd eaten out a few times, joining Ace and Diane, and had taken in a Tyler Perry movie the previous Saturday. All traces of Quintin Bright, including the gonorrhea, had disappeared. Now Candace longed for the penis she once took for granted. There was nothing she wanted more than to make love to her husband. But she knew that would only happen when Adam made the first move. Candace sighed and sipped her tea.

"I'm worried about Toussaint," Candace said into the silence. "I don't like the way he looks, and I think he's losing weight."

Adam grunted and turned to the sports section of the newspaper. "Who's this girl anyway?"

"Her name is Alexis. She's the interior designer who worked on his house."

"Humph. Looks like that's not all she worked on."

Candice smiled. "That's the same thing Ace and Diane said."

"I know the boy's hurting. But I still hated to let Shyla go. She was a damn good marketing manager."

"Yes, Adam, but she crossed the line."

"But it wasn't the first time."

"She and Toussaint were together for what, a couple years?"

"Off and on. He swears they were never an item. But personally, I like the girl, thought she'd make a good daughter-in-law. But Toussaint was adamant—either her or him."

"Like we'd choose..."

"Right, but still. I just hope the settlement keeps her from filing a lawsuit. If that happened, this could get ugly."

"She's bound by the document, which is sealed. If she breaks the terms and starts talking, then we're the ones who will be suing."

Adam took a couple sips from the cup Candace had given him. "A hundred thousand dollars, and from Toussaint's personal finances. I hope this Alison—"

"Alexis."

"Alexis. I hope she's worth it."

"If the redo she did of his place is any indication, she's on the ball—a very talented woman."

"Yes, evidently in more ways than one."

"I invited him over for dinner tomorrow."

"Think he'll come?"

"I hope so, if for nothing more than to get a good meal. I'm so concerned..."

"First time the boy's heart has been broken. He'll come around."

"Second time, actually," Candace said, a bittersweet smile

accompany the words. "The first time was when he was thir-teen."

"That ain't heartbreak then, Can. That's just a hard knock."

"Not when you're thirteen," Candace responded softly. "Your son thought life was over . . . for about a week. Then, as I remember, some new girl came to town, and the girl he said he'd never forget was soon forgotten."

They laughed, and Candace rose to take the tray of empty dishes to the kitchen.

"Here, Can." Adam lifted his cup for her. When she took it, their fingers touched. She felt a tingle and knew that he felt it too. Their eyes met and held, just for a second. Candace shivered. *Could it be? Is tonight the night I get to move back into the master suite?* A second later, the electricity was gone. Adam stood abruptly. "I'm going to shoot a few holes on the golf course," he said, walking away from his wife and the moment. "Don't wait up."

Moments later, Adam was in his car headed to the golf course less than five minutes away. True, he'd needed the exer-cise, but even more he needed to get out of the house and clear his head. He could feel Candace tugging on him, knew she wanted him. He'd never paid attention to it before, Can-dace's sex drive. Through the years, their sex had been average, but it had been regular. It went without saying that they screwed at least once a week. He'd thought that enough, had never dreamed that she was anything less than satisfied.

But now Adam's manhood had been called into question. Ever since his run-in with Quintin, where he'd taken in the tall body, ripped chest, and bulging arm muscles, Adam had viewed himself critically, wondering if he measured up. Pride and sheer willpower prevented him from asking Candace the obvious: Was that punk bigger than him, better? Did he have more stamina? *Did he hit your spot? Do I?* These are the thoughts Adam pondered as he reached for his clubs and began walking the familiar greens, which were tranquil and calming, like the breeze.

He'd just teed off when his phone rang. *Forgot to turn this thing off.* When he saw the caller ID, however, he was glad he hadn't missed the call. "Jon, how you doing?"

"Fine, Adam. You?"

"Good, man, I'm doing good. I'll be doing even better if you have some news for me."

"Matter of fact, Adam, that's why I called. That little situation you asked about? It's been taken care of."

"There's an out-of-business sale going on?" Adam asked, in code.

"There will be by the end of the week."

"Well, I always love a bargain, man. Thanks for letting me know."

Adam turned off his phone and placed it in his bag. There was a lightness in his step as he walked to the first hole. He began to whistle, and anyone watching would have sworn his chest expanded. By the end of the week, a tiny bit of justice would have been delivered on the man who dared touch what belonged to him.

It was after eleven when Adam pulled into the garage and placed his clubs in the storage unit. He'd run into a couple buddies and enjoyed a few drinks and laughs at the clubhouse. Even though tomorrow was a workday, Adam wasn't ready to go to sleep. So after going to his room and taking a quick shower, he walked down the hall to the guest room at the end. He opened the door slowly and, after walking over to the bed, stared for a long moment at Candace, who slept peacefully.

I've loved you for a long time, girl. I still do. He reached out, lightly touched her on the arm. "Candace."

Candace stirred, her eyes fluttered, and then she was wide awake. "What is it? What's wrong? Is it Toussaint?"

"No, it's me," Adam responded, reaching out and taking her hand. "Come to bed."

53

Toussaint lay on the couch in his living room, exhausted yet unable to sleep. It had been this way for a week, since coming back to the Ritz from a wonderful dinner in Marina del Rey to find Alexis fleeing their suite because his *wife* had shown up.

Where is she? he wondered for the umpteenth time. After searching the area for her to no avail, Toussaint had blown up her cell phone, leaving messages until her mailbox was full. Instead of the extended vacation he'd planned, he'd flown back to Atlanta the next day, with the others, and had driven straight to Alexis's loft. Not only was there no answer to his incessant knocking and doorbell ringing, but also her car wasn't there, and a little detective work with the friendly older lady next door revealed that Alexis hadn't been home in quite a while. Toussaint was beside himself.

Shyla was gone, out of the company and out of his life. But he felt no better. He wondered what he'd ever seen in her, to mess around with her for so long. Yes, she was smart and beautiful, but so were dozens of other women in Atlanta. Ego, he'd finally decided. Ego and greed. From the time he'd gotten his heart broken at thirteen, Toussaint had filled his coffers with a multiplicity of women, rarely dating less than two or three at a time. He labeled himself honorable because he'd never lied to a woman, never told her that she was the only one or that he was faithful. To the contrary, he told them up front that he didn't do serious, monogamous relationships, that he lived for the moment, for a good time. The women then decided whether they wanted to stay or go. Most stayed. In fact, they all had, until he tired of them, or they tired of waiting and moved on to a more available man.

Toussaint rolled off the couch and went into the kitchen. *When was the last time I ate?* He couldn't remember. He also couldn't remember the last time he'd done what he'd done this week—take a hard, long look at himself in the mirror, examining his past and pondering his future. *I'm thirty-two years old, and what do I have to show for my life?* He was handsome, rich, had the trappings of success. But what did any of that matter at the end of the day if one wasn't happy? He'd asked himself if he was really, truly happy with all that he owned and all that he managed. And the answer was no. Until he'd met Alexis, he hadn't realized these things. Only with her had he experienced just what it meant to be not only happy, but also blissfully content. For once, his own satisfaction was not his primary concern. In the twenty-four hours of joy they'd shared in the hotel suite, her physical and emotional satisfaction was the priority, and his heart had soared knowing that his actions were the cause of her smile. He'd gotten past the defensive wall she'd built, a wall that he knew was erected as a result of the immense pain she'd felt over the loss of her father, the only man Toussaint felt she'd ever truly loved. *And you.* "Yes, and me." Toussaint said these words matter-of-factly, not boastful, because he knew it to be true. She hadn't said it, but no one could look at him the way she did, give of herself, to her very soul, the way she had, and not be in love with him.

"That's why I'm not going to give up on us, Alexis. I'm not going to let you go." That decision made, something in Toussaint shifted. It was as if he'd awoken from a dream. Suddenly he realized he hadn't showered, nor had he eaten. With a smile on his face, he headed to his master suite. He was going to get dressed, go to the restaurant, and let Oliver feed his body the way Alexis had fed his soul. And then, next week, he was going to find his woman.

54

"Does Victoria know how lucky she is?" Joyce asked as she massaged Malcolm's tight shoulders. He was sitting in an over-sized leather chair in her living room, only the second time he'd been to her home. The first time was a week ago, after having dinner at McCormick & Schmick's. That night, Joyce was sure she was going to get some Livingston loving, but a call from Malcolm's grandfather, of all people, interrupted the moment, and Malcolm had fled her home as if the devil were giving chase.

"Hmmm . . . ," Malcolm responded, his body becoming to-tally relaxed under Joyce's expert ministrations. "Do you know how lucky the man is who is going to get you?" Malcolm knew he was navigating dangerous territory by coming to Joyce's house. But he couldn't help it. Somewhere between the harmless flirtations at the club, the listening sessions when he shared his dreams, and the counseling sessions when he gave her advice on growing her business, he'd developed feelings for her. He was having an affair, pure and simple. An emotional affair, but he was cheating nonetheless.

Joyce finished massaging Malcolm's neck and then began planting tiny kisses along it. "Feel better?"

"Much." Malcolm didn't hesitate in reaching for Joyce's

arm, leading her around the chair, and then pulling her down into his arms. The kiss was hot, urgent, tumultuous, his hands feeling her everywhere, his body yearning to do more. Joyce massaged his throbbing heat through his pants, helping him find the release he craved. She'd tried to go further last time, had reached for his zipper to feel his erection in her hand, but Malcolm had stopped her. The closest she would get was feeling him as she did now and helping him find release, before he cleaned up and went home to the wife who ignored him.

Victoria tossed and turned, trying to find a comfortable position. There were none. She was miserable, pure and simple, searching for the love she'd felt at the first feelings of flutters in her stomach. Now, all she wanted was for the little crumb snatcher pressing down on all of her body parts to be out of her. As if in on cue, a tiny foot (or was it an elbow?) poked her insides. "Ow! Maria!"

Within seconds, the housekeeper was at her side. "Yes, ma'am? What can I get for you?"

"Help me up. I want to move to the chaise and watch TV."

The diminutive housekeeper was strong for her size, and soon Victoria was on her feet. She took one step, and a splash of liquid hit her foot.

"Oh, Mrs. Livingston, your water just broke."

"Thanks, Maria, for stating the obvious. Quick, get a towel." While Maria scurried to the bathroom, Victoria reached for her phone and sat on the bed. "Mom, my water just broke."

"Oh, goodness. Where's Malcolm?"

"Still at work. I'm getting ready to call him now."

"Call me back. I'll meet you at the hospital."

Knowing how Malcolm and her mother got along, Victoria almost told her not to come. As she opened her mouth to tell her, a pain hit. "Oh!"

"Dear, you need to get to the hospital."

"Okay, Mom. I'll see you there." To heck with how her mother and husband did or not get along. Valarie Saunders had been present for every delivery. Victoria needed her mother, bottom line.

As Maria dabbed up the water, another, stronger pain rocked Victoria. She grit her teeth, but a cry still escaped her mouth. It was much too early for labor pains to be coming this quickly. *Something's not right.* She tried to ease back onto the bed. "Maria, get my husband on the phone!"

Maria dialed and put the call on speaker. They heard it go to voice mail.

"Call his office phone!" Victoria cried. She took deep breaths to try and calm herself. But her heart was racing. *God, please let my baby be okay.*

Maria dialed Malcolm's direct office line. Voice mail. She retried his cell phone once more. Voice mail, again. Then they tried both his parents' and his uncle's house. No one had seen him. All the while, Victoria was experiencing more and more pain.

Maria, who had four children herself, was no stranger to childbirth. She looked at Victoria and knew they had no time to waste.

"Get my bag," Victoria panted. "It's in the closet. Then help me downstairs so we can get to the hospital."

"I'll get your bag, Mrs. Livingston, but you are not moving. I'm calling an ambulance, now."

At almost midnight, after they'd watched a movie, Malcolm pulled himself away from Joyce. "I've got to go."

"You know that I don't want you to leave," she murmured, her hand reaching for his privates.

"And you know that I can't stay," he countered, stopping her movement. He'd come close to actually having sex with her tonight, had almost taken her up on the offer to give him head. But Malcolm drew the line at having her help him release—anything more and he felt the legacy would be jeopardized. It was already tainted, and Malcolm felt bad enough about that.

"Congratulations again on the completion of the smoker's mass production."

"Thanks, Joyce. I'll call you tomorrow to finish talking about QVC."

There was a spring in his step as he left Joyce's apartment. Being with her was invigorating, and not just physically. He couldn't understand why some man hadn't snatched her up. Goodness knew if he were single . . .

He got into his car and reached for his phone. As soon as the face lit up, he noticed missed calls from his mother, father, uncle, aunt, the job's answering service, and home. That could only mean one thing. *But she's not due for another two weeks,* he thought as he dialed the home number. When he didn't get an answer at his home or his parents' number, he called Candace's cell.

She picked up on the first ring. "Malcolm, where are you? We've been trying to reach you for hours."

"Forgot I had my phone on vibrate. Is Victoria in labor?"

"No, she's in her room, recovering from an emergency C-section."

"Is . . . is the baby all right?"

"She is now, but it was touch and go for a moment. You need to leave Joyce's house, Malcolm, and come see your child."

55

Alexis had forgotten that sometimes she liked her mother. Loved her, of course, that emotion was required for your parent. But Jean Barnes had a funny, likeable side. It had been a while since Alexis had seen it, or paid attention. But today she'd been reminded: while they'd shopped at Big Lots and Goodwill and before eating at a hole-in-the-wall that served up some of the best catfish Alexis had ever tasted. Now, four hours later, she was eating a simple dinner, having spent the afternoon cleaning Jean's two-bedroom apartment from top to bottom—with the help of a cleaning crew from Happy Maids— and then redesigning her mother's living room, dining room, and bedroom with simple fixes like slipcovers, rugs, and accessories.

"This is good, Mama," Alexis said as she helped herself to another serving of spaghetti. "I haven't had any of your food in a while."

"That's because you rarely get back here," Jean responded. "You're busy, though. I understand."

Both women were silent, knowing that Alexis's schedule wasn't the only reason her visits were sporadic at best. It was no secret that no love existed between Alexis and her stepfather, who'd been blessedly absent all day and almost every time she'd come over to visit during the five days she'd been in St. Louis. And while Alexis loved her brothers, she didn't like them most of the time, because of how they leeched off society in general and their mother in particular. She'd seen Sean, her older brother by five years, only once since coming home, and that was when he'd stopped by just long enough to ask to "borrow" five hundred dollars, then he had "someplace he needed to be" when she said no. Sebastion, or "Bass" as everyone called him, hadn't shown his face at all, even though he hadn't seen his sister for over a year and knew she was home. Alexis had decided it was probably for the best, given he thought she was trying to be bougie, and she thought he was trying to be gangster. But all in all, the trip had been a good one, one she hadn't even known she'd needed before losing herself in her mother's hug.

Her heart still hurt. Not a day had gone by when she hadn't missed Toussaint. She'd listened to his messages over and over, his impassioned pleas to return his calls, and she had purposely kept her voice mail box full so he couldn't leave any more. Aside from the one call to Kim and the short conversation with Zoe, Alexis hadn't talked to anybody about what had happened. And as much as she'd enjoyed her mother's company this visit, they'd never discussed Alexis's personal life. It was her father who'd given her the talk about dating and had encouraged her to set her standards high and not fall for the first man "wearing some nice cologne and a smile."

Alexis had just taken the dishes into the kitchen when she heard her stepfather come into the house. Rather, she heard the front door bang against the wall as he flung it open.

"What the hell?" he slurred, stopping in the middle of the living room, his hands on his hips as he looked around.

"Alexis," Jean said cautiously. "She did this for us. Don't it look nice?"

"What was wrong with how it was? Where's my *Jet* magazines? Where the hell are my shoes I leave by the door? I likes my shoes by the door!"

"Now, Frank, it's all right. They're in a special place, right inside the room there. In the bedroom. If you look next to the couch, your magazines are stacked real neat and nice like, in that wicker basket."

Frank walked over, grabbed the wicker basket, and flung it across the living room. "Nobody told her to bring her high-falutin ass in here and mess with my got-damn stuff. This is my got-damn house!" The sound of another slamming door, this one to the bedroom, provided the exclamation point to the outburst. For Alexis, the sound was her cue that it was time to go.

"I'm sorry, baby," Jean said, hurrying into the kitchen as soon as Frank slammed the door.

"It's all right, Mama. I'm all done here."

"Baby, I don't want you to feel like he's run you off. I've enjoyed you, Alexis. It's been a long time since we hung out, mother / daughter like. And I really appreciate what you did to the house."

"I was leaving anyway," Alexis lied. She'd actually planned to ask her mom to bring out the photo albums and reminisce about her dad. Instead, she asked her mother if she could have them.

Her mother hurried to comply, pushing the dusty, yet treasured memories into her hands. "I know you don't understand it, baby. But Frank's life ain't been easy. There's a heart underneath the alcohol. I'm one of the few he shows it to. I love him."

"I know, Mom. I love you." Alexis gave Jean a heartfelt hug.

"I love you, baby. Don't stay away so long next time."

Alexis's cell phone rang as she reached the car. She'd taken few calls while visiting her mother but now was ready to get back to work. "Alexis St. Claire."

"Hi, Alexis. This is Diane Livingston."

Toussaint's aunt? Alexis was shocked, to say the least. "Yes, Mrs. Livingston. What can I do for you?"

"Girl, somebody who enjoys soul food the way you do can definitely call me Diane. How are you?"

"Fine, and you?"

"I'm fine, Alexis, and I hope you don't mind that I asked Toussaint for your number. But I'm worried about him. I've known that boy all my life, Alexis, and I've never seen him like this. He's hurt, confused, and frustrated as all get out because you won't talk to him."

"Look, Diane, I—"

"I know it's not my business, and I can certainly understand why you're upset. Trust me, if I walked into a suite that Ace and I shared and found a woman lounging in the bed, my reaction would be like yours, with a good amount of violence thrown in for good measure. I also know what it's like to date a man who's attractive and successful, with women throwing themselves at him left and right. I've dealt with that situation for almost thirty years. It's not easy, but when the man is one like my husband, or my nephew, Alexis, it's worth it."

How am I supposed to respond to this?

Before Alexis could formulate a comment, Diane continued. "I talked to Toussaint, and I believe him when he tells me that he knew nothing about Shyla's visit to Los Angeles. I've never seen him so furious as when he found out she was there. Alexis, he had her fired. She's no longer a part of the Livingston Corporation."

For the second time in as many minutes, Alexis was stunned. "Mrs. Livingston, Diane, I don't know what to say."

"You don't have to say anything, Alexis. Just think about what I've said. That's all I'm asking. Well, not quite. Like I said, what happens between you and Toussaint is none of my business. But Toussaint is a good man. If you'd talk to him, for even five minutes, you might decide to try and work out whatever y'all had. Even if you don't, at least you'll have made your decision based on all the facts."

Alexis thanked Diane for calling and after saying good-bye, closed her eyes and put her head in her hands.

What do I do? She cared deeply for Toussaint, wanted to give him a chance. But she was afraid. Loving somebody cost too much, could hurt too deeply. She'd done that once, with her dad. And yes, it was unrealistic, even stupid perhaps. But she wanted a love guaranteed to not hurt.

Like Jon. Alexis knew that Jon Abernathy had been disappointed to learn that they'd only do the one date and that she'd begun dating Toussaint. No, she didn't see fireworks or hear trumpets when she was with him; her heart didn't soar or her nana tingle when he came near. He'd probably be described as more distinguished than handsome. But he was a gentleman— nice, respectful. Most of all, someone like Jon Abernathy was safe and as close to a guaranteed drama-free relationship as Alexis would get.

Alexis packed her bags, feeling better with each passing thought. Diane was right. Toussaint at least deserved a conversation, a chance to be heard. Alexis decided that she would listen. And then she'd invite Jon Abernathy out for dinner and get on with her life.

56

"Q, somebody's here asking for the owner."

Q, who'd been bench-pressing an impressive two hundred pounds, dropped the weights. They fell with a clang. "Who?" He took the towel from around his neck and wiped sweat from his face.

"Health department."

"Health department? What do they want?" Q swung his legs to one side of the bench and stood.

His assistant manager shrugged. "Something about an inspection or something."

Q strolled over to the men and woman standing in the middle of his gym. He was not impressed as he took in the middle-aged, balding man in a bad-fitting suit, the woman with mousy brown hair and pale skin, and the man dressed in drab khakis and a Cardinals baseball cap.

"Quintin Bright," he said, offering a hand to first the man and then the woman. He nodded at the third person, who looked like a maintenance man. "Y'all here for a membership?" That they all needed the benefits of his gym was obvious.

The balding man stepped forward, looking around nervously. "Uh, we're here to inspect your establishment, for mold and lead."

"I've already been inspected," Q replied easily. "Had to, in order to get the business license."

"Yes, well, we've been sent to do a special inspection. It shouldn't take long."

Q's eyes narrowed. "Sent by who?"

"Higher-ups in the department. Don't mind us. We'll just have a look around, take some samples, shouldn't be more than fifteen minutes, half an hour tops." The balding man nodded to the maintenance worker, who began walking toward the office area.

"Whoa, whoa, wait a minute. That's off-limits to the public, son. Y'all can't just walk up in here talking about checking me out. How do I even know you're who you say you are?"

"We're sorry," Miss Mousy said, her voice appropriately high-pitched to go with her face's pinched features. She reached into her briefcase, showed Q her government employee badge, and handed him a notice for the inspection.

Q looked at each of their badges, read the notice, and then called over his assistant. "Stay with them while they look around," he said with feigned casualness. "I don't mind them looking. I have nothing to hide."

Q's nonchalant attitude lasted exactly forty-eight hours—until he got the notice that the city was closing him down.

57

Malcolm and Victoria's home buzzed with activity and tension. After four stressful days in the hospital, Victoria and Victory were home. Mother and child had survived childbirth. Whether they would survive this postdelivery gathering of relatives was another matter.

So far, after the initial strained round of greetings, the camps had kept their distance. Malcolm, Adam, and Ace were holed up in the library, smoking cigars and drinking brandy. Candace and Diane were in the family room, eating cake that neither of them wanted and bonding with Malcolm's two older children. The twins were with Victoria, Valarie, and the baby, in the formal living room. If words were bullets, this showdown would have been a draw.

"I can't believe she's acting so snooty," Diane muttered after Justin and his sister had left the table. "Acting like her shit don't stink."

"And what was with that 'baby-making machine' comment?" Candace asked. "To hear her tell it, Victoria's pregnancy was all Malcolm's fault. Hell, it takes two to make a baby, which, since she's had one, she should know."

"I don't know, sis. Since she thinks she walks on water, she might also believe that Vickie came here by way of immaculate conception."

"Maybe I'm being too hard on her. She's still upset at Malcolm for missing the childbirth, and I can understand that." Candace pushed the saucer of half-eaten cake away from her and reached for the glass of sparkling water. "At least the baby's healthy."

"And already looks like Malcolm spit her out. Did he ever tell you where he was that night, and why we couldn't get a hold of him?"

"No, but I have an idea." Candace sighed, thinking about the son she had thought the least likely to stray yet was MIA when his daughter was being born. She knew she was the last person to talk to someone else about cheating, but Malcolm was her son, his marriage was in trouble, and Candace would bet her house that Joyce was ready and waiting in the wings. Sooner or later, they'd have to have a conversation.

"I sure hope you're not thinking what I'm thinking."

"Let's just say that he's more like his mother than she realized."

"Dear, don't you think you should lie down?" Mrs. Saunders cast a cautious eye on her daughter as she sipped her tea in ladylike fashion, pinkie high in the air.

"I'm okay," Victoria replied. "I spent so much time on bed rest, it feels good to enjoy my living room."

"Still, you don't want to tire yourself out. Having a baby is no small feat."

"I know, Mom. I've had five, remember?"

"How can I forget?" Valarie's expression resembled someone who smelled rotting cabbage. "Married to a cheating scoundrel. A mongrel. If divorce weren't so public, and humiliating..."

"Mom, let's not go there. I've talked to Malcolm, and he swears he hasn't been unfaithful."

"And you believe him? Victoria, I was not aware that I had raised a fool."

"There's a lot of things you're not aware of, Mom." *Like how I alienated my husband by revolving my life around my children and the church.* True, he hadn't been there for Victory's birth, but she hadn't been a real wife, a wholly participating partner, for years.

"On second thought, I think I will go lie down for a while. The baby's asleep, and now I find myself more tired than I thought. It'll only be a catnap. You're welcome to stay."

"And cavort with the enemy? I don't think so."

"Mom, it wouldn't hurt for you to try and be friendly to Candace and her sister. Whether you like it or not, they're family. After more than a decade of me being married, you should know that that isn't going to change."

"One can always hope," Valarie mumbled as she straightened out a nonexistent wrinkle. "Oh, by the way, Victoria, the nurse will be arriving this afternoon."

"Mom, I thought I told you that wasn't necessary. Between the housekeeper and the nannies, I'll manage just fine."

"That may be true, dear, but I'll feel better with Doris here. You've had surgery. I don't want to take any chances." Valarie had known Doris for years. She was an excellent nurse. She was an excellent snoop as well and had been enlisted to find out exactly what was going on in her daughter's house.

Victoria hugged her mother, too tired to argue. She was tired about a lot of things in her life, especially her mother's overbearing attitude. But Victoria silently vowed that as soon as she was back on her feet, a change was going to come.

For now, the drama between the women upstairs had ended. But downstairs, in Malcolm's beloved man cave, it had just begun.

"You know she tried to fuck me, don't you?" Adam rarely used this type of language, unless he was very angry. With Malcolm having just come clean with where he was the night his daughter was born, now was one of those times.

"Joyce told me that harmless flirting is all that happened between you."

"And you believed her? Joyce is determined to get to the top, by any means necessary. She evidently decided to climb the Livingston ladder, and when she couldn't secure her footing on the father's rung, she moved to the son."

"Why can't you just believe she loves me, Dad?"

"I don't give a damn what she's telling you, boy. You're getting ready to throw away over fifty years of history and three generations of legacy for some strange poontang. I'm telling you, son, it ain't worth it." Adam came precariously close to saying "Ask your mama" but stopped himself just in time.

Malcolm rolled a cigar between the balls of his fingers before methodically snipping off the end and lighting it. "So I should just spend the next thirty, forty years of my life being unhappy?"

"You should spend the rest of your life being faithful to your wife. How you feel while you're doing that is up to you."

58

Alexis nervously twirled a loc as she sat perched at the bar, sipping a strawberry daiquiri and watching the cook entertain the crowd. When Jon had suggested they meet at Taste of Soul, Alexis had initially refused. She didn't want to take any chances on seeing Toussaint—or, if she was being honest with herself, having him find out she'd dined with Jon. But then she changed her mind. What did she care if Toussaint found out about it? It might even be advantageous, she'd reasoned. He'd know that she had moved on.

Now that she was here, however, she was having second thoughts. The truth was, she missed Toussaint, terribly. And what Diane told her was weighing heavily on her mind. She'd talk to Toussaint one day, when she was stronger. But not now. *Enough already! Quit thinking about him!* Determined to refocus, Alexis looked around the room. She liked how Taste of Soul had been remodeled, how a wall had been torn down to allow those at the bar waiting to be seated to see the chef and line cook in action at the meat station. The cook, a wiry young man with a flashy white smile, effortlessly flipped two large cleavers, before bringing them down on the marble counter and slicing through a slab of ribs with synchronized precision. The audience clapped, nodded, and murmured appreciatively as he plated the succulent meat, sprinkled on wisps of fennel tops, and, with a flourish, presented the dish to the waiting customer. *He's good!* Alexis's spirits felt lighter as she spun back around to the bar counter and reached for her drink. And then she quickly spun back around. *That's Bobby! Wow.* With the chef hat, new pearly whites, and entertaining flair, she hadn't recognized him.

"I've missed that smile." Jon walked up to Alexis and placed a kiss on her temple.

"Jon! Hi." Alexis leaned into Jon's welcoming embrace and kissed him on the cheek. "Good to see you."

"Is it?" Jon, debonair as always, wore a dark navy suit, white shirt, and striped tie, looking ready to go to the office or speak at a function even though it was a Saturday afternoon.

"What are you drinking?" he asked Alexis.

"A daiquiri, want one?"

"Naw, that's a girl's drink." Jon placed his order, and after receiving it, turned and watched the show happening over at the meat station.

"Wow, wouldn't want to meet up with Bobby in a dark alley," Jon said, sipping his Seagram's 7. "He's dangerous with those knives."

"Yes, but he's a sweetheart, quite skilled. And look at those muscles," Alexis continued as Bobby hoisted a hefty piece of beef onto a hook before slicing paper-thin strips that fell into a decorative mound on a plate below. "Surprising in one so . . . compact."

"You don't have to be six feet to be strong," Jon said, a pointed reference to the reason his and Alexis's communication had been interrupted.

"You are absolutely right about that, Jon Abernathy," Alexis replied, adding a touch of seductiveness to her voice. "Good things come in small packages, right?"

Jon sipped his drink and eyed Alexis thoughtfully. "So,

Alexis St. Clair, to what do I owe the pleasure of your company? Like I said when you called, I was surprised to hear from you. Thought that since the project was finished, and you were all hot and heavy with Toussaint Livingston, our friendship was over."

"I don't ever think we can have too many friends. Do you?"

"Depends..."

"Give any more thought to the outdoor living space?"

"Sounds good, but I'm not interested. I've heard that you don't date your clients."

"That's true, Jon. But there's an exception for every rule."

There was a bit of an awkward silence, interrupted by the hostess who came over and told Alexis that their table was ready. Jon caught Bobby's eye, lifted his glass while giving an appreciative nod, and followed the hostess to their table.

After they'd placed their orders, Alexis began the spiel she'd planned since getting on the plane in St. Louis the Tuesday before. "Jon, there is a reason I invited you here."

"I'm listening."

"I owe you an apology."

"For what?"

"The way I ended things with us."

"There was no 'us,' Alexis. We went out on a couple dates, that's all—actually only one that wasn't work related. You finished the project and moved on. Yes, I was hoping something more might develop but...looks like that wasn't in the cards."

Alexis took a drink of water and waited until the salads had been set on the table. She picked up a fork and picked through the lettuce. "That's just it," she continued softly. "I've been working with that deck of cards and...was wondering if there was any way they could be reshuffled."

"What do you mean?"

"Toussaint and I aren't dating anymore."

Jon's fork stopped halfway to his mouth. "Oh, I see." He placed the bite in his mouth and chewed thoughtfully. "What happened?"

"Nothing I want to relive, or discuss. Let's just say that the Livingston lifestyle is too complicated. I don't like drama, Jon. I give my heart fully when I'm interested in someone and want to know they do the same. I went back home for a little while, thought a lot about my priorities and what I want out of life. I have a great career, love my work, but I've finally admitted to myself that work is not enough. I want someone to share the good times with as well. And that's when I started thinking about the man that you are—kind, considerate, smart, successful . . ."

"Safe? I don't strike you as the type of man who has a gaggle of women chasing him? Like your boy Toussaint?"

"I, well, uh, no, Jon, it's not like that. You're an influential political figure, a force to be reckoned with, here in Atlanta and elsewhere. I'm sure you have no lack of suitors. But you strike me as a man with integrity, a man who is loyal. I know it was short, but I enjoyed the time I spent with you . . . and, well, I'm putting my cards on the table. I'd like to start seeing you again."

"Wow, what can I say? You're full of surprises, Alexis St. Clair."

The waiter delivered their rib platters, and while they ate, the conversation flowed to other topics—Alexis's visit to St. Louis and Jon's recent trip to D.C. Jon laughed at Alexis's recounting of how she "designed on a dime" and transformed her mother's modest apartment with bargain finds. Alexis appreciated Jon's sharing his lobbying in Washington, working to get some of the stimulus money distributed in Atlanta's inner-city schools. They both praised the succulent ribs they ate, which were perfectly complemented with Macaroni and Chubby Checker Cheese and Sam Cooked Green Beans. Conversation continued to flow smoothly as Alexis marveled at the flakiness of her peach cobbler's crust while Jon groaned his pleasure at the sweet potato pie.

An hour and a half later, two very full customers walked to the parking lot. Jon walked Alexis to her Infiniti, which was parked only three spaces down from his BMW.

"So," Alexis said after giving Jon a long hug. "You never did answer my question. Can I shuffle my deck of cards so that we can start seeing each other again?"

"Well, Alexis," Jon began slowly, and for the first time Alexis felt a slight trepidation. "I'm flattered that you've asked me. But the truth is, right now somebody else is playing that hand."

Alexis was stunned. Fifteen minutes later, as she pulled into her loft's parking area, she still reeled. That Jon would turn down her request to date had never entered her mind. True, she didn't know him all that well, but she'd gotten the impression that political functions notwithstanding, his was a fairly mundane lifestyle. That, like her, he was mostly all work and no play. Yes, part of the reason she'd thought to date him right away was to get Toussaint out of her mind, but the more she'd thought about it, the more she'd believed someone like Jon Abernathy was the perfect person for her, the type of man with whom she could feel safe and protected—the way she had felt when her father was alive.

She got out of the car, walked to the elevator, punched the button. *Now what am I going to do?*

59

The elevator came and Alexis stepped inside, feeling more lost than she had when she'd stepped into the Ritz-Carlton master suite and saw Shyla Martin lounging in the bed where Alexis and Toussaint had made passionate love merely hours before. Head down, she was subdued as she walked to her door. Spending the night alone, in her empty house, was not something she looked forward to. She hesitated at her front door, key in hand. *Maybe I should go to a movie,* she thought. *That's what I'll do. I'm not ready to go inside yet.* Alexis turned, and jumped.

"Hey, baby." Toussaint stepped out from the column at the end of the hall. "Sorry, I didn't mean to scare you."

"Toussaint!" Alexis clutched her throat, having almost come out of her skin at the sound of his voice. Anger quickly replaced fear and covered the instant heat Alexis had felt at the sight of him. "What do you think you're doing? You scared me half to death."

Toussaint stopped a few feet from her. He wanted to crush her in his arms, wanted to kiss that succulent mouth that he'd dreamed of all week. But he held himself in check. *My baby. How I've missed you.*

"You haven't returned my calls."

"Yeah, well, that ought to tell you something." Having recovered, Alexis brushed past him and walked briskly to the elevator. Toussaint effortlessly fell into step beside her, her hurried steps no match for his long strides.

"I've missed you, Alexis. There's so much I want to say."

"I think Shyla in our suite said it all, don't you think?"

"What it said was that I hadn't effectively ended that relationship. That she hadn't gotten the message, hadn't understood it when I told her that she and I were finished."

"Well, was she still half naked when you went back to the suite and had the conversation?" Alexis hissed as the elevator doors opened and she hurried inside. She was more than thankful that her ire kept her mouth from watering at the sight of Toussaint's lips or from licking the cleft in his chin. When she got to her car, she pressed the unlock button on her key fob, knowing that if she could just get inside her car and close the door, she'd prevent herself from doing something stupid, like throwing herself into his arms.

"Wait," Toussaint demanded, placing his hand on the glass and preventing Alexis from closing the door. "I want to talk to you, Alexis. Don't you think I at least deserve to tell my side of the story, to tell you what happened in LA and, more importantly, what happened when I got back to Atlanta?"

Alexis slumped back in the seat. "I know you fired Shyla," she said, sighing.

"Then you know that she is out of my life, in every way." Toussaint's heart leaped, and he felt a glimmer of hope that he'd get things back on track with the woman he loved.

"I'm late," Alexis said, starting the car. Her emotions were roiling. She needed time and space away from Toussaint. Where she could think. And breathe.

"So just like that, you're going to drive away. Even though I've tried nonstop for seven straight days to reach you and am wearing my heart on my sleeve?"

Alexis put the car into gear. She took a deep breath and

looked up into Toussaint's chocolate, bedroom eyes. For the first time, she noticed a wisp of a mustache. *Great, so he can look even more fine.* "Can I close my door, please?"

Toussaint looked at her for another moment, then stepped back and allowed the door to close.

Alexis backed out of her space. She looked in her rearview mirror and saw Toussaint's folded arms and wide-legged stance as he watched her drive away. She almost made it to the parking structure exit before she stopped, put the car in reverse, and backed up to where her lover still stood. She rolled down her window with quiet resignation. "You want to go see a movie?"

They didn't get to the movies. Instead, Toussaint directed them to a quiet bar in the area. There he poured his heart out, telling her how he'd turned the hotel upside down until he'd gotten to the bottom of how Shyla ended up in his room. How the concierge worker had been fired and how management heads had rolled. He told her how he'd talked with Ace that very evening, and by the time he'd returned to Atlanta, he had Shyla's severance package ready. How he'd presented it to her the following Monday in a take-it-or-leave it, one-sided conversation, where there was no room for discussion or compromise.

"Your aunt was right. I should have talked to you immediately, listened to your side of the story. But I was so hurt."

"Of course you were. I can't imagine how you felt, walking in and finding Shyla in the same bed we'd shared just hours before. Given my history, your assumption was wrong, but it was justified."

"I'm sorry, Toussaint."

Finally, Toussaint felt it okay to leave his side of the booth and sit next to Alexis.

"I've missed you, baby," he said, gently stroking her cheek.

"I've missed you too."

He lightly rubbed a finger over her mouth. "I've missed these."

Alexis eyed Toussaint's lips and licked hers. "I've missed yours too."

Toussaint's voice dropped to a husky whisper. "May I have a kiss?"

Alexis nodded, already melting by the look of love and longing in his eyes. He aggressively tongued his way into her mouth, crushed his lips on hers, and wrapped her in his arms. Alexis felt a jolt of electricity as she wrapped her arms around his broad shoulders and turned to deepen the kiss. Warning bells of self-preservation went off in her mind, about the danger of dating a Livingston, the potential hurt, deception, deceit that could lurk behind every business trip, every closed door, every female customer at a Taste of Soul restaurant. Alexis heard the bells, but soon their sound was drowned out by the desire in her heart and by the love that encouraged her to throw caution to the wind.

When Toussaint requested the check and they walked back to Alexis's car, she knew something for sure: She might again hear the bells of caution tomorrow, but she was going to dance to the music of ecstasy tonight.

60

"She looks just like you." Joyce stood behind Malcolm, who was seated in his office. They were waiting on Joyce's friend Bernice, who worked with QVC.

"Yeah, I guess she does," Malcolm replied. He fingered the picture of his fifth child, taken one month ago, when Victory was just one week old. He ran his finger over the cherubic face, his daughter's eyes tightly closed and lips puckered. Lips that looked like his. Malcolm's mind went back to the night in his man cave, when his father had demanded he do the right thing and support his wife. He'd gone to the master's suite shortly after they left and found Victoria lying in bed, chatting with her mother.

"I need to speak to my wife, Valarie, alone."

Valarie paused, and then continued talking to Victoria as if Malcolm hadn't spoken.

"Now, please."

Slowly, Valarie turned to face him, a look of pure disgust on her face. "Oh, so when you finally decide to pay Victoria some attention, I'm supposed to scurry off somewhere, fade into the scenery? Whatever you have to say to my daughter, you can say with me present. I'm not going anywhere."

"Mom, please..."

"Please what? This is the man who left you alone, Victoria, who wasn't present when you labored for three hours before giving birth!"

"Mom, enough!" Victoria winced from the pain that yelling had caused her. Malcolm rushed to her side. "Please leave, Mom. I want to talk to Malcolm—alone."

"And just so you know, I relieved your nurse, Doris," Malcolm said. Valarie turned to argue but he put up his hand. "Don't worry, a new nurse will be here in the morning, one that her doctor recommended. I appreciate all you've done, Valarie, but this is still my house and Victoria is still my wife. Thank you, and good night."

"Well...I..." A stuttering Valarie rushed out of the room and down the stairs. The slamming of the door marked her departure.

Malcolm gingerly sat on the bed and took Victoria's hand. It was the first intentional touch in months. "I know I said it before, but I'm so sorry I wasn't there for you and Victory. I should have been, and I feel awful about it."

Tears welled up in Victoria's eyes. She placed her hand on top of his. "And I forgive you, Malcolm. True, you weren't at the hospital when Victory was born, but I haven't been here for you either. Your mother warned me years ago about giving all of my love to the children and leaving none for you. But I didn't listen. I made excuses. And the next thing I knew, we were like strangers in our own house."

"It wasn't just you, Victoria. You focused on the kids and I focused on work."

"We've made a mess of our marriage, Malcolm. But I'll do everything in my power to make things right again. I'll lose the weight, quit that church, even go back to working for the company if that's what you want."

Malcolm looked at Victoria, and for the first time in

months, maybe years, saw the woman he married—the caring, adoring woman he once loved.

"I know it's a lot to ask, but do you think we can get it back, the magic that was there when we first got married?"

Malcolm's eyes were misty and his voice hoarse as he answered, "We can try."

Malcolm stood abruptly, shaking off the hand lightly kneading his shoulder. Joyce felt and saw the change in attitude immediately. "Do we have the numbers from consumer testing?" he asked. He walked over to the desk in his office, papers strewn everywhere even though it was the weekend.

"Yes, they're right here, along with the testimonials. I've also compiled a promotion with the video footage that was shot of customers who tested the smoker. Would you like to see it?"

Instead of answering, Malcolm crossed to his office's sitting area. A flat-screen television was mounted on the wall, viewable from both the chairs and love seat. Joyce scurried to her briefcase, retrieved the DVD, and joined him there. He put the disc in the player, turned it on, and sat on the love seat. Joyce took a tentative seat beside him, close but not touching. Her eyes watched the people on the screen, heard their words of praise about the device that produced a perfectly cooked piece of meat every time, but her mind whirled. Malcolm had been different since shortly after Victory's birth. She'd asked him what was wrong, had tried to gauge where he was in his marriage and whether there was a chance for them to have anything more than they already did, but he'd shut down emotionally for the first time since they shared that dinner at FGO.

"She's excellent," Joyce commented as she and Malcolm watched a charming redhead clasp her hands in glee after the chicken she'd pulled from the soul smoker fell off the bone.

"They might be able to use her testimonial in promotions leading up to your appearance on the show."

"I appreciate everything you're doing," Malcolm said, eyeing Joyce intently. "I'm going to make sure you're compensated for all the help you've given me."

"I'm not helping you just for financial gain," Joyce said, hurt evident in her voice. "I love you, Malcolm. I—"

Joyce was interrupted by a knock on the door. Upon Malcolm's directive, the security guard entered, escorting Joyce's associate, Bernice, the QVC producer.

"It is a pleasure to meet you," she said after Joyce made the introductions. "I've heard a lot about this Soul Smoker!"

"Well, I hope you're hungry," Malcolm replied with a grin. "Because I'm getting ready to let you taste what all the hype is about!"

It was well after ten p.m. when Malcolm entered the kitchen from the garage. He was exhausted but elated at how the meeting with the QVC producer had gone. She had raved about the ribs she ate and was equally impressed with the chicken and links. Joyce had given her a copy of the DVD, which the producer planned to take back to the network in order to develop the strategy for introducing Malcolm Livingston's Soul Smoker to America.

Bypassing the den and his usual two-finger cognac drink, Malcolm climbed the stairs and headed to the nursery. Opening the door slowly, softly, he tiptoed inside. The plastic sunshine on the nightlight bathed the room in a soft, golden glow. He walked over to the crib where Victory lay on her back, sleeping soundly. A smile played across her lips, and she squirmed slightly at Malcolm's touch. Malcolm reached out a thick forefinger and smoothed down a wisp of his daughter's straight, black hair. With that same finger, he touched her tiny hand. Victory opened her small palm, clasped her father's finger, and continued sleeping. Malcolm's heart clenched as it opened up. This was his daughter, his fifth, beautiful, wonderful child.

"Hi, Victory. It's Daddy," Malcolm whispered. He leaned down and breathed in her fresh, baby scent. *She's perfect,* he thought as he folded back the blanket and rubbed a light hand over her long limbs and round, milk-full belly. "I think you're going to be tall, like your uncle," Malcolm said softly to the still-sleeping child. He leaned down and kissed her. "Daddy loves you," he said, and quietly left the room.

Malcolm walked to the guest bedroom he still occupied. He opened the door and was surprised to see Victoria there, sitting on his bed. She wore a sheer white, floor-length negligee. He stood just inside the door, standing, waiting.

"I had my six-week checkup yesterday," Victoria said. Her voice was soft, tentative. "The doctor said I was healed enough for intercourse. I want to have sex with you, Malcolm, tonight."

Malcolm stepped inside and closed the door. He pulled off his jacket as he walked to his wife. He stopped in front of her, and without a word began to strip. When he was naked, he reached for her hand. "Are you sure?"

Victoria stood. "I've never been more sure of anything in my life."

They reached the master suite and lay on the bed. Slowly, but surely, Malcolm became reacquainted with his wife's body. He ran his finger over her scar and then kissed it. Victoria explored his body and soon rubbed him into hardness. She turned on her side and directed him to enter from behind. *You should spend the rest of your life being faithful to your wife. How you feel while you're doing that is up to you.* Malcolm couldn't predict the future. There was a lot of hard work ahead to get back to the love he and Victoria once shared. But as he parted her folds and began the physical journey of their reconciliation, for the first time in a long time, Malcolm was optimistic.

61

"You're back in the bedroom, Candace. Be thankful for that."

"Yes, Diane, but we still haven't made love. He says that whenever he gets ready to, he thinks about me being with Q. It's messing with his mind, and I don't know what to do about it."

Adam had invited Candace back into the master suite right after hearing that Q's gym had been closed down. That night, he'd hugged her close to him, and she'd fallen asleep in his arms. But when she'd reached for his penis and began to stroke it, he'd turned away from her—something he hadn't done in thirty-plus years of marriage. They'd talked the next day, and he'd bared his soul, told her how her cheating had affected his manhood, made him doubt his ability to satisfy her, made him feel that he'd be compared to a tall, buff brothah twenty years his junior. Candace still cringed as she remembered these revelations and how they were met with her silence. Quintin Bright was like no other man she'd ever known, a stallion who'd sexed her to within an inch of her life. He was nine inches of hard, pounding flesh, and on his weakest days had far surpassed Adam on his best. So how, she'd wondered, was she supposed to answer a statement like that?

"Look, girl. That's Adam now. Thanks for listening to me ramble."

"Call anytime."

Adam stopped just inside the front door. He raised his nose, much like a greyhound tracking prey. Was that dinner he smelled cooking... again? "Candace?"

"In here, baby."

Adam smiled and walked toward the kitchen. "I know that isn't Candy's candied yams I smell." He came around the corner, put down his briefcase, and took Candace in his arms.

"It is indeed," she replied after a kiss. "Dinner will be ready in about ten minutes."

"The chef does all right, but I could get used to this, you know. Having you cook dinner every night, like you used to when the boys were young."

"You were so tired in those early years, putting in sixteen-hour days at the restaurant. And then coming home and bottling sauce, ready to peddle on the weekends."

"We thought we'd died and gone to heaven when that first contract for the sauce came through."

"Yes, and we got real distribution, just in the tristate area at first, remember?"

"Woman, how can I forget? Me and Dad went to each of those stores personally, met the managers and the store's staff. Shared some sauce-slathered ribs and turned them all into barbeque salesmen!"

"We've come such a long way, baby. Thinking back to those early days almost feels like a dream."

Adam put his arms around Candace again, his hand cupping her backside. "This feels like a dream."

"Hmmm. So does this," Candace said, reaching between them and stroking Adam's dick. They kissed, a melding of the lips that went from soft and tentative to hot and wet. Candace reached for Adam's buckle, unzipping his pants at the same time. Soon, she palmed his manhood, which was hard and throbbing. She went to her knees, right there beside the island in the center of her kitchen, and put the length of him into her mouth.

"Ahhh." Adam rocked back on the island, placing one hand on the cool marble and another on the back of Candace's head.

"Mmm," Candace moaned, slathering her man's dick with her saliva. She opened her mouth wider, sucking him in deep. It had been too long since she'd tasted him, too long since they'd shared intimacy. She licked and sucked and bobbed her head, her time with Q becoming more and more of a distant memory with each passing second. Candace's knees scraped against the slate-tiled floor, but she ignored it. Her focus was only on the moans, groans, and thrusts that signaled Adam's nearing release. He grabbed the back of her head as it happened, as he spent himself inside her, and she swallowed every drop.

"Baby, oh...baby." Adam slumped against the island, unable to pull up the slacks that were now down around his legs. "That was...amazing." She'd never given head like that before. The thought of how she'd honed these new skills, riding a strange cock when she should have been riding a treadmill, killed the mood. "Move, baby. I've got to use the bathroom." He pulled up his pants and began walking away. The phone he'd placed on the island began to ring.

"Candace, grab that. It's probably Ace. Tell him I'll call him back in a couple."

Candace hurriedly retrieved Adam's phone from his briefcase. She was still reeling from what happened, still rubbing her knees to stop the burning and get the circulation back in her legs. But she'd been with her man again. Adam and Candace were back!

"Hello?" she almost sang, with a smile so wide it could practically be seen through the phone.

Almost, but not quite, as was evident seconds later. "Where's your punk-ass husband?"

Candace almost dropped the phone. "Q?"

"Damn right."

"Q, have you lost your mind? What we had is over, so why are you calling my husband?"

"Don't act like you don't know, and don't try and play the part of protective wifey. Your ass wasn't so concerned about him when I was knee-deep in that pussy. But you should be concerned about him now."

Candace paused. She'd never heard Q talk like this: somber, threatening. *But why?* Several doses of penicillin was proof that she hadn't been the only one Q was screwing. So why was he so angry that they were through? "Q, look, I don't know what your problem is. If anybody is angry here, it ought to be me. You're the one who gave me the clap, remember?"

"Yeah, and that bitch you're married to is the reason my business is shut down. But that's all right. I want you to deliver a message to his ass. He's fucked with the wrong player, believe that."

"Q, what in the . . . Q? Q!"

Candace was still holding the phone when Adam walked back into the kitchen. "Who was that?" he asked, immediately noting the concern on Candace's face.

"It was Quintin, Adam. Something about his business being shut down and that it's your fault?" As Candace watched the emotions play across Adam's face, a sense of foreboding began to beat in her chest. "Adam. Talk to me. What is going on?"

62

Toussaint was walking on clouds, had been ever since Alexis waltzed back into his life. What started out as a night of passion after surprising her at her loft had turned into them practically living together. Whether at her loft or his penthouse, they'd spent almost every night together. In between thoughtful, tender lovemaking or sometimes rough-and-tumble sex, Toussaint and Alexis had talked, sometimes for hours. Her diverse interests equaled his, and she could talk about fashion one minute and then hold her own in a conversation on basketball the next. Toussaint didn't think he could be satisfied with just one woman. It's why he'd never married. But Alexis appeased every one of his hungers. Which is why he'd told every woman who called him that it was over, and when they kept on calling, he had his number changed.

Toussaint reached the front door of Ace and Diane's house. He was overdue for a visit and knew his aunt would make sure he knew this.

"About time you came to visit," Diane said, giving Toussaint a hug once he'd stepped inside. "I was about ready to hire a detective to track you down."

"I've been busy, Aunt Di. You know, work and all . . ."

"Work my foot. Come on back to my office. I'm working on your Food Network stuff."

In the Livingston Corporation's early days, Diane had handled marketing and PR. When Shyla was fired, Diane volunteered her services during the transition and was now determined to see her nephew become the next Food Network star. They reached the comfortably lived-in office and sat down. Diane eyed Toussaint closely. "Looks like somebody's happy."

"Somebody's ecstatic, Aunt Diane. I don't think I've ever felt this good."

"Something tells me this has nothing to do with the cooking show."

"I could never keep anything from you. It's Alexis. We're back together, and closer than ever. Which reminds me. I need to thank you."

"Me?"

"Don't even try it. Alexis told me that you called her right after the incident. When you told her that I'd fired Shyla and encouraged her to give a brothah a chance."

"I'm happy for you, baby," Diane said, putting her hand in the air. She and Toussaint high-fived. "I guess I don't have to tell you how to keep her happy."

"When I make my vows, it will be for keeps, like all of the other Livingston men." During a recent conversation with Malcolm, Toussaint had found out just how hard it was to keep those vows. But he was determined. "I've played the field and sowed my oats. When I marry Alexis—"

"You've proposed?"

"Not yet. But let's just say I've already purchased Alexis's Christmas gift. And once she says yes, I'm going to spend the rest of my life showing her why she married me."

"Baby, the whole country is getting ready to see why any woman would be crazy not to say yes to you."

"I don't know about that, Aunt Diane."

"I do." There was an unmistakable twinkle in Diane's eye.

"Wait a minute. Did you hear from..."

Diane nodded slowly.

Toussaint's eyes widened slightly as realization dawned. "You heard from the Food Network?"

Diane continued nodding. "They played the tape of you and Oliver to several test markets. The camera loves you, darling, and Oliver's warmth oozes from the screen. Those are the words from the producer's mouth. They want to set you up on a test basis, six shows. But I know this is just the beginning—"

"Wait a minute. They've already green-lighted this? We're getting ready to go national?"

"In three months, more than twenty-million households are going to know about Taste of Soul, and other soul and ethnic restaurants across the country."

"But they didn't even see me cook. It was mostly Oliver, with me...you know..."

"Flirting and being your loveable self. And that's what sold them. Your personality, Toussaint. We've got to fly to New York next week, where we'll be discussing specifics about your show. And you watch. It's just a matter of time before that West Coast location opens. Ace has been telling me about your plan, and I love it."

Toussaint looked at his watch. He stood and walked over to the desk. "Did I ever tell you that you're my favorite aunt?" he asked, bending over to hug her.

Diane chuckled. "Yes, but you can tell me again."

63

Diane walked with Toussaint to the door, waving a final time before he jumped into his car and sped off. Then she turned and raced to her phone. "It looks like we're gaining a new family member," Diane said as soon as Candace answered the phone.

"Oh my God, Bianca's pregnant?" Candace asked, referring to Diane's daughter, the only girl in the Livingstons' fifth generation. For the past year she'd lived in Paris, where she was currently finishing up culinary school.

"Heaven forbid," Diane hastily replied. "I think it'll be a while before I see any grandchildren. You, on the other hand..."

Candace's heart leaped to her throat. "Victoria?"

"Ha! No, girl, I think she's done. I'm talking about Toussaint."

"Oh, Lord. Alexis is pregnant?"

"Calm down, Candace. Nobody is with child. But you're getting ready to have another daughter-in-law. Toussaint is giving her a ring for Christmas."

"Giving her a ring? He's barely introduced her to the family! I don't know how I feel about this. What's her last name again? I need to do a background check."

"Careful, sistah. You're starting to sound like Valarie."

"Or Marietta. Remember she wasn't too pleased with my baby news."

"But she came to love you, as do we all."

"Okay, I'll lighten up, give the girl a chance. But I'm still going to check the background. Can't have just anybody in Livingston territory."

"Speaking of territory, has Adam reclaimed his?"

"Didn't I tell you? We're back, and better than ever."

"I still don't understand it, Can. What happened? A midlife crisis?"

"Girl, I don't know what to call it, except stupid. No, that's not true. I know what happened."

Diane waited, silent.

"Okay, here's the deal. This fifty-three-year-old grand-mother got dick-whipped."

"Girl, stop."

"I swear to God, Diane, whipped!"

"Ooh, Lord, was he that good?"

"Don't even get me started—"

"No, don't, 'cause I don't want to know."

"Had me ready to give up my house, my man, my kids, my everything! Nine thick, solid inches. I still miss it."

"Notice that you said *it,* not *him.* You can order *it* online, any shape, size, or color. So remember that the next time you get the itch to go creepin', no pun intended. You can still get your pleasure without putting your family through hell."

"You're right, Diane," Candace said, all humor gone from her voice. "There's no excuse for what I did."

"No," Diane said, her voice also softer. "But at least it's over."

Candace became quiet. "I sure hope so."

"Wait a minute, Candace. What does that mean?"

"Q called last night."

"What in the hell is he doing calling you?"

"It's even worse. He called Adam."

"Adam? Why? How'd he get his cell number?"

"I don't know, but he did. And I answered his phone. Q ranted about Adam having had his business shut down."

"Oh my gosh, is that true?"

"Adam wouldn't tell me, but something's going on. I've got a bad feeling."

They chatted for a little while longer, before Candace received another call. Diane sat in her office, her stomach churning. *Should I have told her?* No, she couldn't. She'd promised Ace she wouldn't tell anyone about the dream he'd had last night. The one in which his twin got shot. And died.

64

Zoe pulled into the convenience store near her house. She was feeling lucky, had dreamed all day about what it would mean to buy a lottery ticket and have her life change overnight. One thing she'd decided, even with a windfall, she'd still continue working at the Livingston Corporation. She loved her new position, loved working with Drake Benson. He'd been extremely helpful, ready to share information, staying late to help her get acclimated to the marketing department. They both were giddy that Shyla Martin was no longer with the company. The entire marketing area seemed lighter, more accessible without her around.

After making quick purchases of chips, soda, and her lottery ticket, Zoe hurried to her car. If she got all the green lights, she'd make it home in time to watch one of her favorite reality shows, *American Idol*. She agreed with Chardonnay that it hadn't been the same since the likes of Jennifer Hudson, Ruben Studdard, and Fantasia had graced the stage, but it still provided Zoe with an escape from what had turned into a routine life. *What happened?* Zoe pondered this as she covered the short distance to her car. What happened to the party girl who used to close down the club and then head over to the Waffle House for the All-Star Special? Who used to not miss a concert when it came to town? True, she'd somewhat lost her running buddy when Chardonnay started having babies, but Zoe was an attractive, single woman. *What in the hell is going on with me, and where is my life?*

"One thing for sure," Zoe said to herself as she got into her car. "I'm not going to date anybody I work with." Not that she'd taken Drake's invite seriously, the one where he'd asked her if she liked red-hot hockey and ice-cold beer. He had two tickets to the Thrashers game and had wanted her to go. She liked Drake and could tell he liked her. But when it came to men, she liked her meat dark.

Zoe jumped at the knock on her window, but her heart went back into her chest when she turned and saw Bobby standing by her car. "Hey, Bobby," she said as she rolled down the window. "What are you doing in my neighborhood?"

"It might be mine pretty soon. I just checked out an apartment complex down the street. How's the area? Do you like it over here?"

"It's pretty cool, quiet. Not too far from work. Speaking of which, how'd you manage to get a Saturday night off?"

"Oliver had to fly to New York, so I helped out in the test kitchen all day. So Chef got somebody else to work my shift, gave me the night off. I haven't had a weekend off in so long, don't even know what to do." He looked at Zoe. "What are you getting into?"

"Laundry."

"On a Saturday night?"

"Works for me. The laundry room is almost empty on Saturday nights, and I like waking up on Sunday mornings to a clean house."

"Nah, that shit ain't happening tonight. You're coming with me. We're going out."

"What?"

"Yep. One of the customers gave me tickets to a party. I wasn't going to go solo, but since I ran into you . . ."

"What kind of party?"

"One where you have to dress up. So give me your number and then go home and change. I'll be by to pick you up in an hour."

Two hours later, Bobby Wilson and Zoe Williams stepped out of his Hyundai and into a world that neither had inhabited. Cascade Heights was a posh neighborhood located about twenty minutes from downtown Atlanta and thirty minutes from where Zoe lived, but it was worlds away from what they were used to. The private party was being hosted at the Cascade Mansion and Gardens facility, an antebellum-style house with a huge nod to what Georgia must have looked like before the Civil War. After giving their name at the door and taking flutes of champagne from the passing waiter, Bobby and Zoe openly gawked and didn't care who knew that they were fish out of water. They oohed and aahed at the cascading fountains, sipped champagne in a garden pavilion, and talked about the bourgeoise black folk and a spattering of whites who mingled under a full moon that was outshone only by the myriad of diamonds dripping from the ears, necks, and fingers of the women in attendance.

"Let's go check out the food," Bobby said after he and Zoe had drank their second glass of champagne.

"That's cool. Just don't ask me to dance to that whack music."

"Girl, what are you talking about? That's the good stuff. That's straight-ahead jazz."

He and Zoe continued to joke about people's hairstyles, clothes, and siddity greetings as they made their way to the large buffet. Halfway to their destination, Bobby smiled and waved at a distinguished-looking brother in a sharp, black tux.

"Bobby! So glad you could make it," Jon Abernathy said, his hand outstretched as he reached Bobby and Zoe.

"Thanks for the invite, sir. This is a real treat. I'm not used to stuff like this."

"Well, you should get used to it, Bobby. The word is out about you. You're a top-rated cook, and I have a buddy looking to open a restaurant in the next year or so. I told him about you. In fact, I'd like you to meet him. But first, who is this lovely lady?"

Zoe blushed and preened as Bobby made the introductions. True to what she'd told Chardonnay, she'd been focused solely on her career and hadn't had a date in months. But standing here talking to Jon Abernathy, she found herself rethinking this position. Aside from casting a vote for Obama, Zoe hadn't participated in politics. What happened on Capitol Hill, or even city hall for that matter, seemed too far away from her world. Until now. Now, Zoe found herself becoming much more interested in politics . . . and politicians.

65

Joyce bustled around her office, excited about the day and her life. One, she'd just landed another great client and event: the Jack and Jill Christmas Party. The event planner they'd selected had backed out at the last moment due to a death in the family. A true example of how one's loss could be another's gain. With the festivities less than a month away, it put Joyce behind the eight ball. But she'd told the organizer that she could pull it off, and she would. Making this event a success would open the door to a whole slew of new clients with weddings, debutante balls, anniversary parties, elaborate birthday bashes—the possibilities were endless.

Such excitement, and this wasn't even the biggest event of the day. No, the biggest event of the day was that Malcolm's Soul Smoker would make its debut on QVC. This afternoon, she and Malcolm would be taking the corporate jet to Philadelphia and would then be chauffeured to West Chester, Pennsylvania, where the shows were taped. Diane's help had been invaluable and was the reason that they'd secured celebrity personalities and Atlanta residents Evander Holyfield and Tyler Perry. They'd eagerly lent their name to the product, especially when told that by doing so, a fifty-thousand-dollar donation would be made to the charity of their choice. She'd bought two bottles of Dom Pérignon—one for the inaugural celebration and a second for the private party she hoped to have with Malcolm afterward. They hadn't hung out socially since the night his daughter was born. She admired him for wanting to bond with his latest family addition, but she missed him. That last night at her house, they'd almost made love. Tonight she hoped to pick up where they'd left off.

A light tap at her office door pulled Joyce from her thoughts. "Hey, Sherri, if those are the tablecloth samples, just put them on the table. I'm trying to decide on what crystal to use. In fact, I could use your help. What do you—" Joyce turned around, and the sentence died on her lips. "Victoria."

"Your assistant must have taken a break. There was no one out front to announce me, so I hope you'll forgive the unexpected intrusion. As it is, I'll only be a moment. What I have to say won't take long."

Joyce crossed her arms and leaned back against the desk. Never in a million years would she have thought Victoria Livingston would be standing in her office. Joyce had to admit that her adversary had dressed for the occasion. Though a size eighteen, Victoria looked rather sleek in a kimono-style print top, black leggings, knee-high boots, and a silver fox fur. Her hair and makeup were flawless. All in all, Malcolm's soon-to-be ex-wife was more beautiful than Joyce remembered.

She has to know about me and Malcolm. Maybe he told her. Maybe he's let her know that their marriage is over and that his life is now with me. Just keep your cool, Joyce, and you'll get through this just fine. And then you'll have even more of a reason to celebrate tonight! "Yes, Victoria. How may I help you?"

"Actually, Joyce, I'm here to help you."

"Excuse me?"

"I'm here to help set some things straight, because you've obviously gotten them twisted. My name is Victoria Saunders Livingston," Victoria stated in a voice as calm as if she were discussing the weather. "I am the wife of Malcolm Livingston, and the mother of his five children. I've been married to my husband for eleven years and plan to stay married. To Malcolm, no one else. I am the woman who will manage his home and his personal affairs, the one who will be on his arm in public and in his bed in private. I am his *wife*. I will remain his *wife*. You are just a temporary diversion who's already gone beyond the fifteen minutes of Livingston fame most women like you are allowed."

The two women eyed each other for a moment. Then Joyce looked at her watch. "You're right," she replied in a voice as equally friendly as the one Victoria used. "That didn't take long, which, considering my schedule today, is a good thing. Perhaps some other time we can have a longer chat, over coffee and a Danish, let's say. But for now, I'll have to ask you to leave. Sherri?"

Joyce's assistant came around the corner. "Oh," she said upon seeing Victoria in Joyce's office. "I didn't know you were with a client." She turned to Victoria. "What can I get you? Coffee? Juice?"

"I was just leaving," Victoria said, her relaxed smile totally hiding the mixture of anger and nervousness warring for domination inside her. It had taken all of her "brought-upsy" to get through the moment without conducting a beat-down in heels. But she'd done it. She'd said what she had to say. The rest, well, Victoria thought that she could show her better than she could tell her.

Two hours later, Joyce was all smiles as she parked her car in the lot of the airport's private airstrip and made her way to the Livingston Corporation jet. She pulled her car up next to Malcolm's Mercedes and then walked around to the trunk for the carry-on she'd packed. She wanted to be ready for anything, including a night spent at a hotel in Philadelphia should Malcolm decide against flying back late. Along with the bottle of Dom Pérignon, she'd packed a small picnic basket of fresh-baked olive bread, caciocavallo podolico cheese and Beluga caviar. As she approached the jet, she saw her friend and producer, Bernice, and Malcolm's assistant just getting ready to board the plane. Both women looked rather serious, Joyce noticed, but understood why. This was a big day, the day that would change the rest of Malcolm's life!

"Hey, y'all," Joyce sang out as she neared the plane. "Are we ready to get this show on the road?"

"Hey, Joyce, let me talk to you for a minute," Bernice said, her voice low and firm.

"In a minute, sistah. I want to speak to Malcolm and get this champagne on ice." Joyce hurried up the steps, entered the plane, and stopped short.

"Hello, Joyce," Victoria said from the first seat, where she sat next to Malcolm. Behind them sat Diane and Ace. Candace and Adam sat on the other side of the plane.

"Uh, hello, everybody," Joyce managed to squeeze out between clenched teeth. Stunned, she looked at Malcolm, who glanced up and said hello before becoming very preoccupied with whatever he typed on his phone.

"And you brought champagne, how thoughtful," Victoria purred. "Wasn't that thoughtful, honey? For your business partner to bring champagne? Don't worry that you don't have enough. We keep two cases of bubbly stocked at all times, for moments such as these. Thanks so much for all the help you've given my husband," Victoria said, her voice full of sincerity. "We owe part of what is sure to be monumental success to you."

Joyce remained standing at the front of the plane. She'd planned to sit next to Malcolm and, along with Bernice, map out final strategies for the show taping. Now she didn't know where to go.

"Bernice is sitting in the back," Diane said casually, waving a hand in that direction. "Feel free to join her. We have some family business to take care of up here."

Joyce nodded and began moving shaky legs toward the back of the plane. Livid didn't even begin to describe how she felt. She wanted to take the bottle of champagne and bust it over Victoria's smug head.

"This isn't over," Joyce whispered to Bernice once she'd sat down.

"I tried to warn you," Bernice replied. She hadn't agreed with her friend going after a married man but didn't like to see her hurting either. "It's all going to work out," she said at last. "You'll still get paid."

"Oh, you don't know the half. There's no way I'm going to work my ass off to help him get launched and then get tossed out like yesterday's newspaper."

Bernice saw Malcolm's assistant stop and talk to him. She spoke hurriedly, wanting to finish before the woman came to take her seat. "Maybe you shouldn't make this trip," she whispered. "Seeing them together isn't going to make you feel better. Her getting all the glory while the cameras roll."

"She might be on one arm, but I'll be on the other," Joyce said, her voice determined. "I'm not going to give Victoria her husband back. She's going to have to take him."

66

Toussaint winked at Alexis, who watched from the other side of the room. It was ironic that both he and Malcolm were taping their inaugural shows the same week. Malcolm had beat him to the company jet, but in celebration of the show, Toussaint had chartered a private jet for the trip to New York, with plans to stop back through the Poconos for a romantic weekend before returning to Atlanta. His aunt was well aware of the long-standing rivalry between brothers, which was why Toussaint hadn't hesitated to let her know he wanted his show to air before Malcolm's did. Fortunately for Diane, scheduling was totally out of her hands. As it was, Malcolm's show was airing live, while Toussaint's show was airing next week, in a special time slot following the popular show *Throwdown with Bobby Flay.*

"We're ready, Mr. Livingston," the cute, blond producer announced. She'd been flirting with Toussaint ever since they'd met, in love-at-first-sight with him just as all of the viewers would hopefully be.

"Mr. Bouvier?" she called out to Oliver, who paced nervously on the side of the set, looking like a supersized culinary genius in his stark white jacket and chef's hat. "Remember what we talked about. Just be yourself—relaxed, conversational. This is when you're going to ask everyday viewers to come into their homes and cook in their kitchens. Make sure you convey someone they want to meet."

Toussaint rolled his neck to relax. The makeup artist came over to dab him one last time. The show producer counted them down, and he began. "Hello, America. My name is Toussaint Livingston, and I want to come cook at your house."

The producers all stood amazed as they watched Toussaint work the camera as if he were a pro. Much as they'd felt when they saw Bobby Flay, Rachael Ray, and Paula Deen, they knew that Toussaint's show was going to be a hit.

"Change the order from six to twelve shows," the executive producer said at the end of the taping. "And double his contract—triple it if you have to. We want to lock this guy in and keep him around. He's one of the next Food Network stars."

When Malcolm entered the greenroom, everyone in there broke out in applause. Joyce stood slightly in front of the Livingston family, next to the producer she'd worked with for months, beaming like the proud . . . mistress. Malcolm walked over and hugged the producer before turning and giving Joyce a big, warm hug. "We did it," he said when he raised his head.

His eyes conveyed a myriad of emotions that caused Joyce's heart to flip-flop. *I knew this was real. I knew that he loved me.* The Livingston family's unexpected appearance had caused Joyce's world to teeter on its axis for a minute, but that hug had just helped life right itself. Her confidence was such that she even managed to smile at Victoria when Malcolm walked over and embraced his wife, mother, and rest of the family. *Enjoy the moment, Victoria. It is going to be one of the last ones you share with your husband.*

Before the end of the evening, QVC knew that a new star had been born. The night had been one of their most successful ever. The phone lines had jammed, and the initial order of smokers, one hundred and fifty thousand, had sold out within the hour. After five years of planning, two years of testing, and several months of bringing his dream to reality and then to the masses, Malcolm was an overnight success and a multimillionare.

Two weeks later, Diane and Ace joined Adam, Candace, Malcolm, Toussaint, Victoria, and Alexis for dinner. Adam had big news. "I got a call from the president of the bank this morning."

Malcolm, who always kept one eye on the company's bottom line, perked up instantly. "What did he say?"

"He said he liked your smoker infomercial, that he'd tried to order one but they were sold out."

"What?" Diane said. "Mr. Bank President watches QVC?"

"And the Food Network, from the sound of things. Because, Toussaint, he knew about your show as well."

"That's crazy," Toussaint mumbled. But he was pleased.

"So what did he call you to do?" Ace asked. "Congratulate you before we go into Chapter Eleven?"

"No," Adam replied, his eyes twinkling. "He called to extend the line of credit we requested." He looked with pride from one son to the other. "After seeing what he saw last night, or at least getting the information, he knows we're good for it."

Victoria held up her glass of juice. "To Malcolm and Toussaint!"

Everyone around the table picked up their glasses. "To the Livingstons," Malcolm added.

Their glasses clinked. "Hear, hear!"

67

Adam and Candace sipped drinks in their master suite. It was a Wednesday night, but they were treating it like a Friday. In celebration of their sons' success and of the renewed flame of their marriage, the couple had decided to take a quick trip to Vegas. Not only that, but with Christmas just two weeks away, she also knew it would be one of the last times she'd have her husband all to herself. Her in-laws practically lived with them during the holidays.

"Baby, Diane and I are planning a small party. Nothing major, just a small gathering of family and close friends."

Adam grunted. He knew what happened when his wife and sister-in-law started planning things: His bank account took a serious hit. *Which reminds me. Dang! I need to get those numbers for the accountant.* With everything that had happened, Adam had totally forgotten about a meeting that had been scheduled for weeks. The accountant and Adam's assistant would do most of the work, but there were some receipts and line items that he wanted to go over, just to be prepared.

He finished his drink and stood. "Baby, I'll be right back. I have to go to the office."

"Now? Baby, it's nine o'clock."

"I know, but we're leaving first thing in the morning. But

there are a couple of items I want to get to peruse on the flight. I've got a meeting with the accountant as soon as we get back. You don't want Uncle Sam riding my ass, now, do you?"

"You know I want to be the only one riding that," Candace replied with a grin. "But can't Ace get them for you and give them to our guy tomorrow?"

"Probably, but I'll feel more comfortable doing it myself. That way, I know it's done and can have my mind clear when I sit down at that blackjack table tomorrow."

"Okay, baby. Well, since you're going out, can you stop by the restaurant and get some sweet potato ice cream?"

"Sure, but you know"—Adam lightly kissed Candace's lips—"you"—kiss on the right cheek—"are"—kiss on the left cheek—"all the sweetness"—kiss on the nose—"this brothah needs." Adam got ready to turn, but Candace cupped his face and planted a sloppy wet kiss on the man she loved. She began to grind herself against him as she rubbed his back.

"Hmmm, baby, keep that kitty hot for Big Daddy," Adam moaned as he gently took her arms from around his neck. "I'll be back in about thirty minutes. And then there's a thing or two I'm going to do with that ice cream."

"Mmm, I can't wait." Candace walked him to the door and then went to take a long, hot shower and wait for her man.

Adam and Candace lived just ten minutes from the office, but he broke a few speed limits and got there in five. He felt better than he'd felt in months, since the first time his burning dick had alerted him to a problem. The credit belonged to Candace for helping him get his manhood back. Adam's confidence had been admittedly rocked following her infidelity, but now he and his wife's sex life was better than ever. Adam walked to the office, retrieved what he needed, and walked to his car humming the latest song they'd added to the Taste of Soul jukebox—Bobby Womack's "Woman's Gotta Have It."

"I told you I'd get you, muthafucka." That's the only thing

Adam Livingston heard before he heard the shot, felt the pain, and fell to the ground.

Candace frowned at the sound of the doorbell. She looked at her watch and was surprised to see that it was ten o'clock. She'd stayed in the bath longer than she'd intended. *Who's at the door at this time of night? And where's Adam?*

Her frown increased along with her heartbeat when she looked through the peephole and saw two uniformed cops. "Yes?" she said, after opening the door.

"Mrs. Livingston?" the older, silver-haired cop asked.

"Yes."

"Candace Livingston?" the younger cop prodded.

"Yes, I'm Candace Livingston. What is going on?"

"We need you to accompany us to the hospital."

"Hospital?" Candace asked, her hand going to her throat. "Why, what's happened? What's this about?"

"It's about your husband, ma'am. Adam Livingston. He's been shot."

68

Victoria sat naked astride Malcolm. She luxuriated in the feel of his skin as she massaged his back and shoulders. For the past two weeks, since reconnecting with her husband and since he'd moved back into the master suite, she'd tried to figure out how she'd lived without him, without this. She'd beat herself up for the time they'd wasted, merely existing in the same household instead of living as man and wife. Perhaps that's why she reached for him every night, making the first move, letting him know she wanted him.

She slid off his back and continued rubbing the massage oil over his body. Malcolm wasn't lean and firm, like Toussaint. He was shorter, stockier, with growing love handles. But she loved every inch of him, just the way he was. "Okay, I'm done," she whispered into his ear. "Feel better?"

Malcolm turned over. The evidence of how he felt stuck up straight in the air. Victoria immediately went to work, doing the thing she didn't particularly care for but her husband loved. She licked his throbbing manhood before taking it into her mouth and was immediately rewarded with a loud hissing. Within minutes, Malcolm rolled over. "Get on your knees, Victoria. I want you doggy style."

Victoria turned and grabbed the headboard. Malcolm

reached between her legs, stimulating her clit. She took his manhood and guided it toward her entrance. "Now, Malcolm, please. I don't want to wait."

"Me neither," he said as he slowly slipped inside her.

Victoria moaned as happy tears hovered at the sides of her eyes. Malcolm held on to her hips and deepened his thrusts. They settled into a nice, steady rhythm. And then the phone rang.

"Let's not answer it," Victoria panted. *It's probably Mom.* Valarie had an uncanny ability to call just in time to interrupt an intimate moment. *Not this time, Mom. Not this time.*

Shortly after the phone stopped ringing, it began again, followed by the ding of Malcolm's cell phone.

"Maybe I should answer it," Malcolm said, still stroking slowly. "It might be important."

"What can't wait until we're done?" Victoria asked reaching behind her for Malcolm's hand and placing it on her breasts.

Both phones stopped ringing and then immediately began again. At the same time, there was an urgent knock on the door. "Mrs. Livingston?"

Malcolm pulled out and sat up at the same time. "Wait. Something's wrong." He bounded out of bed and stood just on the other side of the door. "Maria, what is it?"

"Your brother's calling. He says it's urgent."

Victoria immediately picked up the phone. The color left her face as she listened to Toussaint. She swung her legs over the bed as she hung up the phone. "We have to get to the hospital."

"What happened?" Malcolm asked, reaching for the pants he'd left beside the bed.

"It's your dad. He's in surgery."

"Surgery? Why?"

"Toussaint wouldn't tell me. He just said get there. Fast."

69

Zoe walked to her office door and closed it. She was still getting used to the fact that she even had an office and was thankful for the privacy it afforded.

"Chardonnay, this is Zoe," she said when her friend answered the phone. "Girl, what is going on with you? I've been leaving messages and blowing up your phone. I heard that you were the one who found Adam? I can't believe you haven't called!" It had been three days, and Zoe was still in shock. To hear that someone she knew had almost been killed during a robbery was one thing, but to hear that it happened in the parking lot of the place she worked was something else.

"I've been busy," Chardonnay snipped, mad that she'd answered the call.

"I can imagine. Since you're the one who called nine-one-one. Are you helping with the investigation, being interviewed about what you saw?"

"Something like that."

"I can't believe it. And Adam Livingston of all people, someone who is always trying to help us. That's how it always happens, bad things happening to good people."

Chardonnay snorted.

Zoe frowned. "Chardonnay, what's the matter?"

"Oh, please. Like you don't know? How long did you think it would take for me to find out you've hooked up with Bobby?"

A full beat went by before Zoe responded. "You know what? I'm going to act like I didn't even hear you come at me like I'm not your best friend, accusing me of something without even asking if it's true."

"Okay. Is it true you were at some political fund-raiser, getting your grind on with my ex?"

"Oh, so Bobby's your ex now? I thought he was just another f-ing partner."

"I knew all along you liked him. Y'all were probably even fucking when he was with me! You're scandalous."

"No, what's scandalous is that you would accuse me of something without finding out the facts. But that's not even the main thing. The main thing is you don't give a damn about Bobby yet you're willing to jeopardize our friendship over some bullshit."

"Well, check this out, tramp. I'm pregnant. With his baby. So I'm still going to end up with his big dick."

"You know what, Chardonnay, this phone call is over."

"Yeah, whatever, bitch."

Zoe's mouth flew open as she stared at the phone. *Did she just call me the b-word?* "No, she did not just call me a bitch. And she did not just hang up on me!" Zoe couldn't get to her keys fast enough. She was heading over to the restaurant where it was about to go down!

She was moving so fast that she almost ran over Drake, who was getting off the elevator just as she was getting on. "Zoe, I'm glad I caught you. Come on back. We need to talk."

"Can it wait, Drake? There's, uh, something I need to take care of."

"Sorry, Zoe, but no. Ace has called an emergency meeting. The entire company. We're meeting in the boardroom in ten minutes. Come on."

Zoe attended the meeting, and afterward, too drained to confront Chardonnay, she went straight home. When her phone rang several hours later, she said yes to the invite. Any other time, she probably wouldn't have. But today, too much had happened for her to be alone.

Bobby's hard, round ass was poised in the air, bouncing up and down like a basketball. He grunted with every thrust. "Umph. Umph. Umph. Umph." He moved to the side and went in deeper as he slowed his movements to a leisurely groove, bringing his dick out to the tip and then easing it back inside. "Umph. Is this good? Umph. Yeah, I had a feeling you would like it like this."

"Yeah, just like that . . . mmm, slow feels good."

"Umph. Take this big dick, then. Take it!" Bobby's thrusts increased. He squeezed the hips in front on him and pounded with all his might. When his orgasm came, it was fierce and strong, causing him to shout out his release before collapsing on the bed.

"Damn, that was incredible," Jon said, flopping on the bed beside Bobby. "I don't want anyone else to have you."

"Fuck that. I told you I'm not gay."

"Not because you're gay. I know you like women too. I want exclusivity, so that you can be mine. I'll make it worth your while, Bobby. With me, you'll go far. You'll go all the way to the top."

Bobby was stiff at first, but after a moment he took a deep breath and allowed himself to relax in Jon Abernathy's arms.

Zoe relaxed, too, as she watched the men skate faster and clamber around a hard, black puck. She didn't know if hockey would ever be her thing, and she preferred wine to the cold beer she now sipped. But as Drake Benson slipped an arm around her shoulders, Zoe nestled into his side and began to rethink her preference for dark meat.

70

She read it, but she couldn't believe it. Shyla sat at an ocean-front café, in Ocho Rios, Jamaica, where she'd been for the past month. She'd needed time and space away from Toussaint and the Livingston Corporation to help heal her heart and clear her head. She'd gotten a good price on a six-week rental and now wished she could have it for longer. She loved the island life, much more than she'd expected, and had experienced a peace that was almost blissful. Until it was shattered with the arrival of a Fed Ex package from her mom.

She'd sent articles about Adam's shooting, and Shyla had devoured each one as soon as they'd arrived. In addition, she'd scoured the Internet, soaking up the news and trying to read between the lines to learn exactly what happened. Because try as she might, she couldn't think of any reason someone would want to hurt Adam Livingston. Did it have something to do with Malcolm's invention? she wondered. Or was it related to what Toussaint was doing on Food Network? Shyla repositioned her hat, took a sip of her virgin piña colada, and read the clip again:

> According to police reports, an unidentified assailant accosted Livingston as he got into his vehi-

cle. Although robbery is suspected as the motive, Livingston's wallet was still on his person and his car was not taken. Police conclude that something or someone scared off the attacker. The attack was caught on tape by a security camera; however, because of where the attack took place and the dark clothing worn, the identity of the attacker remains a mystery. Police are asking anyone with information to contact the department at 424-555 . . .

"Ah, such an ugly frown on a beautiful lady. What are you reading that has you looking so sad?"

The waiter, who'd introduced himself as Marley, had befriended Shyla on her first day there. She'd welcomed the friendship. He was one of the few other Americans she'd met on the island.

"May I?" he asked, and sat down at the table once Shyla nodded her assent. "Okay, tell me what's wrong."

"Some bad news . . . from back home." She shared a brief version of what she'd read. "He's a rich, powerful man, and I'm sure he has his share of enemies," Shyla concluded. "But I can't imagine that anyone would go so far as to try and kill him! But this robbery story doesn't make sense."

"Why not?" the waiter asked

"Because the article says that neither his wallet nor car was taken. Adam drives an Escalade and is known to carry large amounts of cash. And nothing was taken? It doesn't add up."

"Well, sweetness, I say have another piña colada and soak up some of this Jamaican sun. The day is too beautiful and so are you to have this crime worrying that pretty little head of yours."

"Thanks, Marley. You're probably right."

"Sure I'm right. Another drink, coming up."

"Thank you, handsome. You always make me feel better."

"That's my job, baby."

Shyla cocked her head, smiling at the tall, dark, kind man with the gorgeous smile. She'd felt a little rhythm between them and knew it was just a matter of time before they had sex. Maybe it would be tonight.

By the time Shyla had finished the expertly made piña colada, she reached for her purse. Marley was right—the day was too beautiful to have thoughts of robberies and shootings filling her head. She scribbled her phone number on the napkin and walked over to where Marley was busy wiping off a table. She placed a hand on his bare back, not missing the muscles that rippled as he worked. "This is for when you get off work," she said, slipping the napkin into his waistband. Without waiting for an answer, she walked away, not stopping until she reached the edge of the bar area. When she turned around to look, Marley was smiling.

"Will I see you later?" she asked with a smile.

Marley's smile was equally wide. "Yeah, mon."

71

The Livingstons gathered, en masse, in Adam's hospital room. Ace sat in a corner, staring straight ahead. Diane sat next to him, rubbing his back. Their son, Jefferson, sat in the seat across from them, eyes red from exhaustion and from crying.

Toussaint stood by the window, looking out but seeing nothing. "Try and relax," Alexis whispered, knowing the suggestion was pointless. But she felt so helpless at seeing the strain of the last week on her fiancé. She'd lain next to him while he tossed and turned, filled with thoughts of revenge against whoever had done this to his father. Alexis knew that he had been filled with fear, too, filled with "what ifs." But no one had voiced those. There was no choice in what had to be the outcome. Adam Livingston had to live.

Malcolm looked up in time to see Toussaint turn and lean a heavy head on Alexis's shoulder. It was a rare moment of vulnerability for the kid brother who'd stuck his chest out from the time he was two. The days had been filled with introspective thinking for Malcolm, since he and Victoria had reconnected and since he'd told Joyce that she could stay on as a partner with the Soul Smoker but that they would not share any type of intimacy—emotional or otherwise —again.

Toussaint had bested him in TV ratings, but due to demand, Malcolm had tripled his next Soul Smoker production order. He was a selling sensation. They were both winners, had both achieved their goal. But what did it matter when none of that could help the man who lay on an operating table, fighting for his life?

He walked over and wordlessly put his arms around Toussaint. It was the first time these brothers had shared this type of hug in years. Not ones for affection between males, these brothers now pulled on the other's strength and knew that no matter how strong their competitiveness ran, their love for each other ran stronger.

"You know, baby brother," Malcolm began, "I've been thinking. It might be interesting to use the Soul Smoker as a giveaway item on your show. It's a perfect item for those busy families you reach and would, you know, be a good promotional move for both the product and the network."

Toussaint smiled. He knew what his brother was doing, and he was grateful for the opportunity to think about something else besides the prospect of his father dying, if even for a moment. "I was thinking that too," he said with a nod. "A partnership between us."

"We'd make an unstoppable team."

"For sure. Especially with me as the leader."

Malcolm looked up and noted the twinkle in Toussaint's eye. "You know big brothers rule," Malcolm said, his voice catching.

"He's going to pull through, isn't he?" Suddenly Toussaint was three and Malcolm was five, and they'd just found out the ten-year-old family dog had failing kidneys.

Malcolm had been the strong one then. Now was no different. "He's going to pull through, brother," he said, hugging Toussaint again. "I just know it."

Victoria, who'd been quietly praying in a corner, came over to where the two men stood. "I thought I'd go for coffee. Would you guys like some?"

Candace sat in a chair, her head in her hands. Ace and Diane's daughter, Bianca, sat next to her, a hand of comfort lightly perched on her arm. Bianca was bewildered by what had happened and had been stunned since being pulled out of class in Paris and put on the next plane to Los Angeles. Now she sat in the hospital where her adored uncle was clinging to life. What puzzled her was why? His shooting made no sense. And her father. He'd been acting so strangely. Bianca knew that something was going on. She had a feeling that unlike what the news and the papers had reported, this had been no random act of violence. But who would want to hurt Uncle Adam? And why?

Suddenly the air shifted, and everyone looked up. Two older versions of almost everyone in the room walked in the door. Ace shot up and quickly crossed to the room Marcus and Marietta Livingston had entered. For the first time since Candace had called him a couple days before, he felt that things would truly be all right.

"Where is he?" the matriarch, Marietta, asked.

"Still in surgery, Mama," Ace replied, hugging her and then shaking his father's hand before hugging him as well. "Come on, y'all. Sit down."

"I still don't understand what happened," Marcus said, his deep voice gruff with emotion. "Somebody needs to help me understand why my son got shot."

Ace's explanation was interrupted when the doctor, obviously weary, entered the room. He was immediately surrounded by Livingstons wanting to know Adam's status.

"How is he?"

"What's going on?"

"Is he going to make it?"

The doctor held up his hands, quieting the questions. "The surgery went well. There were no complications. That's a strong man you've got back there. But somebody in here must have said their prayers too. If the bullet had been just another half inch to the center, this would have been a very different outcome."

"Is he awake?" Ace said, stepping forward. "Can I go see my brother?"

"I need to see him," Candace said, her voice eerily quiet. "I need to know my husband is alive."

"Well, I'm the one who saw him first when I birthed him over fifty years ago," Marietta said, a touch indignant. "But I guess you should see him first, Candace. And then the rest of the family."

"He's very weak, so I want to limit this first visit to a couple people, for a couple minutes. You guys decide among yourselves who that is going to be."

A few moments later, Candace, Ace, and Marietta walked hand in hand as they followed the nurse down the hall. All of them steeled themselves for what the doctor had warned them they'd see: a very bandaged, drugged Adam who might not recognize them.

A sob caught in Candace's throat as soon as she saw her husband. She rushed over to his side. "Baby," was all she could say before putting her head on the bed and crying.

A very weak hand brushed the side of her cheek. She looked up. Adam attempted a wink and then closed his eyes.

"Glad to see you back, twin," Ace said, clenching his jaw to maintain his composure. "I don't want you to worry about anything but getting well. Leave everything else to me."

Adam turned his head, and when he opened his eyes, they bore into his twin brother's.

Ace nodded, having clearly received Adam's unspoken message. "Oh, yes, brother. We'll handle the reason this happened. Don't you worry none. As long as I have breath in my body, I vow we'll handle this."

A couple more comments and a light kiss to the forehead and the nurse shooed the family out of the room. Candace wiped away tears as they walked down the hall.

"It's my fault," she whispered to Ace, her voice again breaking.

"Shhh, don't even go there. You don't own a gun and you didn't pull the trigger."

"I know but—"

"But nothing," Ace cut in. "Adam is going to need you to be strong. To help him recover. You keep your mind focused on that and let the men handle . . . that other stuff."

The Livingston family gathered at Candace's that night, all breathing easier now that they knew Adam would live. The clan had taken a hit, for sure, but they stood taller, stronger, closer than ever. As she surveyed her family room, Candace was overcome with emotion, with the knowledge of how special the Livingston love was that she'd taken for granted. What she'd almost thrown away for seconds of pleasure.

"He's really going to be all right?" she asked Adam's mother, who came up and hugged her.

"Baby, he's a Livingston," Marietta said, her voice filled with faith-fueled confidence. "He's going to be fine."

That's right, he's a Livingston, Candace acknowledged. And so was she. That meant that not only would Adam survive, but so would their marriage.

72

The mood was much brighter as everyone congregated in Adam's hospital room. There was even laughter after Marcus, the patriarch, made a teasing comment about Victoria's cooking. The door to Adam's room opened, and when all eyes turned and saw who it was, the laughter stopped.

"Who are you?" Candace demanded. "This is a private room. You have no business here."

Toussaint rushed forward. "It's okay," he said to the woman who stood just inside the door. "This is Chardonnay, Mama. She works at the Buckhead location. She's the one who found Daddy. . . ."

"Yes, now that you mention it, I do recognize her. Sorry, Chardonnay, I'm not thinking clearly." Candace stood. "I want to personally thank you for calling nine-one-one and saving my husband's life. It's rare for anybody to be there at that time of night. Thank God you found him."

Various thank-yous and accolades were heard around the room. "I'm curious, Chardonnay," Toussaint said. "What were you doing there that night? I don't remember ever seeing you at corporate."

Chardonnay shifted from one foot to the other. There was no way she could tell them the reason—that she'd heard rumblings about a bankruptcy and had planned to sweet-talk the guard into letting her up in the offices. She'd been determined to find out if that was true and if it was, to get out while the getting was good. What she'd found instead was much more than she'd bargained for.

"And how did you get back here?" Candace probed. "We gave very specific instructions that only family members be allowed in this room. It's not personal, Chardonnay. We appreciate what you did. But we're discussing private matters and—"

"Yeah, well, I told them I was a cousin, because I need to be a part of your discussion." Chardonnay's voice dripped with attitude—being dismissed from the room of the man whose life she'd saved.

"Excuse me?" Malcolm asked, rising from his chair.

"Chardonnay, watch your tone," Toussaint warned. "That's not only the wife of the man who signs your checks, but also my mother."

"Young lady," Marietta Livingston began, her voice filled with seventy-something years' worth of don't-start-none-won't-be-none. "I don't know who you think you're talking to, but we're discussing family business. So unless you're a Livingston—"

"I know who shot Adam."

It was as if time stood still in the room. Nobody moved or breathed.

"Who?" Ace finally asked, although he believed he already knew the answer.

Chardonnay hesitated in giving her answer. She didn't think there was any tactful way to exchange information for money, but that is exactly what she was planning to do. "I'm risking my life by telling you what I'm getting ready to tell you. How much is this information worth to you?"

"And how much is your living worth to you?" Toussaint growled, his steps deliberate, menacing as he walked toward her. "Because you're risking your life if you *don't* tell us. Now, out with it! Who shot my father?"

One look at his face and Chardonnay knew Toussaint was serious. She knew when to back off, and did. "Quintin Bright."

Candace gasped. "Oh, no!"

Toussaint and Malcolm looked at each other. Ace stood and headed for the door.

"Ace, wait!" Diane rushed over to stop her husband, grabbing his arm before turning to Chardonnay. "How do you know this? Did you see him that night? And if so, why didn't you tell the police?"

"Because I didn't see anything that night."

"Then how do you know who it is?" Victoria asked.

"Because Q told me when he called me last night. We used to . . . hang out. We're friends. He called me because he knows I work for y'all. He wanted to find out what was going on."

"That's why you're here?" Candace asked, a myriad of emotions crushing her heart, anger being the strongest. "To spy for your . . . lover?" Candace had no doubt that that was how they'd "hung out."

"No! I'm here to help you."

Malcolm cursed. "You're here for money."

"Yes," Chardonnay answered. "I'm single, two kids and another on the way. Ain't no shame to my game of putting food on the table." When no one responded to that, she went on. "Quintin left the state, said he's not going back to jail. He wouldn't tell me where he was, but he did tell me who was with him."

"Who?" was the collective question from the room.

"Shyla Martin." You could have heard a pin drop. "Now," Chardonnay said as she crossed her arms. "Y'all still think I'm here just trying to get all up in your business? Or can I work for y'all a different way . . . and get paid?"

ALL UP IN MY BUSINESS

Lutishia Lovely

ABOUT THIS GUIDE

The suggested questions that follow
are included to enhance your group's
reading of this book.

Discussion Questions

1. There was love but also sibling rivalry between Malcolm and Toussaint. How did this hurt their relationship? How did it help it?

2. Malcolm married young and felt trapped in his marriage. Was he justified in feeling this way? Did Victoria contribute to his unhappiness and, if so, how?

3. Victoria became wrapped up in her children and in the process neglected her husband. Do you know women like this? Has it happened to you? And what part, if any, did Malcolm play in this alienation?

4. Toussaint was a player who felt fine in having multiple partners because he never lied about being monogamous. Do you know people like this? Is it okay to engage in sex with multiple partners as long as this is known up front?

5. Yes, Alexis is smart and gorgeous, but why else do you think Toussaint was so attracted to her?

6. Alexis had reservations about dating Toussaint. Would you date a known player and, if so, under what conditions?

7. Shyla wanted to become a permanent part of Toussaint's life, so she flew to LA to take their relationship to the next level. How far have you gone to secure a relationship or take it to the next phase?

8. Were you surprised to learn that Candace was having an affair with her trainer? When did you begin to suspect their relationship?

9. What do you think about how Adam reacted to Candace's betrayal? Should he have taken her back? Why or why not?

10. Was Adam justified in ruining Q's business? Was Q justified in the way he retaliated?

11. After being rebuffed by Adam, Joyce went after Malcolm. Was it all about the money, or did Joyce and Malcolm develop real feelings for each other?

12. How do you feel about Victoria hiding her pregnancy from Malcolm?

13. He wanted to divorce her, but the Livingston legacy kept Malcolm and Victoria together. Do you think their marriage will survive?

14. Speaking of the legacy, do you think it's possible for a man to stay faithful for ten, twenty, thirty years? Do you know of a long-term couple who have achieved this?

15. Atlanta has been referred to as the "black gay capital," with down-low brothers a part of that mix. Both Jon Abernathy and Bobby Wilson dated women. Bobby swore he was not gay. What do you think about this? Were they bisexual? Can someone sleep with someone of the same sex and still be heterosexual?

16. Zoe believed that Chardonnay had a chance at love with Bobby. What do you think?

17. Chardonnay believed that Zoe was attracted to Bobby. Was she? Is it ever okay to go out with someone your friend has dated? Why or why not?

18. How do you feel about Chardonnay using Adam's shooting for financial gain? Is she a shameless hustler or a shrewd businesswoman?

Stay tuned for a second helping of
Lutishia Lovely's new series, which follows the
hot tempers and tantalizing temptations of a family
whose restaurant is *the* place for a tasty meal....

Mind Your Own Business

Coming in September 2011 from Dafina Books

Here's an excerpt from *Mind Your Own Business. . . .*

"Why can't a woman be on top?" Bianca Livingston demanded, tossing shoulder-length, naturally curly hair over her shoulder. She stood over her brother as if ready to strike, looking totally capable of kicking butts and taking names. Her quick smile, short stature, and girly frame had caused many men to underestimate her—to their peril. But anyone seeing her now—shoulders back, hands on hips, and perfectly tailored black suit and four-inch heels—would believe her capable of running almost anything. "I'm as qualified to run the West Coast locations as you are, even more so, matter of fact."

"You're qualified to run the kitchen, *maybe,*" her older brother retorted. Jefferson suppressed a smile. He'd taunted Bianca from birth, and did so now. Her fiery personality was the perfect foil for his laid-back teasing. But even with his ongoing provocations, this time Jefferson's antics masked the seriousness of his quest. He had every intention of being the Livingston who moved to LA to establish the Taste of Soul restaurants both there and in Nevada. He just didn't like confrontation, or competition. He'd quietly made his bid to run the West Coast locations the same way he cooked his ribs—low and slow. "Isn't that why you spent the last nine months in Paris?" he queried to underscore his point. "Learning the fine art of cooking so that you could give our soul food some class?"

Actually, Bianca had fled to Paris to get away from the chain around her neck otherwise known as Cooper Riley, Jr., her fiancé. But only one other person knew this truth. Initially, forestalling the marriage everyone else believed was a fait accompli was also why she'd expressed interest in running the West Coast locations. But now, after months of talking with her cousin Toussaint, her confidant and the brainchild behind their company expanding out west, Bianca wanted to relocate to continue spreading her independent wings, expand the Livingston dynasty, and make the brand shine under her direct supervision.

"Need I remind you that I have not only a culinary certificate from Le Cordon Bleu, but I also have an undergrad and a graduate degree in business administration?"

"No, little sis, you don't need to remind me." Jefferson's smirk highlighted the dimple on his casually handsome face, his tan skin further darkened by the August sun. His brown eyes twinkled with merriment. "But do I have to remind you that I have a double master's in business administration and finance?" After receiving an MBA at Morehouse, Jefferson had garnered a second one from the Wharton School of the University of Pennsylvania.

Bianca, knowing that she couldn't go toe-to-toe when it came to her brother's education, tried a different route. She walked away from Jefferson and sat in one of the beige leather chairs in the artistically appointed office. Reaching for a ballpoint pen that lay on his large and messy mahogany desk, she adopted a calmer tone, yet couldn't totally drop the petulance in her voice. "Jefferson, the only reason Dad is promoting the idea of your heading up the location is because you're the oldest."

"And the son—don't forget that. You know Dad doesn't want to see his baby girl fly too far from the nest."

"Okay, probably that too," Bianca conceded. It was no secret that when it came to her father, Abram "Ace" Livingston, she was the apple of his all-seeing eye.

"Besides, how are you even considering relocation when you've got a fiancé chomping at the bit to get married? Cooper has been more than patient with you, Bianca. Not many men would let the woman they love move to the other side of the world, even if—as you successfully argued—it was for the union's greater good. What did you call it? Increasing your company value and the marriage's bottom line? As if being a Livingston isn't value enough? No, Bianca, Cooper allowed the wedding to be pushed back once already. He's not going to delay it a second time, and you know he isn't moving to LA."

Bianca abruptly rose from the chair where she'd been sitting and walked to the window. "You're probably right," she said, quickly wiping the tears that had leaped into her eyes. "If everyone has their way, I'll be married in six months with a baby on the way in nine." *But how can I marry Cooper after what happened in Paris?*

"Hey, sister, are you all right?"

Bianca jumped. She hadn't heard Jefferson rise, hadn't been aware that he'd walked from his desk and joined her at the window. "Actually, no, if you want to know the truth. Jeff, I—"

"Hey, man . . . Oh, Bianca, I'm glad you're both here." Toussaint Livingston burst into Jefferson's office and rushed toward his cousins on the other side of the room. "We need to roll to your parents' house right now. Emergency family meeting."

Their conversation forgotten, both Jefferson and Bianca turned and talked at once.

"What's the matter?"

"What's going on?"

Bianca's heart raced with concern. "Why are we meeting at Mom and Dad's house, Toussaint, and not in the conference room?"

Toussaint turned and headed for the door. "That's what we're about to find out. I'll meet y'all there."

Fifteen minutes later, Toussaint, Jefferson, and Bianca joined their family members in the living room of Ace and Diane's sprawling Cascade residence. Toussaint's parents, Adam and Candace, and his brother, Malcolm, were already there.

Toussaint and his cousins were the last to arrive, and as soon as they sat down, Ace cleared his throat and stood. "We've got a situation," he began without preamble. A pregnant pause and then, "Somebody's stealing company funds."

Reactions were mixed, with bewilderment and anger vying for top billing.

"Who is it?" Bianca angrily asked, ready for battle though the culprit remained unnamed.

"We don't know," Ace replied. "But it's definitely an inside job."

The family members looked at one another, a myriad of thoughts in each of their minds. *Who could it be? How did this happen? Is the guilty party somehow connected to someone in the room?* One family member even pondered the unthinkable: *Is the thief one of us?*

"What kind of money are we talking about?" Toussaint asked. "Hundreds, thousands . . . more?"

"*Several* hundred thousand," Ace replied, his tone somber and curt.

Again, responses were symphonic.

"What the hell?"

"Who could do such a thing?"

"Oh, hell to the no. We're not going to take this lying down."

"You're absolutely right, baby girl," Ace said to Bianca. "We're not going to stand for this at all. Nobody steals from our company, takes from our family, without feeling the wrath of a Livingston payback."